Though this is a work of fiction, references to Marilyn's life before 4th August 1962 are – except for Stella Cruz – based as much on fact as possible; a lifetime of love meant that the research had already been undertaken to give a complex life the accurate detail it deserves.

This book is dedicated to Grandma Roberts, whose idol was the Virgin Mary. I grew up with Mary watching us from photos and statues, in toilets and kitchens and hallways. It is also dedicated to those who have sadly gone, too soon like Marilyn, and who I miss dearly: Scottish Sue Marwood, Uncle Lapwim, Zoe m'big love, and Christine Prattley, the mum to everyone.

It is also dedicated to the Norma Jeane in all of us.

Marilyn Monroe is the most misquoted icon of all time. People come up with inane words and slap them over her face; voila, Marilyn said it! Stop putting *your* words in *her* mouth.

Stella Cruz in *Icon* magazine, 1981

The Virgin Mary looked down on me from my Grandma Lil's living room and kitchen walls for most of my childhood; she was serene, pure, and perfect, everything my grandma said a woman should be. On my bedroom wall though, Marilyn Monroe watched me sleep; perhaps not as pure, but definitely serene, with a tiny bird held aloft on one finger, perfect to me.

Flora Baker

I'm not interested in money; I just want to be wonderful.

Marilyn Monroe

1

Marilyn buys her first house

January 1962, Brentwood, Los Angeles

Chill winds gusted angrily from the ocean as though to reproach the frenzy of journalists pursuing a man and woman along a tree-lined lane. Guiding her, the man led the way, papers scattering like large, white leaves from a folder in his other hand. He abandoned them on the grass verge, looking far more nervous than she appeared to be.

'Marilyn, Marilyn, *Marilyn*,' the mob cried, their words punctuated with the pop of camera flash, and the pounding of footfall on damp tarmac.

She disappeared inside a gate, and the man followed, slamming it shut and leaning on it, breathing hard.

'Are you OK, Marilyn?' he asked.

She smiled and nodded, but was more interested in looking up the curved driveway towards the main door of the Mexican-style Colonial Revival house, obviously keen to get to it. 'I'm used to it, honey,' she said, and inhaled the scent of eucalyptus trees, bougainvillea vines, and citrus fruits. She tried to let her senses decide her fate. Should she go inside the house with this real estate agent or turn back, fight the paparazzi, and surrender the dream of her *own* home?

This is the place, the foliage whispered.

She longed for a sanctuary; a secret abode where she could lock the door; a haven where she could stop running and learn to walk more slowly again.

This house, in its secluded position at the end of a cul-de-sac, had enticed her in the brochure with windows protected by wrought iron and tall pines standing guard. It would be the first place she owned if she bought it.

'Shall we go inside?' asked the real estate agent, still red-cheeked from their frenzied run.

He had told her his name earlier and she felt terrible that it had slipped her mind. Of course, he wasn't likely to forget hers. It was a name that had been chosen because a studio executive liked a certain Broadway star named Marilyn; he thought it was pretty and suited her too. It was a name that had taken ages to get used to, one *new* Marilyn had asked her first autograph-hunting fan how it was spelled, partly joking, and partly making sure. It was a name that had meant she could finally forsake the one given at birth, one she associated with abandonment and shame.

'Yes, I'm excited to see the house,' she said. 'I hardly ate my breakfast this morning!'

'How do you cope with it?' He studied her.

'With what?' She had forgotten already; it was so customary. 'Oh, the press? I try and please them with a snap, mostly, but today … well, I wanted a little privacy.'

They headed towards the front door, which he declared would lead into a delightful living room with terracotta floors, wooden beams and a blue-tiled fireplace. Marilyn smiled; announcing what she was about to see felt redundant. He was clearly nervous, reading from the few remaining notes in his folder, not looking her in the eye.

She was accustomed to such reactions and wanted to put him at ease. Men behaved in two ways around her; they were aggressive and flirtatious or they trembled like a windchime in an idle evening breeze. She hated the aggressive ones – they were a reminder of a long ago face that she endlessly tried to bury.

'I like it already,' she admitted gently, to make him feel better.

'I think it has all you, um, said you wanted, um, the privacy.'

'Remind me of your name, honey?'

'Bill.' He fumbled with his folder. He was young, his sandy hair neatly brushed; she pictured him running a comb through it, fingers clumsy. She wondered why they had sent him rather than a more qualified agent. The thought didn't occur through arrogance only due to past experience.

For previous house showings, they had sent older agents who pawed at her, who squeezed into narrow spaces to get close, who stood arm to arm so their hairs tickled her skin. She was public property. She was there to be enjoyed.

'There are more expensive houses than this one,' a greying agent had said at one property, leering down her blouse. 'Why wouldn't you want one of those with all your money?'

But Marilyn didn't have the wealth many believed she did. Years ago she had told a Twentieth Century Fox executive who offered a contract to improve her finances that she wasn't interested in money – she just wanted to be wonderful.

'Shall we go inside?' she said to Bill.

He opened the front door with a light creak. 'There are eight rooms,' he said, though she knew, 'and most lovely to the left, a sunroom offers views to th-'

'Oh, wait.' She put a hand on his arm.

He studied where she was touching him. 'Yes?'

'Look at this.' She crouched by a small tile near the front door, tracing a finger along blue swirls and floral indents. Shivering, she whispered the words etched there: 'Cursum Perficio. It's lovely.' She glanced up at him. 'What does it mean?'

'Ah yes,' he began, obviously pleased to have an answer. 'It's, um, Latin and loosely translates as "here ends my journey" or "my journey is over".'

She rubbed the goosebumps pulsing along her arm and pulled the lemon cardigan around her body. 'How interesting. I think I'd like my journey to be over, at least for a bit; it's been a tough one at times. I love that kind of thing. Don't you?'

'I suppose, yes. It's rather … special.'

'Has it always been here?'

'I'm not sure but I can find out.'

'Oh, please do.' Marilyn thought of something else and leaned closer to the tile again. 'The blue … it's exactly like her dress...'

'Whose dress?'

'Mary's.'

Long ago, when she was a child called Norma Jeane and lived in an orphanage, a girl called Joanie in the next dormitory bed handed her a small card embossed with a fancy silver chalice. On the front was a picture of the Virgin Mary with pink cheeks, her dress as blue as the tile; her head was bowed, and she held a bloody rose in the place where her heart should have been.

'She's my mom now,' said Joanie then.

Norma Jeane had thought sadly of her own mom, one not in a plastic wallet, who had russet hair and a delicate frame, who she had never lived with for longer than a few weeks, and who she had now been told to forget because the woman was 'crazy'.

'If you need my mom tonight,' said Joanie, 'you can have her.'

Norma Jeane had kept Joanie's 'mom' under the alien-smelling pillow – one of many she would sleep on over the years – and held her tightly when night shadows grew tall and strange sounds in endless corridors loomed large. The next day, Joanie had gone, like many children who disappeared overnight. It left Marilyn with a lifelong anxiety about the what the dark could steal.

But she had kept the Virgin Mary for the rest of her orphanage stay, feeling protected by her kind face, only giving it to another child when she finally went into her Aunt Ana's care.

'Shall we continue?' Bill broke into Marilyn's reverie.

Nodding, she followed him into the house. He showed off a pretty sunroom, a simple kitchen and dining room, two bedrooms, a kidney-shaped pool, and a small guesthouse between the main building and the garage, keeping his distance from her, respectful. She imagined hand-picking décor to enhance the house's style. In later weeks would visit Mexico City and Tijuana to purchase mirrors and textiles and tiles. She had never imagined what she might do with any of the previous properties she viewed.

It was a good sign.

Marilyn liked signs.

As Bill finished his summary of the facilities, a question popped into her head. 'The house number... 12305... it's odd, isn't it?'

She always voiced thoughts the moment they arrived. It was useful when journalists wanted witty quips to print next to semi-nude photographs. But then similar responses to stuffy, middle-aged men's questions at dinner tables often silenced rooms. People tittered, thought her dumb. She wasn't clever the way educated people were – her limited schooling had ended at fifteen before she was married off to a neighbour. But she read books with passion and loved listening to those she felt knew more, absorbing their experiences, finding in them a belated education.

Men, however, preferred her to smile and look pretty.

Smile and *be her*.

She realised Bill was studying her, his eyebrows meeting sharply. 'Odd how?' he asked.

'The missing four sticks out; it counts up, one, two, three, but then there's a zero instead of a four, before the five. Do you think it means something?'

'I...' He clearly didn't know quite how to respond.

'It *must* do,' she insisted. 'I've always liked the number four.' She felt she should explain. He nodded but still didn't speak. 'Do you know what it means?'

'The number four?'

'Yes.'

'Um,' he said. 'No. Do you?'

She shook her head. 'No, but I like it. I lived at 444 in New York. My psychiatrist said I should put down more permanent roots,' she added, simply because, as usual, she had just thought of it. She laughed. 'Don't mind me going on, you must be bored senseless!' She paused. 'Do you think this house would be a good place for putting down roots?'

'I think it would be perfect. It's solid and there's lots of scope for putting your own mark on it.'

'That's what I intend to do.'

The small hacienda gave Marilyn a sense of safety with its Mary-blue (as she had always called that colour) tile by the front door and the abundant foliage. If she purchased it, it wouldn't be rented like her previous properties, it wouldn't be shared or temporary, it would be *hers*. Perhaps here, she would finally sleep.

Suddenly her eyelids were weighted with fatigue.

If she lay down here, she might sleep without a massage; she might not need to follow her nightly ritual of blackout curtains, chloral hydrate taken with milk, and an eye mask. Recently, childhood night terrors had returned. She woke with a scream, shaking violently, and had to get up and sit in a chair until it subsided. There were nightmares – men loomed over her, bigger than houses, angry and long-toothed. Then she was drowning, seawater choking her.

'You can't ignore what's inside you,' psychiatrist, Dr Greenson, had once said of her dreams. 'What is it you're not facing? Who are the looming men? That's what we should talk about.'

She hadn't responded.

'If we ease the inner child, you'll sleep,' he said.

She still hadn't responded; her inner child, Norma Jeane, kept her secrets.

Bill led Marilyn back outside.

This is the place, the foliage whispered again. Yes, it was true, she had felt safe within the house's thick walls.

Nervously, Bill opened the gate. Outside, just his dropped papers trampled into the grass verge, and a black car parked opposite, windows dark. Marilyn often saw them.

'Are you OK?' asked Bill kindly.

'I will be, honey,' she smiled. 'Because I think this is the place.'

2

Flora moves into yet another dingy flat

March 2016, Hull, England

It was Flora's third flat in two years. Each one had progressively grown dingier and damper, a descending spiral into hell. This time she was on the third floor. There were two rooms – the largest housing the pathetic makings of a kitchen in one corner – and a bathroom with mould growing like alien spawn around the sink.

Flora had only been here an hour, not even unpacked a mug, and already she wanted to leave. But where would she go? She *must* make it home; she had signed a six-month lease.

Greg, her boss at the club, had been kind enough to help move the few, cheap pieces of furniture, which now convened in the main room like refugees from some land even more hopeless. Small boxes sat on the patio table and chairs, patiently waiting to be opened.

'You don't have a garden,' Greg said of her plastic furniture, confused.

'It's my dining set,' admitted Flora. 'From a skip.'

He shrugged. 'I guess it'll be hardwearing. Should get some for the club.'

'You should see my "bed",' she had joked.

Understandably, Greg left as soon as he was done.

Now, Flora went into the second, smaller, room. Her double mattress (the frame had broken ages ago) and sister Bella's single one (also frame-free) were leaning against the wall like a mother and her child side by side. Flora was happy to co-sleep but when

Bella stayed she liked 'space'; she could share a room, she said, but she liked to be 'cocooned in her own womb' at night. Though Flora knew these words weren't intended to hurt, they did. She felt protective of her younger sister – twelve years separated them – and therefore she put up with a lot.

She placed the two mattresses flat in opposite corners; the distance between them choked Flora. Though she was in fact nearby, it felt like her sister was a million miles away. A mental health ward was Bella's current home. She'd been held there by a Section Three for the last five months due to suicide attempts. Despite insomnia that no pills helped, despite pacing and begging to be 'put out of her misery', despite nights Flora held Bella all through the dark, she would still rather have her sister here. The only pro to her living on the mental health ward was that constant monitoring meant she couldn't drag a razor over her skin until blood flowed.

Buzzing in the other room.

Flora's phone on the plastic table.

A message. Bella: *Thanks for sitting with me all day yesterday. Wish you could be with me at night too, but I know you work. How's the new place? X*

Flora wasn't at work until tomorrow evening but she didn't have the energy to go out into the night to a depressing hospital. Guilt gnawed at her. But she gave as many of her days as she could to Bella. She was the only person who did. Their mum didn't bother.

She sent back: *I'm happy to sit with you. See you soon. The new place makes the last one look like a room at the Ritz. X*

Now, to try and make this Godforsaken place home.

Aside from Bella's presence, three things would do that.

First, Flora's books weighing down the scratched second-hand bookshelf. Arranging them would take time though so maybe she'd start tomorrow morning.

Second, her flowers. Never having had a garden, she nurtured more resilient buds in windowsill boxes and pots. This was no place for much to thrive, but even on the coldest days primroses and peonies and snowdrops and daffodils had been a bright splash of hope, and bloomed with fervour. Right now, the tubs were lined up along the wall like trucks in a traffic jam, their soil spilling onto the cheap cord carpet. A job for tomorrow too.

Third, Flora's two favourite pictures.

Marilyn and Mary.

They would hide some of the wall stains.

And they were easily hung, right now.

But first, some tea. Flora found the kettle, switched it on. Nothing. She tried again. Still nothing. Damn. It must have broken in the move. She rummaged in another box and found a pan, filled it with water, and boiled it on the filthy hob.

Then she found the large, framed print of Mary; the Virgin Mary. In the image, the holy mother stood on a small cloud, palms open and welcoming, tiny gold stars circling her head and a ring of roses at her feet. Of course, her robe was the iconic blue she always wore. She had looked down on Flora and Bella from their grandma's kitchen wall throughout their childhood; she was serene, pure, and perfect, everything Grandma Lil said a woman should be.

But there was another goddess Flora loved.

A poster, also from childhood

Marilyn Monroe had watched her sleep back then; perhaps she wasn't as pure as Mary, but definitely serene. Flora had seen the black and white print in a record shop, been mesmerised by the image of a light-haired woman, large daisy above one ear, small smile playful, with a tiny bird held aloft on one finger. There was something comforting – *motherly?* – about her. Flora had saved a month of pocket money from Grandma Lil and stuck the poster above her bed.

'Who is she?' Flora asked her grandmother.

'Ah Marilyn,' said Lil. 'Such a beauty. Such a mystery...'

'Really? *Why?*' Young Flora was intrigued.

And she remained that way into adulthood, always haunted by the icon, by a woman who invited questions and answered none.

Now, she placed the two images, side by side.

Maybe life would improve here.

Maybe.

3

Marilyn is tired of being seen that way

July 1962, Brentwood, Los Angeles

The LIFE magazine photographer arrived at Marilyn's house early, saying his colleague was running late and would be there in a few hours for the interview.

Marilyn showed him the garden, talking animatedly about her 'little flowers', saying she had taken root here like the violets she had added that spring, along with rose buckwheat and oriental bulbs and sweet olive trees. Seeing them blossom through summer had given her great joy. Maybe having some pictures taken here in this lovely patch might help her summon the goddess she was expected to be.

Though Marilyn had suggested this, suddenly, she changed her mind.

'No,' she said.

'*No*?' repeated the photographer, frowning.

'I don't want pictures out here. I don't want everyone to see the garden.'

The photographer dropped his camera lens cap in the soil, his face falling at the same time.

Marilyn tried to explain. 'I know what I said... but it's... just *mine*. Not for the world.' She saw in his face – as she had seen many times before – that he was thinking, *but you've revealed every inch of your body, all the aspects of your love life, every contour of your face in close-up, what difference does one more exposure make?*

'Whatever you want,' he said.

They went back inside the house and he stayed long enough to snap her – *turn this way, turn that, turn this way, turn that* – in a variety of outfits. She was too tired to be *her*: to be beautiful; to summon the glorious creature this man wanted. No, she was *exhausted*. The sleep she had hoped would come in this home still evaded her. Even so, in her waking hours, she adored the place.

But was she blossoming like the new shrubs?

Were the weeds of the film world still suffocating her?

She had been fired from her latest movie, *Something's Got To Give*, due to repeated absences caused by painful sinus infections. She had dieted, losing too much weight, seeing that gauntness in her face. She had enjoyed a love affair or two, been condemned for it while the men involved escaped judgement-free.

Soon she would turn thirty-six.

A watershed age for actresses.

The end of the road for many female Hollywood stars.

*

An hour after the photographer left, the journalist arrived. Marilyn summoned her usual cheery *hello* – one she was famous for – and intended to make him welcome, and talk freely about the effects of fame on her life, the requested content.

At times, it was the usual interrogation.

'Will you get married again?'

'Well, I...'

'Are children on the cards?'

Quiet sadness; failure.

'I love the profusion of flowers outside.'

Quiet joy; success.

'Will you return to the screen?'

'Well, I...'

She saw herself and the Twentieth Century Fox production

chief in the living room, a week earlier. She had wooed him with chilled caviar and canapes from a Brentwood gourmet shop in the hope of being reemployed to finish *Something's Got To Give*. She hadn't played the dumb blonde, like for previous negotiations, instead showing her true self; she wore a simple beige dress, was savvy, serious and spoke with confidence. The production chief not only reinstated her – with filming scheduled to resume in seven weeks – but he offered more money too.

That hadn't been the point. It never was.

Since then, however, she hadn't been sure she wanted to go back into the movies. The thought of returning to long hours, the need for uppers (amphetamine) to get through the day, and downers (barbiturates) to sleep chilled her.

But who *was* she without the films?

Marilyn offered the journalist some grapefruit juice. 'I've finally put down roots here,' she said.

'And what about fame?' He sipped his drink.

'It's fickle,' she said, laughing. 'And I'm not. Can we talk about my–'

'But what about *fame*?' he pushed.

The only recent interview where she had felt valued as a human had been with Stella Cruz for *Icon* magazine. She had spoken to Stella a few times over the years and felt the woman *got* her. Recently, she had shared very private thoughts with the writer, but then changed her mind about wanting them to be used in a piece, and had asked Stella not to.

She never did.

'I think we're done now,' said Marilyn to the journalist.

*

Another photographer, Larry, turned up out of the blue the following morning while Marilyn knelt at the flowerbeds, pulling up weeds. She had spoken to him months ago about being featured in *Playboy*, a deal that had been dragging on for weeks. He wanted approval of Hugh Hefner's idea for her posing on the front and back covers of the magazine.

She knew why she had stalled; was this what she still wanted to do at almost thirty-six when she was striving to be taken more seriously?

'Your publicist told me you're no longer interested,' said Larry.

'Well, she wasn't authorised to say that yet.' Pat Newcomb had handled Marilyn's publicity for two years, been there for important moments; been at her side when she sang Happy Birthday to President Kennedy, attended divorce hearings and hospital stays, soothed illnesses and heartbreak. She was a friend as much as anything else, but sometimes she spoke for Marilyn without checking in.

'So, you *are* interested?' Larry tried.

'I haven't made my mind up.' She was annoyed, as much with herself for considering it as she was with him. 'I'll call you Monday and give you my answer.'

When she showed Larry out, and he opened the gate, two black cars sat on the grass verge like panthers stalking prey. She was accustomed to being watched, being followed, being snapped; she had chased and encouraged and wanted it in the past, but today she felt violated at the presence of shadowy watchers. She knew then that she didn't want to do the *Playboy* shoot.

She was tired of being seen that way.

As a child, she had dreamed of beauty; of being so attractive that no one would ignore her again, not her absent father, not her mentally ill mother. She felt no shame in her nudity; beneath the orphanage clothes, her gown of poverty, she was like other girls. Naked, she was equal. Yet now she feared aging, becoming invisible again. The celebrated, self-created, but exhausting persona had given her so much.

What was there without her?

Without Marilyn Monroe?

4

Flora arranges her flowers

March 2016, Hull, England

The first morning in her new flat, shivering at the inadequate heating, Flora tended her flowers.

The windowsill, thankfully, was spacious. She had found most tubs in skips, got soil from nearby patches of land, bought cheap bulbs. Spring meant the bright primroses and tiny snowdrops and tall tulips were full bloom. She liked to arrange them in conflicting colour order, a vibrant blast. In summer, when the marigolds and roses reigned, she would open the window wide and sit with her feet on the sill, enjoying the sun like it was a balcony in Spain.

How far away the good weather seemed.

As Flora worked, she looked out over grey roofs, dreaming of brighter days. She frowned; squinted; recognised something. A sign. Though she couldn't see them from here, she knew that yellow letters like daffodils against sky were enclosed within a circle of gold hands holding hands. She had seen them many times before. It was the CARE charity centre, just visible between two crumbling council buildings.

She hadn't realised it was so close.

Was the universe nudging Flora?

How many times had she walked past the place, put a hand on the door, wanting to offer her service, but then hurried away, too nervous?

CARE was the biggest women's charity in the world, subsidised by wealthy sponsors, celebrity patrons, fundraising, and kind volunteers. They always had adverts in supermarkets and libraries appealing to people for their time. There were sanctuaries in many cities for women in need, whether they were escaping abuse, enduring poverty, recovering from an assault, or had survived a difficult childhood. They could stay within its walls until they were back on their feet.

In the past, Bella had stayed there. CARE had been a lifesaver when there wasn't a free bed in a single mental health unit, and Flora was between flats, sleeping on a friend's sofa, so couldn't put her sister up.

Should she finally volunteer there?

She needed to earn money though, not give her time away for free.

Flora patted soil but her eyes were drawn to the sign, over and over. She pulled them back to her flowers. As she stared at the small gathering, a vision unfolded, vivid, within the colour. A woman. In a garden awash with vibrant shrubs and trees, probably alien to this climate. She was blurred as though Flora viewed her through net curtains, and she was on her knees, planting bulbs. Turned the other way; no face visible.

Then gone, in a moment.

Flora frowned. What was *wrong* with her? Hormones? Maybe. Tiredness? Definitely; paper-thin walls had not blocked Beyonce full blast in the early hours from a neighbouring flat. Flora felt like – all at once – life was coming closer.

I feel life coming closer...

Strange.

Some things were getting further away though.

Tonight there would be a hike home from work in the early hours. It was two miles now from where she lived, not one. The last bus had always gone by the time the club shut, and she didn't have a car and couldn't afford a taxi. She supposed it kept her trim.

She should eat something hearty before heading out but she knew beans on toast was likely her evening meal.

As the pan warmed them she arranged her bookshelves. She put the stack of her favourite, now-out-of-print *Icon* magazines at the bottom, within easy reach for when she wanted to flick through the glossy pages. She lined the rest of the shelves with paperbacks, in size order, hearing Bella say she was '*so* OCD'.

She messaged her sister: *How are you? I'll come by tomorrow. X*

Once she had finished the bookshelf, eaten, and showered, it was time to go to work.

She was tired just thinking about it.

But she hoped, at least, that Neil would be there.

5

Marilyn sees the light

4th August 1962, Brentwood, Los Angeles

Tonight, Marilyn couldn't settle within the thick walls of her haven. It had been an odd day. She had walked endlessly through the rooms, a desperate ghost seeking someone to haunt. Now, she paused by the front door, feeling the pull of the dying day, listening, as still as death.

For what? A sound? Movement?

She had heard something earlier, had opened the door and peered out, heart beating. Nothing. She had been tempted to run; it was a curious impulse, heavy with history, dotted with dusty orphanage corridors where she once sprinted to get her heart beating, to be warm.

She continued listening, hand gripping the iron doorknob.

Why did she feel like she wanted to escape?

In the six months of living here she had known restless nights and restful nights. But tonight was the strangest. She hadn't been able to remain in one room for longer than ten minutes, had moved from a chair to a rug to the fireplace.

'Here ends my journey,' she whispered, picturing the tile on the other side of the door.

Finally, she let go of the door knob and went to her bedroom.

She ignored the papers on the bedside stool and the overflowing floral bin and the scattered clothes, and she opened the doors to the courtyard patio. In the fading August light the pool was still. She listened to the night's birth; the cicadas, the crickets and the katydids, the hummingbirds, and the distant throb of traffic. High in the trees her antique, bronze windchime stirred, its lyrical waltz soothing.

Was she just mad at friend and publicist Pat?

Had that caused the restlessness?

Last night Pat had slept in the guest quarters. Over dinner they gossiped like college roommates. Pat then retired early, leaving Marilyn alone to face her torment; the night. The phone rang intermittently throughout, piercing the blackness. Strange men flirted. One was angry that she hadn't kept their date (she had forgotten the arrangement and felt bad). One muttered obscenities. Women screamed abuse down the line until in the end she unplugged it. Her number wasn't listed and yet still they found her. Lurid headlines and sensational (false) claims made people think she was cheap and that they could treat her like garbage.

These phone voices followed her into delirious dreams where, as always on the worst nights, men as big as rooms towered over her, reaching to cover her mouth, to open her up, to do worse.

She had argued with Pat that morning, snappy and envious of her friend's ability to sleep well. But they parted at noon on good terms once more, as was always the case, with promises of talking soon.

No, she wasn't mad at Pat.

She felt... *untethered.*

Needing company, she found housekeeper Eunice washing dishes in the kitchen, violets from the garden in a vase nearby. Soon they would die. It had been cruel to pluck them from the ground so she could enjoy their romantic scent indoors. Eunice had been with Marilyn a year, selected by her psychiatrist Dr Greenson. It was good to have a constant in her life. Their relationship was complex; strained yet tight; close yet devoid of intimacy. Eunice often slept over, though she had an apartment nearby.

'Are you staying tonight?' Marilyn asked.

Marilyn's agitation meant they had been squabbling over minor household things, and she had come close to dismissing the sixty-year-old nurse, but resisted. There was a curious drive to end things, get rid, have a clear out.

'I can, dear, if you want me to,' Eunice said.

'Thank you.' Marilyn knew the housekeeper was concerned about her low mood today; Dr Greenson had turned up suddenly earlier; 'just checking in on you' he had said. Eunice must have alerted him.

'Are you…?' began Eunice.

'Yes?'

'Expecting any... callers?'

She knew Eunice meant men, though most of those in her life were make-up artists and publicists and her masseuse. The others, she didn't want to see. 'No... not that I know of.'

The strange need to run was back, but Marilyn suppressed it.

Where would she go? This was her home.

She flicked through an *Icon* magazine on the worktop to occupy her mind, smiling at the picture of Stella Cruz next to an editorial piece. Maybe she should give her an exclusive. Tell her… Tell her *what*? What was it Dr Greenson insisted she needed to face? What would calm the night terrors?

Marilyn closed the magazine, shook her head. 'I'm going to bed.'

'So early?' Eunice glanced at the clock. 'It's five past nine.'

'Yes. I think... I feel like... it's time...'

'Are you *sure* you're alright, dear?'

'I'll take the phone but if it rings all night, I'll put it out in the hallway. Please, don't disturb me for anything.'

Marilyn poured a glass of milk and took it to her room, grabbing the white telephone from the hallway; its wire snaked under the door like a line guiding a drowning diver to the surface. She loved the telephone; that immediate connection, chatting into the night when insomnia closed in with suffocating hands. Friends often said, 'if it's 2am, we know it's you'.

Suddenly, she returned to the kitchen where Eunice was wiping the surfaces down.

'I've changed my mind,' she said, surprised at the words.

She felt she *must* be alone. No idea why.

'You can go home. Your family must miss you and I'll be fine.' Marilyn knew that Eunice reported all her comings and goings to Dr Greenson. Tonight she wanted privacy.

'You're sure? I can stay.'

'I'm sure. I'll see you tomorrow.'

She returned to her room and looked at the bed, at the unmade expanse of crumpled white eternity: her nemesis. There was always a sense of dread when withdrawing for the evening. Usually she delayed it. She pottered in the garden, called friends, read one of the many scripts she got sent, hoping for a serious role. Here she was though, long before midnight.

She heard the front door closing.

Eunice had gone.

'Here ends my journey,' she whispered.

Where had that come from?

Lethargy dissipated; it always did in here. In an endless quest for sleep, Marilyn had often overdosed. The intention had never been to die. Even once when sitting in a previous apartment window, looking morosely on the busy street far below, she had resisted. Even when she wrote a poem about the Brooklyn Bridge's capacity as an escape route (*I've never seen an ugly bridge*) she had never wanted to die.

She wanted to be the garden shrubs: nourished, reborn each spring, shedding old leaves, growing new, responding to the light and the wind.

She sat on the bed, picked up the vial of chloral hydrate. It rarely had the desired effect. Immunity from years of abuse meant she needed more, and she would lie to a variety of doctors to acquire prescriptions. She poured four capsules into her palm, counting aloud. Four like the absent house number. Today was August 4th too.

A sign?

She poured four more. And another four.

Then she heard a sound.

A whisper, like a blackout curtain moving across a window.

Marilyn waited. Must have imagined it. She lifted the pills to her mouth.

Then light, a white strip of purity, beneath the door.

Had Eunice returned?

She put the pills back in the vial and stepped into the hallway that separated her bedroom from the living room. The light came from beyond. She walked through the shadowy living room where embers died in the hearth and where a cushion was askew in the wicker chair, then through the dining room with hard-backed chairs that guests said weren't comfortable, and into the kitchen. The light didn't come from a lamp or from the moon filtering through the window.

It came from a lady.

Not from behind her but from within.

She stood in the centre of the kitchen.

Her face was olive-skinned, young but full of age, devoid of make-up, line-free and serene; she didn't smile but joy glowed in her eyes, their colour changing from green to blue to brown, as though technicolour movie consultants had manipulated the irises. She was shrouded in a robe the blue shade of the tile by the front door, girdled at the waist by a silky ribbon that flowed to the floor.

Her dark hair was mostly hidden by a hood. One slender hand was over her heart; in the other she held out a familiar flower: a bright pink bloom from the bougainvillea vine.

She spoke.

It was a language Marilyn had never heard, one heavy on *k* and *h* sounds, lacking consonants at the start of each word, vowels brief. She thought she heard a word in English, but then it dissolved before she could decipher it.

Then the lady said three particular words.

'Cursum perficio, Marilyn.'

6

Flora sees the light too

March 2016, Hull, England

The Great Neillusionist dominated the small stage.

Flora was seduced by the spectacle. She didn't know how he had made a torn-up ten of hearts appear in boss Greg's top pocket. He had finesse in spades, with thin, deft hands, a willowy frame, and mousy hair swept to a side. He never spoke during his act, a silence that added tension. But despite this talent, Neil Fletcher was in a backstreet club on a Wednesday night, barely sixty patrons as witness, and they were mostly there for Psychic Pat.

He finished his set by disappearing and materialising next to shocked office workers at the back. Flora watched him leave, her heart aching.

He was chattier offstage, with a wicked sense of humour softly spoken. He once told Flora that magic was *I'll show you this, so you don't notice that*, the way good liars dazzle you with details so it sounds true. She had once sneaked a peak of him practising in the dusty backstage room, repeating an action over and over and over until the movements appeared ordinary, natural, flowed.

Now she collected the empties, her back aching, and feet hot inside her charity shop trainers. Almost ten-thirty. Two hours to go. The hardest thing about working late wasn't the great length of time on her feet; it wasn't the long walk home or the drunk patrons harassing for dates/sex/a phone number.

The hardest thing was that this was *it*.

The Cave Comedy Club, beneath a street where the homeless

found warmth near a restaurant kitchen, where a lap dancing club on the corner enticed, with limestone walls and rows of low-hanging lamps swinging above black metal tables. Initially opened to support new comedians, it now offered its stage to all entertainers, to singers, theatre groups and magicians

Greg grunted, 'More glasses,' at Flora.

She grabbed some from the dishwasher and filled them with beer for the thirsty hoards. The rush between acts was always a stampede.

'Smile, it might never happen,' said a blonde man in a flat cap.

Flora hated being told to smile but bit her tongue.

'You'd be pretty if you did,' he continued.

She banged his pint down on the bar.

'Ooooh, someone needs a good shagging,' he said to his mate.

'Oy,' interrupted Greg. 'Give it a rest.'

'Just being friendly.'

A crackling sound filled the air. The compere – Denise, the manager, with an offstage mic – announced that Psychic Pat was here to 'thrill and astound'. Patrons took their seats where they could switch on a small table lamp when they wanted service while the act was in progress, an illumination Flora dreaded from certain men who then groped her when she got close.

Eerie music provoked a melody of titters.

White smoke billowed from a machine.

It dispersed and Psychic Pat sat on a stool, snake-like hair on her shoulders, crushed-velvet gown faded at the elbows, face caked in orange foundation, and eyes smoky. It was her fifth appearance in four months. Flora knew that before she went onstage, Pat sat in a toilet cubicle, listening to conversations.

'The spirits are with us tonight.' Her voice was a snarl of Hull accent and cigarettes. 'They're among us, whispering, I can let them in.'

'Are they buying the drinks?' someone at the back called.

Unperturbed, Pat continued. 'If I call on you, turn your lamp on so I can see you.' She held a hand aloft and stared with demonic eyes into a space above the heads. 'Oh, yes… I hear you. I'll tell... *her*?' She looked to the far corner, hand still high. 'I'm getting the word... oh, it's an odd one... I'm getting the word *foodbank*.'

A lamp switched on. 'I volunteer in one,' cried a woman with bleach-blonde hair. She turned to her friend, said, 'You know I do, Gee, don't you?'

'She does.' Gee nodded.

Psychic Pat looked as though she was listening to a song in a foreign language. 'Is your brother in spirit, darlin'?' she asked.

The blonde was obviously disappointed. 'He's in prison.'

'Could be... your *dad*? Was he tall? Loved by all…?'

'Oh, yes,' gushed the blonde.

'What's your name, love?' asked Pat.

You should know, thought Flora, collecting more empties.

'Marge,' she said.

'Marge, your beloved dad is with us. And he wants to say how proud he is that you're volunteering at the foodbank.'

Marge put a hand over her gold vest. Flora shook her head. Neil emerged from the backstage door and sat under the Upcoming Events poster. Flora got him a beer and they exchanged raised eyebrows.

'Your dad was taken in the prime of life,' said Pat.

'He was eighty-nine,' said Marge.

'A youthful man though. It was unexpected. You never got to say goodbye.'

'He had pancreatic cancer.' Marge's voice broke. 'It was... slow... we were there at the end...'

Pat seemed irritated. How dare this patron have had a goodbye with her dying father when she hadn't foreseen it? She moved her attention to the word chrysanthemum and a man who had seen them everywhere since his wife died.

'You OK?' asked Neil.

He and Flora occasionally had a drink on her break. She wondered how he felt about her, though what was the point – she'd only ruin anything if it happened.

'Flora?'

She realised she hadn't responded. 'Just... you know…'

'I don't.' He paused. 'Tell me.'

'I moved yesterday.' Would it be nice to unburden her anxieties? Might it put him off, knowing her flaws, her secrets, her past? 'It's a real dump.'

With a swift movement, he produced a pink carnation out of nowhere. She took it, their fingers touching for a moment. She was moved; he knew she adored flowers, she had mentioned her window pots once.

Neil's eyebrows were knitted in confusion. 'That's crazy.'

'What is?'

'It was supposed to be... a *daffodil.*'

'You're teasing.' She knew he planned a trick well ahead.

But now he was frowning at something else. Psychic Pat was looking their way, hand trembling like Death pointing out his next victim.

'I can't see you back there,' she croaked.

Neil manoeuvred Flora forward, his eyes full of mischief.

'Flora, darlin', it's *you.*' Had Pat excepted someone else? Was Flora going to ruin the big finale by being the wrong person? 'I'm getting the word kitchen. It's real. I mean they all are,' she hastily added, 'but it's a powerful one. Kitchen. Does it mean owt?'

'Mine's just a few cupboards and a small hob…'

The audience tittered. Greg leaned on his elbows at the bar, shaking his head.

'You're gonna get a visitor.' Pat seemed surprised at her own words.

'*I* am?' asked Flora.

'Out of the blue. She's telling me. Shit, she really is.'

Flora hated surprise visitors. They only ever brought bad news or wanted money.

'A woman. I don't... this has never... she said you...'

Pat left the stage, first going the wrong way and then stumbling in the opposite direction.

No one applauded. The lights came up and hearty discussion ensued. Flora wanted to find Pat but knew Greg would need her so hurried to the bar. From there, she looked for Neil. Gone. Damn. Pat emerged from backstage – hair hidden beneath a beret, long coat blanketing the purple dress – and headed for the main exit.

Flora abandoned a put-out patron mid-order, and caught Pat.

'What happened up there?' she asked.

'I don't know, darlin'.' Pat shook as she took a cigarette out of her pocket. 'I sort of chide the spirits along. But she spoke right in me bloody ear, like she was next to me, except I couldn't see nowt.'

'Who did?'

'A woman. Gentle, sweet, not like any of 'em in here.'

'What exactly did she say?' asked Flora.

'She said *kitchen* first, and then that a woman will call on you soon. Oh... she mentioned *that*.' Pat motioned to the carnation in Flora's apron pocket. 'That messed with me head. She said it was supposed to be a–'

'–daffodil,' they both said softly.

Pat shuddered. 'I don't think you should worry though.'

'What do you mean?'

'I think it'll be a nice visitor. I have to go, love, my husband'll be waiting.'

'No one knows my new address though,' said Flora. 'I just

moved…'

But Pat had gone.

Flora touched the carnation and returned to the bar. Once the place was empty, she wiped down tables, and took out the rubbish. Sometimes, if he was in a generous mood, Greg dropped her off at home. Tonight he had a new lover waiting at his flat and left Flora to lock up.

Outside, the night world shook off its evening attire and settled into comfortable apparel, into shut curtains, soft lighting, locked doors. She walked briskly, trainers quiet on the tarmac, not inviting attention. She thought about running, like she used to long ago, but was tired.

How had Pat known about the daffodil? That kind of thing, you couldn't guess. Most of 'being psychic' was the art of cold reading: high-probability deductions, broad statements, and picking up on positive responses while ignoring missed guesses. Like Neil's act, it was an illusion, except it wasn't honest in its trickery; it hurt those who longed for messages from dead loved ones.

Flora stopped, realised she had left the carnation in her apron pocket in her locker. Damn it. By tomorrow night, it would have likely died. It would be foolish at this time of night to go back for it. It was just a flower.

No, it was a flower from *Neil.*

At the flat, she locked the door, dropped her keys onto the plastic table and sank into a chair, removing her trainers and rubbing her aching feet. She filled the pan; she couldn't afford a kettle until payday. The fridge was empty so she grabbed some biscuits, made tea, and went into the bedroom.

Lying on top of her duvet, she glanced at the single mattress, imagining Bella there, headphones on, thin arms poking out of a faded daisy-covered nightie and marked with scars of varying depth. She and Flora hadn't had the best childhood, with a mother who came and went, and absent fathers.

*

Flora must have fallen asleep, half a biscuit in hand, because she woke in the dark, crumbs chafing her elbow, wondering if the chill had stirred her.

Then she realised.

Light filtered beneath the bedroom door.

She knew she had switched it off. This light, however, wasn't the wan luminance of an economy bulb; it was a strip of purity. She went to the door, paused, then opened it.

The light came from a lady.

She stood in the centre of the make-shift corner kitchen, by the hob and the fridge donated by a friend.

Her face was olive-skinned, young but full of age, devoid of make-up, line-free and serene; she didn't smile but joy glowed in her eyes, their colour changing from green to blue to brown, as though Instagram filters had manipulated the irises. She was shrouded in a robe the same hue as the dress in Flora's beloved print, girdled at the waist by a silky ribbon that flowed to the floor. A white hood gave a brief glimpse of dark hair. Her feet were bare. Flora thought they must be cold on the cheap lino. One slender hand she put over her heart, and in the other she held out a flower: one daffodil.

'Oh,' Flora's knees gave a little.

The daffodil?

'Am I… dreaming?' whispered Flora.

The lady spoke.

Flora first heard the words in a language she didn't recognise, one heavy on *k* and *h* sounds, not poetic, lacking consonants at the start of each word, vowels brief. Then she heard it in English, the lady's native tongue a soft echo behind the sentences. Two languages, one story.

'Don't be afraid of me,' the lady said. 'I'm the Holy Mother; I'm here with a special message.'

Flora couldn't speak.

Then the lady said three words, a few times, as though to stick them firmly to Flora's heart. Words she didn't understand though she shivered because it was like they were from a poem someone might have read her long, long ago.

'Cursum perficio, Flora,' the lady said.

7

Marilyn wonders if she is dreaming

4th August 1962, Brentwood, Los Angeles

Marilyn sank to her knees in disbelief.

She recognised the lady from the card she had cherished in the orphanage but couldn't understand why she was here, in this modest house half a mile from Sunset Boulevard, close enough to Santa Monica beach to hear children's joy when the wind carried their laughter this way.

Marilyn tried to speak but her voice was a dry croak. Perhaps she was half-asleep and had wandered in here, as she often did, waking and wondering where she was. She hoped not. She felt joy at the sight of this lady, at the bright pink bloom from the bougainvillea vine she held out.

Mary.

'Your journey ends here,' she said.

Marilyn noticed that her feet were bare, felt terrible that they were cold on *her* tiled floor. 'Let me get you some slippers,' she said. Then she saw a circular disc of white around where she stood, wondered if this was warming the soles of her feet. Marilyn's knees should be cold but they weren't: her whole body hummed with heat.

'Don't be afraid,' continued Mary in a breathy voice people associated with Marilyn. Marilyn's true voice, however, was quiet, more earthy, real. She realised that Mary must also experience expectation, have to speak a certain way, *be* a certain way.

'I'm not afraid,' Marilyn managed.

'I'm here to give you a future.'

'But what should I call you?' The question popped into Marilyn's head; it wasn't the most apt after such profound words. 'N-names are important,' she explained, stammering as she had during childhood. 'Th-that's why I ask.'

'Call me Mary,' she said simply.

'My name's yours! Mary and Lynne. I chose it at Twentieth Century Fox. We didn't think Norma Jeane was right and I was glad to say goodbye to her but new names make you confused about who you are.' Marilyn put a hand over her mouth, realising she had gone on. 'Sorry.'

'This is not the place you are supposed to be.' Mary's eyes shone; Marilyn had never been looked at in such a way, not by lovers, or fans, or her own mother. 'This is the place you are supposed to *leave*. Cursum perficio.'

'The words on my tile.'

'Words you knew to be true.' Mary joined her hands, the flower between them. 'You are not happy in this world of fame. Leave here and be free of sadness.'

'Leave this *house*?' Marilyn finally withdrew her gaze from Mary and looked around the room. 'But it's my first real home.'

'We make our home inside ourselves. We are not the place where we dwell, we are the place where we love.'

Marilyn couldn't imagine leaving. Old childhood fears resurfaced; Norma Jeane never knowing from one day to another where her next home might be.

Mary said, 'Your life is your choice but if you don't leave this house... you might leave this world.'

'What does *that* mean?' Marilyn shrank back.

'There is death. This night.'

'*Death*?' Marilyn went cold now.

'Leave, find who you're supposed to be.'

But who was that?

'Then you will be wonderful, my child.'

'I *will*?'

The word had followed Marilyn everywhere since her quote about just wanting to be wonderful; it had been a headline, filled interviews where there was nothing new to include. The word mocked her now. She knew her faults; she was often ill-tempered and had rages that rendered her incoherent. She often ran late, holding up filming and infuriating the crew, and she got emotional at times. These flaws were not allowed because she was supposed to be perfect.

As soon as she wasn't, they tore her apart.

Mary's light flickered. 'Wonderful means *full of wonder*. It does not mean astonishing but to be *full* of astonishment.' She paused. 'With fame, you *gave* great joy but never found it for yourself.'

Fame wasn't waiting when you got home late at night, exhausted. It couldn't hug you in the dark, or give you children. But where would Marilyn go? Was it possible to abandon such global celebrity?

'Shine your light on other women,' continued Mary. 'Tell me this. When did you sleep best?'

'There was a day,' Marilyn said softly. 'I visited an orphanage back in 1952, when I was first famous. I gave candy to the children... spoke to them for a while... I *knew* how they felt. That night, I slept like a baby.'

'Follow your heart,' said Mary, 'and then the tiny white shoe, one you will know, which will take you up into the place you should go first.'

'The place I should first go?'

'And then onto she who is named after the stars.'

'She who is…?'

'And finally, to the place of your ancestors.'

'To... but where *is* that?'

Mary moved towards Marilyn, her trailing gown soundless. She put the bright pink bloom into Marilyn's hand and pecked her on the cheek, her lips cool, brief: an ethereal kiss. She left. Even if Marilyn had wanted to follow her, she couldn't move.

The kitchen shadows were now sadder.

Marilyn cried the way she had when her mother abruptly left years ago. She recalled the apparitions religious Aunt Ada had described long ago. Hadn't the Virgin Mary appeared to a peasant girl called Bernadette in Lourdes? Hadn't a miracle occurred in the form of holy water from a spring? Hadn't others said Bernadette had a mental illness and should be put in an asylum?

Marilyn would not tell anyone about this.

They would say she had been drug addled. She certainly wouldn't tell Dr Greenson in case he suggested a stay in a psychiatric unit, like two years ago when a previous doctor had had her committed. She had thought she was going to rest, but instead got escorted to a padded cell. The four days in its isolation had been the most distressing of her life, and she didn't want to experience that again.

If she *had* imagined Mary, it didn't matter because there was a calm, like she had been bathed in warm milk.

Mary had said there was death.

Hadn't Marilyn felt strange all day?

What time was it? Barely nine-thirty.

She walked through the house, hoping to find evidence of Mary's visit, footprints or an errant hair. Then she remembered the pink flower, lifted it to her nose. This was no proof. They would say she had picked it herself.

And soon it would die.

In the bedroom, Marilyn looked around. Everything appeared just as she had left it: the glass of milk, the phone on the bedside stool, the vial of pills she now had no desire to re-open. The bed was still unwelcoming. Marilyn knew, suddenly and absolutely, that she would not place her head on that pillow tonight.

It was still 4th August. She thought of the absent four in her house number: 12305. What if she too went missing? What if she disappeared? What if she was the number zero?

Then the phone began ringing.

8

Stella Cruz, Icon magazine, August 1963

Marilyn Monroe was not a person; she was a goddess. She was an image. A body and hair and lips. A poster on the side of a building, a flickering image in a movie, a fantasy for men to devour, an ideal for women to emulate.

But when I interviewed her in May 1962 at her Brentwood home, she looked tired. She wore a simple beige dress, and said,' I started it, you know. That's on me. I created this Marilyn Monroe, this other creature that I could hide behind. But I didn't know where it would go. I didn't know that the woman I hoped would give me a new life, grant me all these opportunities, would ultimately let me down. Because she's a cover up. A facade. And when I take off my make-up, she's gone, and there's nothing left. I created her but now I can't find my way back to myself. I'm afraid of all the flaws and failings I've hidden for so long behind this invention.'

At the end of our chat, Marilyn put a hand on mine and asked if I would not include that segment of our talk. She looked sad, said that I probably would, because 'they always do'. She said she had been talking to me, woman to woman, not for an audience.

So, I didn't print them.

I wrote about the joy Marilyn found in the simplicity of planting seeds and watching them grow. About where she bought her shrubs and how she selected each one based on their complementary colours, the way that 'peas and carrots always look so pretty together in the pan'.

It wasn't my first interview but it felt like Marilyn opened up more than she had previously. I found her articulate, warm and sensitive, different to the woman on the screen.

Why then have I fifteen months after that interview broken my promise? Because I'm done with reading salacious headlines and demeaning stories about her. I'm tired of her name being used to sell pages, products, documentaries.

When I began this magazine in 1960, I wanted to publish thought-provoking and well-researched pieces that explored the lives of our biggest cinema icons. My Elizabeth Taylor interview in our first issue, where she opened up about how she had been used by the studios, earned me the coveted prize of that year's Front Page Award, and launched the magazine into the stratosphere.

Now, I want to pay tribute to the blonde woman who proudly showed me her new house, who offered me grapefruit juice and made sure I had the most comfortable chair in her living room. I want to give you the woman who wore little make-up, who looked vulnerable in that bareness, who answered my questions with wit and honesty, who showed anger over how she had been treated.

Marilyn Monroe was not allowed to be human. She was not allowed to be imperfect. She was not allowed a break. She was not allowed privacy.

I speak of her in past tense because I'd like to think that she made peace with her creation, that she moved on from Marilyn Monroe. Perhaps this is what happened on that ever-mysterious night in Brentwood, exactly one year ago. Perhaps Norma Jeane finally found her way back to herself.

9

Flora doesn't feel worthy

March 2016, Hull, England

Flora knelt in Mary's glow, the grimy lino sticky against her bare skin. It was what she had done in church as a child when prayers were said. Grandma Lil had taken her and Bella there while their mother was with yet another unsuitable man.

'You're…' tried Flora.

'Cursum perficio, Flora,' Mary said again.

Flora glanced briefly at Grandma Lil's print on the wall. 'They got you wrong,' she said.

'People see me how they want to.'

Flora put her face in her hands, overwhelmed by this vision in her threadbare flat. Why would Mary come to a building that housed drug dealers, to a town often on the UK's Worst Cities list?

Perhaps she was dreaming.

But the colours in the dull room were sharp like super HD. The daffodil in Mary's hand was the yellowest of yellows, like it had stolen rays from the sun. Flora could hear the sounds of a spring day – birdsong, a breeze, a stream. Her imagination was not strong enough to create this.

'Here ends your journey, and here begins another.'

'I should *go* somewhere?'

Now, at this time of night?

'Divine journeys don't require our feet to move, only our hearts.' She held out the daffodil. Flora thought of Neil's face, the carnation. She imagined sharing this with him, saying look, your magic was real. 'This flower symbolises hope.'

Flora pressed it to her chest.

'I don't feel worthy,' she whispered.

I'm thirty-six and I work in a bar, she wanted to say. I swear and I have crap trainers and no kettle and trouble forming long relationships. My sister is on a mental health ward and my mother can't cope with visiting her there. I've done terrible things.

Flora had questions; why her, why here? But she was mute. She recalled Grandma Lil's tale about two girls who saw the Virgin in Chandavila in Spain. They called her the Lady of Sorrows, and described a black gown covered in stars, and overwhelming sadness in Mary's face. One girl had crawled over rough ground at Mary's request, yet no injuries were apparent. It was deemed a miracle.

'I ask something simple,' said Mary, 'and in return the beautiful one will be saved.'

The beautiful one?

'Bella?' Flora's question came out as a whisper.

'There's a sanctuary you're to serve. Heal others and in return be healed.'

Flora was keen to please. 'Is it a church?'

'It's your turn now.'

'My turn?' This suggested that it had previously been someone else's.

'You should *care*,' said Mary.

'I do. But what place do you mean?'

'You know it.'

'Grandma Lil's church?'

Mary's brilliance was waning. The room took on its everyday shadows again. The daffodil in Flora's hand would die. And what did Mary want?

'You're leaving,' said Flora quietly.

'You made a great sacrifice once.'

'Did I?'

'You surrendered a blessing and carry the scar inside. You ran and ran and ran.'

Mary made the sign of the cross with a slow flourish before joining her palms in prayer. Flora could smell the flowers in their windowsill boxes. Why did she suddenly, again, think of a garden awash with vibrant shrubs and trees, see a woman kneeling, planting bulbs? Why did she feel a connection to a pale-haired woman who did not seem aware that she was watching her?

'I bless the sacrifice that hurt your heart.' Mary broke into the vision. 'You had no say in it and did not ask for it.'

Flora sagged, knees agony now.

She knew the sacrifice Mary spoke of.

'Go and *care*.'

Mary moved, making no noise. She pecked Flora on the cheek, lips cool, brief: an ethereal kiss. She moved through the living room, departed. Even if Flora had wanted to follow her, she couldn't have moved.

She remained in the prayer position. Eventually the sun filtered beneath the curtains. It must be past six. She had been kneeling for three hours. She got up, joints clicking like the heating when it came on. She touched the daffodil. She should press it between book pages to preserve it as evidence.

Did that mean she was going to tell someone?

God, no.

They would ridicule the idea of Mary coming to her grotty flat.

After a while, she filled the pan with water and put it on the hob. Then she opened the curtains and smiled at the blooms in the morning sun. She put Mary's daffodil in a glass of water and placed it on the windowsill too.

And in return the beautiful one will be saved.

She checked her phone; there were messages from her sister saying she couldn't sleep. Flora apologised for not replying, said she would be there later. She made tea and sipped it.

Had Mary really just been *here*?

Belief faltered. Perhaps Flora had had a breakdown. Perhaps she created the woman Grandma Lil always said was there in our hour of need. She went to Lil's Mary print on the wall. Stared hard at it.

Remembered Psychic Pat earlier.

You're gonna get a visitor.

Our of the blue. A woman.

Flora needed to speak to her. Neil had witnessed Pat's vision. Could she tell him about this? Would he think her mad? He wasn't performing tonight but he might turn up, as he occasionally did.

Flora's eyes felt heavy. She would close them for an hour and then think about what had transpired. Go see Bella. As oblivion took her, Flora thought again of the sacrifice Mary mentioned; the sacrifice that hurt her heart.

She pushed it away, buried the face that came to her like a tiny, acute jab.

Let the darkness suffocate it.

There's a sanctuary you're to serve.

As she drifted off, Flora suddenly realised what Mary meant, where she wanted her to go. CARE. Of course.

And in return the beautiful one will be saved.

10

Marilyn follows her heart

4th August 1962, Brentwood, Los Angeles

Marilyn looked at the ringing telephone.

It sounded angry; *don't delay, everything hinges on this.* But she didn't have time, she must decide what to do. The disturbance went on. It would stop, eventually. It seemed to get louder. Marilyn thought of the calls last night. On it went. She wanted to scream.

In the end, she picked it up.

'Hello,' she said quietly into the receiver.

'Honey, it's me.' Pat, her friend and publicist. 'Where *were* you?'

'Oh, hi.' Relief had Marilyn sinking onto the bed. 'I was in the bathroom.'

'Are you OK?'

'Yes. Are you?' Marilyn recalled their argument that morning, wanted to make sure they were good again. 'I'm sorry about earlier. I'm always so envious of people who sleep easily.'

'Oh, I'd forgotten all about that,' said Pat.

Marilyn felt great affection for her friend.

Why did she feel like she might never see her again?

'You're sweet, Sybil,' she said gently. It was a nickname; it stood for sibling rivalry, because she saw her as another sister. She had a real sister too, Berniece, who she had only known recently. They had grown up separately because they had different fathers, and Berniece had lived with hers. Marilyn finally met her aged eighteen, her sister twenty-five, after they had been pen pals for six years. Marilyn got the train to Detroit and they met in the busy station; Berniece's familiar face lit with joy. They now spoke on the phone occasionally, most recently when Marilyn wanted advice on new curtains.

Pat was speaking: 'I called because I had such a strange feeling about you.'

'You did?'

'I felt like... I might never see you again. I was so sad.'

Marilyn didn't know what to say. She felt it too. Should she tell Pat what she had seen? She didn't know what she might think and dreaded the press finding out. She trusted Pat with her life but feared that her phone had been tapped, a concern suggested by Dr Greenson. The press would go wild. She could see lurid headlines: Mad Marilyn Claims Virgin Mary Visited Brentwood Home: Sad Star Says Holy Apparition Appeared In Kitchen: Desperate Monroe Committed To Asylum Again After Losing Mind.

'Are you still there?' Pat, urgent.

There is death. This night.

Marilyn heard the words like a delayed echo. Could she go on with this life now? Could she accept the film obligations, the pressure, painting on her make-up for the cameras, forcing a smile for photographs, over and over and over, click, flash, click, flash, until she shrivelled and died and was forgotten?

'Marilyn, are you there?' Alarm was sharp in Pat's tone.

'I am,' said Marilyn, quickly. She caught her reflection in the doors leading to the garden – a waif sitting on a bed, hair messed, phone in one hand, pink flower in the other; it verified that she was still Marilyn Monroe.

'I was going to come and sleep over again.'

'Another time.'

Pat didn't sound sure. 'I guess, sleep well.' She paused. 'I'll call you in the morning.'

Would Marilyn be here?

Would the phone ring and ring and ring in an empty house?

'Sure,' she said. 'I'll talk to you then. Pat…'

'Yes?'

'I love you, honey.'

Silence. Had Pat hung up?

'Are you *sure* you're OK?' she asked.

Marilyn laughed. 'Can't a gal tell her friend she loves her?'

'But it sounded so… *final*.'

'Goodnight.'

Marilyn hung up. Then she unplugged the phone, wrapped the wire around it and put it in her wardrobe. She had never done that before. It felt like a preparation.

Was she going to walk away from everything?

Her life flashed by, disappearing: twenty-nine movies, many with the greatest actors in the world; founding Marilyn Monroe Productions in the hope of acquiring better roles; a Crystal Star Award and a David di Donatello Award for *The Prince and the Showgirl;* having a script written for her by Arthur Miller.

But what were those things really?

Not things you could touch. Not things you could hug. Not things you could be sustained by. Fleeting transitory highs that gave brief pleasure, like a spring day cooling before it's even begun.

A draught tickled Marilyn's ankles.

She spun towards the bed, the origin of the breeze.

Gasped.

There she was. Sleeping. Sheet pulled over her inert body, a shock of hair showing, one hand near her head, which was face-down as though she was forbidden to speak. But she *never* slept that way. Marilyn slept on her side with the covers tucked around her body to keep the night monsters at bay.

Who was this slumbering twin?

Shadows moved around the bed, dozy creatures with no clear shape, huddling together then moving apart. Marilyn started when she felt them pass by. Voices said odd things, words clumsily overlapping words, growing in urgency and volume.

Did you try to revive her? Did she take the pills? How did she swallow them all? Who was here earlier? Has this body been moved? Who positioned her like this? When was she discovered? Who called us? You rang the movie publicity department before you contacted us? Why did you wait so long?

How long has she been dead?

Dead?

Marilyn cried out and covered her eyes.

When she removed her trembling hands, the vision had gone. What ghastly thing had she seen? Herself. Who were the other people though? Why so many? Of course: it had been Marilyn Monroe on the bed. (She often spoke of herself in third person, not to be pretentious, but because this woman was a separate entity.) Was she losing her mind like her poor mother had done? Had the whole evening since Eunice left been one long hallucination? She pinched her skin.

She was here.

It was real.

Was she to end up dead if she stayed?

She glanced at the vial of pills on the bedside stool. She had poured twelve earlier, counted in fours because that number was in her head. She had taken eight before and woken in the morning heavy-headed, tongue like a ball of cotton. She could probably survive twelve with her high tolerance.

Marilyn needed to leave; she knew it now.

She bustled about the room, sleep forgotten, picking things up and putting them down, flapping her hands like when preparing for a movie scene. But this was the real world not a set. This was a vast undertaking not a moment captured on film.

What did you take if you were leaving forever?

Marilyn got a small holdall from the wardrobe and selected the beige dress she had worn when wanting to be taken seriously, found underwear in a drawer, and toiletries. She ignored her make-up. She no longer wanted those face-changing cosmetics. Nor did she want valuable items, the jewels and furs gifted by husbands and lovers. But she might need money; she had a hundred dollars in her purse.

There were so many precious things; letters from fans, her books – perhaps close to four hundred – some signed by the author, a photo of her mother, and her poems and thoughts in a variety of notepads, all in the wooden travel trunk from childhood.

She could not carry that.

Then she saw her favourite photograph, propped up in the bedside stool. It had been taken by Cecil Beaton in 1956. Marilyn was lying on a patterned sheet, wrapped in chiffon, hair short and curly, eyes dewy, not smiling but looking sleepily into the camera. In her hand was a carnation; the colour wasn't apparent in the black and white image, but Marilyn knew it was pink, like the one in her hand now.

She put the print in the holdall and found the platinum eternity ring from Joe DiMaggio; its value might help in whatever she decided to do.

Then she zipped the bag up. Paused, luggage in one hand, flower in the other.

How the hell was she going to execute this?

It was ridiculous.

She was the most recognisable woman in the world. She might disappear into the shadows while it was dark, but in the morning when the sun cooked the pavement and the hordes herded, there would be no hiding. When she lived in New York she had got around incognito by hiding her hair beneath a scarf, her body underneath a too-big coat, and her eyes behind sunglasses. But someone always saw through it, asked for an autograph. Then she was obliged to become *her.*

Marilyn quickly put on black slacks and a matching blouse, and a plain brown coat Eunice had left in the house, and then a tan scarf tied around her hair and knotted tightly to hide every strand.

She needed somewhere safe to go until she could figure out what to do next. Until she could metamorphosise into someone who wasn't Marilyn Monroe; a butterfly in search of a cocoon so she could become a caterpillar once more.

A sound outside.

She gasped. Froze. *Mary?*

Every instinct told her not.

And she was terrified.

11

Flora looks different

March 2016, Hull, England

Flora woke from her nap like it had been a yearlong sleep.

Had the Virgin Mary really been here, sharing messages about saving the beautiful one? Flora went into the kitchen, paused at the daffodil in its glass of water. The flower said so.

She put a pan of water on the hob, opened Google on her phone, and typed in *who was the Virgin Mary*? The top result was Wikipedia, and on that page she was described mainly in holy terms, as the mother of Jesus, and therefore the mother of God, as being the holiest and greatest saint, the eternal virgin. But what about the actual *woman*?

Next Flora searched for *Virgin Mary apparitions*. The same website said that Marian apparitions were considered expressions of her motherly care. There had been three hundred and eighty-six cases, though most were not recognised by the church. An appearance in Giza, Egypt in 2009 seemed to be the last one.

Flora sipped tea, wondering if everyone Mary visited had shared their experience. Stories online suggested that doing so resulted in a Catholic Church investigation into the authenticity of the miracle. If deemed worthy, the apparition would be verified. However, few were recognised by the Vatican.

Flora didn't want such attention.

Should she tell someone she could trust? Bella. What if her sister disclosed it in therapy? What if, while on medication, she told someone in the hospital? Maybe keeping quiet was best.

'But why *me*?' Flora whispered to the wall.

*

At noon she headed for the bus. The hospital sat just outside the city. Flora knew the drill; she signed the log and waited to be buzzed through the doors. The residents were not necessarily dangerous, but they did try and escape.

Bella's room was small, square, uninspiring. Even her childhood trinkets – Barbie coasters and a jewellery box made of painted shells – and her artwork didn't make much difference, like the vacuous space sucked away their colour. Flora's eyes landed first on the tiny Virgin Mary made of ivory plastic that she knew glowed in the dark. Grandma Lil had given it to Bella, who took it everywhere because it 'had her love in it'.

'How are you?' Flora sat on the narrow bed.

Bella paced the room, phone in hand. 'The battery's at one percent and they won't let me charge it,' she snapped. Phone wires weren't allowed due to their other function – strangulation device. Any ligature risk was barred; belts, shoelaces, dangly light switches. 'Mum messaged me and it's about to die.'

'*Mum* messaged?' Flora was surprised.

Though she only lived a few miles away, she had never visited Bella. The girls saw her only when they went to her house, or if a family event required the presence of all its scattered members. 'You're grown up,' Mum said. 'What do you need me for? It's *my* time, my twilight years.'

'She said she hoped I was better,' said Bella, 'and I should see her when I'm out.'

'That's nice.' Flora didn't know what else to say. A physical visit might have helped Bella, and yet their mother expected them to go and see *her*.

Bella studied Flora. 'You look... different.'

'Do I?' Flora looked at her sweatshirt and jeans, faded from many washes.

'Like you've lost weight, but not that. No, it's more... I dunno.' Bella shook her head and threw her phone on the bed. 'Bloody thing. Sis, I want to get out of here.'

'You've done most of your Section, you've only another week or two. But you need to show them you'll... behave.' Flora hated that word but she couldn't think of another. 'Prove that you won't…'

'Hurl myself off the railway bridge? Yeah, yeah. I know. Keep doing my paintings, keep taking my meds, keep being sane.'

'You *are* sane,' sighed Flora.

'My scars are healing. Look.'

Flora didn't like these cuts. Luckily, most were now a mixture of soft pink and white lines overlapping. Still, Flora feared Bella resuming when she came out.

Bella flopped on the bed, put her head on her sister's shoulder. 'Are you mad at me?' she asked in a small voice. 'Are you gonna stop coming?'

'I'll always be here.'

This was how it went; Bella ranted and raged, then worried that Flora would desert her.

'I had a bad night. Remember when she disappeared that time?'

Flora knew who Bella meant. 'Which time?'

'I was five, so you still lived at home. I'd been sick all over my bed. Mum's bed was empty when I went there. You sorted me out but I was hysterical. I thought I was going to die and never see Mum again.'

'I remember,' said Flora softly.

'She was gone for days that time.'

Flora nodded knowing Bella would feel the response.

'I dreamt I was looking for her.' Bella's voice grew shrill. 'The hurt was like this angry demon ripping out of me. I woke and I swear that demon was in the corner, growling.' She paused. 'How are you fine and I'm not?'

'I'm not always fine.' Flora was suddenly exhausted.

She knew things Bella did not. She had hurts of her own, hidden away like stolen money in a secret safe. She was made of something different, not better just different; they were the same colour jumper knitted from different wool. But Flora couldn't tell Bella this. Bella wouldn't cope with it.

'Sometimes I hate you for it,' said Bella quietly.

'Do you?' Flora was stung.

Bella touched Flora's face. 'No, not hate. More... jealousy. I'm sorry. The wrong words jump out sometimes. You've made something of your life. But look at me…'

'Stop it.' Flora grabbed her sister by the shoulders. 'My life is a mess. You let it all out, which is good.'

'Really?' Bella held out a scarred arm.

'Not that, your ranting. I bottle everything up.'

'I'm never going to live like normal people while I'm in here.'

'That's down to you,' said Flora calmly. 'When you get out, stay on your medication. Keep seeing the therapist. Keep doing your paintings. Maybe you can finally go to uni, do an Art degree?'

'I want that.'

'Then *do* it,' cried Flora.

'I'll try.'

'Good.'

They sat in silence. Flora realised Bella had fallen asleep. It often happened. The medication made her drowsy. The screams and clanking doors in the night stopped her getting quality rest. Flora lay her down and pulled a blanket over her. She stood, picked up the tiny Virgin Mary, glancing back at Bella.

And in return the beautiful one will be saved.

Bella woke after half an hour and they went to the communal area to make coffee and toast and took them into the small garden where benches on a grey patio surrounded tubs of budding flowers. A nurse asked if they wanted to join the Bingo in the Games Area, but they declined.

'How does gambling help people?' Bella sat on a bench, grumpy now.

'I guess there's therapy in crossing out numbers,' said Flora.

'How's work then?'

'Same old, same old.'

'How's the Great Neillusionist?' Bella was smiling.

'Stop it.'

'Stop what?'

'You know what,' said Flora.

'You like him.'

'As a friend, yes.'

Bella nudged her. 'I reckon he likes you.' Bella had come to the club a few times in the past. 'He studies you.'

'He does not.' Flora was indignant but hoped it was true.

'I'd do him.'

Flora laughed then.

'Wish there were some decent men in here but they're all demented. And that's just the staff.' Bella giggled.

Flora laughed but inside she felt morose.

She was thirty-six. She should have made a relationship work by now. There had been a few over the years but none had lasted more than six months. As soon as a man hinted at children, marriage, she found herself causing arguments. Now, she resisted relationships, fearing she would push them away.

'Drink your coffee,' she said. 'I'm cold now.'

Inside, they watched reruns of *Judge Judy* in the Day Room, where a man in a high-backed chair sang Bon Jovi hits in a delicate voice. Bella grew drowsy again. Flora held her hand, the acapella songs merging with Judy's harsh judgement. Before she fell asleep again, Bella whispered something.

'You do look different. It's like... the inside of you changed. Also, I painted you a picture. It's drying on the radiator in my bathroom.'

Bella fell asleep in the chair, hands over her tummy as though to protect a growing child. Flora went to the bathroom. On the radiator was a bright, Andy Warhol-esque painting of Marilyn Monroe. Bella had used her favourite pinks and reds to create the image; her face, thrown back in rapture, appeared like a multi-shaded rose. Flora found a large notepad on the bedside cabinet, slipped the artwork inside and put it in her rucksack.

She caught a bus back to town. After ten minutes, it juddered and stopped abruptly. The driver stood up, told passengers, 'I dunno what's wrong but she aint gonna start. This is as far as we go.'

Passengers groaned and dismounted. Flora followed, glad her flat wasn't too far. She looked up at where they had broken down. Outside the CARE building.

You should care...

She climbed stone steps littered with MacDonalds cups and newspapers before she could change her mind. She told the woman at the desk on the other side of the bars that she wanted to volunteer, and the gate opened with a heavy squeak. The woman said to go to Carla's office at the end of the corridor.

And Flora was inside the building.

12

Marilyn folds in her colourful wings

4th August 1962, Brentwood, Los Angeles

Heart pounding, Marilyn waited for another sound outside.

Nothing.

But even if it was just Pat or Eunice, she needed to leave. Now. The noise had come from out front, so Marilyn placed the pink flower on her pillow, as though in memory of the woman she had seen there, and headed to the kitchen where a door led to a passage and side gate. As she stepped out, there was a knock on the front door, so soft she could have missed it, had her senses not been super alert.

She didn't wait for the rapping to get louder.

Escape, she thought. *Run...*

As she left, she thought suddenly of her garden.

Of the lovely colours she might never see again. She was tempted to steal back, catch a final glimpse, but knew the flowers would be closed for the night. It was those shrubs she was the saddest to leave. Who would water them and whisper words of encouragement in her absence?

There was no time to dwell on it now.

Marilyn stole out of the side gate and onto the street, pausing by a tree, sick with fear. Two black cars had parked on the roadside grass, their engines idling, and windows smoked so she could not see the occupants.

She did not want to.

She weaved between the trees on the lane, breath ragged, and at the end she turned right onto Carmelina Avenue, heading towards the lights of Sunset Boulevard. There she turned right again, and headed inland, away from the ocean.

At just ten o'clock, it was still busy. The Saturday night hustle and bustle was intense. The flashy Coca Cola sign above a favourite restaurant that usually made her smile now had her hurrying past, afraid of being seen in its light.

A newspaper wrapped about her legs as though to trip her up. She pulled it free, saw the headline: Marilyn All Washed Up. She had seen it last week, read how her career was on the 'downward slide' and how she was 'losing her looks now she was thirty-six' and how 'she might never have a much longed for child'. The latter had stung. Their source was an unnamed friend, often the case; how could someone who said such things be classed as a friend?

She tried not to walk like *her*; she didn't unfurl her torso, lengthen her neck or sway her hips like Monroe. She scuttled along like ten-year-old Norma Jeane in shabby clothes, trying to be invisible. She walked and walked and walked, the collar of her coat pulled high, scarf covering her head.

'It's *you*!' A gravelled voice from the shadows.

Marilyn shrank back with a shriek.

She should run.

But then she saw a frail man, clothes filthy, cardboard box his home, bottle of vodka his sustenance, sheltering as best he could from the night. 'It's *you* who has what I need.'

He was just confused; her heart went out to him. She usually spoke to homeless guys, bought them coffee, but tonight she hurried away, heart pounding.

She needed to get off the main street.

She continued, on and on, until her feet ached, and the city folded in on itself like petals in the moonlight. She passed the Chateau Marmont where she and Arthur Miller used to meet in secret, and Hollywood Boulevard with Grauman's Theatre where she and Jane Russell put their hands in cement; it was showing *West Side Story*.

Marilyn's life was flashing by.

She didn't know how long she had walked when she came to an unfamiliar area. She continued uphill, along a wide avenue, maybe towards Glendale and the Verdugo Mountains, passing red-roofed Spanish houses that cowered behind bushes, and fried lawns that needed watering. After a while, she came upon a lane that curved up into an overgrown hill. It had no street sign; she might have missed it had it not been for the single shoe sitting on a wall by its entry.

Follow your heart, and then the tiny white shoe, one you will know, and which will take you up into the place you should go first.

The shoe was white satin with silky ribbons criss-crossed over the top.

Marilyn picked it up.

She *had* seen it before. Two, very similar, bought when she was briefly pregnant while filming *Some Like it Hot*, now in a box at the Brentwood house. That pregnancy, like two before, ended suddenly and with a great deal of pain. One of them, an ectopic pregnancy in 1957, had meant a rush to the hospital. Newspaper photos the next day showed Marilyn smiling, face flushed, gripping Arthur Miller's hand. Monroe had given them joy, said she was fine, while *Marilyn* had cried all the way home in the car.

She put the shoe back on the wall and walked up the lane, curious. It eventually revealed iron gates flanked by white-washed walls covered in vine. A large board hung on chains from the gate. It read: *Angels of the Immaculate Mary. Chapel of Divine Peace Open, Roman Catholic Nuns.*

Would it be open at this time of night? Could Marilyn shelter until dawn and she knew what to do next? She tried one of the gates. It opened with a gentle squeak, as though it had been sleeping and she had roused it from pleasant dreams. Was it OK to walk in? What choice did she have?

She went inside.

Perhaps this could be her cocoon. Perhaps here she might fold in her colourful wings, wrap them about her body, and let herself be entombed in a chrysalis while Marilyn Monroe turned back into an everyday creature, free in its everyday nothingness to wander about the world and find its true home.

13

Flora decides to care

March 2016, Hull, England

Halfway down the high-ceilinged corridor, an emotional scene was taking place.

Flora wondered whether to wait a moment before passing. A girl with flame hair in a tangled mess about her teary face was curled in a foetal position on the floor, screaming. She looked sixteen. Two staff members – women in blue and yellow T-shirts with the CARE logo on the chest – tried to calm her, but she thrashed about, crying, 'I want my baby.'

The anguish of the words pulled Flora closer.

A blonde staff member spoke in soothing tones, telling the girl to return to her room, and that they would get Marjory as soon as she arrived. Marjory, Flora recalled, was a large woman, like a graceful but sturdy ship built to withstand any sea, one of the counsellors – no, *Listeners*.

'Amelia,' said the other staff member gently, 'this won't get her back.'

Amelia caught sight of Flora then and said to her, 'I want my baby.'

Flora moved closer. 'Where is she?'

'They took her away.'

'I'm sorry.' Flora knelt down, held Amelia's gaze. Perhaps Flora's unfamiliarity was compelling. We can tell strangers things never shared with family, dropping our pain into an ocean that will drag it to the bottom never to surface again.

The staff members didn't move.

'*I'm* her mum,' insisted Amelia, 'but they won't let me be.'

'Who?' asked Flora.

'My family. They said I'm too young.'

Flora felt the pain as though Amelia had transferred it through the air. She took her hand.

Silence. Breathing only.

Carla emerged from her office, a napkin tucked in her green blouse, crumbs spilling. 'Sorry, I was on the phone.' She assessed the scene. 'Amelia, shall we get you some tea and a bit of toast?'

Amelia, docile now, allowed herself to be helped up.

Flora rose too.

'Sharon, stay with her,' said Carla to the blonde woman.

As she walked away, Amelia turned and looked at Flora, eyes sad.

'You're Bella's sister,' said Carla. 'I didn't recognise you at first. You look... *different*.' Hadn't Bella said the same. 'How's she doing?'

'Good.' It was a lie but easier than explaining.

'Are you here about her?'

'No... I'm here to volunteer.'

Carla smiled and her austere, bespectacled face changed entirely. 'You couldn't have come at a better time. I was just putting an advert together. Come into the office.'

Flora followed her into the cluttered room where plant pots nudged one another out of the way to grab the best spot on a windowsill, and where folders were piled haphazardly on a cabinet. Flora sat opposite Carla at the scratched desk. A sandwich curled on a paper plate, like one of those shiny fish you won in a Christmas cracker that was supposed to predict your mood.

'Flora, isn't it?'

She nodded.

'Well, this is serendipity. Our longest serving volunteer Mabel just retired, we need a replacement, and here you are, no advert needed. What brought you?'

Flora wasn't sure what to say. Then: 'You helped my sister.'

Carla looked proud. 'We recently celebrated fifty years but it's an endless battle. I did a talk at the university and got heckled for not including men. I suggested *they* start one. My dad was a victim of childhood sexual abuse, so I know it happens.'

'I read that a local man is turning a warehouse into a refuge for men experiencing domestic abuse.'

'That's great,' said Carla. 'We could support one another. So what kind of service would you like to offer us?'

'What do you mean?'

'As you know, we have all kinds of volunteers; those who do nightshifts, the Nighters, those who cook, the Nourishers, and then the folk who offer their time as Listeners.' Carla studied Flora. 'What are your skills?'

Flora wanted to say that she didn't have any.

'Something brought you here.'

Flora shook her head, embarrassed at her silence.

'I think you'd make a great Listener. You have a kind air about you. When Bella had that bad night and we called you in, you just sat with her until she calmed down.'

'That's because I know her.'

'I saw it with Amelia too.'

Flora felt self-conscious.

Carla changed tack. 'How many hours could you give?'

'I work evenings so it'd have to be days. But not every day – I see my sister.'

'We can work something out. There's some training, three days, plus a day where our current Listeners will tell you about their work. The rest you learn by volunteering. Can you manage that?'

'I'm sure I can.'

'We'd have to wait for your DBS check, which can take a few weeks.'

'Oh, I got one last year so my sister could live with me.'

'Brilliant. Can you start training next week?' asked Carla.

'What time would it finish?' Flora could go into work afterwards, though it would be tiring, and she wouldn't be able to visit Bella.

'Five.'

That was doable.

'Why don't you call me when you know, and we'll go from there?'

Flora nodded.

'Do you have any questions?'

She shook her head.

Carla handed Flora a form. 'Fill this application out and bring it back with you.' She paused. 'In this work, you get a sense of a person. There are those who are trained and there are those that don't fit into a category but just feel *right*. You.'

'Thanks.' Flora didn't know what else to say. She put the papers in her rucksack with the notepad-encased Marilyn painting, and stood.

She headed back along the now quiet corridor, pausing where Amelia had broken down. Had her presence really soothed the girl? Was it a quality Flora had always possessed or had it developed it now?

She was let out of the secure gate and headed in the direction of work, stopping only to buy a sandwich, and to tie the suddenly undone shoelace of her cheap, tired trainer.

14

Marilyn is lifted

Angels of the Immaculate Mary, Los Angeles, 5th August 1962

Marilyn walked along a wide path illuminated by the occasional lamp, and up brick steps that climbed higher into the hill. On one side the Los Angeles lights twinkled like the camera flashes that had blinded her. Midnight heat shimmered over the city; layered passion. On the other side, dense shrubbery.

She emerged at the top, breathless, holdall heavy on her shoulder. Ahead was a neat lawn split by the continuing path and bordered by rose bushes, two benches, and a marble statue. At the end, a long white building paralleled the lawn, a tower stretching from its slate roof into the sky, metal cross atop.

Marilyn wondered where the chapel was.

She stole across the lawn, around the back of the building, and found a square, brick construction with clunky doors that opened stiffly. Inside rows of pews underscored dark wood beams and stained-glass windows. Raised steps led to an altar where Jesus looked down from his cross. Four candles shimmered.

Marilyn sat in the last pew, afraid she was intruding and shouldn't sit near the front. She put her holdall beneath the seat. On the wall was a plaque with the word HYMN carved into the wood and the numbers four-four-four below. She had left the number four behind. It was August 5th now.

A new day.

One she wondered if she had been supposed to see.

Exhaustion tugged her eyelids. There were thick, oblong cushions on the floor where the praying could kneel. She put one on the bench, curled up and placed her head on it. She would rest until dawn arrived, and then sneak away.

She should figure out what to do next but sleep stole her.

*

'You're her, aren't you?' A voice dragged Marilyn back into the world; words said with the same worship she had felt seeing Mary.

Marilyn opened her eyes.

The chapel was a new place. Sunlight crisped the walls, splashing colour from the tinted glass onto every surface.

The voice came from a young woman wearing a long-sleeved, dark robe with a white bib at the neck, and a black veil with a pale headband beneath, covering the forehead; a nun. Only the girl's agreeable face was visible; it reminded Marilyn of her sister Berniece's. The young nun knelt by Marilyn.

'You came,' she said softly.

'You were *expecting* me?' Marilyn sat up, surprised.

The nun looked proud. 'I dreamed you'd come and told Mother Superior. Sometimes my dreams happen, sometimes they don't. We're not supposed to idolise humans, only God, but I loved you before I came here.'

Marilyn laughed, touched by the girl. 'Oh, gee, please don't hold me in high regard.' If she only knew. 'I'm sorry I intruded, I just needed to rest before…'

'Before?'

'Before I decide what I do next.'

'Are you going somewhere?'

Marilyn shrugged. 'I guess I am. I just don't know where yet.' She wondered whether to tell the girl about Mary, after all she was adored in a place such as this. But might they find it disrespectful if she claimed to have seen her?

'I'm Sister Joy,' said the girl.

'I'm…' Marilyn paused.

Though Sister Joy obviously knew her name, she wasn't sure now. She had left Marilyn Monroe at the Brentwood house. For a moment she imagined her there, wraithlike, wandering the rooms, not visible to Eunice, Pat, Dr Greenson. Was she Norma Jeane again? It didn't feel that way. Maybe she was Marilyn without the weight of the Monroe, her mom's family name.

'The other sisters didn't know who you were,' said Sister Joy. 'I told them you're a worldwide star. I'm new, so I saw your movies before I came here. They've been here years, and we don't leave once we commit to God.'

'Not *ever*?' Marilyn was shocked.

'No.'

'Not even to see your family?'

'*This* is our family now,' she said simply. '*This* is our world now. We give ourselves entirely to the Lord and do his good work. Let me take you to Mother Superior.'

'I should be on my way.'

'Please, at least have breakfast. It's at seven, so we'll have to whisper until then because it's quiet praying time.' Sister Joy picked up Marilyn's holdall. 'Please, come with me, Sister Marilyn.'

She smiled at the name and let herself be taken, be fussed. It was nice, attention that fame had never given. They went inside the white building, onto a long corridor where paintings and tapestries of bible scenes broke the pale expanse. Sister Joy kept touching Marilyn's arm as though to make sure she existed.

They went into a simple room, clearly a dining hall, where a long table with benches on either side was set with cutlery and bowls.

'The other sisters will be here soon.' Sister Joy bristled with excitement. 'I sit here. Squeeze in next to me.'

Marilyn did. 'Is there a way I should address everyone?'

'Just call us Sister.'

'Won't you be in trouble for letting me stay?' asked Marilyn.

'We never turn anyone in need away. We've found homeless women in the chapel and cared for them until they felt strong and had somewhere safe to go.'

Sister Joy studied Marilyn; her bright green eyes were full of soul. Marilyn used to have such life in her face. Now she had to dig deep to bring that to her expression; the effort it took was a drain. It had been natural, once upon a time, and that translated via the camera into a language others felt. Recently, it had been destroyed by years of pills and long hours and breakdowns.

The door opened, pulling Marilyn from depressive thoughts.

Women dressed the same as Sister Joy came into the hall, faces composed.

'We have a guest,' cried Sister Joy. 'I told you about her. This is Marilyn. Marilyn, this is Sister Sofia, Sister Margaret, Sister Jean, Sister Deborah…'

The women nodded, kind, interested. It was liberating that they didn't know her. There was no expectation. She could be herself, whoever that was.

More nuns arrived, old and young, some chatty, asking Marilyn questions, others quietly observing. Sister Joy softly explained that they had taken a vow of silence, and Marilyn should not address them. Also, no talking was permitted during the meal unless Mother Superior spoke. Other sisters brought in bread and great metal teapots and jugs of milk.

'Are you from nearby?' they asked. 'What brought you to us?'

Marilyn held back from saying that Mary had guided her here.

Then Mother Superior arrived.

The room fell quiet.

Everyone stood. Marilyn did too. She was slight, elderly, with laugh lines and wise eyes. Once she took a seat at the top of the table, everyone resumed theirs. They bowed heads as she recited a prayer, concluding with 'Amen'.

Then tea was poured, and bread cut and buttered. The only sound for a while was soft sipping, teaspoons clacking against teacups, and coughing. Marilyn ate the bread, washing it down with strong tea. It was an unusual breakfast but surprisingly satisfying, perhaps because of the peace in the room. As the meal concluded, Mother Superior said more prayers and then they all stood while she departed the room.

'What happens now?' asked Marilyn.

'Lauds – that's Morning Prayer – in the chapel and then our duties,' said Sister Joy. 'I take care of the garden.'

'I loved mine,' said Marilyn sadly.

'Will you join us in the chapel?'

'I'm intruding. I should…'

But Marilyn was pulled along the corridor with the sisters, carried on a wave of determination. Sister Joy clutched her hand tightly, carrying the holdall in the other. Halfway along the passage, some artwork caught Marilyn's eye. She pulled free to observe the image more closely.

Pastel watercolours portrayed the holiest of scenes – Christ's birth in the stable. Mary held her new son close to her chest, face aglow with the purest elation. She was the Mary that Marilyn had witnessed last night; the baby was the many Marilyn had never had. She touched the layers of paint, fell to her knees.

Pain came.

Pain that had been buried, ignored, glossed over.

Was it exhaustion that let it in? The intensity of the last twenty-four hours? The safety she felt in this refuge?

Sister Joy called out her name.

Mother Superior heard the commotion and came to where

Marilyn was curled over on the floor, trembling violently.

'Our guest is indisposed,' she said briskly. 'Sisters, help her to my chamber. Sister Helene, lead the songs in my place this morning. Sister Joy, thank you for your care of our guest, but continue now to the chapel with the others and then assume your duties.'

Marilyn felt herself being lifted, many hands cradling her. Her head lolled against a warm chest; she hadn't the energy to move. She was taken back to a journey down a hospital corridor, on a gurney, writhing in agony, terrified that this was the end of another pregnancy. Now *she* was the child, nurtured, safe, held.

The air changed; she had been taken into a cool room, where she was deposited onto a hard, narrow bed.

'Thank you, Sisters.' Mother Superior's voice was low.

A door closed. Silence then.

Marilyn hugged her knees, shivering. Hands placed a scratchy blanket over her body. Warmer then. Protected. Eyes closed.

'Breathe, child.' Mother Superior must be close by. 'Sleep. It will heal you.' Pause. 'I feel in you a great, heavy unhappiness you have suppressed for a long time. Sleep for as long as you need. God is looking over you.'

Marilyn succumbed to oblivion.

15

Flora is the magician

March 2016, Hull, England

The first thing Flora did at work was find the pink flower in her apron pocket. It was still surprisingly perky. She held it to her chest, then looked around, embarrassed that someone might have seen her. She filled a glass with water, placed the bloom in it, and put it on the cloakroom windowsill.

Then she went into the bar. The table lamps were not yet shouting her. Greg was inspecting the taps. Manager Denise spoke angrily on the phone to a performer who was cancelling. Evie the cleaner mopped the floor.

'Can you get some fresh tea towels?' grunted Greg when he saw Flora.

'Bloody Sheena Turner.' Denise hung up. 'She put her wig in the washing machine and it's ruined, and she doesn't have a spare. What am I supposed to do now? People come from as far as Goole to see her. Simply the best, my arse.'

Flora put tea towels on the bar shelf. 'Who else is on tonight?'

'That new comedy double act, Two Bitches.' Denise straightened one of the tables. 'Not sure if punters will stay once they know Sheena's cancelled.'

'Don't tell them,' said Flora, 'then they'll stay.'

Denise smiled, her lips cracked. 'You're more than a pretty face, you know.' She lightly pinched Flora's cheek and headed into her office.

Greg and Flora finished opening duties. 'It's just us,' he said, brusque. 'Georgie rang in sick, and Abby's off. But we'll manage.'

Two Bitches arrived, older women with green hair and bags of threadbare costumes, who grumbled that backstage was 'barely a cupboard', and asked for free drinks. The club opened and patrons filtered in.

'When's Psychic Pat in?' Flora asked Greg as they pulled pints.

'Not sure.' He cursed at a spillage. 'Ask Denise. Why?'

'Oh, no reason.'

Flora asked a patron for two-fifty and gave him change. It was the blonde man in the flat cap who had told her to smile, it might never happen. He stared at her; she ignored him, and he returned to a table with his friends.

'Oh, of course,' said Greg suddenly. 'Pat said you were gonna get a visitor. Did you?'

'Not unless you count a large spider with red legs, no.'

Greg laughed.

The usual crackling sound filled the air and Denise announced that new comediennes, Two Bitches, would have them laughing in the aisles. They launched into a Victoria Wood and Julie Walters sketch, badly mimicking the iconic pair gossiping at a sauna, their voices not strong enough.

Flora responded to illuminated lamps. Her feet sweated inside her cheap trainers, and her back ached from lack of sleep. The man in the flat cap asked what time she was going on stage; said he had a large pole she could dance around. Flora 'accidentally' spilt a drink into his lap. He cursed, his mates roared with laughter.

Two Bitches smiled, thinking it was for them.

Flora spotted Neil at the back, sitting beneath the Upcoming Events poster, the light making his hair a saintly halo. Once the interval rush was done, she joined him.

'I didn't think comedy was your thing.' She motioned to the stage.

'That wasn't comedy.' He sipped his beer and studied her. Hadn't Bella said that was what he did? But this was study like he hardly knew her. 'Did you change your hair?'

'No.' Flora shook her head. 'Why?'

'You look... I don't know…'

Different, thought Flora. That's what Bella said. Then Carla.

'Different?' she suggested.

He nodded. 'Did you get your visitor last night?'

Flora knew what Neil meant but pretended ignorance. 'Sorry?'

'What Psychic Pat said.'

The words suddenly itched to get out. She was sure Neil would take her seriously, and even more importantly that he would keep it to himself.

Static, then Denise's voice; 'I'm sorry but due to unforeseen circumstances, Sheena Turner won't be performing tonight. We apologise for any disappointment.'

Boos came thick and fast. Someone smashed a glass. Within ten minutes most patrons had supped their beer and left, the blonde in the flat cap saying to his rowdy friends, 'Let's go to the casino, this place is shite.'

Greg collected the glass in a shovel and poured it into a bin. 'You may as well go,' he said to Flora. 'Doubt we'll get anyone else in now. See you... Saturday?'

'Yeah, Saturday.' She had tomorrow off. She looked at Neil. 'Maybe you should've gone on stage instead of Sheena.'

He shrugged. 'I wasn't prepared. I'm learning a new trick.'

'Are you allowed to tell me about it?'

He paused. 'I want to make myself disappear... and change.'

'Don't we all,' laughed Flora. 'How would you do that?'

'You know I can't share my magic secrets.' He winked.

We all have secrets, thought Flora.

'Can I…?' she began.

He finished his beer, eyes not leaving hers.

'Can I share something with you?' She looked around. Greg was clearing up behind the bar; Denise must be in her office. 'Come with me while I get my coat.'

Neil followed her into the cloakroom. Flora blushed when she saw him notice the pink flower in the glass on the windowsill. He would know she hadn't discarded it with the rubbish at the end of her shift.

'I still can't believe it wasn't a daffodil.' He touched it.

'Isn't your other magic real?' teased Flora. She paused. 'Something happened to me last night.' The words jumped from her mouth, lit fireworks going off too soon.

Neil raised his eyebrows. Flora wanted to reach out and stroke his slightly stubbled cheek. Instead, she took off her apron, hung it on a peg, and indicated with her finger for him to come closer.

'Can I trust you?'

'Of course,' he said.

This was the moment to change her mind. Neil waited. 'Right, promise you won't laugh.'

'Yes,' he said.

She braced herself. 'Last night, I was asleep.' She leaned into the coats, smelled unknown odours. 'I woke and there was this light under the bedroom door. I hadn't left it on so obviously you'd think I'd be scared. But I wasn't. I went into the kitchen where it was, and…'

'And?'

'I *did* have a visitor.'

'Who?' asked Neil.

Flora took a breath. 'Mary,' she said.

He frowned. 'Mary Who?'

'The *Virgin* Mary.' Flora said it so quietly that she wondered whether to repeat it. But she knew Neil had heard; his face didn't show mockery, only curiosity. He waited for her to go on. 'I can't believe it happened. I wasn't dreaming, but saying it aloud, I know the words sound insane.' She paused. 'The Virgin Mary was in *my kitchen*.'

'Did she say anything?' asked Neil, still no mockery.

Flora thought about the specifics but wasn't sure whether to disclose them. 'I felt sure she was speaking in her own language, but I heard her in English. She said this weird phrase: Cursum Perficio. I dunno what it means but I'm sure I've read it before.'

'What did she look like?'

'Not like in paintings.'

'What did you do?' Neil's questions seemed to come from trying to understand.

'I knelt down. I listened to her.'

'And then what?'

'She said what she said, and she left.' Flora remembered an important aspect. 'She gave me a daffodil.'

'Psychic Pat predicted a visitor in your kitchen.' Neil seemed to be trying to process it. 'Do you believe in God?' He was so close to her now that she could have leaned forward and kissed him.

'I'm not sure.'

'Are you religious?' he continued.

'We went to church as kids and one of my schools was Catholic. But not since my Grandma Lil died. Does that matter? I saw what I saw. You don't have to believe in magic for it to work, do you?'

'You do,' said Neil.

'You *do*?'

'Yeah.'

'But do you believe *me*?' Flora feared the answer.

'I do. More importantly, do *you* believe you?'

'What does that mean?'

'If you believe what you saw then it's true, isn't it?'

'It's happened before.' Flora was afraid he was beginning to doubt her.

'Mary? To *you*?'

'No, to others. You must have heard of Bernadette, the peasant girl in Lourdes?'

'Maybe.'

'Mary spoke to her two hundred years ago. That's why the place is a shrine. And she appeared before three children in Fatima, and a woman in Walsingham. Those are approved cases.' Flora paused. 'Do you think I'm crazy?'

Denise put her head in the door. 'I need to get my stuff, we're locking up.'

Flora jumped away from Neil as though they had been caught in a compromising position. Greg followed, grabbing his biker jacket. They made their way outside, saying goodbyes and going in opposite directions. Neil loitered.

'Do you want to talk more?' he asked.

Flora was glad he wasn't rushing off. 'It's late. You must have work tomorrow?' She realised she had no idea what he did when he wasn't making magic.

'No,' he said. 'Want me to walk you?'

'It's quite a way.'

He shrugged. 'I like walking.'

They set off. Flora set the pace, took short cuts she normally avoided because of how deserted they were. Then she realised that was reducing their time together and returned to the main road, to being splashed by cars as rain crashed down.

'Coming back to your question.' Neil pulled his hood up against the sudden weather change. 'I don't think you're crazy. But I wonder if you *made* it happen.'

'Why would I do that?' Flora was indignant.

'Magicians create illusions by taking advantage of how people perceive stimuli and process information. Maybe you saw Mary in a film recently and she triggered something in you. I'm not saying I don't believe you.' Neil crashed into her as he avoided a large puddle. 'I'm very logical when creating a trick; it makes you look at things a certain way.'

'You just made magic sound dull.'

Flora couldn't help but feel sad. The downpour didn't help. Neil looked at her. She couldn't read his expression. A drip ran down his nose.

'Maybe it just happened.' Flora couldn't keep the annoyance out of her voice.

'That's also possible,' he admitted.

'You thought I looked different.'

'Did I?'

'So did my sister this morning.'

'Sorry.' Neil spoke kindly. 'I should have kept those thoughts to myself. You shared something personal with me.'

Flora shivered, didn't respond.

'What are you going to do?' he asked.

'How do you mean?' She knew she was being brusque.

'Will you tell anyone else?'

'God no.'

They turned onto the street where she lived.

'This is my building,' she said.

'Can I see the daffodil?' Neil asked. 'Sorry, ignore that.' He was blushing and she smiled.

'You want to come up and see my daffodil?' teased Flora, and they both laughed. It relieved the tension. 'I'll make us a hot drink.'

He followed her up the rubbish-strewn stairs and into the flat. She was embarrassed at its shoddiness, at having to fill a pan for coffee. She put their wet coats on the radiator, which she turned on despite worrying about the cost. Neil went to the daffodil on the windowsill.

'Now you'll think *me* crazy,' he said.

'Why?' Flora spilt coffee granules on the worktop.

'It looks *exactly* like the daffodil I chose to give you. Same colour, same length of stem.'

'Really?'

'*Really.*'

'And how do you explain that?' Flora looked at him.

'I can't.'

She gave him a mug of coffee. He wrapped his hands around its curve.

'Sit down, if you want.'

He didn't. 'Where did she appear?' he asked.

'There.' She pointed to the small kitchen area. It seemed incredulous now, when the place was ordinary again.

Neil looked around the room, at her books and the two images on the wall.

'It was my grandma's,' said Flora when he looked at Mary. 'It doesn't mean I willed what I saw.'

'Marilyn,' he said instead, stopping in front of her poster. 'What do you reckon happened to her?'

'I don't know.' Flora joined him in front of it.

'I saw a documentary on Netflix,' Neil said. 'They reckoned she was killed by the Mafia and they chucked her body out to sea, so it was never found. Doesn't quite fit with the regular reports that she's alive and well and lives in Wigan.' He paused. 'Do you think she's still alive?'

'I hope so. But it'd be hard to hide being *her*.'

'Lots of people have reported seeing her over the years.'

'She won't look the same now,' said Flora.

'I guess not.'

'Oh, my picture.' Flora went into her rucksack and took out

Bella's artwork. 'My sister painted it.'

'That's gorgeous.' Neil seemed genuinely impressed. 'It needs framing.'

She leaned it against the paperbacks on her shelf. 'She's very talented.'

'Does she live here?'

'Marilyn?' Flora smiled.

'Your sister.' Neil smiled too.

'Sometimes.'

'Sometimes?'

'It's complicated,' she admitted.

Neil finished his coffee. 'I should…' he began.

Flora didn't want him to go but knew there was no point in anything happening. She was incapable of forming relationships that lasted. She grabbed his coat from the radiator; it was still damp. She walked him to the door where they stood on opposite sides of the frame.

'When are you next performing?' she asked.

'Not until the week after next. You're in on Saturday though?'

'Yes.'

'OK.'

She didn't know what else to say. Neil seemed to find something acutely interesting in his feet. Then he looked at her. 'I like you, Flora.'

She smiled.

He leaned close and touched her cheek with one hand. It was cold; the sensation made her shudder, with surprise and anticipation. The tenderness of the gesture warmed her though. Then he kissed her. His lips were chilly too, but didn't detract from the pleasure. Their tongues met. She pulled him nearer, roughly, not shy now, bodies crashing together. He was stronger than she imagined when he gripped her waist; she sank into his hands.

He stopped after a few minutes.

'I should go,' he said, voice husky. 'If I don't... I won't...'

She didn't want him to, but knew it was best. 'Yes.'

He put a finger to his mouth as though savouring her taste. 'Shall I come by the club on Saturday then?'

'If you want to.'

'Well,' he said. 'I'll see you.'

Not if I see you first, Flora thought, and tried not to laugh.

She watched him go down the stairs, wondering if he would turn and look back again. When he did, with a small smile, she felt like a teenager catching sight of her favourite pop star in the street.

Inside, she went straight to the daffodil. She removed it from the glass, dried it off, found a heavy hardback on the shelf and two sheets of paper. She placed the flower between the sheets and put them inside the book. Then she put it on the floor and piled more on top, hoping it would work.

She could not hang onto love, onto lovers.

But she would preserve this yellow remnant.

16

Marilyn doesn't want to be her anymore

Angels of the Immaculate Mary, Los Angeles, 1962

When Marilyn woke, she had no idea how long she had been asleep. She was in the same curled up position; usually, at home, she woke in crumpled sheets, having tossed and turned and woken repeatedly.

The room was empty.

It was a simple place. Aside from the narrow bed the only furniture was a wooden desk that one knelt at, on a thick cushion, and a sink in the corner. She sat up; the walls wavered. She lay back down, tried to breathe slowly. After a while, the door opened, and Mother Superior came in with a steaming teacup.

'I'll go now.' Marilyn tried to sit again. 'I've imposed on you enough.'

'Please, child, don't trouble yourself.' Mother Superior sat on the corner of the bed and held out the teacup. 'There is no imposition here. Drink your tea. Take as long as you need.'

'Thank you. What time is it?' Marilyn propped herself up, sipped the strong liquid.

'Almost six.'

'In the *evening*? But I must have slept for... nine hours?'

'You needed it,' said Mother Superior. 'Do you feel better? I was quite concerned earlier.'

'Please don't feel you have to stay with me.' Marilyn felt terrible that there must be other things for this woman to attend.

'I've chosen to give this hour to you. God sent you to us and I don't question his reasons. Tell me about yourself.'

'I'd rather know about you,' said Marilyn.

'Maybe another time. For now, you.'

'What do you know?' Marilyn could never help but be guarded.

'Young Sister Joy told me you were someone of note in the film industry. I've lived here many years so I know little of this world. She said she dreamed of your arrival. We love our little chatterbox, but she dreams vividly, and has excitedly declared many things that never realised. But here you are, so I guess I know nothing.'

Nothing.

It felt like Marilyn was being born. Given a blank page. A new start. She could write herself as she wished. She was her own God, Goddess, whatever you wanted to call it. This was no reporter hoping for a witty one-liner to titillate readers.

'I began with nothing,' she said.

'We all begin that way.'

'With nothing you don't expect anything. I never knew my father, other than an old picture, and I couldn't be sure it was him. Illegitimacy is a shame put on a child, not on the absent parent. I carried it around like a bag of dirty laundry.'

'I was illegitimate too,' said Mother Superior quietly.

'You were?'

'Yes. It…'

'Yes. It does.' Marilyn knew the unfinished sentence. 'My mother,' she continued, 'was very ill. In her mind, you know, which is harder to deal with. I lived in lots of different foster homes and in an orphanage for a while, and then with friends of my family. They married me off to the boy next door as soon as I turned sixteen – Jimmie – he was sweet, and I did love him, but you like to choose who you love, don't you?'

'That must have been difficult.' Mother Superior spoke matter of factly which gave Marilyn great comfort. She didn't want histrionics; these things only reminded her of how hysterical her mother could be, which was frightening for a child.

'I never expected to be happy. It was safer that way. But one joy I had was going to the movies.' Marilyn remembered it with a surge of nostalgia, being seduced by Harlow, Swanson, Garbo. 'I'd escape for a day, watch one after another. It was a magic world where everyone was beautiful and got a happy ending. How I wanted that.'

'I can see why a child might feel that way.' Mother Superior spoke carefully, studying Marilyn as she did. 'But it's all pretend, isn't it? Like the stories in books except on a screen.'

Like the bible? wondered Marilyn, but didn't say.

'It is. I discovered that for myself.'

'Have you been in lots of movies?'

'I was about to resume my thirtieth film before I left.'

'You hardly look old enough. It's no wonder you are so exhausted, child. I feel it in you. There are things you are not saying to me, that perhaps you haven't said to anyone. You should let them come to the surface. You have nothing to fear here.' Mother Superior paused. 'Where is your mother now?'

'Rockhaven Sanitorium. It's a private hospital for women with mental disorders. I send them a cheque every month.' Marilyn realised that this might stop in her absence and suddenly felt sick; how could she ensure it continued? She could only hope that someone would intervene.

'That's very generous of you,' said Mother Superior.

'She's my mother. I *should* care for her.'

'To do so after a childhood where she was absent shows great compassion and, most importantly, forgiveness.'

'But she was ill. I've always feared that illness consuming me too.'

Perhaps it already had.

Marilyn finished her tea and placed the cup back in the saucer. Mother Superior put it on the desk. 'Do you have children?' she asked.

The question was a natural one following discussion of her mother, but it always cut deep. 'No. I tried. That's the best way I can describe it. My body is viewed as perfect. But it isn't. I can't…' She felt sick. 'I can't carry a baby to term. I tried three times recently. I think it's because I… I got… ruined long ago.'

'How so?'

'I… I can't… please.'

Mother Superior graciously changed track: 'What brought you here last night?'

Should Marilyn tell her about Mary? Perhaps now was not the moment. Marilyn still wasn't sure what she planned to do.

'I just need time away from the pressures to find … myself, I guess. Fame has been my life for years. But I'm not happy like when it began, when it was exciting and new, and I hoped to find a great life.'

'Stay with us a while,' said Mother Superior. 'Until you have your answers.'

'I can't do that.'

'Why not?'

'I don't know.'

'I'm inviting you. We have the room and the heart. Last year we found a lady in the chapel who had escaped from a cruel husband. She had terrible injuries. We nursed her to health and, once strong, she left. I don't know where she went, but I hope she found peace.'

'That's so sad.'

'Indeed. But God sent her to us.'

'What can I give you in return?' asked Marilyn. 'Let me cook.

No, perhaps not, I'm not the best. I've burned things you wouldn't imagine *could* be burned! I could help Sister Joy in the garden. You must let me if I'm to accept your kind invitation.'

'I'm sure Sister Joy would love your help.' Mother Superior paused. 'Should we let anyone know where you are?'

Marilyn pictured Eunice, who must have gone to the Brentwood house today and found it empty. She thought of Pat, the morning call she had said she would make, perhaps now anxious about her friend's whereabouts. Did she feel bad to have simply gone without a word?

Yes.

But she didn't want to go back. And contacting anyone from that life would mean doing so. She needed this. Mary had been right.

'No, thank you,' she said. 'Will you keep quiet about me being here?'

'Not a word shall be said.'

'My life has been selfish,' said Marilyn quietly. 'Fame makes you egotistical.'

'Then you have somehow come out of it well.'

Marilyn wasn't sure. 'Tell me more about *you* now?'

'Let's save that for another day,' said Mother Superior. 'You must be hungry? We eat supper in fifteen minutes, and then we have Vespers – evening prayer – and then we do not speak between the hours of eight in the evening and seven in the morning. It's our time to converse with God. I will show you to a room.'

'Thank you.'

'Our quarters are simple, perhaps not what you are accustomed to, but if it is peace you seek, then our home will serve you well. You are not obliged to take part in prayers, and I do not ask what your beliefs are, but if you could join us for meals, I would be grateful.'

'I will.'

Marilyn followed Mother Superior along the corridor, holdall in hand, knees still weak, to a room much the same as the one she had left, smaller, but with a window that looked onto the lawn. Mother Superior left her to unpack, which Marilyn knew wouldn't take long, and asked her to join them in ten minutes in the dining hall.

Once alone, Marilyn opened the holdall. There was no wardrobe or drawers, so she left the underwear, toiletries and platinum ring inside the bag but hung the beige dress on the back of the door, and placed her favourite black and white photograph with the carnation on the desk.

I'll remember you, she thought, looking at the picture. *I just don't want to be you anymore.*

Then she washed in the sink and went to the dining hall.

17

Flora worries about sudden happy endings

March 2016, Hull, England

The morning after she kissed Neil on her doorstep, Flora was woken by the phone; she rarely put it on silent in case Bella needed her. It was past ten, which often happened after working late. Bella's name flashed. Flora's heart tightened; she always feared the worst.

'Are you OK?' she asked.

'I feel wonderful,' Bella said.

'You *do*?' Flora couldn't have been more surprised. She wanted to ask if the doctor had put her on new drugs but that felt unkind. She should be delighted but fear of things gone before tempered her reaction.

'Yeah, I woke this morning and I swear I've never felt so well. It's like... something lifted.'

'Lifted,' repeated Flora quietly.

'And guess what?'

'What?' Flora went into the kitchen and filled the pan.

'They said I can come home.'

'*What*?' She spilled water on the hob. 'When did they say that?'

'Just now. I can leave today. It's actually nothing to do with how good I feel this morning, they said it's been discussed this week.'

'But … just like that?'

'Aren't you happy?' Bella sounded sulky.

'Of course, it's just…' Flora was afraid to trust good news.

'Can I stay with you?'

Flora sat on the stained sofa, listening to the water in the pan softly bubbling. 'Wasn't there a meeting? This should be discussed with me, *and* with you.' She had always attended them with nurses, social workers and psychologists, putting forward her thoughts on major decisions.

'Maybe it's a miracle.' Bella laughed, but the word struck Flora hard. 'I can leave at lunchtime. I told them I'll come to you, they're happy with that.' Flora knew they would only let her leave if she came here or went to CARE. 'Don't worry – they'll be checking in with me for the next few weeks like always.'

Was this sudden joy a manic episode? Flora had witnessed weeks where Bella cleaned and painted and hardly slept. But this didn't seem frenzied. Though she spoke excitedly, there was a calmness. Was she different in the way that Flora appeared to be?

'Make sure you have all your medication with you.'

'Stop worrying. It's all good.'

And Bella hung up.

Flora was unsettled. It was a happy ending too soon in a story; one that didn't quite fit the previous narrative.

She made tea and stood in front of Bella's Marilyn painting. She remembered them watching her movies as kids, often when Flora was looking after her sister in their mother's absence. There was a comfort in Marilyn's sweet voice; she somehow reached out, beyond the camera, and spoke to them. Even in posters flat against a wall she had a gift for emerging from the photo. Reading Marilyn biographies as a teen, Flora learned they had things in common; absent fathers (Flora's had left before she was born), unstable mothers, little education … and other things that Flora never spoke of.

However, Marilyn had made something of her life.

Flora opened the book with the daffodil inside, expecting it to be gone; that Mary's visit had never happened. But it was there, flat, dehydrating, preserving, still bright. A few more weeks and it would dry out fully, so she stood on a plastic chair, and put it on top of the bookshelf.

She saw the CARE application form on the kitchen counter and realised that if Bella was living at the flat and Flora didn't have to travel to the hospital, training would be easier. It would be exhausting to work evenings too but it was just three days.

She rang the number on the form, asked for Carla.

'I can do next week if you still want me,' she said.

'How about Monday through to Wednesday?'

Flora was only working Wednesday night. 'Is there anything I need to bring?'

'Just bring you.'

*

Bella arrived at the flat, her hair plaited and curled around her head like sleeping snakes, her clothes smelling of the sterile hospital room, and her things in the scruffy sports holdall she took everywhere. They hugged.

'You're right.' Bella looked around. 'This place *is* worse than the last. But this looks lovely.' She went to her Marilyn painting. 'I think it's my favourite. I'm glad I chose pinks and reds. I didn't feel those shades when I painted it – I felt grey – but something made me choose them.'

She looked well.

Different.

Flora tried to recall the last time Bella had been that way. Not since depression changed her from sweet girl into difficult teenager. It was unnerving. Like Flora couldn't fully trust it.

'Are you hungry? I don't have much but I can do an omelette?'

'Fab, I'm starving.'

While Flora found eggs, Bella took her stuff into the bedroom. Flora knew she'd be putting her things on the windowsill and her nightwear under the pillow on the mattress. They ate at the plastic table. Bella's hearty appetite was another good sign; during difficult times she barely ate a morsel.

'I feel lighter.' Bella shovelled food into her mouth.

Was this because Flora had gone to CARE?

There's a sanctuary you're to serve. The beautiful one will be saved.

'But surely that can't be why they suddenly released you.' Flora chewed slowly.

'I heard them talking about a lack of beds. Someone more desperate must have needed mine.'

'I'm annoyed they didn't speak to me.'

Bella finished her food. 'So, what have you been up to?'

'Not much.' She wondered whether to tell Bella about Mary. Instead, she told her about Neil. Her stomach turned over when she thought of their intense kiss. 'I had a visitor last night.'

'*Who?*'

Flora, smiled, coy. 'Mr Magic himself.'

'The Great Neillusionist,' cried Bella. 'You shag him?'

'No, I didn't! But we did kiss.'

'About bloody time. I know I've only met him a few times, but there's a chemistry. What are you gonna do?'

'What do you mean?'

'Are you gonna see him again?'

Flora shrugged.

'Come on, Sis, you're cracking on a bit now. Thirty-six. You should be thinking about weddings and babies and all that.' She said more softly, 'Don't you want kids?'

Flora looked at her empty plate, unable to speak.

'You're not that old,' said Bella kindly. 'I'm only teasing.'

Flora nodded, still mute. The question scraped a nerve, a dentist's instrument against a rotten tooth. Their mother had been twenty-three when she had Flora. Neither of their fathers had stuck around; Flora's had been a soldier passing through town, and Bella's had been a fling. Perhaps the absence of a father figure had made Flora reticent about relationships.

'I think you like Neil,' said Bella simply.

'I'd just mess it up.'

'Maybe not with him.'

'It's easier to be alone. I don't want the kind of home we had, men causing fights, leaving when they feel like it and returning drunk for a shag.'

'But you wouldn't choose anyone like that.'

Flora piled their plates up, took them to the sink.

'Give Neil a chance,' said Bella. 'I'd love to see you happy.'

'Why do I need a man for that?' Flora was indignant. 'I'm volunteering at CARE. *That's* the fulfilling stuff. By the way, I'm training on Monday so you'll have to entertain yourself. Why don't you apply for university? I know you missed the deadline but a guy at work said you can apply until June.'

'Maybe I'll pop in. Put the kettle on.'

Flora filled the pan again.

'For fuck's sake, where's the kettle?'

'It broke. I'll buy one when I get paid.'

'It's like *Benefits Britain: Life on the Dole* in here.'

'I'm glad you're home.' Flora was sarcastic but meant it. 'Will you see Mum?'

'Who needs her when I've got you? How long will that pan take to boil?'

'Only about eight hours.'

They laughed, heartily. Maybe the sudden things weren't miracles. Maybe they were just life when it happened without anyone else interfering.

*

That evening they pooled money and bought cheap chocolate and wine from the corner shop. At eleven they went to bed. Flora let Bella use the bathroom first. Sitting on the mattress, she was filled with anxiety. Bella had often needed to cut before she retired. She always cleaned up afterwards, but Flora still faced missed bloodstains, distraught at the pain her sister was in. Now, as Bella came into the bedroom and Flora went to clean her teeth, she braced herself for that crimson.

But the sink was clean.

She gripped it, flooded with relief.

Flora wiped the mist from the mirror with her sleeve, looked at her tired face. *Don't you want kids?*

The question haunted her.

In bed, she listened the soft thud of bass as Bella fell asleep, headphones on. She swiped her phone and typed *Marian miracles* into the search engine, then read the stories online.

When Mary appeared to a poor man in Guadalupe, Juan Diego, she asked him to tell the bishop to build a church. The bishop didn't believe it, so he asked for a sign, and she gave him a bunch of roses that were not in season. Numerous receivers of Mary had also reported health problems being miraculously healed. Flora read the reports with scepticism. Had these people willed such things because they wanted affirmation of their faith? Grandma Lil had always found comfort in a higher power keeping her safe.

Was Bella happier because Flora had done as Mary asked, or simply because the right medication had finally kicked in?

Flora closed the search engine and went on Instagram. Found Neil's account, which had a decent number of followers and featured short videos clips of his best performances. She clicked on a video where he was making rose petals dance in a circular pattern a foot higher than his open palm. They ascended, spinning, the gap narrowing, then disappeared. His face was serene. He was at his most natural onstage.

She couldn't let further feelings develop.

She couldn't take that chance.

She switched her phone off. No need to leave it on in case Bella called. Flora realised that her sister had put her plastic glow-in-the-dark Virgin Mary on the top of the wardrobe, and she watched the room as they slept.

18

Marilyn un-Monroes

Angels of the Immaculate Mary, Los Angeles, 1962

For the next few weeks in the convent, Marilyn's life was a simple one.

She rose with the sun and walked around the garden, inhaling the sweet, tart scent of the roses. Sometimes she joined the sisters for Lauds after breakfast, and then Vespers later, enjoying particularly the Rosary, where each delicate bead meant a different prayer. Marilyn loved the Hail Mary, which she learned easily. She often fluffed her lines on set – something newspapers loved to report – but that prayer stuck.

Here, Mary was everywhere. But, just like in the watercolour that had caused Marilyn to collapse, she was different to the lady who visited Brentwood. She was sketched as an angel, as perfect, like Monroe on screen.

Marilyn spoke privately with the sisters, fascinated by why they chose to live in such a place. 'I was a social worker,' said Sister Sofia. 'But the calling to a holy life grew stronger in me so I gave it all up and devoted myself to Jesus Christ and his teachings.'

Could Marilyn do such a thing? Was that what she wanted?

No, she didn't think so.

She just didn't know exactly *what* yet.

She learned that everyone within the community had a specific role. Just as Sister Joy was responsible for the garden, other sisters took care of administrative issues, some cleaned the premises, some oversaw laundry, and others did DIY.

Though they didn't venture out into the world, they invited others to enter theirs. On Mondays, weather permitting, the poor ate with them on the lawn, which was a jovial affair. Marilyn didn't join them, fearing recognition, and life at this refuge being over. Wednesdays, every other week, they had a craft and cake sale, inviting people to buy baking, paintings, and hand-sewn wares, which funded the place, alongside community donations and work taken in for a fee, like dressmaking and book-keeping. Thursdays, they held a meeting to address problems or needs.

When the sisters entered the convent, they gave up their lives, their families, and their personal possessions, taking a vow of poverty. Sister Joy explained to Marilyn that it was the truest sacrifice.

'Our needs are met by God,' she said. 'Not by things.'

*

Marilyn slept deeply at night.

The first evening, having slept for nine hours during the day, she did not expect to, and her customary anxiety reared its grey head. But she fell asleep in the early hours and still woke at dawn, feeling refreshed.

After that, she would retire to her room following supper, and found that she drifted off easily in the quiet solitude, no pills or milk or eye mask needed. The tranquillity gave space to reflect more than she ever had; when there was nothing else to consider, there were only your flaws, your truth, *you*.

The silence was a mirror, and into it she looked.

Every day that she was there, the outside world – or the *other world* as she now called it – moved farther away, dimming like a movie set when the lights had died. Marilyn often wondered if her *other world* friends missed her? Had her ex-lovers and husbands searched for her?

Did the press speculate wildly?

Should she let someone know where she was, high on this hill, so near and yet so far? Would knowing her whereabouts satiate them or cause more commotion?

She wasn't prepared to find out, not yet.

*

Her hair began to grow out; the natural mousy brown with the odd streak of reddish gold came back through. She un-Monroe-ed. Though there weren't any mirrors in the convent, at night the darkness made one of her window. Marilyn watched with interest the progress of her darker roots.

She had rather liked her original hair colour.

In her early days as a model, she wore it long, waves cascading around her shoulders. Then she was told that in order to get more work, she should lighten it. 'Look, darling,' the head of her modelling agency said, 'if you intend to go places in this business, you've got to bleach and straighten it. Your face is too round. A good hair job will lengthen it.'

Marilyn knew from her most recent stylist – who always marvelled at how fast her hair grew – that the average yearly growth was six inches. She figured that by then she could cut it and resume her own shade, which would help her be anonymous.

Having arrived in black slacks and a blouse, with only one other dress, Mother Superior gave Marilyn a couple of plain gowns to wear. They were not the dark robes the sisters wore, but grey, cut from the kind of cheap cloth Norma Jeane's orphanage dress had been. Marilyn rather liked the simplicity, how practical they were for working in the garden. This attire would be her cocoon while she metamorphosised into who she was supposed to be.

Marilyn's need for drugs diminished. There had always been sleeping pills at night, but during the day, especially when working, she often needed uppers to last the eighteen hour shifts on set.

Now, she detoxed naturally, and enjoyed the wellbeing that came from that.

She did, however, occasionally have nightmares that were so vivid she forgot where she was and woke thinking she was back in the orphanage; flashing images from the past grabbed at her as though to say, *you can't just abandon what was, you don't deserve this escape, this chance at happiness, look at the past, look at me, look at it.* In that long-ago place men as tall as houses loomed over her, reaching to take what they wanted, to take and destroy.

*

Marilyn always feared her demon – insomnia – and one night, he came for her.

She'd had a rare bad day, enduring flashbacks of long ago days, dark incidents that she tried desperately to quash. She paced her chamber in the blackness, wringing her hands, and counting to ten, again and again. Then, not sure what she might do, she crept out of the convent, wearing her grey gown, hair hidden beneath a scarf Sister Joy had loaned her for gardening.

She stole down the road, and hailed a passing cab.

'Where to?' he asked gruffly.

Where to?

'Well?'

Then she knew. 'The ocean,' she said, mindful he might recognise her voice so lowering it.

'Which beach?'

'The nearest.'

He took her there. In the dark, she was not sure which one it was, but she didn't care. 'Can you wait for me?' she asked the driver.

Are you coming back? whispered an alien voice. *Do you need him to wait?*

'Sure. It'll cost you,' he said.

She nodded and went onto the sand. The place was deserted. She kicked off her shoes. God, it felt good. The moon scattered silver coins across the water. Marilyn discarded her robe and scarf and went into the waves, as naked as the day she had been born. That was how she preferred to swim. It was glorious. Just her and the elements.

She still felt grimy inside though.

What if she swam right out?

Sank. Never came back.

Was that what she had come for?

No. There was hope now. She had simply needed to disrobe.

When she left the sea, chilly, glistening in the moonlight, searching for her dress and scarf, she spotted the silhouette of a man sitting on a nearby upturned wooden boat. He was smoking, the tip red in the dark, like an angry, all-seeing eye. This had been a bad idea. She had risked her new refuge for a dip in the ocean. She found her things and quickly donned them, hurrying up the beach towards the waiting cab.

'I know who you are,' called the man. 'They're looking for you.'

She ignored him.

'Come here, let me see your cunt!' He stood.

Again, she ignored him.

'Come here, I'll give you a nickel.'

No. *No.*

She must have heard wrong, must have imagined it…

Marilyn ran.

She was not shocked by his language – men on the street often talked to her that way – but he was a reminder of everything she was trying to escape. A reminder of how anxious aggressive male attention made her, a reminder of a long ago face.

No, don't think of that.

She jumped into the cab, asked the driver to take her back, and shivered for the entire journey. At the convent, he waited while she crept inside to get ten dollars.

Then, alone in her room, she stripped once more and got into bed. The risky adventure only further cemented why she wanted to escape the *other world*. She was not yet ready to leave the convent. There were ghosts not laid to rest, and they were rising, higher than ever before.

No, don't think of that.

She finally fell asleep, exhausted.

*

In the morning, still shaken, Marilyn knelt to tend the roses in the garden. Mother Superior came to admire her work.

'You're a natural.' She knelt beside her as though they were worshipping the flowers in unison. 'You have green fingers. You touch plants and they spring to life.'

'Not really.' Marilyn felt shy about the praise.

'Are you alright, child?'

Marilyn couldn't speak. Instead, she cut a pink rose and gave it to Mother Superior. 'For your room,' she said. 'Can I ask you something?'

'Of course.'

'Tell me more about the Virgin Mary.' Marilyn still hadn't told anyone about her visit. 'I'm fascinated with who she *really* was.'

Mother Superior joined her hands as though about to pray. 'Mary is the Mother of God,' she said. 'She was free of original sin from the moment of her conception, a singular dignity higher than all the blessed souls in heaven. God chose her to bear his son, Jesus Christ, to give him life on earth.'

No, thought Marilyn, disappointed. *Not the story, not how the*

Catholic Church sees her, but the real her … as a human, as a woman, as a girl. 'She was very young,' she said, 'when she was chosen.'

'Yes, but life was different in her day. Jewish girls were married at fourteen, often mothers by fifteen.'

'That's just a baby,' said Marilyn quietly.

She couldn't imagine it.

Suddenly she pricked her finger on a thorn and gasped. The blood was rich and ran down her finger. It triggered a memory, one of pain, damage, bleeding afterwards; one she had tried to supress yesterday; her whole life. 'How could she agree to do such a huge thing at so young an age?'

'She was asked by God. It was her destiny.'

'But... the *weight* of it…'

'She was strong. She was pure.'

'That's when someone should be left alone,' said Marilyn to herself, angry. She sucked the blood from her finger, shook her head. Heard Dr Greenson encouraging her to face the unspoken thing that haunted her.

'Tell me what troubles you,' said Mother Superior.

Marilyn staggered to her feet. 'Mary was far too young,' she said softly, and went to her room.

19

Worldwide, August 1962

MARILYN MISSING!

Marilyn Monroe, who was last seen by her housekeeper Eunice Murray at nine o'clock on August 4th, has been missing for a week. Murray reported that Marilyn's Brentwood home was empty when she arrived for work early August 5th.

'Nothing appeared out of place,' she said. 'The car was on the drive and only a holdall, a few items, and a photograph were missing. The side door was unlocked, and there was a single pink flower on the bed that I don't recall being there the day before. I've been to the house every day, dealing with the mail and the ringing phone. Marilyn, however, hasn't called the house once.'

Publicist, Pat Newcomb, expressed her concern, saying she had had a 'bad feeling' when she called Monroe the night she was last seen, and that the star had been 'odd' when they spoke on the phone.

'I might have been the last person to speak to her,' she said with emotion. 'I've no idea where she might have gone. I've heard nothing since.'

Close associates are baffled by the disappearance. The troubled star was recently fired from but then reinstated by Twentieth Century Fox on the movie, *Something's Got To Give*, starring alongside Dean Martin, who told Fox, 'No Marilyn, no picture'. A spokesman said they were concerned, but the show must go on. The film is due to restart next month. Dean Martin may have insisted on Marilyn's return when she was dismissed, but another actress will play her role now.

Police have checked local hospitals, searched the area, and followed possible leads, but are not 'too worried yet'. 'Sometimes we need a break,' said Sergeant Mullins. 'She'll probably turn up next week, relaxed and ready for the camera again.'

New York Times

MONROE STILL MISSING

Marilyn Monroe, who has dominated headlines for more than ten years, is still missing after three weeks. The search has widened. The Los Angeles Police Department have spoken to Monroe's friends and ex-husbands, as well as executives at Twentieth Century Fox. With no evidence of foul play, they think the star might have taken a vacation but are also taking her absence 'very seriously'.

Joe DiMaggio, baseball star and Monroe's ex-husband, who she was photographed in Florida with recently, said, 'Marilyn loves to chat on the telephone. Even if she has taken a vacation, she would call. I'm very concerned.'

In November 1954 the star donned a black wig, boarded a plane as 'Zelda Zonk' and escaped to New York. At twenty-eight she said she felt overworked, underestimated, and underpaid, having played dumb blonde after dumb blonde. For the next fourteen months she lived in the city, telling friends that it was the 'happiest of her life'. It meant freedom from derogatory labels such as starlet, sex symbol, and slut.

When she returned to Hollywood, she had a new confidence, and had formed her own company – Marilyn Monroe Productions – with photographer Milton Greene. It looked like her life was on the up. Then, however, the world knew where Monroe was. Now the world is mystified by the star's sudden disappearance.

Los Angeles Times

MONROE SPOTTED NUDE ON BEACH

Missing star, Marilyn Monroe, was alleged by a local man to have been seen swimming nude at Venice Beach. 'I wish I'd had my camera,' said William Norris, who reported that he saw the star emerge naked from the waves one night. 'She looked stunning. She came over and gave me a salty kiss, and then disappeared. I'll never forget it.'

Parade magazine

When Marilyn was here, still among us, the press photographed her from every angle – high up to caress the rise of her bosom, low down to capture some thigh, behind to see her ass. Now she's gone, they still swarm, their buzzing more desperate. It's been two months and none of the 'witnesses' who have come forward saying they've seen her in Mexico, Spain, Egypt, and – most ludicrously of all – in a convent in Austria, have led to anything.

Where is she?

I hope she's OK.

Stella Cruz, *Icon* magazine

20

Flora is on fire

March 2016, Hull, England

The sisters slept late. Flora woke first and lay quietly for a moment, listening to Bella snoring softly, anxious that she wouldn't be as happy today as yesterday. She got up, filled the pan; as it bubbled, Bella emerged.

'God, I slept well.' She sank into a plastic chair.

'That's good.' Flora paused. 'How do you feel?'

'Great.' Bella shrugged. 'Have you got any bread?'

'I think it's past the date.'

'Past date doesn't matter for toast. You should eat the shit I had in hospital.'

'You're sure you feel good still?' Flora studied her sister.

'I'm sure. Stop worrying. I slept like a baby, I'm starving, and I'm happy.'

*

Later, Flora left for work. Bella said she'd come by at some point.

There had been a leak in the kitchen. Greg was ringing around for someone to sort it and swearing about Denise being off. Flora and young barman Georgie, a drama student, helped mop up the mess.

'Just hope the punters like the new act,' grunted Greg.

'Kerry Loggins,' cried Georgie, face alight. 'I'm here for this.'

Kerry was a female Kenny Logins tribute act; she also dressed as Tom Cruise to sing 'Dangerzone' and recreated the various dancing feet when performing 'Footloose'. She had – according to the poster – sold out in Scunthorpe.

'Aren't you a bit young for *Top Gun*?' said Flora.

'No one's too young for *Top Gun*,' said Georgie.

By seven-thirty, the club was full. Flora knew Neil rarely arrived early, but still watched the door as she served drinks. The blonde man in the flat cap was back with his mates, already drunk.

'Psychic Pat's in on Friday.' Greg put a bottle of Prosecco in an ice bucket for three women dressed as brides. 'Barry Lung cancelled and she's covering.'

Flora nodded and pulled another pint. She needed to talk to Pat. It was three days since Mary appeared in her kitchen. Was that distance making her question whether it had really happened? No: she recalled it the way you see fond memories – more rose-coloured with every recollection.

'Anyone in?' It was flat cap guy, aggressive. 'Talk about the lights being on but nobody home. For the third time, *three pints of Stella*.'

Flora walked away, leaving Georgie to serve him.

As Kerry Loggins took to the stage on a motorbike, Bella arrived. Flora couldn't help but smile. She had piled her hair up in a messy bun; soft strands fell around cheeks the colour of rose petals. She had chosen flame-red lipstick and borrowed Flora's favourite sleeveless top, which added glamour to her usual jeans. She never hid her arms, was never ashamed of the scars there. She wore them like statement tattoos.

Even though she was twenty-four, she looked too young to be out drinking. She sat in the left corner and Flora took her a sneaky glass of wine. She couldn't talk because lamp after lamp demanded attention while Kerry Loggins belted out the hits.

At the interval, still no Neil.

The thought of not seeing him made Flora sad.

'No Neil?' asked Bella, buying another glass of wine.

'Hadn't noticed,' said Flora.

'Yeah, yeah.'

Then he arrived, as though the two women had conjured him with their words. He came to the bar, nodded at Bella, and ordered a beer. Flora tried to act like he was just any customer, sure her tight voice gave her away.

'Who's on?' he asked.

'The one and only Kerry Loggins,' cried Bella.

He laughed. 'I knew there was a reason I came.'

Bella looked pointedly at Flora, but she ignored it. Neil held Flora's gaze for a second and took his usual seat beneath the Upcoming Events poster.

'Don't you dare harass him,' hissed Flora when her sister looked mischievous.

'I need to find out if his intentions are honourable.'

'Stop it. You'll put him off.'

'I thought you weren't going to take things any further?'

'I won't get chance if you go causing trouble, Madam.'

'As if.' Bella winked.

Music blasted and Kerry Loggins returned to the stage, dressed like George Michael now, shades and leatherette biker jacket in place. Georgie danced between tables. The lamps occupied his and Flora's time for the next hour, but she kept an eye on Bella, who kept motioning to Neil.

Eventually Greg took over so Flora grabbed a ten-minute break. She headed towards Bella, who shook her head and gestured to the back; to Neil.

So, Flora joined him.

'Bet you wish you'd perfected your disappearing trick right now, eh?' She looked at Kerry crooning 'Careless Whisper' with one of the hen party women.

'I'm saving that for when Psychic Pat's on.'

'How's the disappearing trick going?'

'Getting there. I'm adding a new element to it.' He paused. 'How are you?'

'Good. Remember my sister?' She glanced over at Bella, who was nodding her head along to the music. 'She's back with me again.'

'At your flat?'

'Yes.' Flora felt sure Neil sounded disappointed, and smiled.

'There's another disappearing trick I might be doing soon.' He changed the topic abruptly.

Flora's heart tightened. 'What do you mean?'

'I'm going to Vegas.'

'Forever?' The word escaped before Flora could stop it; a split-second pause in the music gave it added volume.

He smiled. 'I wish. Well, I don't, not really. No, just for a week. Next month.' He paused. 'You're gonna think me a total nerd.'

'Why?'

He looked thoughtful. 'I saw David Copperfield in Vegas when I was fifteen. My dad got free tickets to his show. I'd never seen anything like it. I mean, what did we have in the UK back then? Paul Daniels.'

Flora laughed. She noticed Bella watching them, her face a picture of exaggerated encouragement.

'He did the Lucky Thirteen trick where he made thirteen random audience members disappear on stage, and reappear at the back,' said Neil. 'It blew my mind. I wanted to know how he'd done it. Back home, I started reading books about magic, tried a few tricks with cards. I wasn't popular at school – too gangly and I wore glasses – but suddenly the kids loved me.'

'You're like Dynamo,' said Flora. 'Both working class kids.'

'Another hero of mine.' Neil looked sad then. 'Look at his success and look at me.' He paused. 'Do you think my magic is good?'

'Better than good.' Flora meant it. She almost admitted that she had looked at footage of him last night but stopped herself, embarrassed. 'You just haven't had your lucky break yet.'

'That's why I'm going to Vegas.' He was happy again. 'There's a big competition at the Magic Theatre. I found out yesterday that I got a place to audition. God knows where I'll get the money to travel there, but I can't miss such a chance, can I?'

'No, you can't.'

'Everything's been done. You can't outdo the big ones; David Blaine suspended above London for forty-four days, Dynamo walking on water. People want *more*. But for me, it's about…'

Neil undid his cuff button, pulled his sleeve back and turned his palm up. On his forearm was an intricate tattoo. It pulsated with life, the way Marilyn Monroe did on a flat surface. A woman wore a crimson robe of flickering flames. Her hair was wild too. Flora recognised the face.

It was *her*.

She gasped.

She reached out to touch it; in a deft movement, Neil pulled his sleeve over it, then back again.

It had gone.

'*How*?' she whispered.

'Magic,' he smiled. 'Flora, I want to disappear like no one ever has before.'

'Onstage I presume?' She arched her eyebrows, still stunned by the tattoo. She wanted to see it again.

'Yes.'

'They'll call you the Marilyn of the magic world.'

'Ha. I like that.' He paused. 'Better still, I want to change. Not just disappear but transform into someone *else* live on stage. I've sort of figured out how I could do it. I just need…' Neil leaned in, his breath warm against her ear. 'Flora, before I go to the US…'

'Yes?'

'Can w-'

They were interrupted by Greg shouting Flora to attend the lamps.

She dragged herself back to work, her patience with the flirtatious drunks limited. Kerry Loggins finished her final song and the place slowly emptied. Flora collected glasses and noticed flat cap guy chatting to Bella. Bella looked like she was enduring him rather than interested. Flora put the empties on the bar and began wiping tables, keeping an eye on them. Neil was still at the back, looking at his phone. As the place got emptier, Flora could hear flat cap guy.

'So, where you goin' after this?' he slurred.

'Wherever you're not,' said Bella.

That's my girl, thought Flora.

'You don't fancy a shag then?' He dropped clumsily into the chair next to her. His mates were finishing their drinks. One of them urged him to hurry up, saying they wanted to go clubbing.

'I've just painted my nails,' said Bella.

'Think you're pretty special, don't-cha?'

'I've just got taste.'

'I bet you're a little slag.' He leaned over and tugged her ear lobe.

Flora threw the cloth down and marched over. 'Get your hands off her!'

'Oh. It's... *you*.' He could hardly get the words out. 'Jealous a bit?'

'She isn't interested,' hissed Flora. 'She's out of your league.'

'What's it got to do with you?' he slurred.

'It's fine, Flora.' Bella started to get up.

'Wait.' Flat cap guy pulled her arm so she fell onto him.

Flora had never felt such rage.

She moved her sister out of the way – carefully, the way you would a small child out of danger – and hurled him to the floor with strength that felt like fire. Stunned, he tried to gather himself, but Bella pinned him to the ground by his neck, while he gagged, bright red; his ridiculous cap fell off. His mates pulled at Flora, telling her to calm down, it was just a bit of fun.

'Fun for *who*?' she screamed.

Neil put a hand on her elbow, which she almost pushed off.

'What's going on?' demanded Greg, Georgie not far behind.

Bella was looking at Flora like she had never seen her before.

Am I different? she thought.

'She should be sacked.' Flat cap guy was on his feet, unsteady, hat in trembling hand. 'She's a fucking maniac. I won't be coming 'ere again.'

'Good,' spat Flora.

'You go, Girl,' cried Georgie.

'Cloakroom, now,' ordered Greg.

Flora sagged, as though his words had released a valve. She wanted to cry. She headed for the cloakroom, hearing Greg telling flat cap guy he was barred, and Neil asking if Flora was OK.

Flora buried her face in her jacket, embarrassed at her behaviour. Why had he made her so angry? She had endured many a drunken harassment in this job.

Because it was Bella.

A hand on her back and she jumped.

Bella and Neil.

'Are you OK, Sis?'

'Yeah. Can we go?'

'Of course,' said Bella. 'Wow, you were … scary.'

Neil looked like he wasn't sure if he should stay. 'You were on fire,' he said softly. 'Like the tattoo.'

'What tattoo?' asked Bella.

Flora ignored the question, pulled her coat on, and they headed into the bar. 'Can I go?' she called to Greg.

'Are you alright?' Greg was his usual gruff self but seemed genuinely concerned.

'It's been a long week.'

'Well, see you…?'

'Wednesday,' said Flora.

'Great.'

Outside, the night had turned cold; their breath fogged the air. The three of them stood shivering, glancing at one another, Bella's face still full of awe when she looked at Flora.

'I should…' started Neil.

'Come back to ours,' said Bella. 'I'm off to bed so you two can do whatever.'

Neil laughed but Flora was mortified. He looked at her, the question in his eyes clear; did she want him to come back? She did.

'Can we get a taxi,' said Bella. 'I can't be arsed to walk.'

'I'll get one.' Neil made a call.

When it arrived, Bella got in the front and made conversation with the driver. Neil and Flora sat in the back. Halfway home, without even looking at her, Neil found her hand and wordlessly held it inside his until they got to the flat.

21

Marilyn finds the words

Angels of the Immaculate Mary, Los Angeles, 1962

After her secret escape to the beach, Marilyn dreamed she was drowning.

Four nights in a row, she woke gasping, sure that saltwater was choking her. In the nightmare, men swam out to save her, but instead they rose from the sea like liquid devils, faces dissolving into ghoulish masks, screaming, 'I'll give you a nickel,' over and over and over.

Norma Jeane had loved the beach. But, as Marilyn lay shivering in the aftermath of the dream, she recalled a day long ago when she had wanted to rip off her bathing suit and run naked into the ocean, desperate to be cleansed by the chill water, wanting to swim out as far as was possible and sink to the bottom.

She had wanted to scream words into an abyss: No, no, *no*.

*

Mother Superior approached one morning as Marilyn pruned roses, knelt at her side once more.

'You look tired, child,' she said. 'Do you miss your home?'

Marilyn shook her head.

'Your family?'

She began to cry.

Mother Superior let the tears fall, didn't push for explanation.

'I was eight,' said Marilyn. 'He was supposed to be looking after me.'

Mother Superior waited.

'He was one of my foster carers.' Marilyn paused, shame lowering her head. 'That was... that was the first time…'

'Don't speak if you can't,' said Mother Superior.

Marilyn rocked back and forth.

Then the words came, like blood.

She let them.

'He told me to be a good girl... so I *was*. I liked to be a good girl. He gave me a nickel when he was done. I thought, oh, I'm worth something because that was a lot of money to me.' Amidst the roses, Marilyn curled over; the words were muffled by her knees. She had developed a stutter after the abuse, which caused further trauma, and now it returned. 'I s-s-suppose the next time I should have endured it better. Because it h-h-happened again … in a different foster home, but this time I was older, and somehow that made it much worse … because now I knew about s-s-sex, and that made it all the more shameful … as though it was my fault, *my* shame, and I had caused it.'

She had spoken of this abuse before in casual words, like it didn't matter, belying the gravity of the hurt, with Pat, with her sister Berniece, but she hadn't *felt* it like now. Like she was that little girl again, afraid, trying to fight him off. She didn't just speak her story to Mother Superior; she relived it. The pain peaked in her belly, the place it often manifested; in her womb where all the grief gathered.

'I told you, M-M-Mother Superior. I got r-r-ruined long ago.' Marilyn sobbed, violently.

'You are not ruined. You are strong, like Mary was.'

'I'm n-n-not.'

It had been difficult to speak back then because after it happened Norma Jeane told her foster mother, who slapped her and told her not to tell lies. That silenced the child for many years, and into adulthood. When you are humiliated into such quiet, the words you want to say are then laced with shame.

'You have survived,' Mother Superior said simply.

'But have I?' Marilyn sat up again, anger now fierce. 'Sometimes I don't even know who I am.'

'What do you mean?'

Marilyn shook her head.

'You told me you created this Marilyn Monroe who you were in the movies,' said Mother Superior. 'And I thought *created* was such an interesting word. How does one do that?'

Marilyn took a breath; remembered. 'A woman in the orphanage let me try on her lipstick. She powdered my nose and curled my hair in ribbons. I was about twelve. I felt beautiful for the first time in my life. And in the mirror, I was *her*! This other wonderful creature, long before Marilyn Monroe was born. I caught a glimpse of *her*. I liked that other girl. She was better than me.'

'I see.'

'And then when I got made up to do my first modelling assignment, long before the movies, there she was again, smiling at me, radiant. She was a means to escape my past, to be loved, to replace all the ugliness I felt inside. I thought, I'll create a beauty so bright no one will look any deeper.'

'She was a safe place?' asked Mother Superior.

'Maybe … but she's not real, is she?' said Marilyn.

'She must be a real part of you. We can't create what isn't there. God loves all the aspects of you, that I know. God forgives, even those cruel men who hurt you.'

'Well, I can't!' cried Marilyn.

She was exhausted now.

She wondered if the breathing space she had given herself here meant trauma she had buried deeply was working to the surface, if the midnight swim had washed away the last of her resistance to it. But now it was here, she felt sick, choked, like black tar was trickling up her throat.

'Praying could help,' said Mother Superior.

Marilyn wanted to shake her head, but resisted.

'Nothing is too dark to share with God,' continued the Mother. 'Speak with him privately, find solace there in His grace.' She paused. 'When I first came here, many years ago, it was just after the first war. I was a young widow with no children. My beloved husband, Clint, was killed. I had no one else. I grew up mostly in care, like you did. I had never felt more alone. I intended to commit the gravest of sins.' She bowed her head. 'I wanted to die. I tried to make it happen. While I was unconscious, God spoke to me, told me to come here. I had never felt such love.'

Marilyn was filled with compassion, wanted to show it with a touch but didn't know if she should. In this empathy, she felt the black tar ease, felt her own trauma lessen. It had always made her feel better when she felt for *others*.

'When I was in the orphanage, they made God seem like a scary thing,' she said instead. 'Someone always watching and judging. But I've often thought, if there is one…' She paused, nervous that she was rude to question his existence, but Mother Superior waited for her to go on. 'If there *is* a God, he's the same, no matter what religion or name we give him. Surely he loves all of us, so why would he judge?'

'So why do you judge yourself harshly if He does not?'

Marilyn didn't know what to say.

Sister Joy joined them then, basket of cut roses over her arm. 'Oh, sorry, am I interrupting?'

'No, Sister Joy, I must get on.' Mother Superior stood with a groan, and Marilyn followed. 'Your garden is lovely, sisters,' she continued. Looking at Marilyn she added, 'Out of the most undernourished and uncultivated soil, great flowers can bloom.'

When she had gone, Marilyn and Sister Joy continued with their duties, Marilyn quiet while her young companion chattered happily. The revelation had exhausted her. Perhaps the more she shared it, the lighter it would become, and the more she would heal.

Perhaps it was time to write her thoughts down again. She had often scribbled away in the past, finding it soothing, and now was the perfect time to do so.

*

The next day she asked Mother Superior if she might have a notepad; she gave her a slim black book with lined pages inside.

At night, Marilyn put herself between those lines.

The weeks passed and became months.

Her natural hair emerged alongside the new poppies she had planted in the garden. She liked how blue her eyes looked in contrast with the darker shade, how pink her cheeks were from good sleep and simple food and daily work.

Some days she wondered about contacting someone from the *other world*, just to let them know she was safe, but she feared being persuaded to go back into that place. She knew she'd have to, one day, but until she knew *how* she would re-emerge, and where she might go, she would keep her whereabouts secret.

She knew this was not the place she belonged forever. But every stopover was important on the journey. This place was showing her a glimpse of the changes she wanted to make, the things she wanted to do, the person she wanted to be.

And soon she would make that happen.

22

Flora finds words too

March 2016, Hull, England

At the flat, Bella made a show of getting a glass of water, yawning, and saying she was going to bed. She came to the sofa where Neil and Flora sat, ruffled her sister's hair, said, 'Don't go beating him up, will you?'

'I'm sorry about her,' smiled Flora when she had gone.

'She's sweet,' said Neil. 'You're alike.'

'Are we?'

'Have you told her about…?' He faltered.

'About?' Did he mean the kiss?

'About Mary,' he said.

'Oh. No.'

'Why not?'

Flora felt bad that she'd told Neil and not her own sister. 'I'm not sure,' she admitted. 'When she was little, I was all she had. I took on a care role and I've never shaken it off. I think I'm nervous it might be too much for Bella. She's been unwell but seems a lot better now.' She realised she was rambling.

Neil studied her. 'You didn't like that man pawing her.'

'No.' The rage bubbled again, deep in Flora's gut.

'That was intense.'

'I don't want to talk about it,' she snapped.

'Maybe you should?'

'Who the hell are *you*?' The words ripped from Flora's mouth like squeaky aliens from a stomach in a sci-fi film. She saw the shock in his eyes, died a little inside. 'Sorry. I'm not angry at you...'

'No,' he said quietly. 'But you're angry at *someone*.'

Flora didn't respond. She glanced up at the book that was preserving the daffodil, heard*: I bless the sacrifice that hurt your heart. You had no say in it and did not ask for it.*

Had those words opened a scar Flora was sure had healed over? Did such wounds ever close?

It had been years ago. She had survived. More than survived. She had made a life, left home young, always worked, even if the jobs were minimum wage, never asking for anything from anyone. She paid her bills – maybe late occasionally – and she'd only had to go to a foodbank twice when she was unemployed. She had returned that help by donating tins when she had spare.

'Where did you go?' It was Neil, concern in his eyes now.

Where *had* she gone? Not just to the past but inside. Deep inside where she never went, into her gut, her *womb*. It was hard now to pull free from that place, to know that she was in the flat, safe, with a kind man who she liked.

'When he touched Bella,' Neil said, 'you were a wild animal.'

'I was assaulted once,' she spat, regretting it immediately.

'I'm so sorry.'

'It was nothing.'

'I'm sure it wa–'

'Can we not?'

'Sure,' he said kindly. 'Whatever you need.'

But it had been said. It sat in the room between them, demanding to be acknowledged. She had looked into hell, and it was looking back. If Neil had returned to the flat after she shared the story of Mary's visit, then he *must* be trustworthy. Instinct said he was. Hadn't that instinct saved her from disastrous relationships before, an inner voice whispering, 'Get out'.

Now it urged, 'You can tell Neil.'

But she didn't want him to see her as a victim.

'I can go,' said Neil kindly.

That was the last thing she wanted. '*Stay.*'

How could they resume a light-hearted mood now she had mentioned the assault? Maybe she should tell him so they could return to banter again.

'Is… *this*... us... is it…?' Flora didn't know how to finish.

'Is it going anywhere?' Neil responded. 'I'd like it to.'

'Good.'

'Good,' he repeated, and she smiled.

'It wasn't just an assault,' she said quietly.

'Oh.' Neil nodded.

'I was barely a teenager.'

'Shit.'

'It was... my mother's boyfriend.' His name came to her: Malcolm. But she couldn't say it.

Neil held his breath, maybe afraid Flora was so fragile he'd blow her away. She felt like nothing held her down, like she was a child again, voice soft and small.

Hold my hand, she wanted to say. *Like you did in the taxi.*

And then he did.

'You know what I'm saying, don't you?' she whispered.

Neil nodded. 'But... your mother's…'

Flora had blocked his face the way people blocked followers on Twitter. 'Can you see why I'm shocked that Mary would come to *me* of all people?'

'Maybe she... *identified.*'

'What do you mean?'

'Well, she was barely fifteen they say when she became a mother? I liked Religious Education,' he added, as though to explain how he knew such a thing. 'I had a crush on the teacher, so I paid attention.'

Flora smiled, despite the intensity of the moment.

'Mary was a child and maybe she didn't *want* to be the Mother of God.'

'My Grandma Lil always said she carried the burden of the world on her shoulders. She had to be perfect. It must have been exhausting. Maybe you're right. Maybe she came because we have something in common.'

Flora had been able to talk about the attack, even if she hadn't used the real word for it. It was a start. She was still sitting here, still alive. But that wasn't the most difficult part of the story. That had only been the beginning of a long nightmare. The other part choked her. Still.

'You being young, you mean?' asked Neil.

Flora couldn't look at him. 'There's more. We both…'

'Tell me.'

'We both…'

He waited.

'We both... had a baby.'

It was done. It was said. Her greatest pain.

'A *baby*?' Neil repeated it like he didn't know what one was.

'Yes.'

'I …' He shook his head.

'A bit of a shocker, eh?'

'But where is…?'

'Gone,' said Flora simply, sweeping it under the carpet like she had had to do all those years ago. 'My mother made me give it away.'

'It?'

Flora swallowed. Breathed. Spoke. '*He.*'

'Oh.' Small words.

'See,' she said, 'I can make things disappear just as well as you.'

And then she began to cry; it surprised her because she didn't feel it coming. Neil moved closer, put his arms around her. He didn't say a word while she wept. When Flora surfaced, gasping for air like someone rescued from the sea, she feared disturbing Bella, and then drowned more quietly.

She saw again the pale-haired woman she had imagined kneeling at flowers. The lady paused, as though sensing someone behind her, but she didn't turn. Flora's tears subsided. The vision died. After a while, she breathed hard.

She pulled away from Neil. 'God,' she said. 'I'll never see you again after that.'

'You will. Are you OK?'

'I'm starving.' She was. It was fierce. He looked startled. 'Do you want cheese on toast?'

'Sure.'

Flora made it. Neil watched from the sofa. He probably thought she was unstable, going from being distraught to savage hunger, making toast like it had been an everyday evening of Netflix and chat. Maybe she *was* unhinged, suddenly sharing something she had never told anyone.

'Did your mother's boyfriend... did he know you had a…?'

'No.'

'Does your sister know?' Neil looked towards the bedroom.

'God, no. She was too young to have known what was going on. And we... we hid it...' She brought their snack to the sofa. 'The pregnancy.' The word pained her. It was an experience most women enjoyed, but hers had been shrouded in shame because she had been a child. Each little kick she savoured in the dark, cherishing that unique movement, knowing it would be over one day, and she would be empty once more. 'My mother kept me home from school in the last two months when we couldn't hide it anymore.'

Flora didn't want to think about the birth, the pain when it began in full.

'Have you ever looked for... *him*?'

Flora shook her head, bit into the toast.

'Do you want to?'

She was glad to have her mouth full. When she had swallowed, she said, 'I don't want to talk about it anymore.'

They finished the supper in silence. Flora worried that she had ruined things. Neil might have *said* he would come back, but what about when he digested all this?

The silence continued as she rinsed plates and returned to the sofa; it grew, steady and suffocating. Flora feared they would never speak again. Then Neil took her hand once more. It was a simple gesture that touched Flora. She looked at him, afraid of seeing revulsion in his eyes.

Then he kissed her, his mouth warm this time. She sank into him. Neil didn't take things any further, despite a heat growing between them, and exploring, urgent hands.

He pulled away after a while, said, 'Let's save something for next time.'

Next time. Two words she needed to hear.

'Let's,' she said.

'Shall I give you my number?'

'Yes. I'll give you mine.'

They put the new digits into their phones.

'I should go.' He paused. 'Unless you want me to…'

'I'm fine.' She looked towards the bedroom where Bella slept. 'Anyway, I'm not alone.'

'I'll message you.'

'That would be nice.'

Flora walked him to the door. They kissed again, brief, more restrained. Then she watched him go, with so many conflicting feelings: anxiety, happiness, shame, excitement, and *hope*.

She didn't think she would sleep, but oblivion came easily. Flora dreamt of the birth. Of almost blacking out from waves of pain. Of blood, so much, no one warned about that, but why would they, no one knew, no one checked her, or advised her.

And then a baby; warm and small and not hers to keep.

She woke, briefly, sure she could smell that infant.

She thought of Amelia on the floor at CARE; their connection; her distraught words, *I'm her mum, but they won't let me be.* Flora drifted into dreams where they both searched endless corridors for their babies.

*

She woke first in the morning, crept out of the bedroom so she didn't disturb Bella, and filled the pan with water. She liked Sundays. The club was shut, and the day stretched ahead full of nothing. Today, though, there was so much going on in her head.

A knock on the door.

Neil?

She opened it onto a middle-aged man with a too-big moustache and hair brushed over to hide a bald patch.

'I'm John Marse,' he said. 'From the *Yorkshire Post*. Are you Flora Baker?'

She tried to process his words. He must have come to the wrong address. But he knew her name. Was someone hurt? Surely that would mean the police knocking not someone from a newspaper.

'I've been calling you,' he said.

'I don't answer unknown numbers. They're all robots.'

'I left messages.' He seemed annoyed.

'I don't listen to any from unknown numbers.'

'Are you free to chat?' He put one foot inside the door frame.

'About what?'

'About your visit the other night.'

Neil? Why was that of importance?

'From the Virgin Mary,' he said.

Flora felt sick. 'How did you get my address?'

'So, it's true?'

'Get your foot out of my door.' She tried to close it.

'We've spoken to someone but we want your side.'

Flora tried to move his foot.

'Why do you think Mary chose you? Is it true that she gave you a daffodil?'

'Get out.' Flora kicked his foot away and slammed the door.

'Are you afraid you won't be believed?' he called from the other side. 'I believe you and I'll write a very sensitive piece.'

'Go away,' hissed Flora. 'I'm calling the police.'

'I'll put my card under the door. You'd be better talking to me. If your story got in the wrong hands it'd be done in an exploitative way. Call me after you've had time to think.'

'I'm not interested!'

After a moment, footsteps on the stairs. Flora picked up his card and put it in the kitchen drawer without looking at it. Two things came to her as she closed the drawer, heart hammering, stomach churning.

One: if this story got out, everyone was going to know about Mary's visit. She'd be mocked and insulted.

Two: who had told this man about her experience?

Neil was the only person she had shared it with. The only one who knew about the daffodil. No. He would *never* do that. She was certain of it.

But what if she was wrong?

She had trusted before and been let down.

No, he was different. He had listened to her emotional confession last night, knew things about her that no one else did.

Things she realised he could disclose if he wanted.
No. *No.*
Not Neil.

23

Marilyn has an idea

Angels of the Immaculate Mary, Los Angeles, November 1963

Marilyn removed slacks and a sweater to reveal a skimpy, striped bathing suit, and walked slowly across the sand to the water's edge. Young men whistled. She closed her eyes and savoured it and then, instead of going into the ocean, she turned and walked back along the beach. The men whistled more; some approached to speak to her. Even women, sitting on blankets, getting a tan, sat up and stared as she went nearer to them.

She realised she was not Marilyn.

Not yet.

She was Norma Jeane. No. *Two* people. One was Norma Jeane from the orphanage, shy and gangly, and the other was the creature she glimpsed in the mirror the year before, aged twelve, when a kind woman powdered her nose and curled her hair. She didn't have a name for this other woman who incited such intense reactions from people when she assumed her walk, her smile. She only knew that she belonged to the ocean and the sky and the whole world.

Marilyn woke in her simple room at the convent.

It had been a dream. But a lovely one, not a nightmare.

Because it had been a good memory.

The moment she first experienced her power as a blossoming teenager, aged thirteen, on Santa Monica beach. Back then, this mysterious unnamed persona was a beacon of hope. Someone who offered a brighter future.

Where had it gone wrong?

She had enjoyed her early career, the opportunities that came, the fascinating people she met, and the creatives she mixed with. She found a belated education in learning how films were made on set, in being tutored by an acting coach during the early days, in studiously poring over books about the human body so she could use hers to powerful effect before the camera, and in finally having the honour of studying at the New York Actors Studio under Lee Strasberg.

Despite these efforts, all she had was instinct when she stepped in front of a camera. Whatever she tried to learn, whatever advice she took, in the end it was *her*.

But then it began to fall apart.

Now, here in the Angels of the Immaculate Mary, fifteen months after escaping the *other world*, Marilyn was beginning to miss *something*. The slow healing – helped not only by sharing her trauma with Mother Superior but by nightly self-reflection in her notepad – had given way to new hope.

Was she missing her early glittering career enough to try and return there? She did occasionally wonder what roles she might have been offered if she'd stuck it out. Something more challenging? More fitting for a woman who was now thirty-seven, who had quietly celebrated that slow edging towards forty with a small cake and the good wishes of the dear sisters.

Perhaps *this* was Marilyn's greatest role; a woman facing her demons and growing more comfortable in her skin; a woman deciding for herself what she wanted, what she did next, no studio dictating her every move.

She sat up in the narrow bed.

It was November and though the night had been crisp, and the sun had not yet risen, Marilyn knew the day would soon be warm. Her autumnal sunflowers, chrysanthemums, and freesias would outshine the dying leaves. She got the black notebook from beneath her pillow and recorded the dream. For the first time since her arrival she grew restless.

It was time.

But what for?

Follow your heart, and then the tiny white shoe, one you will know, and which will take you up into the place you should go first.

Go first. Two key words. There was clearly another place she was supposed to go after this one. Hadn't she known that?

And then onto she who is named after the stars.

What had that meant?

And finally, to the place of your ancestors.

Who were they?

She didn't know who her father was, and knew little about her maternal family.

Shine your light on other women.

Marilyn needed to talk to someone.

She still hadn't told any of the sisters about the visit, and wasn't sure she ever would. Now she felt the beginnings of an idea and needed to bounce it off someone. She washed and dressed, and went for breakfast, where the silence was an irritation when she wanted to spill thoughts like she used to; to speak first and think later. Then to Lauds, where the Rosary was as familiar as a childhood song.

Tending their flowers in the garden later that morning, Marilyn asked Sister Joy, 'Do you know anything about charity work?'

Sister Joy sat back on her ankles, small trowel in hand. 'I've never been involved with any. I read that you were generous in helping charities. You know more than me.'

Marilyn shrugged. 'I sang to raise money for children in a hospital once – not very well!' She giggled. 'And I gave money where I could, but that isn't much.'

'I read that you helped Jane Russell with an adoption charity.'

Marilyn had forgotten and smiled at the memory. Jane had founded WAIF (World Adoption International Fund) in 1955, a fundraising arm that aided the International Social Services in placing orphans with families. She had asked Marilyn to assist, because of her experience of being in that system.

'I helped Jane raise money and visited children in care – which I loved – but I don't know how to do anything more than that.'

'Anyone would help *you*.' Sister Joy's adoration hadn't faltered.

'But I don't want it to be *me*.'

'But you just said…'

Marilyn tried to explain. 'Helping Jane I used my celebrity, but I wouldn't want to do that with this. I don't want it to be me, you see – as in Marilyn Monroe. People will just come just to ogle. It needs to be anonymous. But how can I do that?'

'What kind of charity?' asked Sister Joy.

'I'm not sure. I want…'

'Yes?'

Marilyn looked around the pretty garden. 'I think I want to create a place.'

'A *place*?'

'Like this. But not this.'

'How so?'

'Not one about God.' Marilyn put a hand on Sister Joy's arm. 'There's nothing wrong with God, he's marvellous, I'm sure.'

Sister Joy laughed. 'He isn't for everyone.'

Marilyn smiled. 'I mean a place for *us*. Somewhere to go where we can blossom safely like these roses.' She touched one. 'The kind of place I needed last year, that I'm sure many in far more difficult situations need. Not where we have to give anything up, just a temporary *sanctuary*.' She shook her head. 'I don't know.'

'It's a wonderful idea.'

'Thank you.'

'Mother Superior might help but she's lived here so long, she doesn't know much about the real world. Is there anyone you can trust to advise you?'

Marilyn had friends she could rely on but she feared being drawn back into her old world if she contacted them.

'How about Jane Russell? She could tell you how she started hers.'

'I wouldn't like to bother her.' They hadn't spoken in a few years and what if the press found out? 'Maybe it's a silly idea. I'd need help from other people. And once they know it's me, they might tell reporters.' Marilyn looked at Sister Joy. 'I'm not being arrogant when I say that.'

'There isn't an arrogant bone in your body,' said Sister Joy softly.

'I'd need money. I have some, but to access it, I'd have to go home.'

'Speak to someone who could do it on your behalf.'

Though she didn't have a full plan, Marilyn was excited. She felt sure this was her path; it just needed to be cleared of weeds and laying with brick. It needed a destination. 'I'll think about it. Thanks for listening, honey.'

'My pleasure,' Sister Joy said.

Marilyn thought of nothing else all day. She was so distracted she didn't hear when the sisters spoke to her as they passed on the corridor.

In her chamber, she read the same page of *The Bell Jar* by Victoria Lucas three times because she couldn't concentrate. The author was poet Sylvia Plath under a pseudonym. She had desperately wanted to read the book but it had only been published in the UK. Mother Superior kindly let Marilyn have it delivered, and she was now on her second read.

She had been heartbroken to hear of the poet's suicide nine months earlier, via one of the sisters, who heard it from a guest at the weekly bake sale. Marilyn had seen herself in Plath's confessional poetry; she felt they both put on a pleasing public face. How sad a loss for the literary world. They were so close in age. When she heard the news, she had recalled that horrible vision of her own dead body on the bed in Brentwood.

Would that have been at her own hand too?

Marilyn tried writing in her black notepad, but nothing came. She thought about her past charitable actions; they had been spontaneous not planned, songs sung to raise money, a hospital visit to highlight its existence.

A memory flashed.

The lovely Ella Fitzgerald. Her broad smile.

Marilyn recalled a time the singer had been refused entry to a club because of her skin colour; Marilyn demanded that Fitzgerald be allowed to perform there, promising that if Ella sang, she would ensure publicity by sitting in the front row every night for a week. She did. Ella broke into the Los Angeles music scene. And the two became firm friends.

These were hardly great things though.

Starting some sort of charity herself, however, would be huge.

But how?

24

Marilyn makes a phone call

Angels of the Immaculate Mary, Los Angeles, November 1963

Evening arrived; darkness fell earlier now November was passing by. Marilyn decided to talk someone from the *other world.*

She knew who.

This person had always hated Marilyn's fame so she knew he would *never* tell anyone that she had contacted him. He had wanted her to surrender the film world back in the early 1950s but she had resisted.

She asked Mother Superior if she could use the one telephone in the convent. It sat next to a directory, notepad and pen on a wooden table in a small, windowless room off the dining hall, and was used only in emergencies.

Marilyn dialled a number she knew well.

'Hey Joe, it's me.' Simple words.

'*Marilyn.*' His voice was emotional. 'Is it really you? Good God, I need to sit down. You're alive! Where the hell have you *been*?'

Marilyn had not even wanted to meet Joe DiMaggio – then recently retired from baseball – for their first date, thinking he would be an arrogant, showy sportsman. But nothing could have been further from the truth. She found him rather shy. They married quickly but it only lasted nine months; it was passionate, explosive, which couldn't endure. They were better suited as friends and had been close again during the last two years. Joe rescued Marilyn when she was admitted to the psychiatric unit against her wishes, and then took her to Florida to recuperate.

Hearing him now was a comfort.

'It's really me,' she said. 'Listen, I'm not sure if you're alone, but don't tell anyone it's me.'

'I won't. It's just me. *Marilyn*. Where the hell are you?'

'You'd never believe it.' She giggled.

'Try me.'

'I'm living with some nuns.'

'I don't believe it,' he cried.

'Told you. It's true.'

'Where?'

Marilyn wasn't ready to share that. 'How are you, Joe? Looking after yourself? Given up smoking like I kept telling you to?'

'Don't change the topic.' He was annoyed, affectionately. 'I know you too well. I've been so worried. What got into you? Why didn't you tell anyone? Just disappearing like that.'

'I did what you always wanted me to. I retired from the movies.'

'But you could have *told* me.'

'I didn't want to tell anyone,' she said softly.

'Let me pick you up, doesn't matter where you are. We'll go to Florida again.'

'Oh, Joe, that isn't what I want.'

'What *do* you want then?' He sounded sulky now. 'Why did you call me?'

'Because you're my friend,' she said simply. 'I trust you. You have to respect that I'm not ready to come back. But I'm fine. I just wanted to talk to someone who wouldn't tell the world where I am.' She realised that Joe probably couldn't advise her on how to begin a charity; it wasn't anything he had ever done. Maybe she had just wanted to talk to someone she was fond of. 'What's happening with my house, do you know?'

'Eunice still goes. She called me at the beginning, upset, saying she would keep it clean until you returned, asking if I knew anything. It's all in limbo, Marilyn. You need to sort that out or at least let someone else do it for you.'

She felt sad, picturing Eunice, quietly cleaning the empty house. Maybe it had been wrong to abandon her housekeeper like that. Wasn't that what her own mother had done, over and over, breaking Norma Jeane's heart? Maybe she should ask Joe to share a statement with the press so the world knew Marilyn Monroe had retired for good, and then she could arrange selling her house.

But would they accept it and leave her alone?

Probably not.

'You're right,' she said. 'I should sort the house out. Do you know how my mother is?'

'I don't, I'm afraid,' he said kindly.

'Can you tell those who matter that I'm OK? Arthur and Berniece. People who won't talk to the press.'

'I'll tell them,' said Joe. 'Berniece called me a few times, upset.'

'Did she?' Marilyn felt sad at the thought of her sister. They might not live close to one another, and they might not have the usual relationship siblings did, having not met until adulthood, but there was a bond. 'Please tell her I'm safe, that I never wanted her to be embroiled in my chaotic life.' Marilyn had always kept her sister's name out of the press, not wanting her to be hounded by them, so the world didn't even know she existed. 'What's the press been like?' she asked. 'Have I been forgotten yet?'

'The papers went wild for months.'

'Were they... unkind?' Why did it matter so much? She was done with all that.

'Not unkind, but it was mixed. There was lots of speculation, most of it ridiculous. They called here for months, but I refused to speak, which they interpreted as me knowing where you were.

One of the papers suggested I was hiding you at my house and they camped outside for days.'

'Oh, Joe,' She knew he would have hated that.

'I told one of my baseball buddies how concerned I was,' he continued, 'and he told a journalist at the Los Angeles Times, so of course they used that quote as though I had spoken exclusively to them.' He paused. 'Stella Cruz from *Icon* magazine was kind. My housekeeper likes that magazine; she leaves copies lying around the house. She showed me a couple of the pieces.'

'I know Stella,' said Marilyn fondly. 'She's one of the few journalists I felt safe with. I felt like we might have been good friends, in another situation.'

'She's written some lovely words about you, real kind and respectful. There was one line that touched me, Marilyn. It was something like…' Joe paused to think. 'Like *perhaps Norma Jeane finally found her way back to herself.*'

A soft *oh* escaped from Marilyn's throat. Tears prickled the corners of her eyes. Stella *got* it. Even without knowing the full story, she seemed to understand who Marilyn was.

And then onto she who is named after the stars.

Didn't Stella mean star? It only occurred to Marilyn now.

'I'm touched by that,' she admitted to Joe.

'It's nice, isn't it?'

'It is,' she said. 'And now?'

'Now?' repeated Joe.

'Has the speculation died down?'

How long before she could risk a quiet return to the outside world?

Joe took a breath. Marilyn sensed he was going to say something important. 'The thing is,' he said carefully. 'There's been some news, something happened and it might eclipse all other news for months.'

'What is it?' Her heart was in her mouth.

'You're going to be shocked. I know you were mixed up with them.'

'Mixed up with who?'

'The Kennedys.'

'Oh, that was exaggerated,' she cried. 'You know it was, I talked to you about it.'

Her relationship with the brothers had not been at all what the newspapers reported. Yes, she had sung Happy Birthday to the president at Madison Square Garden, and yes, she had gone to parties where he was present, and they had talked, but that was all. Bobby, his brother, had spoken to her with great respect, listened to her thoughts on the world.

'What's happened?' she asked.

'It's the president…'

'Yes?'

'He was assassinated.'

'*What*?' Marilyn dropped the phone, scrambled to pick it up again. '*Assassinated*? But no!' She couldn't take it in. 'How? What happened?'

'It was two days ago. He was on tour, in Dallas, in the car. It happened in broad daylight, Marilyn. He was shot, twice, he slumped over towards Mrs Kennedy. They played the horrible footage over and over on the news.'

'But *why*? He was so young. Had so many ideas. Wanted equal rights, opportunities for us all. I can't believe it.'

'Are you OK?'

'No. Yes. I'm in shock.' Marilyn's hand began shaking and the earpiece knocked against her face. She thought of Bobby. How he must feel. His beloved brother, gone.

'They arrested someone,' said Joe.

'Already,' cried Marilyn. 'Well, that's good. I hope they punish him.'

'He's dead.'

'*What*?' It was a wrecking ball repeatedly hitting a building.

'They arrested a young man called Lee Harvey Oswald just hours after Kennedy died. This morning on the news he was being transferred from the police headquarters to a county jail and someone *shot* him, right in front of everyone.'

'Good God.'

'I know.'

'I don't agree with the death penalty,' cried Marilyn, 'but I'm glad.'

'Many feel that way,' agreed Joe.

'The country must be in deep mourning.'

'It is. I must admit, at first, I wondered if that was why you'd called.'

'I had no idea. Oh, Joe, what a world. And there was me going on about myself and being in the newspapers. *This* is a tragedy.'

Marilyn pressed her forehead against the wall and closed her eyes. Sylvia Plath gone earlier that year, and now this. She was suddenly overcome with the feeling that she had not been supposed to outlast either of them. That she had changed the order of things by leaving the other world behind fifteen months earlier. Something else came to her, the way curious things often did.

Marilyn opened her eyes.

'What was the date?' she asked.

'Sorry?'

'When the president…'

'Two days ago. The 22nd.'

She nodded. 'The number four again,' she said. 'If you add them together.'

'I don't understand,' said Joe.

'Sorry.' She felt silly. 'You know me and my signs.'

He sighed. 'I do.'

'I have to make sense of things in my own way.' She smiled, despite the heaviness of his news. 'If I look at coincidences and repetitions, I can process things that are too much. I know, it's silly.'

'It's not. This is intense news to take in.'

'Yes.'

'What are you going to do?' he asked gently.

'What do you mean?'

'Are you coming home now? The world is changing, Marilyn. If you want a quieter life, I think it's possible.'

She wasn't sure. She still needed time. She was in the right place for that. 'Not yet,' she said. 'I just wanted you to know that I'm OK – and to know that you are too.'

'You've no idea how glad I am to hear your voice.'

'I'm sorry for worrying you.' Marilyn felt wretched.

'I miss you.'

'I miss you too.' Now that she had heard Joe's voice again, she didn't know how she had managed to leave everyone behind so easily. Without Mary's guidance, she never would have done. But she was glad it had happened. 'Joe…'

'Yes?'

'Do you have a copy of *Icon* magazine in the house?' she asked.

'I can check.'

'Can you see if there's a phone number in the front?'

'Sure.'

Marilyn heard the phone clunk onto a surface and waited.

She closed her eyes and saw herself walking along the beach in the early hours with Bobby Kennedy, following a dinner party at his brother-in-law's house that she had been nervous about, and tried three dresses on beforehand. 'Some people hate my brother,' Bobby had said of the president, boyish in slacks and an open shirt. 'I worry for him.' Marilyn had been touched by his vulnerability.

Now, he must be heartbroken.

'I've got one.' Joe pulled her from the past. 'There is a number. What are you going to do? I thought you wanted to get away from that world.'

'I'm not sure, I just…' She shrugged. 'I like Stella. I remember her starting the magazine. I went to the launch party.'

Marilyn had expected a glitzy affair, a plush venue and vintage champagne, but been surprised to find herself at Stella's modest house in a quiet spot on the beach, with a few carefully chosen – in Stella's words – guests, mainly female stars, and some members of the press and literary scene. Stella had explained in a softly spoken speech that she wanted to write sensitive pieces about female celebrities that gave them the chance to speak honestly, to not be misquoted, to counterbalance the lurid coverage female stars often received.

Marilyn sensed there was something Stella *hadn't* said; some deeper reason behind her desire to represent these women.

When the pair spoke alone in a corner, Marilyn noticed that Stella wore simple gold studs in her ears, so tiny they might have been missed by a less observant person. They said everything. They said, *Don't look at me, I'm not showy, I'm small and insignificant.* Marilyn had felt Stella was more than that, despite her gentle manner. She learned that she had re-mortgaged her house to fund the magazine. Marilyn had been pleased to see it grow quickly, to garner wide readership and great respect, and to win awards.

'I'm glad her magazine is still going strong,' Marilyn said now.

'Stella was on a news show a few weeks ago and they were discussing you. She said they should just let you be. She didn't look like the usual Hollywood type, and was adamant about her point. Kept saying it, let her be.'

'Let her be,' said Marilyn softly.

And then onto she who is named after the stars.

Stella.

'Sorry?' said Joe.

'That's what I'm doing. Letting Marilyn Monroe be.' She paused. 'Can I have that phone number?'

Joe read it aloud, and she wrote it on the notepad.

'Will you call me again?' he asked.

'I will. It was wonderful to hear your voice. Take care, Joe.'

'You too, Marilyn.'

She replaced the receiver, keeping her hand upon it for a moment. Then she put the *Icon* magazine phone number into her pocket and went back into the corridor. The convent was quiet now it was evening. Most of the sisters would be in their chambers, though some liked to sit in the chapel and pray during this silent time.

Marilyn headed there.

It was empty.

On her first evening Marilyn had sat in the back pew, feeling she was intruding. Slowly, over the months, she had moved closer to the front when she sat with her thoughts. Now she went to the long table of candles at the altar; some shimmered softly, others awaited that luminosity.

She struck a match and ignited three candles.

She watched them shiver.

Three candles for people gone.

One for Sylvia.

One for the president.

And one for Marilyn Monroe.

25

November 1963

It's curious that people miss someone they never met; they mourn the loss of a person they never had; they grieve for an absence in their life that has never physically touched it. I could be talking about John F Kennedy, and I am, or at least I was when I began the piece. But also, Marilyn. Our Marilyn. Because she was ours. And I think we all fear that we've lost her too.

Stella Cruz, *Icon* magazine

26

Neil's name flashes on Flora's phone

March 2016, Hull, England

Still reeling after the journalist, Flora paced the kitchen. What if he wrote a piece? Would anyone care?

Maybe.

People loved this kind of stuff. She remembered a story in the local paper about a woman who had seen Jesus in the mould on her wall. It had been rather beautiful in a bleak way, the messiah, long hair fluid, hands sinewy. The woman in question had ended up on the news and had clergymen visiting her council house to analyse the so-called miracle, which they ultimately dismissed.

But there was no evidence here; nothing to come and view.

Except the daffodil.

It would blow over. These stories always did. But it wasn't as much about Mary as about what else they might unearth. Once journalists began digging, they might find out about the baby.

'What happened with Neil then?'

Flora jumped. Bella was smiling, hair mussed up from sleep, one shoulder exposed because her *Relax* T-shirt was too big.

I told him things you don't even know, thought Flora. *And now I'm scared I can't trust him.*

'Oh, nothing.' She tried to sound blasé.

'Did you shag him on the sofa?' Bella patted the arm.

'No!'

'*Boring*. I'll put the pan on.' Bella clattered about. 'You must have done something. He was here ages.'

'We... talked.'

'*Talked*? Jesus.'

Flora felt terrible about all she had shared with Neil. She *should* have told Bella about Mary. 'Are you feeling…?'

'I know you're watching me all the time,' said Bella, 'but you don't have to. Anyway, one of the crisis team called yesterday to check in.'

'Good.'

'Are *you* OK?'

'Just tired. I start at CARE tomorrow and obvs I'm a bit nervous.'

'You'll be brilliant.' Bella loitered near her Marilyn art. 'Oh, that's brought my dream back. I dreamt it was hanging over my bed and she was crying. I touched the surface, and it was wet. Then she stepped out of it, like the scene in that horror film – what's it called? – where the woman comes out of the TV. Except it wasn't scary. It was nice. She sat on the bed, held my hand.'

'That *is* nice,' said Flora.

Bella studied the picture for a moment longer and then flopped onto the sofa. 'When are you next seeing Neil?'

Flora attended the bubbling pan to avoid Bella's scrutiny. 'Not sure.'

She made tea for them. Her phone pinged on the kitchen counter. Neil's name flashed. Her heart said that there was no way he would have spoken to a journalist but her head asked, who then? Maybe he had told a friend and *they* had shared it. She should trust him – that was her instinct – but what if he hurt her? That was the lifelong fear.

Before Flora could read his message, Bella interrupted. 'Have you seen this?' She hunched over her phone. 'Your club's trending locally.'

'What do you mean?'

'On Twitter. *Look.*' Bella spoke impatiently.

Flora took the two mugs of tea over and leaned close as Bella scrolled down a feed of comments that made Flora's tummy turn over.

The hashtags included: #VirginMary #ReligiousFreak #VirginMarySighting #YouCouldntMakeItUp #CaveComedy and #PsychicPrat.

'Psychic Pat was doing a gig at your club,' said Bella. 'She had a premonition that a woman would have a visit from the Virgin Mary. And apparently, she did.' Bella laughed.

'It wasn't exactly like that,' snapped Flora.

'*What*? You were there? Well, what did she say?'

Flora shook her head, distracted by the social media page. She found the original tweet – from @Psychic_Pat_Powers – which had been shared last night, and she read it with a sinking feeling.

The spiritz been strong this week. On Wed at @cavecomedyclub a soul in spirit gave message for woman said she would receive visitor. My strongest message! I have on good auth that Virgin Mary was visitor! VIRGIN MARY! Book here for readings. #VirginMary #PsychicPat #VirginMarySighting

Was Neil that good authority?

But he had mocked her when they gossiped. None of it made sense. She didn't really know him and yet she had trusted him enough to talk about her deepest pain. She hated being unsure, always pulled back in such situations, a self-protective mechanism. But she needed to know; she should ask if he had disclosed it.

'*Flora.*' Bella was pulling at her arm. 'What did she say?'

'Who?'

'Psychic Bloody Pat!'

One way or another, if Pat continued sharing this, Bella could find out. It would be worse if Flora hadn't told her. She wanted to get up and run and run and run, the way she had when she was a teenager and it was all too much.

'Pat told this woman she'd have a visitor,' said Flora. 'She's making out she predicted the Virgin Mary, but she never named her.'

'Who did she pick out of the audience?' Bella was as excited as when they watched the latest crime drama together.

Flora didn't respond.

'Well?'

'It was me,' she said finally.

27

Flora spends the afternoon on Twitter

March 2016, Hull, England

Bella stared at Flora. 'What do you mean *you*?'

'Me.'

'But you haven't had a visit from Mary. Pat's insane.'

'She's a trickster, yes. But she's not insane.'

'What do you mean?' Bella demanded.

'I did have a visit.'

'*What*? From *Mary*? *The* Mary? The one Grandma Lil prayed to?' Bella put her mug on the floor. 'You're winding me up.'

'I'm not. She was there.' Flora pointed to the kitchen area.

'No way.' Bella shook her head.

'Do you want me to tell you or not?'

Perhaps it was something about Flora's tone, but Bella went quiet. After a moment, she said, 'Tell me then.'

Flora did.

She evoked that moment using a similar pink and red palette to the one Bella had chosen for her Marilyn art. She relived the peace she had felt in Mary's presence; she walked Bella through each action, each word; she gave her sister the glow and the daffodil and the promise that Bella would be saved if Flora volunteered at CARE.

'That night' she said quietly, 'just for ten minutes, I had a feeling of absolute safety. A belief that I was cherished, I was... important.'

Tears built up.

These were things that a mother made you feel, Flora knew. She recognised it not through her own experience but through the things other people said about their mums. She had always been desperate for such love, something she rarely acknowledged because it was too painful.

'Oh, Flo,' said Bella. 'Don't get upset.'

'I need you to believe what I saw,' Flora said.

Perhaps that was the real reason she'd been afraid of sharing it.

'I do. How you described it. Earlier, I just thought you were winding me up, like we always do.'

'I wasn't dreaming and I wasn't drunk and I didn't imagine it.'

'Why didn't you tell me until now?' asked Bella.

'I was scared about overwhelming you.'

'But I've been OK. Can I see the daffodil then?' Bella sounded sulky.

Flora got the book from the top shelf. Between the pages the flower remained, still bright.

'What a *gorgeous* colour,' said Bella.

'Neil swears he was supposed to give it to me.' Flora spoke without thinking. She hadn't told Bella that he knew about Mary.

'What do you mean?' Bella obviously hadn't twigged yet.

There was no going back. 'Oh. He did this trick. Gave me a carnation. Said it was meant to be a daffodil. Then he saw this and said it was identical to the one he'd meant to give me.'

Bella frowned. Flora saw her figure it out. 'Hang on. You told *him*?'

Flora placed the book back on the shelf, didn't respond.

'Of course– you must have told *someone* or else how would Psychic Pat know about Mary?'

'I don't know if he told Pat but … yes, I told him.' Flora sat back down, looked at her sister. 'Look, it just came out of me. It was the day after. Yes, I visited you at the hospital that day but how could I have told you when you weren't well?'

'It might have cheered me up.' Bella was acting like a stroppy kid but Flora could understand it.

'I did what I thought was best.'

Bella shrugged.

'Jesus, Bell, imagine how it's been for me, worrying, never knowing if I'll get a call that you've overdosed. And now you're well, I daren't risk upsetting it.'

'She called me the beautiful one?' Bella smiled.

Flora couldn't help but laugh. 'Yes.'

'Bitch knows her shit.'

'Bitch does,' said Flora softly.

'Aren't you upset that Neil told Psychic Pat?'

'Maybe it wasn't him.' Flora felt defensive despite her own concerns.

'But if you only told him?'

'I did.'

Bella's silence said it all.

'I won't be happy with him,' admitted Flora quietly. 'A journalist came this morning. About Mary.'

'Oh my God, we're gonna be famous.'

'I don't want to be bloody famous.'

'What did they say?' asked Bella.

'He wanted my story. Knew about the daffodil.'

'What are you gonna do?'

'Ignore him.' Flora took the empty mugs to the sink and dropped them into it, not caring if they broke.

Bella jumped. 'But it's on Twitter now. People love this religious shit. It could go big. Remember that woman who saw Jesus in her mould?'

'I don't want to talk about it.' Flora turned the taps on full, filling the cups with an angry gush.

'She still does chat shows.'

'I don't care.' Now Flora sounded like a stroppy child.

'Oh shit.' Bella hunched over her phone again. 'You might not be able to avoid it.'

'What do you mean?'

'Do you know who Nina Ford is?'

'No idea.' Flora returned to the sofa. 'Did she see Jesus in the sand at Withernsea?'

'Remember that documentary about Marilyn where they had that old footage of her visiting orphanages?'

'That was a lovely one; it treated her with compassion.' Flora had watched it with Bella, curled up in her bed at CARE, eating popcorn and drinking hot chocolate. 'But what does that have to do with *my* story?'

'Nina Ford was the producer. She's got a blue tick and 50,000 followers.' Bella paused. 'And she just shared Psychic Pat's post. Not just a share but a quote retweet.'

'A what?' cried Flora.

'For fuck's sake, just read it yourself.'

Bella handed her the phone.

On the screen was Psychic Pat's original tweet, shared by @ NinaFord along with the words: *Sightings of the #VirginMary have happened for centuries and are often met with disbelief and mockery. Are you a believer or a cynic? Look out for my new documentary #MotherOfGod which explores these visitations, coming October 2016.*

Nina had also commented on the original tweet, asking Pat to follow her back so she could speak to her about the experience.

'She wants Pat to contact her,' said Flora softly.

'I saw.'

'But *why*?'

'Isn't it obvious?' cried Bella. 'For this documentary.' She took the phone back and scrolled through the feed. 'She interviewed someone related to Bernadette Soubirous last week. Remember, Grandma Lil told us about the girl in Lourdes.' Bella looked at Flora, eyes misted over with nostalgia. 'I miss her.'

Flora knew who she meant but said, 'Bernadette Soubirous?' They both smiled. Then Flora added, 'Yes, I miss Grandma Lil too.'

'She'd love this. Her favourite girl getting a visit from Mary.'

'I wasn't her favourite.'

'You *were.*'

I wouldn't have been if she'd known, thought Flora.

Flora's mother had her hide the pregnancy from Grandma Lil. Though Flora had been relieved that her grandma never knew her shame, she felt guilty about deceiving her. No matter how many times they knelt side by side at church, Rosary beads glinting in the light from the coloured windows, Flora felt unworthy.

'What if all this stuff leads to me?' she said.

'Speak to that journalist, tell your side before he makes shit up. You know who'll be in touch if it gets out, don't you?'

'Jeremy Vine?' said Flora.

'*Mum*. You know she likes a bit of drama.'

'She can fuck off. She never even came to see you in the hospital, so she needn't think she's getting her fifteen minutes of fame.'

'She messaged me yesterday, saying we should go there sometime.'

'*We*?' Flora frowned. 'No, thanks. She should come here. She never does.'

*

For the rest of the day, Flora barely moved from the sofa.

Everything happened inside her phone; tweets swam before her eyes. Nina Ford got hundreds of shares and comments, from those saying they were excited about the *Mother of God* documentary, and from others criticising religion, God, the church, Mary.

Flora was invisible, for now. She had a Twitter account but had never uploaded a profile picture, rarely posted, and had fifty followers. She could watch the stories unfold anonymously.

She wanted it to stay that way.

Finally, she looked at Neil's message instead.

Hope you're OK. I'm glad you shared those things with me. I'm free Wednesday. Can come to the club if you want? X

She touched his words. She wanted to see him. Trust him. She should just ask if he had, even accidentally, talked to someone about Mary, then she could put it aside and enjoy what was unfolding between them.

I'm good, thank you. A journalist came to the flat this morning, asking about Mary. Did you tell anyone else, because I haven't shared it?

As soon as Flora had clicked send, she realised she had forgotten to put a kiss. Damn. A response arrived: *No, I wouldn't do that.*

No kiss either. She deserved it. She believed him. Maybe she had just needed to hear him say it. Now she had ruined things. She should rectify it; for the first time in her life, she was prepared to risk her heart.

I thought that but had to ask because I've no idea who. I'd love to see you Wednesday at the club. X

She sent it, waited. After ten minutes, a reply: *Maybe.*

What more could Flora expect?

She had suggested that he betrayed her trust. Maybe he would realise that she'd *had* to ask, that she wasn't accusing as much as figuring out who. She was no closer to the answer, and now she had alienated one of the best things in her life.

She cried into one of the threadbare cushions and when Bella returned, she told her she had watched the last episode of *Friends* again and been sobbing at that.

28

Marilyn and the lady of the stars

Angels of the Immaculate Mary, Los Angeles, December 1963

'Hi, is this Stella?'

Marilyn retreated into her goddess-type voice, as she often had in the past when she was nervous; speaking slowly had been a way to curb her stammer. Not everything had been about being sexy. Sometimes the things that made Monroe alluring were the things she did to conceal her flaws. Like the quivering lip as she found the right smile because a photographer once told her to lower it due to the shadow from her nose ruining 'the look'.

Now she was more nervous than when she had met the queen of England in 1956; than when she had first performed a scene before Lee Strasbourg at the Actors Studio; than when she had married Arthur Miller.

No response on the end of the line.

Yet a second ago a soft voice Marilyn was sure was Stella had said, 'Hello.'

'Are you still there?' asked Marilyn.

Why was she so afraid?

Was it because this was only the second person she had spoken to in the *other world* for almost a year and a half? Was it because of the risk in speaking to a woman she hardly knew, who wrote for a major magazine, and who could – if she wanted – expose Marilyn's safe hiding place to the world?

'I'm here,' said Stella. 'Who is this?'

'Marilyn,' she said, then added, 'Monroe,' as she often had

when meeting new people in the past, enjoying their laughter and their comments of, 'I don't think you needed to verify *which* Marilyn.'

'I thought it was.' Stella's voice was shy, even though they had met before. '*Marilyn*. Really? Oh my God.'

'Yes, it's me,' she smiled, voice more like her own now.

'But... where are you…? Why me?'

Marilyn laughed. 'What should I answer first?'

'I guess, what I'd really like to know is, are you OK?'

Marilyn heard the soft flare of a lighter being ignited and then the inhalation of a cigarette. She had occasionally smoked in the past and missed it suddenly; such a civilised habit, one she mainly enjoyed in company. She hadn't had a drop of alcohol or a cigarette in so long, and though she felt good for it, she missed the decadence, the socialising and chat that accompanied it.

'I'm great,' she answered. 'Are you?'

Stella laughed now. 'I'm not the one who's missing. We've been so worried about you. The world, me, everyone. I can't believe you've called *me*.'

Should Marilyn tell her that Mary had visited, said: *And then onto she who is named after the stars*. That Marilyn had realised this meant Stella, that the idea of calling her had grown since her chat with Joe. In the last month she had picked up the phone three times but put it down again, afraid this privacy might end if her location was leaked.

'It's what you said,' Marilyn explained.

'What do you mean?'

'I called Joe DiMaggio last month and he told me how kind you had been about me. You said that perhaps Norma Jeane finally found her way back to herself.' Marilyn realised she was choked up. 'That... meant a lot…'

Stella didn't speak. Perhaps she too felt emotional. Another inhalation of cigarette. 'I'm just glad you're safe.'

'I am.'

'Where *are* you?'

Marilyn ignored the question. 'Stella, it's time for me to leave here. I have some ideas for my future but I need to remain out of the public eye. I'm afraid if I go home I won't be able to do that. I need a... *place*. This is so presumptive of me, I realise, but...'

'You want to come *here*?' Stella didn't say it with outrage, more surprise.

'It's silly, isn't it? We hardly know one another but I feel... I don't know. Just that I'm *supposed* to. Your house is secluded and no one would ever expect me to be there. Gee, you can say no, of course, this is so rude of me, now I think of it.'

'It isn't rude.' Stella laughed. 'And it feels like the most natural thing in the world.'

'It really does.' Marilyn giggled.

'If you want to come here, then come.'

'Really?'

'Sure. There's only me and as you know I live on the beach. Did you have a day in mind?'

'Maybe tomorrow.' Now Marilyn had said it she panicked. Was she ready? She realised that it was a few days until Christmas and Stella might have plans. 'Look, I can wait until after the holidays if that suits you better and you ha-'

'Oh, don't wait. I'm home until the beginning of January. My family are in New York and I've left it too late to travel. I've been busy, so it was just going to be me. *Come*.'

'Honest?'

'*Yes*.'

Marilyn was really doing this.

'Should I pick you up? Are you still in this area?'

'Give me your address, I'll find my way.' Stella did. 'You're sure about tomorrow?'

'It's you that sounds unsure.'

'It's just been a while since I was in the *other world*.' She laughed. 'That's what I've been calling it. I guess, I'll see you tomorrow. And Stella, thank you. Should I bring anything for the holidays... food? Wine?'

'There's no need for thanks, or to bring anything.' Stella paused. 'Marilyn?'

'Yes?'

'Did you find your way back to Norma Jeane?' she asked.

'I'm not sure.' Marilyn shrugged. 'But I am finding my way to... *someone*.'

They hung up after goodbyes.

Marilyn returned to her chamber, passing the rows of intricate hand-made wreaths on the corridor, and resisting the urge to skip.

29

Flora smells marmalade

March 2016, Hull, England

Monday morning, Flora climbed the stone steps to the CARE building, completed application form in hand, heart beating fast.

The hallway was quiet; no drama, no Amelia.

Carla took Flora to the communal area, a room Flora had often thought if it was a school report would get an A for effort and a C for achievement; the walls were the yellow used for road markings; four mismatched sofas had been donated, and the TV was old school and chunky.

'It's a strange day.' Carla turned her nose up at the unwashed cups in the sink and switched on the kettle. 'We've never been so quiet. It's like the calm before a storm. Lots of women left at the weekend, so we've only got seven in. I can't remember a time we had that few. How are you feeling?'

'Good.' Flora nodded to add clout to her weakly spoken word.

She was distracted. Despite Bella's suggestion, she hadn't rung the journalist, even after two more calls from him. He sent a text earlier saying he was interviewing Psychic Pat and did Flora want to give her side.

Neil hadn't texted since his message last night. Flora had been unsure how to reply and in the end, didn't. She should, later.

'Marjory, a Listener, should be here any minute.' Carla handed Flora a cup of tea she hadn't asked for; she could hear the capital letter Carla gave Listener. 'You'll shadow her this morning.'

Marjory arrived, the graceful but sturdy ship Flora recalled had spent many a time comforting Bella.

'Hi, darlin',' she said warmly. 'I know you…'

'Flora. Bella's sister.'

'Of course. How is she?'

'Really well.' It was great that this was finally true.

'Right, I've got to get on,' said Carla briskly. 'This afternoon we'll go through some official stuff, and get you a uniform sorted.'

Flora followed Marjory into a laundry room where she moved damp clothes from the washer into the dryer. 'If it needs doing, I do it,' she said. 'There are cleaners, but I'm not one to leave a job for someone else.'

Then they headed to the dining room, a curtainless space that housed three large tables, one set for lunch. 'We like communal meals,' she explained though Flora knew, having joined Bella for dinner before. 'Some women eat in their rooms. We don't push but we encourage mixing because it's good for the soul.'

'What if a woman never wants to leave?' asked Flora, as they headed to the corridor.

'That's never happened.' Marjorie stopped in her steps. 'I guess we'd find a way. But I don't suppose anyone would want to be here forever.' She shrugged. 'Let's go see Amelia.'

'I met her the other day,' said Flora. 'She was upset.'

'Ah, you're the calm lady.'

'The *calm lady*?'

'She told me there had been a calming lady.' Marjorie smiled. 'Our Amelia is a descriptive one. She's been in and out of here since she was fifteen. She's seventeen now, had a baby that her family take care of. She has a lot of issues so it might be for the best.'

'For who?' Flora couldn't help her terse response.

'It's an emotive issue,' said Marjory. 'I can't predict how Amelia will be. There's no pressure to join me if you'd rather wait until you know the ropes.'

'I'm ready,' said Flora.

They arrived at a door. 'Listening is giving space for someone to speak,' said Marjory. 'Asking open questions, not pushing, encouraging with positive responses. It doesn't come naturally to everyone.' She looked at Flora. 'I have a feeling it will with you.'

They went into the room.

It was small; Bella had stayed in this one. The curtains were closed so it was softened by shadows. Bella used to block the sunlight on her worst days too. The floor was covered in clothes and make-up and odd shoes. Amelia was in bed, a small lump covered by a duvet.

'It's ten o'clock,' said Marjory gently.

Grunt.

'We said we'd have a talk remember?'

Another grunt.

Eventually Marjory said, 'The calm lady is here.'

A tangled mess of red hair popped out. 'I thought I dreamed you.'

Flora laughed. 'I'm not always calm. You should see me when I stub my toe…'

Amelia smiled.

'How are you today?' Marjory sat on the bed.

'Better.' Amelia looked at Flora. 'Did you come to see *me*?'

'I'm here to volunteer,' admitted Flora, 'but I did hope to see you too.'

'So,' said Marjory, gently. 'Tell me more about yesterday, Amelia.'

'I don't wanna talk about it.'

Flora wondered what had happened.

'You upset Bethanni.' Marjory didn't say this in an accusatory tone.

'She pissed me off,' cried Amelia. 'She shit stirs, then walks away. Said I didn't deserve to get my daughter back cos she'll only end up like me.'

'That wasn't kind,' said Marjory, 'but Bethanni is going through a lot too. Maybe both of you should air how you feel?'

'I feel hungry,' said Amelia.

'Why don't you make some toast,' said Marjory, 'and then talk to Bethanni.'

'Will you come?' Amelia put a raggy dressing gown on over her vest and shorts.

Flora realised she meant her. 'Is that OK?' She looked at Marjory.

'Yes. I'll go and see if Bethanni is up.'

As they left the room – Amelia with her hood up like a celebrity hiding from the paparazzi – Marjory opened the curtains and light finally invaded the gloom. Flora followed Amelia to the small kitchen where an older woman with her hair curled around toilet rolls was making tea. 'Just boiled.' She motioned to the kettle and left.

'That's Barbs.' Amelia popped two slices of bread into the toaster. 'Reminds me of my nana. Been here a long time. I think she's lonely.'

'Poor Barbs.'

'What made you want to volunteer?'

You wouldn't believe it if I told you, thought Flora. 'My sister's been here a few times. It's a way of returning their kindness.'

'Your sister's dead lucky to have you. Mine thinks I'm a slag.'

Flora didn't know what to say. But then, she was supposed to be a Listener, and that meant giving Amelia space.

'She's right. Wouldn't have got pregnant otherwise, would I?' Flora wanted to say that anyone can end up pregnant, but Amelia continued. 'I dunno who the father is cos me and Luke broke up and I met Matt the day after, so I *am* a slag.' Flora opened her mouth to say she wasn't, but Amelia barely took a breath. 'That doesn't mean I'm a crap mum though. I love my little girl to bits.'

Amelia's voice broke.

The toast popped and she jumped. She coated the slices in margarine and jam, her action as forced as her words. 'She's with my auntie in Edinburgh so I don't see her much. But I will in summer when I stay there. They called her Jennifer but I wanted Amber. I call her that, secretly.'

'That's pretty,' said Flora softly.

Amelia bit into her toast and chewed. It seemed to placate her. Then she spoke with her mouth full. 'I was having a paddy the other day but I know my daughter will have a better life with my aunt. What can I give her?'

A mother, thought Flora.

'But my aunt doesn't lie awake at night and *smell* her.' The words were less forced now. 'My stepdad said I can get on with my life. But *what* life? I didn't pass my GCSEs and all my mates have gone to college. The lads down our way think I'm the town bike. They shout it at me in street.'

Flora gasped. 'That says more about them than it does about you.'

Amelia finished her toast. 'I suppose I'm lucky that I'll see Amber though. Some women never see their babies again, do they?'

Flora found that she couldn't speak.

'You OK?'

'I…'

Flora looked everywhere but Amelia's face. Her gaze landed upon an open jar of marmalade sitting on the worktop; the lid was nearby, caked in orange goo. She was sure the tangy odour lingered in the air.

Sure she could taste it, sharp and bitty.

Marmalade on toast had been the first thing she'd eaten after giving birth, trembling with exertion and shock. She had never eaten it since; never stocked a jar in her cupboard. Two days after the birth she smashed the jar against her mum's kitchen cupboard; her mother went mad. Suddenly Flora wanted to hurl this one at the wall with that same childhood pain.

'You've gone white.' Amelia looked concerned.

Flora needed to be the calm lady. She forced a smile. 'I think you're brave.'

'I wouldn't be here if I was.'

'You're *seventeen*,' Flora reminded her. 'You're just a kid who's experienced a lifetime of pain.'

'People go through worse.'

'It's not a competition. If it hurts, it hurts. When you see Amber in summer, she'll know who you are. The heart never forgets the first one to hold it.'

Flora spoke with heat. Fuck calm. Why was facing the world with feminine grace revered? Wouldn't it be better if they screamed, broke down, swore?

Had Mary ever lost her temper?

She *must* have done. It just hadn't been written. In many ways, she'd had to give up her child too, not straight after the birth, but later when he died young. How had she coped with that? As perfectly quiet as the narrative suggested for everything else?

Flora wanted to hold Amelia but was unsure if it was allowed.

Then she thought *fuck it*.

She hugged her. The teen was slight and frail in her arms; physical smallness was never a true indication of what strength lay within.

'Bugger calm,' Flora said after a while.

Amelia pulled away. 'I think it's what you made *me* feel rather than it being about you.'

Flora was afraid of it now. It was like getting an A and knowing it might be expected of you for the rest of the school term.

'Are you here all day?' asked Amelia.

'I am. And tomorrow and Wednesday. Training.'

'And after that?'

'I'll have to see what hours they give me.'

'I was thinking I might go home next week but if you're starting here…'

'You can't stay for me.' Though flattered, Flora knew this was wrong.

'Nobody at home talks to me like you have. My mum doesn't listen.'

'Every teenager says that.'

'Did you?'

'Yes,' admitted Flora.

'I'm not going home,' snapped Amelia.

'You don't have to. Just don't let anyone else sway your decision.'

Marjory put her head around the door. 'Bethanni said she wants to talk to you.'

'I don't care.' Amelia crossed her arms.

'I think you do,' said Marjory.

Amelia tutted. Flora smiled inwardly at how she went from mature woman to stroppy teenager again when having to do something she didn't want to.

'Flora,' said Marjory, 'would you help Michelle in the communal area – a couple of new sofas have been donated and she needs help sorting that.'

For the next hour Flora helped Michelle – a vivacious, middle-aged woman who was volunteering to 'get over a philandering ex-husband' – squeeze two red leather sofas through the door into the communal area.

She later shadowed Marjory while she hosted the weekly Speak

Out meeting, where residents expressed concerns and made suggestions. Then it was lunchtime and Flora ate with Barbs, toilet roll curlers now gone, Marjory, Michelle, a bruise-covered woman who wore sunglasses and didn't say a word, and Amelia, and Bethanni, who giggled at something on a phone.

Flora checked hers.

Two messages; her heart soared. *Neil*?

No. One was from Bella, saying she was popping into the university, and one was from the journalist. He was speaking to his source tomorrow, and the piece would go live Wednesday, so she needed to call him to have her say. Anxiety stopped Flora finishing the delicious homemade soup one of the Nourishers had served.

'Smile, it might never happen,' said Barbs with the least happy face ever.

Neil's lack of message said everything. She deserved it after her blunt question. But he *had* said he might come to the club Wednesday. She would apologise then.

'They reckon the Virgin Mary visited a woman in Hull,' said Amelia, huddled over her phone.

Flora went cold despite the dusty heat wafting from the old-fashioned radiators.

'Someone called Psychic Pat sai-'

'I saw her once,' interrupted Bethanni. 'She said me dad was shagging the neighbour.'

'And was he?' asked Barbs.

'Yeah. He ran off with him. Me mam never got over it.'

'Pat's bragging on Twitter about some big interview,' said Amelia. 'Thinks she's Mystic Meg. As *if* the Virgin Mary would come to Hull.'

'She always used to visit the poor,' said Marjory. 'She never made appearances to kings or queens or celebrities, did she?'

'She might've done,' said Michelle.

'You reckon?' laughed Marjory.

Feeling queasy, Flora stood, trying not to wobble.

'You look terrible.' Marjory's face was kind.

'Just a bit warm. I'll get some air.'

Outside, on the steps, Flora was grateful of the crisp late March afternoon.

*

Later, she spent the afternoon in Carla's office, going over protocol, learning where forms were kept, and what was expected of a CARE volunteer.

At three Carla dismissed her, saying she had done well. 'Don't forget these.' She handed over a couple of blue and yellow shirts with the CARE logo on the chest. 'That's if you want to come back…'

Flora stared at the tops in her hand.

Bella had asked that morning if she truly believed that her return to good mental health was because Flora had volunteered at CARE. Flora had admitted that she didn't know but it was worth going, just in case.

'See you tomorrow,' she said to Carla.

*

When Flora got back, the flat was empty. A note from Bella on the kitchen worktop said she was sleeping at her mate's house. Flora boiled water in the pan and made a pot noodle. Tempting though it was to look, she avoided social media. It was better not to know. She watched old *Location, Location, Location* episodes, fantasising about the dream house she could never afford.

She kept checking if Neil had messaged.

Nothing.

It was up to her.

She typed, *Look forward to seeing you at the club*, but then deleted it. What was wrong with her?

The past. That was what was wrong with her.

She needed to see Neil. In person. Then she would know how he felt, how *she* felt, and what to do. She would wait until Wednesday.

If he even came…

30

Marilyn goes back into the other world

Angels of the Immaculate Mary, Los Angeles, December 1963

Christmas was a special time in the convent. The sisters' anticipation of the big day was not so much frenetic excitement as silent expectation, a quiet pause that carried them through the four weeks of Advent.

The Feast of the Immaculate Conception, when they carried a statue of Mary around the grounds and into the chapel, was Marilyn's favourite event. She helped decorate the virgin with a halo of stars, and enjoyed Mary in the festive paintings, cards, and mementoes, and hearing about her in the shared readings.

But she felt, privately, that they were celebrating the wrong parts of her; the stories, the myths, the spun narrative. Marilyn thought instead about the lady she had seen in her kitchen. The woman she had still not told anyone about receiving that night. The woman whose feet had been bare, whose face had been plain but perfect, who had spoken softly.

*

Marilyn was leaving.

In her chamber, she gathered items together. There were the things she had arrived with; her favourite picture holding the carnation; the beige dress she wore in the *other world* to be taken seriously; the black slacks, blouse and dull tan coat and scarf; the platinum ring, underwear, toiletries, and the hundred dollars now minus ten for that midnight cab ride.

There were also things she had acquired while living here – little gifts, postcards and hand-made trinkets from the sisters, books, and the black notepad into which she had poured her thoughts, her grief over Kennedy's death, and her hopes for the future.

She would go to the woman named after the stars.

Mary had also said: *And finally, to the place of your ancestors.*

Where was that?

She would worry about it later.

She looked down at the cheap gown she had worn during her stay, alternating with the spare hanging on the back of the door. Was this how she should depart? Perhaps it would ensure no one recognised her.

She went to find Mother Superior.

She had already expressed a desire to leave, shared the idea of starting a place where women who needed space could go. Mother Superior had responded warmly, saying it was a good plan, one she was sure God would heartily bless.

Marilyn found her in the chapel, kneeling at the front, deep in prayer. She waited. Once done, Mother Superior stood, made the sign of the cross on her chest, and lit a candle.

'I sensed you would come to me.' She didn't turn around.

'You did?'

'I've been praying for you, child.'

'You have?'

Marilyn was honoured – no that was the wrong word. She felt cherished. Norma Jeane always stirred when Mother Superior called her child. The way she used it was soothing, and she would miss it. Marilyn suddenly thought of her mother and swelled with tears; she had often been angry at her, resentful that she had not been around, but now she wanted to say to her that it didn't matter.

She felt that everything had happened how it was supposed to.

'Yes,' said Mother Superior. 'I asked God to watch over you in your new endeavour. I'm sad to see you leave but I knew this day would come. You have taught me a lot.'

'Me? *How*?' Marilyn was stunned. She felt that it was *she* who had learned the lessons.

'I was always a bit of a stick in the mud. That was my flaw. I liked traditions. I could be brusque with the sisters when they wanted to be more modern. But seeing your ways, your openness, your refreshing honesty–'

'You're kind,' interrupted Marilyn, 'but you really mean, my speaking before I think, don't you?'

Mother Superior smiled. 'Whatever you want to call it, you have shown me that transformation is growth. After all, doesn't God transform the world around us every day, in the plants and the seasons?'

Marilyn struck a match and lit a candle too. 'This one is for you,' she said. 'Thank you for welcoming me into your special world.'

Mother Superior headed along the aisle, motioning for Marilyn to walk at her side.

'I've faced some difficult things here.' Marilyn wrapped her arms about her torso. She had finally looked into the terrifying abyss of her childhood trauma, but that didn't mean she had fully come to terms with it. Recovery didn't happen that way, she knew this from her counselling sessions in the *other world*. 'And for that I'm grateful.'

Mother Superior nodded. 'When are you leaving us?'

'Tomorrow.'

'Do you have somewhere safe to go?'

'I do. I need to book a cab. I'll go first thing. Mother Superior…'

'Yes?'

'I'm nervous. I haven't been out there in so long.'

They stepped into the cool December air. Winter had aways been Marilyn's favourite season in Los Angeles, when the days were more comfortable but not cold, when primroses and winter jasmines splashed their sunny yellow everywhere. The smog was worse though, hanging like tired grey washing over the city.

'You'll be fine. Have you told Sister Joy? She has quite an affection for you.'

'Not yet. I'll go and speak to her now. She's become very special to me too.'

They stopped before going into the main building.

'Can I ask you something?' said Mother Superior.

'Sure.'

'I'm only curious – there's no judgement or expectation. Would you say you've found a new belief in God while you've been here?'

Marilyn didn't speak.

She didn't want to insult this holy woman who had been so gracious.

The truth was that she remained unsure, which was strange, because if Mary had spoken to her, didn't that mean God existed? Or perhaps Mary was a woman in her own right, not created by a higher power. A woman free to do as she wished. Marilyn had always felt that in the world of God, women had such small roles to play, and those they did usually required that they be perfect.

The Gods in the movie industry demanded the same.

'Can I just say,' she began, 'that I've found a new faith in people.' The sisters here were not perfect – they squabbled and they made mistakes – but they tried. That was the key. They strived to be good. 'Surely my belief in the sisters and in you says a lot about your God?'

Mother Superior nodded. 'It does.'

And they went inside.

*

Later, Marilyn found Sister Joy in the garden, a place they had worked side by side for many months.

'I know what you're going to say.' Sister Joy didn't look up from her spot on the ground, kneeling at the bright purple pansies and violas. 'I've felt you pulling away. You're leaving, aren't you?'

'I am.' Marilyn knelt too. 'I always knew this was just a temporary home. Well, my dear friend, I've found somewhere to go. And I think I can begin to carve out a new life from there.'

'Then I'm happy for you.' Sister Joy sounded quite the opposite.

'I'm going to miss you too,' said Marilyn.

Sister Joy cut a viola free and handed it to her.

'I'll press it in my notepad and keep it forever.'

Sister Joy touched her chest. 'I'll press you in here.'

Marilyn smiled, kissed her cheek.

*

Early the next morning, two days before Christmas, during the quiet period when no one spoke, Marilyn rose and dressed. Mother Superior had given her one of her own tunics so she wouldn't be recognised – who would expect Marilyn Monroe dressed as a nun?

She smiled at her reflection in the darkened window. How different she looked to the woman who had arrived here seventeen months ago, with her natural brown hair curled about her face – recently trimmed by Sister Margaret to remove that last of the blonde – and her un-made-up face.

Only when she smiled did a softer, more ghostly Monroe appear, as though from another world.

A cab pulled onto the brick drive just after nine. Marilyn had booked it for then knowing the sisters would still be in the chapel for the longer festive Lauds; she didn't want any fuss. But as she gave the driver Stella's address and started to close the door, Mother Superior appeared.

She put something into Marilyn's hand. 'It's the only item I still have from my time in the care home as a child. I'd like you to have it. Be safe, Ma-' Mother Superior glanced at the cab driver and stopped herself saying Marilyn's name. 'Be safe, child.'

Only when the vehicle pulled away did Marilyn look at the treasure in her palm. It was a tiny silver and Mary-blue medal, tarnished with age, depicting a young Mary, her hood up, a starry halo above her head, palms open. The wording around the edge said: *Pray for us who have recourse to thee O Mary conceived without sin.*

Had Mother Superior had an inkling about the visit? Or had she just noticed Marilyn's adoration of Mary during her time in the convent?

She would never know.

She put the gift in the pocket of her holdall.

'Do I know you from somewhere?' The driver studied her in the mirror.

She supressed a giggle. This man had Marilyn Monroe in his car, disguised as a nun. Then she said in a voice she hoped was pure, 'I don't think so. I've been in that convent for most of my life.'

She had been in a cocoon. She had folded in her colourful wings, wrapped them tightly about her body, and let herself be entombed in a chrysalis while Marilyn Monroe turned back into an everyday creature.

Now she was back in the world.

The *other world.*

31

Flora is an arsehole

March 2016, Hull, England

Flora arrived at the club on Wednesday evening exhausted.

She had spent a long but satisfying third day at CARE, shadowing Marjory again, dealing with a new arrival; a woman so traumatised by an assault that she couldn't be left for a moment. Flora had sat in silence with her for thirty minutes when no other volunteers were available. The woman – who hadn't given her name and shook her head vigorously when it was suggested they call the police – sat on a sofa, hunched over her knees, shaking. Flora sat opposite, feeling those waves of pain, saying only, 'You're safe here.'

The club was a different world.

Flora had to shed her coat of care and don one of armour.

The first face she saw was Marilyn Monroe's.

A huge poster dominated the wall. Gold lettering declared that award-winning drag act, Selby lad Daniel Vee, who had been bringing Marilyn to life for fifteen years, delighting fans, was back after sell-out gigs.

Greg joined Flora at the poster, clean tea towels in hand. 'Marilyn tributes are always fucking terrible.'

'Daniel was good,' said Flora.

'They're never quite her though, are they?'

'It must be hard to replicate someone that famous.'

'If anything that should make it easy,' said Greg, 'she's still everywhere.'

Flora thought about it. 'It's because they're trying to recreate what she *had*. Some *look* like her but they make the mistake of thinking it's only about what she looked like. And it's about something far less... obvious.'

'Guess you're a fan,' said Greg.

Flora smiled. 'Suzie Kennedy is good; I think because there's a real joy in her that shows. It's more of a tribute than a mimic with her.'

'I guess it's a living.' Greg disappeared behind the bar.

Flora grabbed an apron from her locker, eyes gritty with fatigue. She had agreed to volunteer two days at CARE next week. Though delighted, she knew it would be intense on top of her shifts here. Also, full of cold, Bella had snored all night. Flora hadn't wanted to roll her over because she was relieved she was sleeping well.

'You're here.' Flora jumped. It was Denise. She closed the cloakroom door after her. 'Can I have a word?'

'Sure.' Flora frowned.

Was she in trouble?

Denise looked uncomfortable.

Then Flora remembered throwing that flat cap guy to the ground. Greg would have told Denise. Flora couldn't afford to lose her job. 'If it's about Saturday night and me and that guy–'

'Oh, no, it isn't.' Denise came closer. 'I think I might've done something I shouldn't.'

'You've lost me.'

'I heard what you said.'

'What I said?' Flora shook her head.

'In here. To Neil. Last Thursday.'

Flora realised what Denise meant.

Everything fell into place.

'*You* told the journalist,' she cried. 'He won't leave me alone! I haven't had the chance to look but apparently there's an article in the paper tonight.'

'Yes, it's in.' Denise looked remorseful. 'There's a copy behind the bar. They didn't name you but they said you work here. Flora, I *didn't* tell him though.'

'What do you mean?' Flora needed to sit down.

'I told my Pete about Pat's prediction, and what I heard you telling Neil. It was just pillow talk. I was fascinated because I went to a Catholic school; that stuff stays with you, Mary watching over you and all that. But I honestly never thought my husband would tell John.'

'*John*?'

'John Marse, his brother-in-law – the journalist.'

'Oh, shit.'

'Yes,' said Denise. 'My thought too. I went mad at Pete. I did *not* give John your number though, I told him he was out of order. I hoped it would blow over but I see Pat's been all over social media since John contacted her. Now tonight's article has gone crazy too.'

'Has it? *Jesus*.' Flora slumped onto the stool by the coat rack.

'Do you want to read it?'

'Yes. *No*.'

The door opened again. 'Marilyn's here,' said Greg. 'Can you look after him Denise, I've got shitloads to do behind the bar?'

'Will do, just a tick.' Denise waited until he had gone and touched Flora's shoulder, said, 'I'm sorry.' Then, more quietly, 'Did you really see her?'

'Who?' asked Flora, distracted.

'Mary.'

She nodded, not caring if Denise believed her. She felt wretched. Neil hadn't done a thing wrong. Denise headed out, pausing in the doorway, the light from a low hanging lamp making her a dark shadow. Flora caught something in her eyes though – judgement, disbelief, *reverence*? – and then the briefest of nods and she was gone.

The night beckoned. There was no time to dwell on problems. She went into the bar where Georgie was putting promotional leaflets for future acts on the tables.

'It's you, isn't it?' he said.

'Me what?'

'The Mary girl in the paper and on socials.'

The Mary girl.

What could she say?

She hurried to the bar. The club didn't take long to fill. Marilyn Monroe was a big draw. Flora was glad she didn't have time to look at the newspaper beneath the tea towels; she pulled pint after pint and poured prosecco after prosecco.

Marilyn burst onto the stage at eight, wearing the pink *Gentleman Prefer Blondes* dress, blonde wig perfectly coiffed, voice breathy. The crowd – mainly Hull's small but loud gay community – sang along to 'Diamonds Are a Girl's Best Friend'.

Flora wondered how Marilyn might feel about her continuing popularity. Would she enjoy knowing she was still loved? If she was alive, she must know. She would have seen the replays of her films, the artwork, the documentaries, the websites, the dolls, memorabilia and books. How curious to be ogled without being seen.

Perhaps that was what she had wanted.

Just before the interval Flora saw Neil sitting under the Upcoming Events poster. He was looking at his phone. Though anxious, it put a bounce in Flora's step. The last time she saw him he said, 'Let's save something for next time'.

Did he still feel like that?

On her break she approached him. He looked up, face unreadable, body language just as closed. She sat in the adjacent seat; her words tumbled out like coins from an arcade game.

'I should've trusted you but I panicked. I should never've

asked if you'd shared what I told you, I should've known, and now I know it was bloody Denise.'

'It's fine.' There was a coolness though.

'It isn't. You listened to me. You were... *kind.*' Flora's voice broke. 'And the Mary thing. You didn't laugh. Can you just accept that I'm an arsehole and move on?'

He smiled, briefly. 'I suppose... *Arsehole.*'

She smiled too.

'So Denise blabbed to the papers?' There still a brusqueness to Neil's tone.

'Long story, but it was an accident.'

'Did you see tonight's newspaper article?'

'No. You?'

'Yeah. They didn't name you but they mentioned the club, Pat's prediction, and the daffodil. It's gone crazy on social media.' He looked at her for a few seconds. 'I know you didn't want everyone knowing.'

'It's only a matter of time until someone names me, isn't it?'

'They might've done already, I haven't been on socials.'

Flora wondered what he had been doing on his phone earlier. Did he have a woman in every bar? The idea of him spending time with someone else hurt.

'What will you do if you're named?' he asked.

'Hide,' said Flora.

'How?'

'You tell me.' She held his gaze. 'You're the one who knows how to disappear.'

Marilyn went into the 'Heatwave' song, and two backing dancers appeared from the sides, dressed for no apparent reason in matador outfits.

'They'll call me crazy,' said Flora. 'There've already been comments like that online. Hopefully I'm enough of a nobody for them to get bored quickly.'

'A nobody arsehole,' said Neil.

'Fine by me.'

'It'll blow over.'

'Maybe.' She paused. 'How's your Vegas trip coming along?'

He looked morose. 'I don't know if I'll get there.'

'What do you mean?'

'It'll set me back thousands. The flights are extortionate cos it's only three weeks away. I need to stay at least a week, but all that's left are expensive hotels.'

'This competition, isn't there prize money?'

'Yeah – ten thousand pounds.'

'Perfect,' cried Flora. 'Put it on your credit card and pay it off when you're back.'

'What if I don't win?'

'You *will* – you're gonna do this amazing trick.'

'I don't know.' He shook his head. 'It could be a stupid gamble. I'm no Dynamo.'

'You're *better*.'

'Get real, Flora,' he sighed.

'Arseholes know best.'

Greg signalled for her to serve some lamps; they shone like annoying smiles about something that might never happen.

She didn't want to leave Neil. He seemed so unhappy. This protectiveness caught her off guard. She wanted to kiss his cheek, but said she had to get back and asked if he would stay until the end.

Then she served the punters.

Once Marilyn had closed with another heartfelt rendition of 'Diamonds', the place emptied. Loading the dishwasher, Flora caught sight of the newspaper on the side, and the headline: *Virgin Mary Visits Local Girl.*

Jesus, the front page.

She picked it up.

The main picture was of Psychic Pat sitting in a living room straight out of the 1970s, her hands floating above a clouded crystal ball. Next to it was a small image of Mary, this time a pious, slight, peasant girl with an angelic face.

Flora skim read the piece.

They had interviewed a Catholic priest who said, 'For this to be classified as an official apparition, the woman claiming to have seen Mary must have done so visually, in her real-life environment. If she *heard* Mary but didn't see her, this is known as interior locution. Also excluded from the category of apparitions are visions experienced in dreams, and any miracles associated with Marian artwork, such as weeping statues. I should like to speak with this woman and hear her story.'

Flora closed the paper.

Should she come forward? Once they knew she was a dull thirty-six-year-old woman interest would fade.

'Why don't you tell 'em it's you?' It was Georgie, end of night beer in hand. 'That shit'll get you on Big Brother.'

'Maybe she doesn't want that kind of shit,' said Greg, counting the till float.

Flora glanced towards the chair beneath the Upcoming Events poster; empty. Her heart sank. Neil had gone without even saying goodbye.

'What did she look like?' asked Georgie. Flora couldn't tell if he was mocking or curious.

Greg paused his counting and looked at her too.

'She… she was lovely.' Flora glanced down.

The whole thing felt worthless now the world was getting its grubby hands on her experience.

'Why do you think it was you?' asked Greg, no judgement

apparent.

'I'm beginning to wish it hadn't happened.'

'If it was anyone but you, I'd say they were a nutter.'

'Why anyone but me?' Flora frowned.

'You're down to earth. If you say you saw her... you did.'

She was touched.

'Someone's said who you are, babe.' Georgie was looking at his phone. 'This lass on Twitter said she knows who, and tagged you in it. Someone else is saying they know you and you're... God, that's harsh. Doesn't matter. Anyway th–'

'What did they say?' interrupted Flora.

Georgie looked unsure. 'Just some slag from the flats.'

'I love people.'

She remembered Bella saying their mum might get in touch once word got out that she was the Mary girl. A curious longing, one Flora rarely had, squeezed her heart. For a mother, any mother. Maybe she *would* call. Maybe – even despite the difficult relationship – Flora would be glad.

'We're closing, love.' Greg made her jump.

A woman approached the bar. She didn't look anything like the usual clientele; she wore the kind of tailored suit that lawyers wore for the office in high-end TV dramas, and had short blonde hair cut in a style that only suited elfin faces. Her heels were sharp on the stone floor.

Flora was sure she had seen her before.

Anxiety rose in her gut.

32

Flora will think about it

March 2016, Hull, England

'I'm here to see Flora.' The woman's accent was softly southern. 'Are you her?'

'Yes, she is,' said Georgie before Flora could lie. 'Are you from the press? I'm her best friend, and she won't do anything without me.'

'Pat told me you'd be here tonight,' said the woman.

'Who are you?' Flora couldn't help but be curt.

'My name's Nina Ford and I'm ma-'

'You did that Marilyn documentary.' Georgie went around the bar as though he might pounce on her. 'I *loved* it. You're doing one about Mary.'

Flora realised what she wanted and ran for the cloakroom.

Nina followed her; spicy perfume filled the small space.

'I'm not interested.' Flora spoke sharply, putting on her coat.

'I respect that you don't want to talk to anyone,' said Nina. 'I gather you won't speak to the press, which I understand.' She must have done some research. 'You're worried about how your story might be portrayed, yes?'

'I don't want it portrayed at all, thank you.'

'You're not the only one,' said Nina softly.

'What do you mean?'

'There are other women. Many of them. One woman who came forward when she knew I was making *Mother of God* had never talked about her experience either. She had a visit from Mary ten years ago while she was hanging the washing out and had never told a soul. But she realised that it was something the world *should* know. Do you really want to wait that long?'

'I'll wait forever.' Flora tried to push past, escape.

'Don't you think Mary would *want* you to tell the world?'

Flora stopped.

She had never considered that.

'Don't you think she came because she *wants* it to be known?' Nina's voice was hypnotic. Flora found herself staring at the woman, despite her resistance. 'That's my theory. She wants to show us who she is, who she *really* was. It seems to be mainly women she's visited recently, except they're reluctant to share it. Men have told Mary's story for years. Perhaps she's tired of it. Maybe she wants us to hear directly from her.' Nina paused. 'Via *you*.'

'No.' Flora shook her head, came to her senses. 'You're very persuasive because you want something from me, but I'm *not* interested.'

She headed outside but Nina was just behind.

'If I told you why some of these women decided to come forward, you might think again,' she tried.

'I wouldn't.' Flora began to walk in the direction of her flat.

'Some of these women wanted to be heard for *other* reasons.' Nina tried to keep up, her heels shrill in contrast with the silence of Flora's cheap trainers. 'They had other stories, more than just Mary.'

'I'm not going to change my mind.'

'Meet me for coffee. I know it's late and you want to get home, but tomorrow before I go back to London?'

Flora realised something and stopped. 'Did you come here just for *me*?'

'Yes.'

'But why?'

'Psychic Pat told me about you. I saw her post on Twitter and she was happy to talk to me.' Nina laughed. '*More* than happy.'

'I bet.' Flora paused. 'But why me when it sounds like you have plenty of others?'

'There are a few, but... your story fascinates me.'

'*Why?*'

'Meet me for coffee and I'll tell you. Take my card at least.'

Flora reluctantly took the card and put it in her pocket.

'I'll tell you my vision for the documentary. What harm can that do?'

Flora studied Nina. Despite the classy clothes and refined accent, there was a steel to her, an earthiness, like the timber frame inside the walls of a luxury apartment. Flora put her at forty, or perhaps she was older but expensive creams and surgical tweaks had given youth. She didn't belong on a rundown backstreet and yet here she was: like Mary in Flora's grubby kitchen.

'Where?' asked Flora despite herself.

'How about the coffee shop in Paragon Station? At eleven?'

'I'll think about it.' She paused and then added, 'I did love your Marilyn documentary though. You treated her like a human.'

And Flora walked home.

33

Marilyn's future starts here

Near Paradise Cove Beach, Los Angeles, December 1963

The cab battled the morning traffic.

Marilyn looked out of the window at the festive decorations adorning the LA streets; rows of gold bells and stars dangled from a wire across Hollywood Boulevard, and fat Santas sat in store windows. She felt like a child, seeing Christmas for the first time.

They passed Grauman's Theatre.

The popular movie palace, with its Exotic Revival style architecture, dominated the street. She tried to catch sight of her handprints in the cement, which were near the doors, alongside Jane Russell's. The cab screeched to a halt as someone ran out onto the street – and she saw them. Marilyn Monroe had never left this world; her mark was forever there on the sidewalk.

Nothing else had changed except the film posters, which were for *Cleopatra* and *Move Over, Darling*. The former had been in production when she disappeared, almost bankrupting Twentieth Century Fox with excessive costs caused by Elizabeth Taylor's unprecedented million dollar fee, her illnesses, and the decision to move production from London to Rome halfway through.

The press had always pitched Marilyn and Elizabeth as rivals but it wasn't true; Marilyn had no ill feeling towards her contemporary, though it had slightly irked her when she found out that her last film, *Something's Got To Give*, was being rushed so it would be in theatres in time to pay postproduction bills for *Cleopatra*.

Marilyn spotted Doris Day on the other poster before the cab moved past.

'What's the *Move Over, Darling* movie about?' she asked the driver.

'Not sure,' he said over his shoulder. 'It opens on Christmas day. I'd rather have seen the original though.'

'The original?'

'Yeah, the unfinished Monroe one. *Something's Got To Give*. She disappeared before they completed it and it got retitled and made with Doris Day and James Garner. I guess you don't see many movies in the convent, huh?'

Marilyn hardly heard his last sentence.

How quickly she had been replaced.

She was happy for dear Doris, but for a moment felt regret, thought; *that should have been me*. No. It would have been *Monroe*. It would have meant the treadmill of pills to sleep, pills to work, a punishing schedule that would ravage her physical and mental health again.

Still, she wondered what the finished movie would have been like. Fox, when they fired her, had said that most of the footage was dire. But she later overheard a conversation between execs who hadn't known she was there. They said that despite her drug addiction and tardiness, she still brought the magic.

But the price for conjuring that was too high.

Regrets about abandoning the movie crumbled, like fragile film prop glass broken in a scene.

'Who is this Monroe?' she asked the driver, pretending innocence.

'Who was she you mean? The biggest star in the world.' He honked violently at a car that overtook them. 'Gee, she was hot though, great ass and tits. The guys at the garage have her all over the wall. She went missing last year. Biggest mystery ever.'

'I see.'

'Do you know what I think?'

Marilyn didn't want to know but said, 'Tell me.'

'I think the Mafia killed her.'

Marilyn shivered. 'Why would they do that?'

'Oh, she was mixed up in all sorts. Gee, I think she was sleeping with everyone, movie men, government men, *any* men. Not that I'd say no, if I had a chance.' He laughed.

'Maybe you've got her all wrong,' she snapped.

'Uh, sorry, lady, forgive my crudeness. I forgot you're a woman of God.'

'Maybe you should treat *all* women like they're women of God.'

He apologised and didn't speak for the rest of the journey.

As they headed in the opposite direction to Marilyn's Brentwood home, she felt a pang of longing. Should she ask him to drive by, just so she could see the place, peer over the gates and check her flowers had been cared for?

No. Too risky.

On they went. Marilyn knew Stella's house was in a quiet spot between Paradise Cove Beach and Zuma Beach, off the Pacific Coast Highway, hidden by a slight incline and rows of skinny trees. After an hour – most of it along the coast where Marilyn was delighted to see the ocean dappled with early light – the cab dropped her at the roadside. She paid him out of her remaining ninety dollars.

'No tip?' he demanded.

'Here's one,' she said. 'Treat women like they're humans.'

When he had gone she gathered herself before descending the sandy path to the side door and knocking softly. The white, three-level house had a generous oceanfront deck, she remembered, made private by the distance between this property and the others, and by tall fencing on each side, leaving views to the front, of ocean and sky. Its privacy had reminded Marilyn of Brentwood.

Now, she noticed a plaque above the door, not unlike the tile at her house. It was Mary-blue and white too, its words in italics; words she didn't understand.

Futurum incipit hic.

The door opened.

Stella was dressed in white, fine hair tied with a scarf, tiny gold studs that said *I'm not showy, I'm small and insignificant* still in place. 'Marilyn,' she said warmly. Then she looked at the tunic. 'But you're a…'

Marilyn laughed. 'Don't ask,' she said.

'Your hair! It looks... lovely. Natural. You look so *well.*'

'Thank you. I love that scarf. Is it silk?'

Though they had only met a couple of times, she felt like she was seeing an old friend. Perhaps it was because she had seen the same women for months and the thrill of a new face was intense.

No, that wasn't it.

There was a connection, one felt keenly now, in this curious circumstance.

Marilyn hugged Stella. 'Thank you so much for this.' When Marilyn pulled away, she pointed to the plaque. 'It's pretty. I never noticed it when I came to the magazine launch but it was dark then. What does it mean?'

Stella looked at it. 'It was there when I bought the house. I took it as a good sign. It means *the future starts here.*'

Marilyn shivered. 'I love it,' she said quietly. 'I had one similar at my house.'

'I know. I remember. Cursum Perficio.'

'Here ends my journey.'

'Come in, come in,' said Stella.

Marilyn followed her through the homely kitchen with multi-coloured tiles around the hob and worktop area, and disorderly racks of herbs, and into the main living area which had bulging bookshelves, and doors that opened onto a wooden deck. A small Christmas tree by the fireplace reminded Marilyn it was the holidays.

'Is that all you have?' Stella looked at the holdall.

'This is it.' She recalled arriving at the orphanage with a similar bag, not knowing how long she would be there, or if she would see her mother again. But this was different. This was a life she had chosen; there was no need to be anxious.

'Do you want to change into something more…?'

'Not nun-like?'

Stella laughed. 'It's a great disguise. Might be worth keeping if you want to go out incognito.' She paused. 'I don't think you've ever looked prettier.'

'I feel the best I have in years. But yes, I'll change. I don't have anything casual though. I need to buy new clothes.'

'I'll lend you something.'

Marilyn followed Stella to her bedroom, a large space with its own balcony. Marilyn chose a simple lemon sundress and cardigan. Stella showed her another bedroom on the top floor with views of the ocean too.

'This is yours,' she said. 'For as long as you need.'

'I can't thank you enough. This is such a huge thing for you to do and I don't know how I'll ever repay you.'

Stella smiled. 'You have no idea, do you? This is an honour for me. I've admired you my whole adult life and now, here you are, a guest in *my* house, except, well, somehow as a different person. Right, I'll leave you to change and then let's have coffee on the deck, shall we?'

'That sounds perfect.'

Marilyn put her few things around the room, then changed in the ensuite bathroom, and joined Stella outside.

It was mild for December, almost seventy degrees. Marilyn took off the cardigan and hung it on the back of the cream wicker chair. Though she had spent plenty of time outdoors at the convent, it was good to feel an ocean breeze on her face, smell salty air. Stella handed her a strong coffee and sat in the opposite chair with hers.

'Do you still want to hide from the world?' she asked.

Marilyn nodded. 'Can you keep me secret?'

'No one will hear a word from me, though we'll have to hide you if anyone comes over.'

It felt to Marilyn like an adventure.

'When I spoke to you,' continued Stella, 'for that interview in the May before you disappeared, you looked tired. I was concerned about you. I thought about you afterwards.' She sipped her coffee. 'But I have a confession to make.'

Marilyn's heart tightened.

She waited for Stella to go on.

'The words you asked me not to use that day … I printed them in a piece on the one year anniversary of you disappearing. I had no idea if we were going to see you again and I just …' Stella was clearly emotional. 'I wanted the world to see a little of the real you.'

'That's OK.' Marilyn meant it. 'Joe told me you were kind when you spoke about me. That means everything.'

'You said on the phone that you have some ideas for your future.' It was a question.

'Can I tell you another day?' Stella was studying her; Marilyn could see the million other questions in her flecked eyes. It must have been hard for a journalist not to ask them. She turned the tables. 'Tell me more about you. Why did you start your magazine? Why are you so passionate about making women's voices heard?'

Stella stood. 'Shall I make some lunch?'

'You're changing the subject.' Marilyn knew she could be

guilty of this when being tackled about personal issues.

Stella laughed. 'No, I'm delaying the subject. I'll tell you. But I'm hungry. Do you like pasta?'

While Stella cooked and then they ate, enjoying crisp white wine, Marilyn learned the truth about the woman named after the stars.

34

Marilyn comes out fighting

Near Paradise Cove Beach, Los Angeles, December 1963

Stella's story began with a sister.

That sister was called Moira and she started out as a model in the late 1940s, much like Marilyn had. As with most girls in that industry, Moira's dream was for a movie career. Stella had always liked the privacy that writing gave her, and pursued a career as a reporter, though she was mostly given 'light' stories, the gossip and society events, by burly editors who smoked as they typed and called her 'little lady'.

But Moira wanted the lights, the fame, the glory.

She was spotted by a talent director at MGM and he arranged a screen test. There was a price though. She would have to sleep with him. Moira confided this in Stella, and Stella begged her not to, warning that if she did, it would be expected every time. Moira had told her shocked sister that it *was* expected every time; it was what you did as a woman if you wanted a big role.

Promised a starring part in the next B movie, Moira agreed.

'Be quiet,' the talent director told her during the sordid deed. 'Be quiet and you'll go far.' Then he put his finger to his lips every time he saw her around the film lot, and at social events where starlets were excepted to entertain top execs.

Moira never got that role.

'You likely won't have heard of her.' Stella pushed away her empty plate, finished her glass of wine.

'I haven't.' Marilyn was sitting opposite at the chunky red

oak table, meal also done, taking her wine slowly. 'I was at a different studio so we probably didn't cross paths. Poor Moira. The casting couch is real, and it's tough. I remember an executive at a Hollywood party offering me lavish gifts in exchange for sexual favours. I refused and asked my agent what I should say to men like that. All he said was, "You'll learn." I tried to.' Marilyn paused. 'Please tell me that Moira chose a different career?'

Stella shook her head.

'She had children?' said Marilyn brightly.

'She hung herself.'

'No.' Marilyn sat up in her seat. 'Oh, Stella, I'm so sorry.' She got up, went around the table and knelt as you do when a holy vision has come into your kitchen. Put a hand on Stella's knee. 'That's just... *awful*.'

'I know.' Stella put a hand over hers.

'Was it... when did it..?'

'Almost five years ago. She was just twenty-three.'

'A kid,' whispered Marilyn.

'She left a note.' Stella closed her eyes. 'She wrote, *Now I'm quiet*.'

So was Marilyn. She didn't know what to say.

What *was* there to say?

Long ago, she had learned how to tolerate the wolves, as she called them. There had been plenty. She discovered who was worth fighting off and who was worth being more submissive with, not because of what power they wielded but because of the harm they might do if not. She rode in their limousines and sat next to them in swanky places if there was any chance a role, and not another wolf, might follow. When she signed with Columbia in 1947, the studio head, Harry Cohn, invited Marilyn to take a trip with him on his yacht. She said she would only go if his wife went too.

She was dropped from the contract.

'Now *you're* her voice, aren't you?' said Marilyn eventually, realising this.

'I'm trying to be. That's why I started the magazine. I was tired of actresses having to keep quiet.' Stella's anger was understandable. 'I decided to make sure they were heard. That they got to voice their stories.'

'And you have done,' said Marilyn with passion. 'Moira would be proud.'

'Thank you. You've been quite the pioneer too. I remember your piece way back in *Motion Picture and Television Magazine.*'

Marilyn returned to her seat. 'I can't think of it?'

'It was called *Wolves I Have Known.* I cut it out. You called out the men who used their power to try and get you in the sack.'

'Ah, yes. I remember now.' She smiled. 'Gee, I was kinda proud of that, though I sure got some stick from the industry. I didn't name anyone but they'd have known who I meant.'

'We need more of that.' Stella stacked the empty dishes and took them to the sink. 'I don't think we live in a world that will listen though. It's run mostly by men.' She shrugged, looked more thoughtful. 'Things are starting to change though, slowly. Women are getting fed up.'

'We are,' said Marilyn quietly.

'I just read a great new book, *The Feminine Mystique,* by an activist called Betty Friedan. I'll loan you it. It explores the assumptions that women are fulfilled merely by housework, marriage, and children, and analyses their unhappiness with such limitations. It's been sparking a new wave of feminism in the US.'

'If women had somewhere they could go.' Marilyn said it to herself, staring across towards the living room and the ocean beyond.

Stella poured another wine and held the bottle out for Marilyn, who shook her head. Having fully detoxed for months she felt a little tipsy after just one.

'What do you mean somewhere to go?'

'I'm not sure. Some sort of place they could escape for a while. Find themselves.'

'Then come out fighting,' smiled Stella.

'I guess.'

'Have *you* come out fighting?' Stella motioned for Marilyn to follow her onto the deck, where they resumed their positions in the sun. 'Wherever you've been,' she continued, 'and I'm not fishing, you don't have to say where it was, it's clearly been good for you. You're a different woman to the one I saw last year. Not just physically but your demeanour.'

Marilyn's time at the convent had been more healing than the months of expensive counselling with Dr Greenson. With distance, she could see how he had overstepped many ethical boundaries put in place to protect both psychiatrist and patient. He had invited her to his home, offered her a drink after each session, let her meet his family, and made decisions for her. Really, he was one more in a long line of men who wanted to bask in, use, and enjoy Marilyn Monroe's light.

'I needed the time I took. But I wish that was available for women in greater need. Like your Moira.' She looked pointedly at Stella. 'There are women who don't have money or a family to turn to. Women who have no education, who have experienced trauma, abuse, who've-'

'Like you,' said Stella kindly.

'I have money though I'll need to find a way to access it, and I ha–'

'No, I mean when you started out. When you were a *child*.' Stella paused. 'I read about things that happened to you.'

'Oh, those were... rumours.' Marilyn shook her head, feeling exposed.

'But I can... I sense it too…'

Even having addressed it in recent months, the shame was acute. 'I... can we…?'

Perhaps sensing her discomfort, Stella asked instead, 'Is this escape your future idea?'

'Yes.' Marilyn was glad to answer. 'I'm not sure exactly how yet, but I feel it calling to me. Does that sound silly?'

'Not at all.'

'It can't be through Marilyn Monroe though. I have to let her go.'

'She could be useful in getting things off the ground.'

'No.' Marilyn was firm. 'Her name could eclipse it. I don't want that. People will treat whatever she does as a curiosity, with contempt. They'll say, *silly glamour star, what does she know of such things*? You know that as well as I do, Stella.'

She didn't respond.

A small grey and white sandpiper bird flew down and walked along the edge of the deck. Neither women spoke as they watched it forage in the cracks between the wood and then – dissatisfied – hop off the edge and search in the sand.

'She'll be refuelling between places,' said Stella, eyes still on the busy creature.

'Will she?' Marilyn was fascinated.

'They breed in the Arctic tundra and then winter along the Pacific Coast. It's a safe spot here, in-between.'

'In-between,' Marilyn repeated softly. She looked meaningfully at Stella. 'I think I'm going to contact Joe, see if I can sign something to give him the authority to sell my house, access my finances, and then I can contribute while I'm here, and begin some sort of new life. I'll need to change my name so I can get a new passport.'

'But you're truly Marilyn now,' said Stella, sadly.

'Maybe. But I'll lose the Monroe. I love it because it was my grandmother's surname, and it worked well with Marilyn. Baker is my original surname but I don't feel that works.'

'Who will you be then?'

'I don't know. For once it's entirely up to me. Maybe I should honour someone I love, like when you get married and take their name. What was your sister's surname?'

'Same as mine – Cruz. Neither of us have married.'

'It's nice.'

'It's Spanish, means cross.'

'Interesting. I have a sister, you know,' said Marilyn. 'Berniece. We have the same mother but different fathers. Though we don't see each other a lot, we used to write one another and talk on the phone. No one knows about her because I didn't want her in the limelight. I've always felt that our relationship is... sacred.'

'What's her surname?'

'Miracle.'

'That's pretty.'

It occurred to Marilyn how fitting such a word was now, after Mary. It might be a tribute to her sister.

She didn't have to decide now. She didn't have to do anything right now except enjoy the company of the woman named after the stars.

'Whatever we do with our lives,' said Stella after a while. 'Let's not be quiet.'

35

Flora finds herself talking

March 2016, Hull, England

Walking home from work, Flora didn't know what to think about first; the events, feelings, and faces of the day piled up like jumble waiting to be sorted in a charity back room.

There was the newspaper headline: *Virgin Mary Visits Local Girl.* There was Denise: a remorseful face, sorry she had revealed Flora as 'the Mary girl'. Then Psychic Pat: an older face in a photo, sitting in a living room, hands floating above a crystal ball. Then Nina Ford: a new face, maker of documentaries and wearer of chic clothes.

And finally Neil.

A familiar face that Flora feared had changed how it looked at her.

She got home at one. There was a note on the kitchen worktop from Bella: *Tried to stay awake but knackered.* Flora was too. She peeled off her trainers and sank into a plastic chair, no energy to fill the pan. Three days volunteering at CARE, work tonight, and the visit from Nina Ford had left her burnt out.

She sent a message to Neil: *Hi, it's the arsehole, hope you're OK? X*

It was late so he likely wouldn't see it now, let alone respond.

Then the blue tick appeared.

And then... *nothing.*

Flora stared at the tick, willing the dots to show that he was typing. Still nothing. Maybe he was half asleep. Maybe he didn't care about her.

She opened Twitter.

Wished she hadn't.

There were hundreds of notifications. And Flora now had over a thousand followers. Someone had tagged her in a post about the newspaper article and said that this was the *Mary Girl.* That had become a hashtag: #TheMaryGirl. And it had been used many times, in tweets that ranged from fascination to downright vile, with posters saying Flora was a blasphemous, attention-seeking, whore.

Psychic Pat had been tagged too and had over fifteen thousand followers; her profile picture had been changed to the image from tonight's newspaper. She had shared a post saying to 'look out for her' in the upcoming Nina Ford documentary, and that she was now fully booked for readings until 2018.

Neil still hadn't responded to Flora's message.

She switched off her phone, threw it on the sofa.

Why had she agreed to meet Nina tomorrow?

Perhaps it was an interest in other women's Mary stories. She had to admit, the idea that others had seen her too was validating. Deep down, humans need that endorsement, and she was curious to hear how they had seen Mary. Would she take part in the interviews? No. She had no desire to be thrust into the limelight. She would have coffee with Nina, sate her curiosity, but say *no thank you* and come home.

*

In the morning, Bella already had the pan on the hob when Flora woke.

Flora feared that her sister's mood might finally have plummeted and tried to study her without being obvious. 'Feels like I haven't seen you in ages,' she said. 'How did it go at university?'

'You were right, it's not too late to apply.' Bella beamed. 'They said this is a good time because the end of January rush is done, and they'll know what spaces are left. I filled out the application to do a degree in Graphic Design cos it sounds fascinating, and they have room.'

'That's amazing, Bell. When will you know if you made it?'

'June.' She paused. 'Can I stay here while I do the course? I'll be able to contribute cos of my student loan.'

'You don't even have to ask.'

'Yeah but…'

'What?' asked Flora.

'You might want to move on.'

'Where would I go?'

Bella shrugged.

'Have the mental health team been in touch with you?' asked Flora.

'Yeah, a nurse called yesterday.'

Flora made tea – the milk had soured so they drank it black – and they sat on the sofa watching morning TV. Flora fired up her phone; her heart shrank when she saw that Neil still hadn't responded to her message.

'I saw last night that someone shared your identity as the Mary girl,' said Bella.

Flora shook her head. 'It wasn't Neil who told that journalist. It was bloody Denise at work, though to be fair she didn't mean to. Long story. Another time.'

'Well, that's good,' cried Bella.

'Is it? Neil's been cool with me,' said Flora. 'I get it. I wouldn't like it if he'd thought for even a second that I'd disclose something like that. But I said sorry. Said I'm an arsehole.'

'Yeah, you are.'

'Thanks.'

'Have you got a copy of the newspaper?' asked Bella.

'I don't want one.'

'I'd have framed it. Is it online?'

'Probably,' sighed Flora.

While Bella searched for the article, Flora wondered whether to tell her about the meeting with Nina; she'd have to leave soon. But Bella would only get excited and want to come, and Flora wasn't even going to take part in the documentary. She felt bad. She hadn't told Bella about Mary for ages and that upset her. But she wasn't going to take part, so there wasn't any point.

Bella studied her phone. 'There isn't a picture of you in the article.'

'Good.' Flora finished her tea. 'Anyway, I have to get ready.'

'Where you going, anywhere good?'

Flora felt guilty as she rinsed the cup out. 'Got to pick some forms up from CARE.'

'How was it yesterday?'

'Tiring. But I enjoyed it.'

'If it didn't work out, please don't stay, just because of me, what Mary said. You're not responsible for my happiness.'

I am, Flora couldn't help but think.

'I know,' she lied.

'I might paint today,' said Bella.

'You should.'

'I reckon she'll def be in touch now.' Bella didn't need to say who; Mum. 'Surprised she hasn't rung the paper herself, telling them *I'm the mother of the Mary Girl*.'

'Give her time,' said Flora quietly.

*

She headed for Paragon Station at ten-thirty, leaving Bella sorting through the paltry paint pots and brushes she had. Flora would have loved to buy her art equipment, but neither of them had enough money.

On the walk, she thought of Neil not having enough to pay for the Las Vegas trip. She wished she could help with it. Anyone who said money didn't buy happiness obviously had plenty; it might not guarantee joy but it certainly gave freedom of choice.

Nina was already in the station café, sitting at a misty window table with a tall latte, reading something on her phone, Louis Vuitton suitcase at her feet like an advertisement for a better life. The place was full of travellers surrounded by cheaper luggage, eating breakfasts, steam from frying bacon fogging the air.

'What can I get you?' she asked as Flora approached.

'A latte, thanks.'

'Anything to eat?'

'No, thank you.'

Flora watched Nina order, her wide-legged grey trousers obviously expensive, and her jacket cut in the sharp way that designer clothes always are. Flora glanced down at her pink sweatshirt that had a hole near the cuff, and jeans that had seen better days. She had said no to food but her stomach rumbled. Pride didn't help. Nina returned; Flora sipped her coffee.

'Thanks for coming.' Nina's nails were as silver as frozen tears in moonlight. 'I know you're worried about how you want your story portrayed so let m-'

'I don't want it portrayed at all.'

Nina nodded. 'But you came,' she said simply.

Flora couldn't argue.

'Shall I tell you about my vision for the documentary?' Flora remained quiet. Nina continued. 'It goes way back. When I was growing up, the men came and went but there were always three women in the house: my mum, the Virgin Mary, and Marilyn Monroe.'

Flora sat up – they were the same.

She shivered.

'Me too,' she said softly, 'except it was my gran.'

Nina smiled as though she now had Flora. 'My mum absolutely loved Marilyn. She was seventeen when she disappeared and kept every newspaper article afterwards. I still have them in a scrapbook in a drawer. Mum always said that her mother had loved Mary the way she loved Marilyn, and that the two icons had more in common than you'd think. I couldn't see it, not then.'

I do, thought Flora.

'Mary was portrayed as pure, virginal, while Marilyn was thought to be highly sexed, some even said obscene. But both of them,' continued Nina, 'had little say in their image. Men glorified Mary's story; she *had* to be a virgin giving birth to Christ, even though she was only fifteen, so the act of impregnating her, whether it was God or not, was pretty terrible by today's standards. But hey, if any other young girl gets pregnant, *she*'s a whore…'

Nina paused as though for effect.

Flora began to wish she had never come.

'It's about the story, isn't it?' continued Nina. 'Like with Old Hollywood. We share images and revere those women, that era, but it was fraught with difficulties. The female stars were loved but they had no control over their careers and were exhausted, trying to be perfect and beautiful.'

Nina looked sad then.

Flora felt it too.

They looked at one another and didn't speak for a moment. Something changed. It was subtle. Flora didn't know if Nina felt it too, but it was like when you're on a third date and you realise that maybe there's a future here.

Except this wasn't sexual.

Flora still didn't want to do the documentary – and hoped

that if Nina had felt the odd shift too, she didn't think it was that she did – but she realised that Nina was genuine. 'I loved how you portrayed Marilyn,' she said.

'Thank you. As you know, in *Marilyn Only* I used her words, no one else's, and footage that showed her in more natural repose, out and about, filmed by fans and people who loved her. But with Mary, I can't do that because obviously there aren't any recordings of her speaking. I can, however, share the voices of the growing number of women who say they've seen her.' Nina crossed and uncrossed her legs. 'I'll be interspersing these interviews with a beautiful, animated story created by a friend of mine, depicting the Mary the world created, the perfect Virgin. He's also making a short film that shows how *I* see her – young, scared, and poor.' She paused. 'How did Mary appear to you?'

Flora couldn't help but be guarded again. She thought of something. 'Wait... are you recording me?'

'No. If you were to be recorded, I'd have you sign a contract. I'm just curious to hear from you. I've read the paper and I spoke to Psychic Pat and to-' Nina shook her head. 'But only you can tell your story.'

'I told you – I don't want to.' Flora finished her latte.

'Everyone wants to.'

'Not necessarily.'

'Not even just to me?'

'Look, I'm not going to change my mind, but I'm here, so tell me about these other women.'

'It's paid,' said Nina.

Flora didn't respond. She hadn't considered that. But she found herself shaking her head, despite the fact that she had no idea what the fee was, despite the fact that she needed a new kettle, needed new trainers, had an outstanding gas bill to pay, and knew the cupboards were bare.

'Makes no difference,' she said less assuredly than she felt.

'Do you want to know how much?'

'No.'

'Paying people to feature in documentaries is generally frowned upon,' said Nina. 'If you're making a commercial release fiction film, fair enough, but documentary takes you into the world of journalism, and journalism has certain rules and standards. One of these rules is, you never pay people to participate. Obviously, the argument is that it'll make interviewees less honest, more easily persuaded to appear a particular way. I don't want that, but also, I respect that this is a huge thing for these women to do. So, I get away with paying them by including a certain amount of *fiction* in the form of my animation.' Nina looked at Flora. 'Most of these women are... shall we say, not well off, and I'm happy to help in some way. I grew up in a council house.'

Flora found that hard to believe but tried never to judge.

'Also, I pay because I want complete exclusivity. If you talk to me, you'll sign a contract saying that you can't share your story anywhere else.'

Flora couldn't help but think that she would be selling her soul if she got money for telling the world about Mary's visit.

'Tell me, how did she appear to you?' Nina asked again. 'Just between us.'

Flora gave in; found herself telling Nina about the miracle of Bella being 'better', about her fears that this good health might fade, about Mary encouraging her to volunteer at CARE, about the daffodil, even about Neil. It felt good to open up.

Nina was a great listener.

But Flora didn't share Mary's words: *I bless the sacrifice that hurt your heart. You had no say in it and did not ask for it.*

She didn't tell her about the baby.

'Flowers seem to be quite a theme,' said Nina when Flora had been silent for a while. 'Mary gave them to a few of the women.' She paused. 'And you mentioned CARE.'

'I noticed you responded to that,' said Flora.

'I think you should watch a couple of the interviews, and you'll know why. Do you want to?'

'You have them with you?'

'Yes.' Nina took a laptop from her bag and opened it. 'I feel like Mary appeared to these women so they could find their voices, because every one of them shared something they never have before. All of them experienced some sort of miracle.'

'Do you believe they saw her?' asked Flora.

Nina paused, just for a second. 'I do.'

'Good.'

'I wouldn't have made such a documentary if I didn't. You have to believe in what you're creating.' Nina untangled some white headphones. 'When you see them I think you'll want to contribute your story.'

Flora didn't have the energy to argue again.

'I paid each of them ten thousand pounds,' said Nina.

Flora tried to hide the surprise, not wanting Nina to think her greedy or that she had been swayed.

But it was a lot of money.

She couldn't help but note that it was the second time in a few days someone had mentioned this exact amount – Neil had said that ten thousand pounds was the Las Vegas prize money. They both had the chance of earning the same fee. He would have to make magic, and she would have to tell the truth.

When Flora didn't respond, Nina plugged the headphones into her laptop and opened a video app. 'These are just short clips,' she said, 'and they're unedited, just thrown together for now. There are only four, but I can send you the others when I go back. You'll get a feel for how natural I want things to be. Are you ready?'

Was she?

'I guess,' she said.

Flora popped the earphones in.

Nina adjusted the volume and then pressed play.

36

Marilyn goes shopping

Near Paradise Cove Beach, Los Angeles, December 1963

Christmas Day was quiet.

Stella cooked turkey and they ate it on the decking under a Mary-blue sky, only a light cardigan needed. Beach walkers passed and cheerfully waved; nervous at first, Marilyn waved back. It seemed the distance and the darker hair – at least so far – was protecting her anonymity.

Later, she called Joe to wish him well. They continued a conversation begun the day before about him consulting a lawyer so Marilyn might sign something that let him sell her property and access her belongings as well as her finances. She also asked Joe to tell officials that she was alive and well, but wished to remain anonymous. At least then they could 'call off the search' so to speak.

Afterwards, she rang her sister Berniece, who knew that Marilyn was safe and living with a friend. The protection Marilyn had given over the years in keeping her sister's name out of the press would now be returned; Berniece promised never to reveal Marilyn's hiding place, and she knew this pledge would be honoured.

As Stella and Marilyn drank red wine into the evening, Marilyn considered telling her about Mary's visit. Wasn't this the perfect moment to share it, on the day Mary's son Jesus was said to have been born?

But something kept her quiet.

Was it shame, embarrassment, or fear of it reaching the press?

No – a desire to retain its sanctity.

*

Between Christmas and New Year, Stella drove them to Bullocks Fashion Square in Santa Ana so Marilyn could shop for clothes and other essentials. It occurred to her that just *being* with Stella – a woman known for *Icon* magazine – was risky.

Before they left the house, she tried on Stella's large glasses and some plain clothes, and practised walking around the rooms in a way that felt stiff. She tried not to smile. Stella said it would be a giveaway because she always threw her head back when she did.

Would this be her life now, never smiling while out in the world?

But laughter was such a big part of who she was.

'You still look a tiny bit like *her*,' said Stella. 'Try something else.'

So Marilyn wore Mother Superior's nun tunic and a headscarf; Stella disguised her identity too with large glasses and her own scarf.

Browsing the fashion rails – quietly, in a way she hoped was nun-like – Marilyn wondered what clothes to buy. The old Marilyn favoured capri pants and simple blouses when not working. Should she go for something different? In the end she chose jeans and loose-fitting shirts, and a couple of cotton dresses.

'Are you…?' An older lady in an elegant trouser suit touched Marilyn's arm.

She recoiled, then felt bad for her reaction.

'You're Marilyn, aren't you?' she whispered.

'Everyone says I look like her.' Marilyn tried to speak gruffly.

'I think you *are* her.' The lady smiled.

'I'm really not.' Gruff again.

'Don't worry, I won't say anything.' The lady touched Marilyn's cheek in such a tender way that she accepted the affection. 'We're not all vultures, you know. Some of us are rooting for you. You're lovely.' Then she headed for the nightwear department, looking back once and smiling warmly.

Marilyn smiled and quickly put her hand over her mouth to hide it.

This was the love she had enjoyed over the years; the genuine fans. But much as it warmed her, it wasn't real. They loved a version of her, one they created from the movie image, the well-lit poster art, and their own desire. But clearly, an essence of that character lingered.

She needed to go back; this was too risky.

'Someone recognised me,' she told Stella quietly at the till.

'It's going to happen. Do you want to go home?'

'Yes. But…'

'What?'

'I should... but not yet.'

Despite her fears, Marilyn was enjoying the world. She suggested they drive to Villa Nova on Sunset Strip for lunch. It wasn't far from her house and she almost asked Stella to go there first but, with regret, decided against it. She remembered the black cars that often pulled up outside, loitering there, sinister and silent. She couldn't help but look for them as they drove through the city, afraid – ridiculous as it was – that whoever they were, they were still watching her.

'Are you sure?' asked Stella when they arrived at the restaurant. 'It's very popular.'

Looking up at the peaked roof of the familiar building, Marilyn felt sad. 'I had my first date with Joe here.'

Part of her wanted the old life, to be able to visit her favourite haunts; but the other part knew the price to be paid for having that.

'Won't the staff recognise you, even in that tunic?'

'I hadn't eaten here for a while, before I left. But you're right. All we need is one photographer.' Marilyn would have to move on from so much more than her home if she wanted a quieter life. The feeling of it all being an adventure waned a little. This was the reality, one she had known for months, but only now did the intensity of such a change hit her.

They found a chain diner further along the Strip.

It was wonderful to be in a restaurant again, the hustle and bustle, the customer chat, the steam, the cups clattering, music Marilyn didn't recognise playing on the jukebox, and neon Coca Cola signs flashing on the wall. In her old life she had frequented the same places, ones where the staff knew who she was so gave her space. Now she noticed everything, seeing it as though for the first time, in technicolour, perhaps because she wasn't contending with fans chasing her.

Maybe it was also due to having seen the same walls for so long.

She was fascinated by the fancy automatic drip coffee maker they used, which Stella explained had been introduced to lots of diners that year.

'Tastes good,' Marilyn said when they found a booth and she sipped her espresso. 'I need one of these. What else is new? It's like I've been away ten years. How quickly things change.' In bed last night, she had read the book Stella loaned her, *The Feminine Mystique*. 'I'm up to chapter four of your book,' she said now. 'She's talking about the suffragettes and how they secured our right to vote and pursue a career.'

'Thank God they did,' said Stella.

'What's going on in the film world these days?'

'Things are finally changing a *little* for women. The studio system is starting to collapse.'

'*Really*? Why?'

'Partly due to the growth of television, partly due to outdated movies receiving less of a fanfare at the box office.'

'That's sad.'

'It is, but I think it's mainly because women have found their voices and are standing up for their rights. They want better pay, and more control over film roles.' Stella paused. 'There might be a place for you, after all.'

Marilyn shook her head. 'Let the new actresses enjoy it. I'm glad they might finally be treated as well as actors are. Maybe we'll even end up with more female producers and directors, who knows?' She looked at Stella. 'You forgot to include your magazine. That must be helping actresses too.'

'Maybe.'

'Don't be modest. I tried to be a strong woman but sadly they thought I was dumb. The irony is that they're the dumb ones to think that a character on screen is the *real* me.'

'You *are* a strong woman,' said Stella.

'I will be now.' Marilyn nodded as though to convince herself.

'It's so weird.'

'What is?'

Stella lowered her voice. 'Marilyn Monroe is in this diner and no one knows.'

The food arrived then and Marilyn jumped, afraid the waiter had heard, but he was lost in his own world and put two portions of fries, two hamburgers, and a side salad on the table.

'I meant to say earlier,' Stella continued, 'I read in the newspaper this morning about a local woman who's planning to open a sanctuary for abused women next year, somewhere in San Gabriel Valley. The first of its kind. She wants to offer women and their children up to forty-five days of help and counselling. It made me think more about your idea. Maybe you could get hold of her, get advice?'

Marilyn bit into her hamburger; it was divine. 'That's not a bad idea. I'll definitely need tips. The first thing though is getting my money, and then-'

A commotion by the door interrupted her words.

A familiar sound filled the air: the deep timbre of cameras flashing, some a single boom, some double-time like a healthy heartbeat.

Instinctively, Marilyn ducked down. In the past that attention – popping bulbs and cries of her name – had been exciting, but towards the end it had caused anxiety, especially when onlookers ripped at her hair, and journalists yelled intrusive, rude questions about her private life.

She put her hands over her ears, taken back to the moment she left a hospital after gallbladder surgery in 1961, sitting in a wheelchair, vulnerable and at the mercy of a mob who bombarded her with questions and took pictures from every angle. As always, she had smiled, and the press reported how pretty she looked.

Pretty miserable, she thought afterwards.

'It's OK.' Stella touched her hand. 'It's for someone else.' She peered over the booth chair. 'Oh my, it's Bette Davis.'

'Really?' Marilyn peered over the seat too.

It was. She looked tired, sad; perhaps the black coat and scarf she wore and the scraped-back hair just made her look that way. Marilyn felt protective of the star she had revered for many years.

'Poor Bette,' she said. 'Wonder what she's doing in a place like this?'

'Looks like she's with her daughter Barbara. I think she's sixteen now.'

They both heard Bette's instantly recognisable gravelly voice, irate, telling them to back off. 'Can the kid just get a damned burger?' she cried.

Another flash, a cacophony of questions, a glass falling to the floor and smashing, a look of fear on the teen girl's face. Some of the diners, realising that a star was in their midst, approached the scene, calling Bette's name.

Marilyn wanted to scream at them to give the woman some space but couldn't risk it; Bette knew her. They had been in *All About Eve* together, a defining film for Davis and a breakthrough role for Monroe. Though their relationship had been rocky on set – due to acute nerves, Marilyn needed take after take – they parted on reasonable terms.

Bette said, 'Good luck, kid, don't let it get you down.'

Eventually, the restaurant manager intervened, and they got Davis out to a waiting car, while journalists demanded to know how she felt about losing out on the Oscar, what it was like to be an aging actress, and whether she and Joan Crawford still hated one another.

'What do they mean about the Oscar?' Marilyn asked Stella.

'She was nominated for *Whatever Happened to Baby Jane?* but lost out to Anne Bancroft.'

'They were filming that when I left. Was it good?'

'Brilliant. Bette deserved to win. It wasn't helped by the fact that Joan Crawford – who was annoyed that she wasn't nominated – campaigned against Bette winning. It was quite vicious.'

Marilyn had never liked Crawford after she criticised a tightly fitted dress she wore at the Golden Globes in 1952. Crawford told the press after the ceremony: 'Monroe should remember that the public likes provocative feminine personalities, but it also likes to know that underneath it all, the actresses are ladies.'

'Poor Bette,' she said now. 'How cruel of that journalist to call her an aging actress. Aren't we all aging? We're certainly not getting younger each day, are we? They seem far more aggressive than I remember.' Marilyn had lost her appetite and put the remains of her hamburger back on the plate. 'Even if the studio system is changing, and women are making progress, it doesn't change the way we're viewed, does it?'

'Maybe it will,' said Stella, softly, 'in time.'

'I'm glad I left that life. But I'm sad that other young women might still see it as a glamorous world that brings happiness.'

'I know.' Stella didn't need to say the name *Moira*.

'Of course you do. Sorry for being morose. Can we go back now?'

Black moods like this had often descended suddenly in the past, triggered by criticism in a review or feeling bad that she hadn't been friendly enough to a young fan wanting an autograph. At least now she could give herself care, retreat to a place that was safe. And that was what she wanted to give other women.

*

On New Year's Eve Stella opened some vintage champagne.

'Here's to 1964.' She held her fizzing glass aloft.

'I never thought I'd be here.' Marilyn touched the glass with hers.

'I didn't either,' smiled Stella.

'No, I mean here, as in 1964. I feel like I wasn't supposed to make it this far. Like something was supposed to happen the night I left, and my departure stopped it.'

'What are you hoping for?' asked Stella.

'Sorry?'

'What do you wish for 1964?'

Marilyn thought about it. 'I need to leave Hollywood, move away altogether. I need to start whatever it is that happens somewhere else. I don't know where but that's my instinct.'

And finally, to the place of your ancestors.

This suddenly came to her now, nagging her to think more

about it.

She would, soon.

'I'd miss you,' said Stella quietly.

'You could come. What's stopping you?'

Stella looked around the room.

'No, you love your home,' said Marilyn. 'What do *you* hope for in 1964?'

'I'm not sure.' She held Marilyn's gaze. 'I think 1963 has ended pretty much incredibly.'

'Has it?'

'With you,' said Stella softly.

'You're so sweet. You won't be saying that in a few weeks when you've seen more of my moods and my bad temper.'

'We'll see.'

And 1964 arrived quietly with two women on a midnight beach toasting the stars.

37

Worldwide, January 1964

Marilyn Monroe's Brentwood home is up for sale. The Hollywood star went missing more than eighteen months ago, having last been seen August 4th, 1962. Monroe's housekeeper, Eunice Murray, continues to maintain the house despite not having heard from her famous employer. 'I still think she'll come home,' said Murray, 61. 'And I want the place to be clean when she does.'

Now, Morgan Real Estate Group are suggesting offers of no less than $100,000 for the Mexican style property on Fifth Helena Drive, which has a kidney-shaped pool and guest house. Monroe paid $75,000 for the four-bedroom property in January 1962. It's thought that the big price increase is due to the star having lived there for six months.

It is not known who instigated the sale, or why the house is on the market now.

'We expect to get a lot more than the asking price,' said Morgan realtor, James Van. 'Viewings have exceeded all expectation. People are fascinated with the mystery of Monroe. Who wouldn't want to live in her home?'

Los Angeles Times

Why do we love her so much? Has absence made the heart grow fonder, as the saying goes? It appears that, in the case of Marilyn Monroe, it has. Since her disappearance, an appetite for all things Monroe – in particular the more sordid side of her life – has grown more voracious. But we love her for the unexpected. For the side people often forget.

She got herself noticed far beyond Hollywood and in bigger ways than the sex bomb image that is the leitmotif of her iconography; she was so much more.

She read serious literature in private, Dostoevsky in particular. As early as 1950, studio executives warned her not to be seen reading politically radical books. She married playwright Arthur Miller when he was being investigated for his dalliance with communism. She supported the civil rights movement and was a founder member of the Hollywood branch of the Committee for a Sane Nuclear Policy.

Hugh Hefner describes her as their first Playmate of the Month, but though Marilyn appeared on both the cover and nude inside the magazine's first-ever centerfold, she never actually posed for the issue. The photos were taken four years earlier in 1949 when she was a struggling actress in need of cash; Tom Kelley paid her just $50. He later sold the shots to Hefner. Marilyn didn't see a cent.

She is a money-maker but was never a big money *earner.* She is still a lucrative asset, selling everything from books to purses to magazines to bras. But what cost when the woman – a *real* woman, not an image on a billboard with her skirt flying above her waist – has gone?

The Ladies' Home Journal – Special Winter Issue

Playmates revisited... ten years ago Marilyn Monroe, in all her glorious form, was the very FIRST Playmate of the Month. This month we celebrate her sensual body with new, hotter than hot, never-seen-before shots from the infamous nude swimming pool scene, which was filmed for unfinished movie *Something's Got To Give*.

Playboy

38

Various, 'Mother of God' documentary interviews (unedited), England, 2016

Georgina Shephard, 58, Leeds

'I was having a bad day.' Georgina sits in a garden, on the second ledge of a rockery made up of mismatched stones and bright flowers. The sky is grey. 'I was here actually. Yes, I was crying, right here. About the washing machine. It had broke. I mean obviously, *really*, it was over more than that, it always is, isn't it?'

Georgina looks at the camera and a soft voice – Nina's voice – asks if she can just look at her.

'I'm sorry, yes. I always wonder why they do that, you know, in these interviews, on the telly, but I guess it's a bit intense and full on having someone glaring down the camera at you.' She laughs, revealing a missing tooth. 'Where was I?'

'Here,' says Nina, off camera still. 'What were you really crying about?'

'It was…' Georgina picks at some soil; the camera zooms in on her dirty fingernails. 'It was the anniversary. I hadn't even realised. Then someone on the news said the date. I felt bad that I'd forgotten. How *could* I? And that was when the washing machine made an awful juddering noise mid-cycle and water went everywhere. I just left it. Couldn't deal. I came out here and sobbed me heart out.'

'What was the anniversary?'

Georgina looks at the camera and then seems to remember and returns her gaze to Nina. 'Of my boy. My baby boy.' She scratches her cheek leaving soil there. 'I've never shared him with anyone outside of my family before. He only lived for two hours. Sean we called him. It wasn't his birthday, no, that was a week ago. This was the anniversary of his funeral. That always hits me harder.' She shakes her head. 'And I forgot.'

She's quiet for a while. The camera captures the slow movements that the pain causes; a laboured blink, a shudder in the throat, a closed mouth.

'Tell me about Mary.'

'She was just there. Near the bins. I never even heard her come in.' Georgina laughs. 'I doubt I would've though cos she had bare feet. She was lovely, sort of glowed, like she had a candle in her heart. I should have been surprised – I mean, this was the bloody *Virgin Mary* – but I was overcome with this warm contentment.'

'Did she say anything?'

'She said something like you have nothing to fear. And then something in another language. And then she mentioned Sean and I fell apart. She said I had known pain but she had a message from him.'

Georgina puts her face in her hands. The camera respectfully keeps a distance. She looks up again.

'She said he was always with me.' Georgina is quiet for a while. 'Then she said something like, you care, or maybe you *should* care. Later on, I sort of forgot about that, and then I got a leaflet through my door about this place that until then I'd only vaguely been aware of. CARE.'

'Care?'

'No, *CARE*. The sanctuary place for women. Something just... well, something made me go and... well, I've been volunteering there ever since. Mary didn't directly ask me to. It's more like she... well, put the idea in my head somehow. And she'd given me a miracle too.'

'She had?'

'Yes. When I went back in the house, the washing machine was fixed. The water was gone. No word of a lie. And I came back out and there was a lovely pink rose on me rockery, sitting right on top of it.'

Melanie Paul, 27, Durham.

'It was dark. Like it always used to be here.'

Melanie sits on a bed in what is clearly a prison cell. There are family photos and children's drawings on the grimy wall behind her. Occasionally, noises from echoey corridors interrupt the scene; clanking doors, jangling keys, angry voices.

'The lights always used to go out and they took forever to replace the bulbs,' says Melanie. 'I could barely see her. Not Mary, she was dead bright. I mean Wren, when I gave birth to her. Here. In a prison cell. Can you imagine?'

She looks at whoever is off camera, her eyes damp. Then she speaks faster, like she wants to get it out.

'I've never told anyone the full details before, but here goes. OK. The light had broken and she was all milky in the glow from that small window that's too high in the wall to be any use. But it was enough to bathe her in moonlight. Her black hair was like the soft bristles on one of me small blusher brushes. There were loads of sounds, you know, the usual midnight noise, sobs, moans, calls for help, as I grunted and breathed and gripped this metal bed frame, expelling her. I could have called for help, but I didn't want it. I wanted her all to myself.'

Melanie smiles wistfully and positions her arms as though she's holding a baby; she rocks it.

'She cried, at first, snug against my chest, and then, I don't know, like she knew our unspoken pact, that it must just be me and her for now, she just stopped. She's gone now.' Melanie looks up and shrugs as though it doesn't matter after all. 'With my mum. This is no place for a baby. I could have had her here with me for six months but it wouldn't be fair to her. She's one now and I see her once a week for an hour. But I'll be out in two years and then I'll make it up to her.'

Melanie speaks without self-pity; the camera is kind to her, she looks angelic, despite the dirty hair and plain clothes.

'Anyway, Mary came the day after they took Wren. The lights were still broken but it didn't matter cos she was glowing. She was right there near the lavvy.' Melanie looks at the filthy toilet. 'She said this to me, and I remember it as clearly as if she was still here: *Words are just one language. The eyes speak another. The breath is bi-lingual. The hands are fluent. And when we care they all come together as one*. Isn't that lovely?'

'It is,' says Nina softly, off camera.

'I didn't know what she meant but I've thought about it ever since. Anyway, she was beautiful and she said she would keep the lights on for me if I volunteer at CARE when I get out of here. I'm gonna too. I already read about them online and there's this woman in here – Cheryl – who did some time there. And Mary must know I'm really gonna go and do it too because the lights flicker sometimes but…' Melanie puts a hand over her chest and glances up at the fluorescent bulb. '... well, in here, in my cell, they never go out anymore.'

Alice Sparks, 49, Goole.

'My period was late the day before Mary came to the foodbank and I told my Brad I felt like I was pregnant.'

Alice leans against a wall. She is overly made-up and has clearly put equal effort into styling her hair in a messy bun and choosing large gold hoop earrings that flash gold in the sunlight when she moves.

'You're forty-bloody-seven, he said to me, it'll be menopause. I insisted I felt... queasy ... odd... but he wouldn't have it. He raised his eyebrows and reminded me I'd never been able to get pregnant in twenty-five years of multiple positions, experiments, attempts. Why would you be now, he asked me, when I can barely get it up and you have a permanent headache? But I swear, I felt... *different*.'

She touches her hair as though to check it's still in position, looks at the camera – a position that clearly means the sun hits her eyes, because she squints – and quickly returns her gaze to the person off camera.

'Anyway, the day after that, still feeling dead queasy, I volunteered at the foodbank – I used to do two days. So I was out the back, taking some rubbish to the bins and having a moment, cos I really did feel crap, and there she was. The bloody Virgin Mary. I knew it was her right away.' Alice laughs. 'But I did think I was just seeing things, and it was all down to how odd I'd been feeling.'

'How did she look?' asks Nina softly, off camera.

'Radiant. Small. Smaller than I'd have imagined. I didn't understand her at first. Not because she spoke quietly – though she did and the world was noisy cos there's a main road just behind the wall at the back – but because she talked in this strange language I didn't understand. Then suddenly I did.'

Alice looks thoughtful. The camera follows her gaze to a porcelain tile nailed to the opposite wall; Mary is painted on it in soft ocean blues.

'She said I was pregnant. I almost sank to my knees. I had known, I had, but now I *really* did and I was delighted. I mean, I was forty-seven then, it wasn't ideal, but God, talk about waiting.

Talk about... well, a lovely, unexpected surprise. Who needs miracles? This was the biggest in the world yet it happened *before* she came.'

'Did you have the baby?'

'Oh, yes.' Alice's face lights up. 'Harry. He's one now. Me and Brad adore him. Mary told me he'd be a boy. She said she had a soft spot for baby boys – I mean she might not have used those exact words, she spoke a lot more eloquently than I do, but that was the gist. And it's understandable. Then she said... what was it? Something about it being great that I made sure they got food but once Harry was older I should make sure they got care. I never really thought any more about that but on the day I had Harry…'

Alice composes herself.

'The day I had my son, there was a leaflet for that big charity, CARE, on my hospital bedside cabinet. I swear, I looked around, thinking Mary must have put it there.'

'Did you tell anyone?' asks Nina.

'About the leaflet?'

'About Mary.'

Alice shakes her head.

'Not until now. I just thought... well, who'd believe me? The Virgin Mary near the bins at a foodbank. Ha. But when you said that other women had seen her too... well, I felt... validated. I mean, *I* know what I saw, but when you say the words aloud... you sort of question yourself. You ask, why me? What makes me so special?'

39

Flora wants to be shown

March 2016, Hull, England

Nina clicked stop on the documentary recordings. Flora pulled the earphones out. The real world crashed back in; the café, cups clinking, voices rising and falling, crackling train announcements, the smell of coffee and cinnamon.

'Why did you stop it?' she asked. 'I thought there were *four* interviewees.'

'There are.' Nina looked uncomfortable. 'Do you want another drink?'

'No, thank you. Can I watch it then?'

'This next lady didn't actually *see* Mary.' Nina couldn't quite look Flora in the eye, and she grew nervous. 'She… well, you'll see. I feel bad now. I should've…'

'Should've what? Who is she?'

'You know her.' Now Nina looked directly at Flora. Someone dropped a glass and it smashed but they both ignored it. 'I should have said from the start, but I thought you wouldn't come. Yet I knew you'd want to see this. I knew... it would matter. I won't be using it because of... well, what she ended up sharing.'

'What did she share?'

Nina ignored the question. 'She approached me on Twitter and I came straight up to Hull.' So Nina *hadn't* come just to see Flora. Why did she feel so sad about it? 'But now I want to hear... well, *your* side.'

'*My* side?' Black butterflies fluttered in Flora's tummy.

'Not side, as such. There isn't a battle. But your version, I guess.'

'Show me,' said Flora.

And Nina did.

40

'Mother of God' documentary (unedited), England, 2016

Allison Baker, 58, Hull

'She always ran in circles.' Allison lights a cigarette and looks at the camera even though a voice – Nina again – asks her not to. She sits in a worn chair, the kind that might have been stylish once upon a time, and blows smoke up towards a yellowing ceiling.

'Circles. Yes. Not back and forth, like someone in one of those races... what do you call them? The ones when you go back and then forward and there are other runners, and you swap something?'

Off camera, Nina says, 'A relay race?'

'Yes, that's the one. No, she never ran like that. She always ran in a circle. I guess it started when she was twelve or thirteen. Not sure. She wasn't always with me, of course. She was half with me and half with her grandma. Maybe seventy-thirty with her grandma. It was hard. I tried, before you judge.'

'No judgment here,' says Nina quietly.

'But anyway, when she turned thirteen she *was* with me. She had been for about a year. I had to totally change the living arrangements in the house. It took a bloody week, all that shifting of furniture and rearranging beds and stuff. Her room was above the lounge, you see, and I couldn't stand it anymore. I had the little 'un, my other daughter, just six months old then, and it woke her, cos she was in the next room. And Stan, my boyfriend then, would be trying to watch *Never Mind the Buzzcocks* of an evening and it'd be thump, thump, *thump*, just like these pervy neighbours we had back then.' Allison pauses, cigarette dangling precariously. 'Can I say pervy?'

'Yes,' says Nina. 'you can say anything you like.'

Allison inhales hard on the cigarette and continues. 'She wasn't fat, that's not why the thumping was loud. She was never likely to be, was she, with all that bloody running? But she was tall. Close to five-foot-six at that age, about five foot nine now. I always thought, *there must be a right tall gene in me family somewhere.*' She pauses. 'I dunno, of course – I was adopted. Could be any bugger she takes after!'

'Did you ever look for your birth family?' Nina, off camera.

'No. Fuck 'em. Didn't want me. Anyway, to get to my point, we moved her into the room above the garage then, so there was nothing but junk below her, and no bugger got disturbed. It got cold in winter, but she never seemed to feel it. How would she? She just ran and ran and ran, round and round and round. I get dizzy just thinking about it.'

'Why do you think she liked running so much?' asks Nina.

'Hard to say.'

'Did you ever ask her?'

Allison shrugs. 'Teenagers don't like you to speak to 'em, do they? She went back to her gran – that's Lil, me adoptive mother – about six months later, with her sister too. I was knackered. All of it. Too much.'

'You must have an idea about the running,' tries Nina again.

'So she saw Mary, did she?' Allison isn't going to be pushed. She lights a second cigarette with the first. 'She always did like to tell stories, to be fair. She'd read 'em to her little sister for hours. But it seems some people believe her.'

'Do you?'

'Well, she hasn't told me herself, has she? She doesn't bother with her old mother that much. I don't mind, I have a life, my friends, the bingo, my boyfriend Ned. I taught my girls to have independence and it's the best thing I ever did.'

'Maybe the running was... an attempt to escape from something?'

Allison stubs the cigarette out in an overflowing, brass ashtray and glares at Nina. Then she looks at the camera, as though to test them. Finally, she rubs her forehead and looks at her feet.

'You can't run from shit forever, can you? God knows, I've tried. I know what you're all thinking, I can see it. Me here in me council house, two daughters who hardly ever come. You think I'm scum. But I never had much. Not when I was a kid, though me mother did love me and do her best. I got pregnant real young but didn't keep it either – like birth mother like daughter.' She sighs and looks at Nina again. 'Then I got caught with Flora at twenty-three, which is still young, I know. But you never expect 'em to be *twelve*, do you?'

'What do you mean?' asks Nina.

'I mean, she was heading for thirteen, but still.'

'Who?'

'Flora.' The word is a bark. 'She had a baby at twelve.'

'Oh.'

'Yeah, *oh*, alright. You don't expect it, do you? I sent him packing of course, bloody animal.'

'Who?' Nina's question is almost inaudible.

'Fucking Santa Claus, who do you think? My boyfriend. I had no idea. It was only once, not that I'm saying that's fine, and he was drunk and I think he thought Flora was a younger me, again not that I'm excusing… But I got rid.'

'And what happened?' Nina's voice is still quiet.

'To him?'

'To *Flora*.'

'She had the baby. It was too late not to. Shit. I've never talked about this.' Allison glares at Nina. 'You're a witch, you got this out of me. You did something to me. You made me talk. You came to ask about Flora and Mary, you said it was about that, and you've tricked me. I don't want to talk anymore. I want you all to go.'

41

Flora runs

March 2016, Hull, England

Flora barely heard her mother's final words.

The black butterflies that fluttered earlier now swirled in a frenzy as though desperate to escape her stomach. She couldn't see beyond the frozen clip that had captured her mother's face; her eyes were half shut as though she wanted to disappear.

How could she have disclosed this long-kept secret, not only to another person, but in front of cameras? She could understand her mother attention-seeking and doing the interview, but this, when *she* had insisted they keep the baby a secret all these years.

Now, it was out.

She saw it in a flash. The birth. The blood. The baby, beautiful, a head of wild hair and sleepy blue eyes. She tasted marmalade, bitter and tart. And she wanted to throw up.

But at least her mother hadn't shared the full story.

'Are you OK?' Nina put a hand on Flora's arm.

'You can't share that clip,' cried Flora.

'I'd really love to hear about this from you.' Nina was obviously ignoring her request. 'I felt such compassion for you and it made me think that your Mary story is extra special – you have this in common with her. You both became mothers very young. Won't you reconsider talk-'

'Hang on.' Flora shook her head, pushed her cup and the laptop away. 'When my mum got in touch with you, it must have been a few days ago, yes? But they only announced yesterday that

I'm the Mary girl. How did she know about it?'

'She knows Psychic Pat.'

'Shit. Hull is such a small city. Everyone knows everyone. Why the hell did you talk to her?'

'I knew you were declining interviews so when she contacted me on Twitter – well, it felt like a gift, I can't lie.' Pause. 'And then she told us about the baby.'

'She had no right.' Flora stood. 'This is private.'

'I agree. But do you maybe think it would help others who've been through the same?'

Flora grabbed her bag. 'Why is that my responsibility? Do *not* share that clip.'

'Tell me privately, without cameras, just us. And then we can work out what you do share in front of the camera.'

Neil came into her head, that night, their intimacy. *I already told someone,* she thought. *That's all the soul-bearing I want to do.*

Flora realised something. 'Did you pay her?'

'A small fee,' admitted Nina. 'Not anything like what the Mary women got.'

'Now I know why she didn't get in touch with me when she found out I'm the Mary girl.'

'What do you mean?'

'She knew she'd done this. She felt guilty.' Flora looked at Nina. 'Don't contact me again. Don't use my mother's footage.'

Then she ran.

Ran like she hadn't for years.

Ran like she had aged thirteen during a two-year obsession that consumed her, when she'd stubbed her little toe so many times on wall corners it turned black, when her knees ached at night, and her soles chafed with every step. She had begun doing it at school when her feet wouldn't stay still, which was great when she won the Sports Day races, but not so much when she sprinted out of the classroom on a whim. She got sent to a school counsellor who asked if she was running away from or towards something. She'd said she was running *with* it.

Now, she did the same – she ran and ran and ran with her anger and pain, hoping it would come loose and fall away.

When Flora stopped, she had no idea where she was. She sat on the stone steps of a solicitor's building and put her head in her hands. Her whole life she had been running from the event that changed her. Now, twelve-year-old Flora was screaming to be acknowledged. She couldn't run anymore.

Where would she go anyway?

She didn't think she could go home; it wasn't fair to burden Bella when she was in such a state. Should she go to Neil? She didn't even know where he lived.

Footsteps, too close.

She looked up. A man, smartly dressed, bald, sweating.

'Smile, love,' he said. 'It might never happen.'

'Fuck you,' she spat.

'Nice,' he sneered.

Something buzzing then. Too early for wasps. The bag. In there.

Phone.

Flora scrambled for the device, saw Bella's name flashing. So many times in the past this had meant her sister's distress, Flora calming her, and then rushing to wherever she was to make sure she was safe.

'Bella,' she cried. 'Are you OK?'

'Of course.' Pause. 'Are *you*? You don't sound it.'

'I was just worried about you.'

'No need. But, Sis, there's a priest here. Father Colahan.'

'*What*?'

'He wants to talk to you about Mary.'

'No.' This was Flora's immediate reaction. 'Tell him I'm not interested.'

'He's really keen.'

'I don't care.'

'No problem.' Bella paused again. 'When will you be home?'

'I don't know.'

'You don't know?' Bella sounded concerned.

'I... yes. I'll... I'll talk to you later.'

'Wait, whe-'

Flora hung up. She saw that there was a message from Neil.

Hi Arsehole, sorry I didn't respond, family crisis. That's why I left early last night. Lot on mind. When you next in work? X

She smiled at the kiss.

When was she next in work?

She couldn't think straight. Tomorrow night?

Suddenly the thought of going there – of real life, of drunken men and abusive customers – had Flora queasy. Was she having a breakdown? Why now? Her mother's betrayal? She felt weak, shaky, yet without feeling. She should respond to Neil's message but she couldn't summon the effort needed.

She stood, unsteady.

Where was she going?

She didn't know. She began walking. There was no energy left to run.

Maybe it was time to stop running and turn around and look back.

She walked past the maritime buildings and marina and shopping centres, which blurred as though they were a painting not yet dry. Her feet led; she followed. They stopped at a familiar building; the place that had helped Bella, the place that had become a part of her imminent future, the place where she was the *calm lady*.

Flora stood where Mary's girls had been directed.

CARE. Her feet had brought her to where she should be.
And then her heart arrived too.
Closely followed by the past.

42

Marilyn has been making plans

Near Paradise Cove Beach, Los Angeles, August 1964

Marilyn opened the door to hordes of reporters.

Their questions were indecipherable in the chaos. They hurled aggressive words at her, held pens to notepads ready to record anything said. Panic rooted her to the floor. This was it; she had been discovered. Her haven with Stella would be over. Her space to grow would be done. She would have to run away again. She felt sick.

She tried to close the door.

'What did Elizabeth say to you?' yelled one man, foot lodging it open.

'Does she care that she wrecked a family?' cried another, face sweaty.

'What have you got to say about it?' from another.

Marilyn realised two things: one, there were no flashing cameras, so they were not here for a star, and two, they had come to interrogate Stella, and thought she was her. Last night Stella had been out with Elizabeth Taylor, who had caused quite a scandal by marrying Richard Burton following their affair. Elizabeth had been chatting exclusively to Stella and the other journalists apparently weren't happy.

It gave them no right to be here though.

'Get the hell away from my door,' cried Marilyn.

She kicked a foot, and slammed it shut.

Once composed, she giggled despite the shock. Marilyn Monroe had been right in front of them – wearing an old dressing gown, make-up free, and with mousy hair – and they had missed the scoop of a lifetime. Then her laughter died. It was too much. The invasion served only to further prove how much she cherished this precious freedom.

Anonymity gave so much, and asked for nothing. But staying hidden was an effort. Every time she left Stella's house, Marilyn had to don a disguise, and had to avoid crowded places, past haunts, her old world.

It was no life.

But she had been making plans.

An hour after the intrusive reporters, another arrival; a new passport.

She opened the package and sat on the wooden decking studying it, feeling a curious sense of detachment. The photograph didn't look like her; not like any of the *hers*, not her then and not her now. With the name change done – now Marilyn Miracle, which her sister Berniece had cried with delight over – she had renewed it so she could travel.

She had made sure the picture taken was as un-Monroe as possible. She wore no make-up and flattened her hair with cream. The requirement that the applicant didn't smile meant she looked almost severe.

'It came,' she cried when Stella returned from another interview.

This time, the interviewee had been Julie Andrews. Julie was a British stage actress who had undertaken her first film role, and *Mary Poppins* had been released that weekend to immediate critical acclaim.

'I look like a strict schoolteacher, don't I?' Marilyn laughed, holding out the document.

Stella grinned too. 'It doesn't even look like you – or *her* I should say. But that's good. You'll easily get through any airport without raising a fuss, even with your first name. And you've deflected many an *almost* recognition now.'

'I did earlier. A group of reporters turned up, wanting to know about Elizabeth Taylor. They thought I was you. I managed to get rid of them.'

'Bloody vultures. Are you OK?' Stella was concerned.

'Yes. I'm just glad I'm no longer their target.'

Stella studied Marilyn. 'It's weird, but you're still changing physically. It's like you're discarding the final remnants of what it was to be her. You hold yourself differently. It's natural. And the longer hair really suits you.'

'They always kept it super short to maintain it. Bleach is a killer of hair. I love that I can finally grow it out a little.' Marilyn touched it with a smile. 'Mostly, I don't fear being recognised as much. People who spot me now just think I just *look* like her. But this morning was a bit of a wake-up call. Reminded me how easily I might be found.'

She had chanced a trip out alone a few months ago, borrowing Stella's car, wearing her nun tunic, hair scraped back. In a store, a woman had studied her and then approached cautiously, said, 'Gee, has anyone ever told you, you look like Marilyn Monroe?'

'I get it a lot, yes.' Marilyn thought it was best to go with that idea.

'If you cut and dyed your hair, and you were a bit younger, you could pass for her,' the woman continued.

'Maybe I'll get my hair done.' She winked. 'I might pass for thirty.'

'Oh, you would. You're actually quite pretty.'

Marilyn had taken her blouses to the till, smiling at the 'actually quite pretty'. Anyone else might be upset at such a backhanded compliment, but she was pleased. *Quite pretty* was what she had often been called before Monroe. *Quite pretty* when she was a girl-next-door model. *Quite pretty* by her first husband, Jimmie, who her carers had married her off to when she was barely sixteen.

Quite pretty came from a simpler life; it could mean a simpler future.

'How was Julie Andrews?' asked Marilyn now.

'She was lovely. She's finding the transition from preparing for a stage performance to preparing for a movie role hard, especially since she has her baby daughter with her and is breastfeeding.'

It was great to hear about that other world, but it only reenforced how glad Marilyn felt to have abandoned it. She felt sad for Julie, even without knowing her. She couldn't imagine being in a strange country, with a new baby, knowing how the studio could treat actresses. At the thought of a baby she put a hand over her tummy; remembered the ones she had lost. She had often wondered in these last few months if maybe now was her chance – she was only thirty-eight, after all.

But who could she date?

They would eventually find out who she was.

Marilyn put her passport on the wicker table. She wasn't interested in a lover, not right now. She had other things to think of.

'Do you want coffee?' asked Stella.

'Sure, honey. Thanks.'

After a moment Stella brought two mugs out.

The beach was sweltering; heat shimmered above the sand as though caressing it with nervous hands. The high fence afforded them some shade on the decking, a place they often sat, contemplating the world. During the last eight months, they had fallen into a pleasant routine; Stella was often out and about on assignments, so Marilyn kept house, enjoying it immensely. She experimented with cooking, failing more often than she succeeded, but eventually perfecting Julia Child's Boeuf Bourguignon after watching episodes of *The French Chef* on daytime TV.

She devoured the books on Stella's shelves, particularly JD Salinger and Daphne du Maurier, and she walked for hours along the beach, both for the fresh air and to remain trim. Then she and Stella often talked late into the night, about the past, their sisters, their hopes for the future.

The only thing Marilyn hadn't shared was Mary.

She couldn't believe it had been two years since she saw her.

Two years since she abandoned the superstar life she had created.

Two years since she walked around her beloved house.

It had sold in February, quickly, and for a great price, fetching $110,000 in the end. Joe transferred the money to a bank account opened in her new name. Marilyn knew it had gotten a good price because she had lived there and wished she could have visited the place one last time. But that would have been too risky. The surprise profit, however, meant she would be comfortable for a long time.

But she didn't only want the money for herself.

Marilyn invested in *Icon* magazine despite Stella's argument. She also gave Joe money to send a large payment towards her mother's care; it couldn't be done in her name or the care staff might alert officials. Marilyn so wanted to reach out to her mother, tell her she was still around, and that she still thought of her. But apparently she was so unwell these days that she barely knew her own name, let alone who her daughter was.

It wasn't worth confusing her further.

Alone, Marilyn wrote in the black notepad Mother Superior had given her, scribbling ideas and thoughts and observations, as was her way. It was emotional to see again the violet Sister Joy had given her, pressed between the back pages.

One night she wrote a list, numbering the items in a column. The pen ran out on the number four. It had taken her back to that last night, to the date, to her house number with the missing four.

Sit up and take notice, she thought.

She realised that the list was what she planned to do, and that she had no idea beyond the first three things: *sell house, change name, get passport.*

What was number four?

She often read old lines in her notepad; the words she had put down while living in the convent.

One line struck her: *I'm here, between worlds, not her, not me, not yet, but she still haunts me and she always will.*

Now, Marilyn sipped the coffee Stella had given her.

'You're quiet,' said Stella. They had come to know one another well, sensing when the other needed space, when comfort was required, when to come forward, and when to step back.

'My passport made it all real.'

'Made what all real, Mar?'

'The new me. The freedom I now have. I can *go* places. I know I had that moment on the doorstep but I feel lucky that it's otherwise been relatively easy to just walk away from it all.'

'I wouldn't say it's been easy,' said Stella kindly. 'You've had to sacrifice the house you adored and seeing people you love.'

'I've found new people to love.' Marilyn raised her eyebrows at Stella.

'You're not too bad yourself either,' she said.

'I feel... not blue. More thoughtful. Like, I can't waste any more time. I have money now, I need to get on with whatever I'm supposed to be doing.' Marilyn shrugged. 'Maybe I'd have left my old life sooner if I'd known it was possible.'

'What really made you leave that night? I remember you said you felt like something bad was supposed to happen.'

Marilyn still didn't feel like sharing Mary, and certainly not the horrible vision of her own body lying dead on the bed. If she gave the moment with Mary away, it might lose its shine; and if she shared the death scene, it might come true.

'There were signs,' she said. 'You know me and my signs.'

'You just said that you need to *get on with whatever you're supposed to be doing.*' Stella sipped her coffee. 'Not what you *want* to do. It's as though you're following a higher power.'

'Did I ever tell you about my brief trip to Ireland?'

'You're changing the subject.'

Marilyn knew she was but continued. 'It was just a stopover, at Shannon airport, barely more than an hour or two. We were coming back from England after filming *The Prince and the Showgirl.*'

'We?'

'Arthur and me. We'd been arguing. Things had been tough on set. You probably know, the press shared a lot of it. Word got out that we were there and hordes of fans broke through security – I didn't mind, I always enjoyed chatting to everyday people but Arthur was grumpy about it.'

'Why?'

'Well, aside from that he disliked my fans, I wanted to linger longer in the airport, especially at the duty free shop, but he wasn't interested in funding a shopping spree and he moved me on to a lounge to wait for our plane back to the States. I felt sad. Not only that my marriage was breaking down but that I didn't have time to stay and explore.' Marilyn looked out to sea as though she might somehow see the Emerald Isle from their spot. 'My ancestors are from Ireland, you know. My grandmother – that's my mother's mother – could apparently trace her ancestry back to Dublin. How exciting is that? And I felt it, you know. Something, in that brief time there. I was... pulled.' Marilyn shrugged. 'I wanted to go back, but I never did.'

And finally, to the place of your ancestors.

This phrase came to Marilyn.

And today her passport had arrived.

'Shall I make us some lunch?' asked Stella.

'Sure, whatever you fancy.' When she had gone, Marilyn whispered, 'And finally to the place of your ancestors.'

43

Marilyn is restless

Near Paradise Cove Beach, Los Angeles, August 1964

Marilyn was restless. She had been in the days since her passport arrived. She woke early, unable to go back to sleep, thoughts racing.

One morning she picked the early newspaper up from the step and skimmed through the pages while sitting on the deck with a strong coffee. The beach was quiet at this time, the sun gentle. She paused at one of the headlines: *The Scandal Of Ireland's Unmarried Mothers*. Shaking her head at the misogyny, she read the piece.

It described the pregnant women admitted to Mother and Baby homes. They ranged in age from twelve to forty-plus, with admissions among those under eighteen rising sharply. Some pregnancies were the result of rape; some women had mental health problems; some had an intellectual disability. However, the majority were indistinguishable from any other Irish women, the only difference being that they became pregnant while unmarried and had failed to secure the support of their family or their child's father. Many were destitute and feared their pregnancy becoming known to the community.

Mother and Baby homes were, apparently, superior to county homes where women with venereal diseases or criminal convictions were sent, as were 'delinquent' pregnant girls. The care given there was grossly inadequate. Marilyn found the descriptions distressing. The writer of the piece suggested that had these girls not 'sinned' they might not be 'paying' in this way.

'Morning.'

It was Stella, hair messy, steaming coffee in hand.

'Sorry if I woke you,' said Marilyn.

'Up early again?'

'My brain won't switch off.' Marilyn threw the newspaper on the table.

'Was that the piece about the Mother and Baby homes?' Stella sat opposite.

'Yes! It's so judgmental and nasty.' Marilyn realised there were tears on her cheeks and viciously wiped them away. 'You can tell the journalist thought those women deserved punishment and that they should be grateful of any place to stay. What about the absent fathers?' Her voice grew shrill. 'What about the predators that left thirteen-year-old girls pregnant? No one writes about *them*. Women are always sent away because they're a scandal. There's no choice. No *care*.'

'I agree.' Stella spoke quietly.

'Sorry, it really gets to me, honey.'

'It should. It's appalling. I read it and immediately wanted to fly over there and report it properly but my readers are only interested in stars.'

'Ireland has been haunting me,' Marilyn said more softly. 'I hope none of my ancestors ever got treated that way. If I had a daughter, and she found herself pregnant and alone, I'd *never* let her go into a place like that.'

'But Ireland's a Catholic country, Mar. These women have little choice.'

Marilyn thought about the nuns' compassion. She had seen the good side of God with them, but here was the cruel, angry God who punished women for things that they hadn't done. 'Babies need their mothers,' she said quietly. 'Not some stranger.'

'They need *a* mother,' said Stella sadly, with an emphasis on the *a*.

'Children who are abandoned require *everything*. And yet, sadly, they often end up with little.'

'That's profound,' said Stella softly.

'I suppose it is.' Marilyn realised she had been rambling and her friend looked sad. 'Are you OK, Stell?'

She nodded but didn't answer.

'You're not. What is it?'

Stella looked out to sea.

'You can tell me,' said Marilyn.

'My daughter doesn't have her mother,' she said gently.

'You have a…?'

'I *did*. She was adopted.' Stella finished her coffee; Marilyn waited. 'I was twenty-five. It's not that young really, but it is when you're alone, when the father isn't interested. She was taken. By an English couple.'

'Oh, Stella, that must have been so hard.' Marilyn knelt by her friend as she so often had during their emotional sharing.

'It was. She was beautiful. Tiny. I held her for a *lifetime*.' Stella put her face in her hands. 'It felt that way, but it was a moment. And then she was... gone. What could I have given her? It was before the magazine, I was living at home, and my parents, they're religious. I would have been quite the scandal.'

'You did what you thought was right for your daughter,' said Marilyn.

'I don't know, but I think she's happy. I get a letter once a year, and it's obvious she is loved. She's seven now and doing well. They're not a rich family, but they wanted her…' Stella looked at Marilyn. 'You said children who are abandoned require everything. I guess they do. They need extra to make up for not having their birth mother.'

'Oh, I didn't mean that,' cried Marilyn. 'I wasn–'

'It's fine. They probably *do* need more care than most.'

'And you gave her that. By doing what you felt was best for *her*.'

'Maybe. But the *guilt*.'

The two women held one another, no more words needed.

Later, Marilyn found some. She finally told Stella about Mary. If her dear friend could share such a painful, intimate secret, then so could she.

*

The following night, as the sun sank exhausted into the ocean and while Stella was sound asleep, Marilyn kicked off her shoes, lay on her bed, and opened her notepad. She wrote: *Children who are abandoned require everything.* Then she added: *More care.* And: *Women are always sent away because they're a scandal.*

'No choice, no care,' she whispered.

She played with the words, circling the word *care* and underlining it.

'Why should women be *sent* away?' she mused.

She reread the first sentence over and over.

Then she crossed out the words *who* and *are*, leaving: *Children abandoned require everything.* She couldn't get it out of her head, sure there was something she wasn't seeing; it teased, like when she tried to learn her lines and the words wouldn't stick in her head.

And then she saw it.

The first letter of each word made CARE. Marilyn smiled. None of it made sense. But she felt something important had just happened. She fell asleep with the pen in her hand, one page open on her scrawl.

In the morning, she was up early and made a pot of coffee.

When Stella came down, sleepy, Marilyn asked how she was.

'I'm good,' she said. 'Slept well. Must have been sharing that stuff with you the other night. And Mary, I still can't quite get my head around it.'

'I'm glad if I helped in any way.' Marilyn felt guilty over what she was about to say; the idea that had lodged in her brain at dawn. 'I think I'll go to Ireland,' she said.

'*What*?' Stella was fully awake. 'Now?'

Marilyn laughed. 'Not right now.'

'*Ireland*?' Stella sat on one of the kitchen bar stools and poured a large coffee.

'I feel it's where I'm supposed to go.'

'But do you know anyone there? Where would you stay?'

'I'd book a hotel, and then just get a feel for the place. Dublin, I think.' Marilyn shrugged. She realised that said aloud it was madness, but as the sun rose earlier it had felt like the most natural place in the world to go.

'What is it you think you'll find?' Stella continued.

'I'm not sure.'

'But on your own? A strange country. Do you want me to come?'

'Maybe once I get settled but first I-'

'Get *settled*?' Now Stella looked horrified. 'You're intending to *stay*?'

'I don't know.' Marilyn laughed and hugged her friend. 'I know I sound crazy, but this feels like the next step. If I don't like it, I'll come back. Nothing is set in stone.'

'Aren't you nervous about being recognised while you're alone.'

'Every month, every year, I'll age a little more; and every month, every year, the press writes less about me, probably even less so in Ireland.'

'You'll never be forgotten,' said Stella sadly.

'Maybe. But now I'm a bit more invisible.'

'And that's really what you want?'

'Yes. It is.'

*

During the following weeks, Marilyn set her plans in motion.

A local travel agent, Gloria, sorted everything out over the telephone, the flights, the visa, and three weeks at a brand new hotel in Dublin. Marilyn didn't want to fly First Class or stay in a penthouse though; that risked drawing attention.

She read books about the city and other areas, shivering a little when she saw that Mary had appeared to the townspeople of Knock, County Mayo in 1879. But it made sense – it was such a strong Catholic country.

Marilyn asked her sister Berniece what she knew about their Irish ancestry.

'Mother got her red, curly hair from that side of the family,' said Berniece. 'And look at yours – that natural curl, the way it turns russet when the sun touches it. I was always a little jealous of your hair. I'm so glad you're back to that colour again.' Pause. 'You're really going there? Shall I come with you?'

'I think I should do it alone,' said Marilyn.

It was time.

44

Worldwide, Autumn 1964

Would there still be a place for Marilyn Monroe in today's Hollywood?

More than two years after her disappearance, with speculation still sparking and occasionally catching fire, it feels more like a world alien to the innocent breathiness of a 1950s blonde bombshell.

The cultural and political growth in recent years means that cinema has undergone radical change. With competition from television, independent producers, and foreign art films, the studio system has crumbled, and the Production Code has been replaced by a new rating system. Movies are grittier, musicals – aside from the grotesquely successful *Mary Poppins* – are dying, and the golden actresses are now less blonde, more brunette, more savvy, and more in control of their careers.

Could Monroe have competed with the quirky, strong-willed and eccentric Shirley MacLaine? How about the Tony Award winning Anne Bancroft? Perhaps Monroe, with that infamous innate instinct, sensed her time was up, and she left before she could be left behind.

Los Angeles Times

No one likes to say goodbye to someone they love. But I think, after more than two years of speculation, it's time to do that with our dear friend, Marilyn Monroe.

Stella Cruz, *Icon* magazine, 1964

45

Flora whispers abracadabra

March 2016, Hull, England

Flora made it through the metal gates at CARE and headed up the corridor, not sure where she was going, or what she was doing there.

Unaware that it was the spot where Amelia had cowered a week ago, she suddenly found that she couldn't walk anymore. It was terrifying; like someone had stuck a pin in her chest and all the life had evaporated in one puff. She sank, and began to shake.

Footsteps then.

'You OK?' A familiar voice. A warm hand on her back. 'Oh, it's *you*. My calm lady.' Pause. Louder: '*Carla*! I think she's ill.'

'*Who*?' came a distant response that Flora also recognised.

'Flora!'

More footsteps. Another familiar voice near her ear. 'You're not supposed to be here until next week.'

Flora's teeth were chattering so badly she feared cracking them. Even if words had formed coherently in her head, she couldn't have spoken them.

'Let's help her up,' said the voice Flora realised was Carla.

Two sets of arms helping then. Moving her, carefully, like she was frail. Into a small room with a bed where they sat, one on either side. Flora couldn't look up, couldn't speak.

'I think she's in shock,' said the voice she knew was Amelia.

'Do you want some sweet tea?' Carla again. Flora couldn't answer. 'I'll make some. Amelia, stay with her. She likes you.'

And then it was the two of them. Amelia's arm was light on Flora's back. The quiet was nice. Perhaps Amelia knew this because she didn't speak, she just stroked Flora's spine. Carla returned with a steaming cup of tea and a plate of toast.

'I put some marmalade on for the sugar,' she said.

Flora felt sick at the sight of the orange spread. 'I can't eat that!' She pushed the plate, sending it to the floor. 'Can't you just let me *be*?'

'Yes,' said Carla calmly. 'We can leave you to rest.'

As though these words had given her permission to surrender, Flora sank back and closed her eyes; she remembered reading about terminally ill patients needing consent from loved ones to 'let go and pass to the other side'. But Flora only wanted rest, not death. She heard the women move away. Heard Carla tell Amelia in a low voice that Flora was here to *use* their service rather than provide it.

'I wonder if it's because of Mary,' whispered Amelia.

'What do you mean?'

It sounded like they had moved to the other side of the door but Flora could still hear them talking. 'I know she hasn't said owt on socials.' That was Amelia. 'Maybe she hates the attention now everyone knows it was her?'

'I don't think it'll be going away anytime soon.' Carla. 'There's that documentary coming about women who've seen Mary. I saw that the producer was in Hull – I wonder if it was for Flora?'

They moved away. Flora didn't drift into sleep but was pulled under by a current of memories and secrets and fears.

She dreamt about that day; the birth.

She wasn't in a hospital because her mum had insisted they hide the pregnancy.

'It'll ruin you if they see,' she'd said, not unkindly. 'People don't forget shit like this. They'll call you a slag, even though Malcolm's the animal. I should know, I've been called one. No, you'll stay home at the end and I'll help you at the birth. It'll be fast, I reckon – mine was with you. We'll do it together.'

They did.

The contractions began before daylight on a cold morning when ice clung to the inside glass of the windows, and the heating didn't come on because her mother hadn't paid the bill. Flora bore it alone for an hour, but when it was too much, she woke her mum, and they moved into the bathroom.

'Get in the bath,' she said. 'It'll clean up better.'

She laid towels in there for warmth, but Flora barely noticed. Fire surged through her almost teen body with every tightening, building to a fiery crescendo. The only mercy was its brevity; the birth was quick, as her mother had predicted, but with that speed came intensity that made Flora scream.

A Marilyn Monroe mirror hung above the sink; her mum had got it in a tacky gift shop in Scarborough. The glass was warped and Flora thought Marilyn looked as though she was throwing her head back in pain rather than ecstasy.

They were united in it.

Flora concentrated on Marilyn's face as she pushed her baby out.

And then afterwards, marmalade on toast.

Emptiness.

*

Flora woke in darkness, disorientated, mouth dry.

Then she remembered she was at CARE; she was safe. No one could visit here, no journalist, no priest, no well-dressed documentary maker. She must have been asleep hours, and felt better for it. Then, as every day upon waking, she thought of Bella. She must be so worried. Flora found her phone. Ten missed calls from her sister and a message from Neil.

She read it: *You OK, Arsehole? X*

Flora hadn't responded to the other one yet.

But first, Bella.

She answered after one ring. '*Flora*? Where the hell are you?'

'I'm at CARE,' she said simply.

'You've been gone nine hours. I've been worried sick.'

Flora realised that being overprotective of her sister over the years had created a situation where Bella panicked if Flora wasn't immediately available.

'I had to get away,' said Flora. With the distance a phone afforded, she felt able to be honest. 'You know the woman making that Mary documentary? She found me at the club, last night. I went to meet her this morning.'

'Why didn't you say?' Bella sounded huffy.

'Because I'm not doing the documentary. But Bella, she showed me some of the women who've been interviewed.' Flora paused. 'One was Mum.'

'What? Wait... has she seen Mary too?'

'No.' Flora wanted to laugh at the absurdity but couldn't. 'It's just because she's my mother. I... the thing is…'

'Yes?'

'She talked about something that I... never have.'

'I don't understand.'

Maybe it was time for Flora to share what had happened. Her sister was an adult now. She could take it. But no; it would mean telling Bella the full story, the story that their mother had edited, thank God, in her interview, leaving out a vital aspect.

'I'm scared Nina will use the footage, even though I told her not to. What rights do I have? She paid her so she can probably do what she wants.'

'What's the thing that Mum shared?' asked Bella.

'Not on the telephone.'

'Can I come and see you?'

'Tomorrow,' said Flora. 'I'm so tired, I can't see straight.' She paused. 'I think I've had a breakdown.'

'Oh, Sis, let me be there for you like you always have for me.'

'No,' cried Flora. 'That isn't how it's meant to be.'

'Why do you get to do the nurturing?' demanded Bella. 'You don't have a monopoly on it. You've always looked out for me cos you're older, but I'm not a child.'

'You're right,' she said. 'But give me today. Then you can fuss as much as you want tomorrow.'

Silence. Then, 'OK.'

'Make sure you lock the door tonight,' said Flora.

'I *will*. You just look after you.'

Flora opened Neil's message again. Was it terrible that she longed to see him even though she had turned Bella away? Perhaps it was because there wasn't any responsibility involved. Perhaps because she needed to know that things were good between them. Perhaps she had... fallen in love with him.

She typed a reply: *Sorry I didn't respond, long day. I'm supposed to be at work tomorrow but might ring in sick. Do you want to meet for an hour? The Arsehole X*

The blue tick appeared immediately, and then dots that showed he was typing.

Neil: *Where? How about the Minerva in an hour? X*

Flora: *Great, yes X*

Though still fatigued, Flora felt better.

She went into the corridor; a TV blared somewhere. All Flora had was a rucksack containing her phone and purse, but she didn't want to return to the flat. The thought of doing so filled her with anxiety. The dingy dwellings she'd endured had often caused that angst. How many times had she opened the door after a long shift, hating the damp smell and bare cupboards?

Suddenly, it was too much.

Stay, whispered a voice, not Mary's, not her own.

OK, she whispered in her head.

She went to find someone to ask if she could.

Carla's office was locked. Of course – it was past seven in the evening. Marjory was in the laundry room. 'Oh, I didn't know you were volunteering tonight, darlin',' she said cheerfully.

'I'm not.' Flora's voice was hoarse. 'I'm staying here.'

Marjory's stance changed, as though this revelation peeled away layers, revealing the Listener. 'Have you been given a room, love?'

'Yes. The thing is, I want to pop out. But I'm not going home. Can I come back?'

'Of course. Do you need a chat first?'

Flora shook her head. 'I'm sorry.'

'Don't be. I'll be here when you get back – I'm on the night-shift. Sign in and sign out, but you know that.'

Outside, the night was as starry as the opening line to a Don Maclean song. Flora headed to where the two-century-old Minerva pub sat on the marina, glad of the Humber breeze, excited to see Neil. She bought a glass of wine and found that the rarely available snug – Britain's smallest pub room – was vacant, so she sat on its triangular wooden bench and waited nervously.

'How cool is this?' she said to Neil when he looked into the space ten minutes later, beer in hand. 'You usually have to book it. Did you work your magic?'

'Yeah – it's an illusion. You're actually sitting in the second cubicle in the Ladies.'

Flora laughed.

He looked tired; his hair was stuck up on one side. 'I've done magic here.' He sat, close enough that his knee touched hers.

'In *here*?'

'No, the Old Brew House Room. They hired me once. A woman stole three purses and blamed me – said *I'd* made them vanish.' He sipped his drink. 'Sorry about last night. I've got some stuff going on.'

'Forget it,' said Flora.

'I saw they named you as the Mary girl.'

Where should she start? 'After you left last night this woman who's making a documentary about Mary came to the club; she made one about Marilyn. She's interviewing women who've seen Mary.' Pause. 'I met her this morning.'

'You're gonna talk about it?' His eyebrows arched in surprise.

Flora shook her head. 'I was just curious about the other women.'

'And?'

'They were mostly from up north, everyday women. Some had had babies that they couldn't keep or had lost.' She glanced at Neil, knowing he knew her hidden loss. 'Mary asked them to volunteer at CARE.' Flora paused. 'And then there she was. My *mum*. One of the bloody interviewees.'

'She's seen Mary too?'

'No. But she shared... something…'

'What do you mean?'

Flora felt the black butterflies unfurl in her tummy again. 'She told them about the baby.'

'Oh, Jesus.' Neil placed his beer on the table and put a hand over hers the way he had in the taxi. She hoped he would never let go.

'I feel trapped,' said Flora.

'How so?' he asked softly.

'If I don't share my story with Nina, she'll just use my mother's, won't she?'

'Did she say she would?'

'Not directly, but she suggested I talk instead. I don't know which would be worse – my mum getting to tell it, or me speaking up.' Probably the only way to get Nina not to use her mum's version would be to share her own.

'Why don't you talk to your mum?' asked Neil.

Flora thought about it. Neither of them had mentioned the birth since it happened. Each wordlessly agreed to a silent pact. What had possessed her mother to now share it? She knew what the full story could mean if it came out; how it could change their lives.

'Our relationship is *tricky*. But something like that changes things. She isn't all bad and I love her... but…'

Black butterflies swarmed, spiralled, rising.

'What's *your* mum like?' she asked.

Neil visibly slumped. His hand left hers. 'She needs a lot of care,' he said. 'I do most of it now my dad's gone – he died last year – although my brother comes from London now and again. She has MS, so there are good days and bad.'

'Oh, Neil. That must be so hard.'

He shrugged. 'I just get on with it. That's why the trip to Vegas may not happen, aside from my lack of cash. Another drink?'

'No, thanks. I can't stay much longer.'

He looked dejected; she was pleased but then felt bad.

'It's only because…' Flora was embarrassed to admit she was staying at CARE. This must be the stigma Bella often said she felt because she was living in a mental hospital. No matter how much depression was openly discussed now, these things still stuck. She changed the subject. 'So, you're not going to Vegas?'

'Even if I had the money, my brother can't stay with my mum for that long.'

Flora took his hand now. 'What if you *did* have the money?'

'What do you mean?'

'I get paid if I do Nina's documentary.'

'But you don't want to do it.'

'The fee is ten grand.'

Neil looked stunned. 'I couldn't take that kind of money from you.'

'I could loan you it. When you win, pay me back.'

'And if I don't?'

'My gamble,' she said.

'I don't want you to do something just to get me the cash. And anyway, I doubt you'd be paid until afterwards, and then it'll be too late.' Neil held Flora's gaze. 'But thank you for offering. No one's ever offered to do anything like that for me.' He looked so touched that she leaned over and kissed him softly on the cheek. The way he looked at her – affection bright in his eyes – was something she would always remember; she would put this moment away in the catalogue of whatever their relationship might become.

'So, no Vegas,' she said sadly.

'Will you do the documentary?' He was changing the subject now.

'I don't know.' Flora sighed.

'My mum reckons that we always know.'

'What do you mean?'

'Deep down, we know exactly what we want to do. We just arse about cos we're scared.' He looked at her. 'You know what you're going to do.'

Flora refused to think about it. 'I have to go.' She shouldn't stay out too long if she was using the service that CARE provided.

'I'll walk you.' He finished his beer.

She stood. 'Not as far to walk tonight.'

He stood too. 'How come?'

Outside she said without looking at him, 'I'm staying at

CARE.'

'A nightshift?'

'I'm there as a... resident.'

'Oh.' He digested this; didn't appear to judge. 'How long for?'

'I'm not sure. I got overwhelmed. It was…'

The baby, she wanted to say.

'It's OK.'

When they walked back, he held her hand. Outside the CARE doors, Flora began trembling. Neil hugged her. She wondered if he'd kiss her like he had at the flat, but he didn't. She sensed that he didn't want to seem pushy when she was upset.

'Abracadabra,' he whispered in her ear.

She smiled. Whispered it back.

When he let go of her, he held another daffodil. 'This one was intentional,' he said.

Flora held it in her hand as she fell asleep that night.

46

Marilyn holds hands with an old friend

Near Paradise Cove Beach, Los Angeles, August 1964

Early on her last morning in Los Angeles, Marilyn borrowed Stella's car and went for a drive, roof down, sea breeze lifting her hair. She wanted to see the old places, her past life, quietly say goodbye; it was chancy but she couldn't leave without doing so. It was silly, really; she might come back anytime.

But she was compelled to put the past to rest.

She ended up on Hollywood Boulevard, left the car, and found herself outside Grauman's Theatre. Her old haunt. She saw a ghostly Norma Jeane, alone, going into the venue, where she spent hours watching movie after movie, paying for one show and then sneaking in to see another when it was done. That child dreamed of being a star like those she idolised.

It had been surreal when she placed her hand and footprints in the theatre's forecourt with Jane Russell many years later.

Now, she approached those eternal impressions.

A small girl knelt before them, her tiny palms inside the shape of Marilyn's long-ago imprints. Marilyn knelt beside her.

'I need to grow a bit,' said the girl, wriggling her fingers.

'Don't be in a hurry for that, honey.'

'I bet you'd fit inside them,' the girl said.

'Shall we see?'

The girl nodded enthusiastically.

Marilyn placed her palms inside the familiar shape; the cement was cold against her warmth. It was like holding hands with an old friend. She had to swallow back sudden tears.

'Did you know her?' asked the girl, awe heavy in her voice.

'I guess you could say I did, yes.'

'*Really*? What was she like?'

'Inside, she was just like you.' Marilyn touched the girl's cheek. 'She was just trying to find where she fit in.'

*

Later that night *Gentleman Prefer Blondes* was on the TV; it seemed fitting since Marilyn had placed her hands in the cement to commemorate that movie. Though the film had reenforced her as the dumb blonde she ended up resenting, it had a place in her heart for being the role that launched her into the stratosphere.

The first television broadcast of what could be termed a recent Hollywood movie had been in 1961 when *How To Marry A Millionaire* was shown. Marilyn remembered thinking how much smaller she looked on the screen than she had in the cinema. But she kind of liked that intimacy. It scored such high ratings that it changed the landscape of TV forever; after that, networks vied for newer films as opposed to black and white movies from the 1930s and 40s.

Stella and Marilyn stayed up late watching the 1953 classic where Jane Russell and Marilyn are lounge singers who travel to Paris, enjoying the company of many eligible men along the way.

'It's such fluff,' said Marilyn, fondly. She felt like a mother watching her little girl perform in the end of semester show.

'You looked radiant,' said Stella.

'It helps that they lit me well, and I had the best make-up artist, and also the best hair styl-'

'No, it was down to *you*.' Stella looked pointedly at her friend. 'Can't you see that? They could light me that way, paint my face perfectly, do my hair, but I couldn't have brought what you did.

Cinema has lost someone special, you know. But then the world gained a much happier woman, and I'm glad.' She paused. 'Do you ever miss the spotlight?'

'Of *course*. Mostly in the middle of night when I'm alone. But, Stella, when I craved fame, I was looking for a mother's love. That's what I realise now. Without that love, Norma Jeane looked for it everywhere else. And Marilyn Monroe gave it to her; she gave *me* a great deal. I wouldn't be here if she hadn't happened. It all lead to this.'

'Sounds like you've made peace with her.'

'I'm fond of her. I even miss her. But I'm happy now to be... *me*.'

*

In the morning, Stella drove Marilyn to the airport.

They were quiet on the journey that paralleled the ocean, though Marilyn sensed that her friend had a million questions to ask. It must seem irrational that she was jetting off to a strange land, alone, with no real plan or vision. But she was not afraid, only excited. She had packed her few beloved items; the black notepad, her favourite Monroe picture, and the holy trinket Mother Superior had given her.

But she was leaving with so much more.

In the departures lounge they hugged amidst travellers who rushed past like water gushing around two stones in a stream.

'Thank you for everything,' said Marilyn. 'For taking me in, for being my friend.'

'You sound so... *final*.' Stella looked sad.

'This isn't a forever goodbye, just a farewell for now. I think when I know my next chapter, you'll be a part of that too. I'll be seeing you soon.'

'Stay safe. Call me when you're there.'

'I will, I promise.'

Marilyn was excited, sure about her destination, her choice.

But still, she cried quietly behind an eye mask for the first hour of the flight.

47

Flora is not always the calm lady

April 2016, Hull, England

When she woke, Flora was confused.

Where was she? It was still dark so she knew it couldn't be later than six. Soft whispers of grey shadow shrouded the room in further mystery. Then she remembered. She had come back to CARE last night.

She thought of Bella alone at the flat.

She grabbed her phone, imagining all kinds of desperate messages but there was just one, from Neil: *I enjoyed tonight. Hope you're OK. X*

She smiled, sat up in the narrow bed. The battery was getting low. She would have to see if someone had a charger. Parting the curtain, she saw the daffodil in the half-light next to her; a splash of sunshine on the pillow.

She responded to Neil: *I enjoyed it too and I love my daffodil. X.*

Then she messaged Greg, saying she had been vomiting and wouldn't make it into work tonight, but hoped to be back Saturday.

She made tea in the kitchen and drank it leaning against the worktop, listening to the unusual sounds; unfamiliar creaking floors, wind through pipes somewhere, radiators clicking into action. Alien as it was, it was nice to be warm, not smell damp, know care was available. Then it arrived – Marjory, pile of bedding in her arms. She must be near the end of her shift.

'Morning, darlin',' she said cheerfully. 'I didn't see you come in last night. We should do your settling in chat but I leave in ten minutes. Carla'll be in at nine.'

'I'm fine now. I might go home. I just feel...'

'Tell me.' Marjory waited, a Listener; Flora felt obliged to find the word.

'Restless,' she admitted.

But like I'm supposed to stay for some reason...

'Ah, we live in a restless world, darlin'.' Marjory patted her hand. 'If you're still here tonight, we'll chat in full.'

Flora took her tea back to the room and saw Amelia in the corridor.

'I was dead worried when I saw you on the floor,' the young teen said. 'It was weird, like we'd switched places! I spied on you at midnight but you were asleep.'

'See,' said Flora, 'I'm not always the calm lady.'

'Maybe I can be yours for a bit then.'

This was Flora's problem; she could not surrender easily to care. She had always been the carer. Always stubbornly refused help. Always stood firmly on her own feet. She had had to, from such a young age, and now it was innate.

'I've got a new photo of baby Amber,' cried Amelia. 'Do you want to see it?'

'Absolutely,' said Flora.

She followed Amelia to her room and sat on the unmade bed while Amelia swiped her phone screen and showed Flora a picture of a chubby baby with a toothy grin, sitting in a large, old-fashioned pram. Flora instinctively touched the screen, her heart in her chest.

'She's beautiful,' she said softly.

'I can't wait to see her. My auntie said she has four teeth now and she cruises around the furniture herself. Isn't that cute?'

These were things Amelia should be experiencing, not getting second-hand like a youngest child receiving worn out hand-medowns after everyone else has discarded them. Flora was angry about this little cherub without her mum, about the experience *she* had had years ago, about all the children without their mothers.

'You OK?' asked Amelia.

'I don't know.'

'What happened yesterday?'

'I should go to my room.' Flora stood.

'Will I see you later?'

'I guess.' Flora felt bad for being vague. Thoughts came so fast she couldn't process them, like images in a PowerPoint presentation whizzing by before she could read the text. Was this how Bella had often felt? 'I just need to…'

She returned to her room; smelled the daffodil.

Her phone flashed.

Bella: *Are you any better today? Gonna get ready and come. X*

*

Flora was sitting on the bed staring into space when a soft knock on the door surprised her. Takeaway latte in each hand, Bella entered, and hugged her so tenderly that Flora choked up.

'It's about time someone fussed you.' Bella looked around. 'It's weird to be here. I stayed in this room once.' She sat on the bed and handed Flora a latte. 'I liked it because the view is of the street not the bins at the back.'

Flora sipped her drink; she hadn't even noticed.

'Nice daffodil.'

'From Neil.' Flora realised that Bella might be sulky that she'd seen him but she didn't react.

Carla put her head around the door. 'Oh, hi Bella. You're back too?'

'I'm here for Flora.'

'Nice to see you – you look well. Do you need anything, Flora?

I can come back if you've got your sister with you.'

'Thank you.' Flora had never been so cared for; it felt like a onesie made of fleece.

When Carla had gone, Bella said, 'Sis, you scared the bejesus out of me when you said you had a breakdown. What happened? I said you seemed different the other day but this is an even *different* different.'

Flora sighed. 'I don't even know myself.'

'Is it what Mum shared in that interview?'

Where should Flora begin? Not with her mother's words, they were biased, but with her own. But how to tell her own version?

'If I tell you, you'll be shocked,' said Flora.

'I'm not as fragile as you think.'

'It's... how you'll see *me* now.'

'I'll only ever see you as my weird sister, trust me.'

Flora smiled. 'God, what to say...'

'Just rip the plaster off. Then we'll deal with it.'

'Well, if you're doing metaphors; this plaster has been on so long that I'm afraid it won't even come off.'

'I'll help you with it.' Bella touched Flora's cheek. How Flora loved her. How she wanted to keep things as they were.

Just do it, she thought.

48

Marilyn is here for the small things

Dublin, Ireland, August 1964

Her first day in Dublin, Marilyn set the alarm to wake at seven and get onto the new time, and then went exploring.

Though she had asked travel agent Gloria to book somewhere simple and central, Marilyn was surprised at the luxury of the Shelbourne Hotel; Dublin's 'Grande Dame' was obviously somewhere the elite stayed. Her room was delightful, overlooking the lush foliage of St Stephen's Green. She supposed she could keep a low profile, maybe choose somewhere less grand when her three weeks here were up.

She first wandered the large park she had seen from her window, drinking in the fresh air. How could air be so *different*? Here, it was... clean. The trees were rich in colour, dense and thick; the ground was damp and bouncy. Everything was so *nourished*. That word felt right.

Marilyn stopped at the Three Fates fountain, transfixed by the bronze statues of three robed females, the highest with her left hand raised, the middle woman with her right hand raised, and the third crouching, each of them holding the same piece of thread. Three women linked.

This was the land of beauty, of poetry, of WB Yeats and James Joyce; she had read and loved both writers, and felt small here in the land of great literature. It was good to have that perspective though; to be kept in check. She was here for small things; they counted as much as the big. Dublin itself was big and yet small.

Marilyn couldn't believe it was a city. Los Angeles sprawled endlessly, was often unfriendly, but here, on streets lined with pubs and red brick buildings, people said hello.

And she loved it.

Said hello cheerily back.

She wandered all day, full of joy and curiosity, going in and out of museums and libraries. She spent an hour staring at the Shrine of Our Lady of Dublin in the Carmelite Church. The tomb housed a medieval statue of the virgin with the child Jesus. This Mary was chubby-faced, whitewashed, and Marilyn was held rapt by the less colourful girl in her plain robes; she felt they were the same.

In the afternoon, it began raining and she loved that too; the downfall felt so fresh. She ran, childlike, splashing through puddles, and laughing at her own silliness.

Later, she left a café after sampling a hearty meat stew and potatoes, and someone grabbed her arm.

Marilyn panicked, pulled back, heart racing.

She had been recognised.

She should have worn the plain tunic and headscarf instead of her more modern capri pants and blouse.

'These fell out of your bag,' said a young woman with a spotted umbrella, the Irish lilt in her voice music to Marilyn's ears. She handed over the postcards Marilyn had bought in a souvenir store earlier.

'Oh, thank you.' Trying to recall her years-ago vocal training, Marilyn lessened her American accent, made her voice neutral.

'Oh, you're from…' tried the girl. 'You're from... somewhere else.'

Somewhere else; it seemed apt.

'Yes, I'm from... Canada.' Marilyn had heard that Europeans often mistook an American accent for Canadian, and vice versa, so she decided that would be her story here.

'I love your accent! You only hear it in films.'

Marilyn wanted to steer away from the movies. 'Well, sure, though I hear it on the streets where I live back home too.'

The girl laughed uproariously. Marilyn smiled. She looked barely out of her teens, and on closer inspection, Marilyn saw a curve of belly distorting the kind of floral mini dress the young ones favoured. She reached out to touch the swell before realising it might be impolite; her hand had spoken without thought.

'How lovely,' she said. 'How far along are you?'

The girl shrank back, face pale now, laughter gone. 'I'm not... it's... I…' Then she looked tearful, said, 'You can see? I thought the tight corset still hid it.'

'I'm so sorry, I didn't mean to upset you.' Marilyn felt terrible.

'My mum told me to stop coming out now I'm almost six months, but I hate being stuck in.'

The girl looked so distraught that Marilyn guided her back into the café, insisting she buy her a warm drink. They took a table near a steamy window. On the wall behind the girl, hung an early black and white Monroe print. Marilyn felt sure she would be outed. But the girl on the poster was a long-gone ghost.

'I'm Mari-' she started. Stopped. Felt that if she said her name, the link would be made, and the girl would see the Hollywood icon sitting before her. 'I'm Mary,' she said. She supposed it was a short version. Maybe she should call herself that with new people? 'What's your name, honey?'

'Trudy.' She sniffed, nose red. 'I'm not supposed to rub it in people's faces.'

'What do you mean?'

'My family, they accept it; the baby.' She went to pat her belly, but looked around the busy venue and stopped. 'The father – he's a soldier – he disappeared as soon as I told him. My mum obviously doesn't support abortion.' Trudy whispered that final word like it was blasphemous. 'I'd have been sent to a Mother and Baby home without her decision to let me stay at home.' Pause. 'You probably don't know about those places...'

'Oh, I do. I've read about how terrible they can be.'

Trudy sipped the creamy hot chocolate Marilyn had ordered for her. 'I'm lucky really, but I don't feel it. I've ruined my life apparently.'

How could a baby ruin a life? Ruin came from trauma. From being abused. Maybe Marilyn was being naive. It was easy for her to think like that – she craved a child, so she saw the image of cradling a newborn through a rose-tinted lens. 'Maybe it won't be so bad,' she said feebly.

'I know other girls have it worse. A friend of mine was disowned by her family, and I never saw her again. Don't know what happened to her or the baby.' Trudy shook her head. 'And you always know that wherever they went, it'll be somewhere bad.'

'There needs to be somewhere good they can go,' said Marilyn quietly.

'Sorry?'

She shook her head. 'Doesn't matter.'

They shared life stories for a while, enjoying a second drink. Marilyn's was vague, one of her leaving behind a job she hated, but Trudy's was descript, full of lively tales of life with twelve siblings, sharing beds and midnight secrets and stolen snacks. Eventually Trudy said she really must get back or her mother would worry.

'I'm sure I know you,' she said as they parted ways.

'You do?' Marilyn shivered.

Trudy shrugged. 'Maybe you're just an angel sent to cheer me up.' And she was gone, swallowed by the alien crowds.

Marilyn returned to her room, haunted by the girl's tale. She longed to talk to Stella about it but that wasn't possible. Though the hotel offered an international service, it could take hours to connect, wouldn't last more than three minutes on a bad line when it did, and cost a fortune. Marilyn sat and wrote a letter on the headed notepaper, knowing it would take more than a week to reach LA, so by the time Stella's response came, it would be a historical document.

This is the place, Marilyn said in her missive. *This is where I think it will happen, and yet I don't know what…*

Days passed quickly, blurring into one. Marilyn explored further afield, walking the beach at Dollymount Strand and the forests at Enniskerry. She wondered where her ancestors had lived, if they too had roamed these roads, inhaled the good air. She felt at home. Like this land had been waiting for her.

When the three weeks at the Shelbourne were up, she booked another fortnight. She had just over two months left before she would have to return to the states, unless she got a work visa. But she wasn't ready to go back yet. She wasn't done here.

She hadn't even started yet.

*

During her fourth week, Marilyn saw a flyer for a local women's book group in a rack in her local café; it was happening that night. How nice it would be, she thought, to chat to people again; she couldn't deny she was a little tired of her own company.

She would go.

The meeting was held in a draughty hall that she presumed by the name – The Old School House – had once been a place of study; sadly many of the latticed windows were broken and patched up with tape, and some of the walls were chipped and crumbling. The place smelled of forgotten dreams.

'Hello,' said a dour woman wearing thin spectacles, with wooden beads swinging angrily from her neck, who emerged from the jostle of gossiping ladies. 'Nice to have a new face. I'm Sheila. Join us.'

They sat in a circle, book on knees, and expected an introduction from Marilyn. She said she was Mary from Canada and was considering moving here.

Sheila said they had been reading a new novel – *The Girls of Slender Means* by Muriel Spark – which Marilyn learned from the lively discussion was about a group of women sharing a converted building, who 'had very little' and were trying to escape the horrors of the post-war world.

'Sounds right up my street,' said Marilyn. 'I'll to find a bookshop today and buy it.' She needed something to read at night.

'You'll love it,' gushed a young woman in gingham. 'It's very eccentric and a bit fragmentary, but the idea of how a progressive, literary mind can reconcile itself with religious beliefs, and of these women finding themselves in this united place is just brilliant.' She took a breath. 'Has anyone ever said you look a bit like Marilyn Monroe?'

Two other women nodded, said there was a likeness around the chin, and the arch of her eyebrows.

'Oh, yes, I've had that before,' Marilyn said quickly; she felt it best to acknowledge the similarity. 'I *wish*! I'm a tad older. But thank you...'

As the book dissection concluded, and tea and homemade cakes were served, Marilyn told Sheila she would love to join them next time.

'Sadly, this is our last meeting here,' Sheila explained. 'The place's been condemned, so no one wants to buy it. Too much work to do to restore it.'

'But it's so full of character,' said Marilyn sadly.

'I agree, I think it's a beauty, and I'm heartbroken. Its history is wonderful. Before it was a school, it was apparently owned by an eccentric spinster called Helen Fields who let it overgrow with flowers.' Sheila laughed, looking less sharp; she held her beads to stop them swinging. 'She was determined to make the world a wild and pretty place…'

'Sounds perfect,' said Marilyn quietly.

While the book group were packing up, she explored the other high-ceilinged rooms, imagined school children giggling, fancied she saw colourful climbing flowers like star jasmine and honeysuckle devour the walls. In the dilapidated bathroom, she studied her face in a cracked, rusting mirror. Leaned closer. She was two, both faces identical in each glass shard.

The Gemini twins; her birth sign.

'Here,' she whispered. 'This is the place. Cursum perficio.'

When she left, she glanced back at the arched doorway, and the notice she had missed on the way in; a For Sale sign. She wrote the telephone number in the back of the book Sheila had loaned her. On a whim, the next morning, Marilyn called to see how much they wanted for the place. It would be auctioned the following week.

Should she go? She had the money.

But did she have the know-how? The ability? The determination?

Marilyn had eight weeks left until she needed a work visa to stay on.

Was this her ticket to that chance?

49

Flora rips off the plaster

April 2016, Hull, England

Bella was waiting for Flora to speak – to rip off the plaster.

'OK. When I was twelve…' she began, heart beating fast.

Bella waited still.

'I had a baby.' There. It was said.

Bella didn't speak. Flora could see the words going in, finding their way to her head, her heart; saw her frown, open her mouth, shake her head. 'You had a *baby*,' she repeated.

'Yes.'

'But... where *is* it?'

'Gone,' said Flora simply. 'Mum said I should give it up. She was right. I was a child myself. She was... she was actually *kind*. We hid the pregnancy. I was glad because I was ashamed. Even Grandma Lil didn't know. When I started to show – not until late because I was skinny then – Mum kept me home from school.' Flora put her empty coffee cup on the bedside cabinet. 'I gave birth in the bathroom. Held... *him*.'

'Oh, him,' whispered Bella sadly.

Flora nodded. 'For a while. And then… Mum knew someone. They came. I was still upstairs. He went... was taken. She said we should never speak of it again. And we didn't.'

'Oh, Flora.' Bella clung to her. Neither spoke for a while. Then Bella asked, muffled against Flora's chest, 'But who was the father?'

Flora felt sick.

'Mum's boyfriend,' she said with difficulty.

'Oh, Flora, no.' She squeezed her even harder. 'But... *who*... how did it happen?'

'Malcolm. He was drunk. I'd fallen asleep on the sofa and he came home from the pub.' Flora closed her eyes. She always did to this part of her story, but flashes of it grabbed her by the neck; his breath heavy with alcohol, grunting, unintelligible words in her ear, futile resistance, then over. 'He told Mum the next day that he'd thought I was her.'

'She didn't buy that, did she?'

'No, she was horrified, got rid of him straight away.'

Flora felt Bella nodding. 'I don't know what to say, Flo.'

'You don't have to say anything.'

So they were quiet for a while.

'Hang on.' Bella pulled away. 'So Mum shared this in that interview?'

'Yes.'

'Even though she's never mentioned it and made you keep quiet?'

'Yes,' repeated Flora.

'What *possessed* her?'

'Nina – the documentary woman – she does have a way about her. The other women who've seen Mary shared things they never had before. I saw the clips yesterday morning. Perhaps it's when a camera's on you? Perhaps it's the way Nina asks questions?'

'I know you said you're not doing it, but maybe you *should* tell your side. You've been silent all this time.' Bella's voice broke.

Flora didn't respond. She didn't know what she wanted to do.

'Let's look for him' said Bella suddenly, excited.

'*Who*?'

'Your son. I'll help you. We can make Mum tell us where he went.'

'*No*,' snapped Flora. Then, more kindly, 'Sorry. Can we leave it now?'

'Did you get a photo of him?'

'No. But I don't need one. I can see…' Flora couldn't finish.

'What did he look like?'

'Perfect.'

'Is that why…?'

'Why what?' asked Flora.

'Why you've never wanted children. I'm sorry I interrogated you, I didn't know *this*.'

'I'm not sure.' Flora shrugged.

They were quiet again for a while.

'I love you,' said Bella eventually.

'I love you too,' said Flora.

'Are you coming back to the flat?'

'Maybe tomorrow.'

'Shall I stay, like you used to with me. We can lie in the bed and watch the *Real Housewives* all morning.'

That's what they did.

They got lost in a world where women appeared to have it all; apartments with the best views, designer handbags, luxury holidays. But who knew what sadness went unspoken? Who knew what silent grief was harboured within their manicured beating hearts?

Who knew what they had lost?

50

Marilyn's baby

Dublin, Ireland, March 1965

The Old School House was surrounded by daffodils, like children in yellow dresses dancing in a ring. The bulbs must have already been in the ground, perhaps planted many years ago by Helen Fields when she owned the place and wanted florae to consume the premises. The narcissi now burst forth with vivid determination.

'Look, Stella,' cried Marilyn, grabbing her friend's arm and dragging her to a patch by the freshly-painted main door. 'Aren't they beautiful?' She ran fingers through the gold gathering. 'I've never seen anything like it!' She had read that they were mainly native to Europe and been excited for spring to come so she could experience them.

'Now I see why Wordsworth put pen to paper,' said Stella.

'And so you'll understand my sign too.'

'Not *more* signs, Marilyn?' Stella laughed, knew her of old.

'No, not that kind of sign. One you can actually touch this time.'

'Oh, you designed it already?'

'I did. And apparently it's inside, ready to be mounted above the door. Come on, let's go and see.' Marilyn pushed one of the double doors open, and they went inside.

This was not the building where Marilyn had first attended the book group seven months ago. It had been Monroe-ed. Damp had been dried, wiring had been ripped out and replaced, the roof stripped and retiled, and the plumbing updated. Patchy brickwork had been plastered, floors had been polished, rugs laid and windows repaired. Leading off the main, brightly painted hall that housed numerous sofas were smaller rooms with beds in. Marilyn had put vases of daffodils in each one.

Stella looked around, eyes damp. 'It's... I don't know what to say.' When she had last come over to Ireland the place still looked like a bomb site. 'You've done all this in a *month*?'

'I'm no plumber, honey,' laughed Marilyn. 'I think you'll find some good men were the key. But you were a part of it as much as I was.'

'I only put my name to it, you *did* it all. You made all the calls.'

Stella had headed the paperwork, just to keep Marilyn behind the scenes. She still feared recognition, knew her project would likely make it into the newspapers, and needed Stella to speak and be photographed when that happened. But Marilyn had got the money together, located the right builders, contacted the council, and organised fundraisers.

'She's *your* baby,' said Stella.

Marilyn nodded, no words needed.

She went to the office by the main doors. Stella followed. A newspaper lay open on the desk; the headline said *New Women's Centre Opening In Dublin*. In the picture below, Stella stood in front of the half-finished building, squinting in winter sun. She had come over for the shoot in February.

'Gosh, I look like my mother,' she laughed.

'He said he'd left it here,' Marilyn said to herself.

'Who... what?'

'My designer, Ed. The sign. Ah. *Here*.' She located a flat box in a drawer and paused, prize in hand. 'We talked at length, and I sketched it for him,' she said. 'But you can imagine how bad *that* was. I just hope…'

She opened it.

Took out the circular plaque.

Said, '*Oh,*' softly and reverently.

The yellow letters like daffodils against Mary-blue sky were enclosed within a circle of gold hands holding hands. Marilyn remembered painstakingly drawing those many hands, thinking they evoked a feeling of being nurtured. She remembered carefully pencilling the C so it drooped like a lazy daffodil, the yellow A and R with grass at their feet, and the E as a more proud, upstanding flower.

'CARE,' whispered Stella. 'That's what you went with.'

Marilyn nodded.

It was perfect.

'When are they mounting it?' asked Stella.

'Tomorrow. A journalist is coming so I'll need you here.'

'I will be. It's what I came for.'

'And then we wait for them to come,' said Marilyn.

'Who?' Stella frowned.

'The women who need us…'

51

Flora dreams hard

April 2016, Hull, England

When Bella left CARE, Flora fell asleep on the bed, daffodil wilting on the pillow. It should be in water. And she should eat something. But she needed to rest. She was glad Bella knew the truth about the baby, if only a part of it.

Dreams came hard.

She was running like she used to, breathless, pounding the floor. A baby screamed in one of the CARE rooms, but she couldn't find it. Then sweet singing drowned that out. Flora followed the sound to the TV in the lounge. On the screen, Marilyn Monroe rehearsed a number, the footage grainy, documentary-style. The film flickered, went out, came back on. She sang a mournful melody, the words lamenting a life given to the world and expressing a desire to leave it behind.

A tap on the door disturbed the song.

Flora woke.

It was Michelle.

'Flora,' she said softly. 'There's a new lady with us and she'd like to speak to you. I said you might not want to.'

Flora sat up, head fuzzy. 'Who is it?'

'She didn't give a name. She's elderly. Keen to see you.'

'I don't know anyone like that.' All Flora could think of was Grandma Lil, but she was long gone.

'She looks tired, the poor dear,' said Michelle, 'but if you're not up to–'

'I'll come,' said Flora, curious now.

Perhaps it was to do with Nina and the documentary. But Nina didn't know she was here. Wait – *no one* knew she was here aside from Bella and Neil.

She followed Michelle along the corridor to the last door. Flora knew that on the other side of it was a cosy room that caught the evening light due to a gap in the adjacent buildings; Bella had stayed in it for a few months, refusing to let Flora open the curtains on the slither of golden sunset each eve. Flora felt emotional about going in there again.

'You OK?' asked Michelle.

Flora nodded.

Michelle opened the door.

The curtains were parted. This was the first thing Flora noticed, even though it was not yet sundown and no flaming sky pulled her eyes there. On the bed sat a lady, perhaps in her late eighties, hair neatly curled in small rows of ovals, skin papery, and eyes the brightest of blue, full of life.

At her feet, was a small suitcase.

In her hand, a bunch of daffodils.

Flora suddenly saw in that flash of gold the one Mary had held, its hue so vivid that Flora again heard the sounds of a spring day, birdsong, a breeze, a stream. Everything felt brighter now.

She almost wanted to sink to her knees like she had with Mary.

'I'll leave you,' said Michelle, closing the door.

The lady on the bed smiled. It reached every part of her face. 'You must be Flora,' she said, accent curious, soft, alien. 'These are for you.'

'Thank you. They're lovely.' Who was she? Why had she brought daffodils? 'I don't understand. How do you know me?'

'It's a long story,' she said.

'Tell me.'
'Soon.'
'But who are you?' asked Flora.
'Cursum perficio,' the lady said. 'I'm Marilyn, honey.'

52

Marilyn heads to the end of the line

April 2016, Dublin, Ireland/Hull, England

A dream woke Marilyn.

Images from the past, edges as faded as old photographs, flickered like a bygone movie in a deserted cinema where only she watched. She saw herself young, blonde, *her*, rehearsing a song she didn't recall. And yet, as is often the way with dreams, it felt familiar. The segment that had her start awake was when Mary walked into that auditorium, light in her wake rather than the expected shadow.

What joy to see her again!

Like that long ago night, she entered quietly, barefoot, holding a single pink flower. She stood in the aisle – the movie's mournful song still playing – and spoke in her curious language that Marilyn's brain translated.

'Cursum perficio, Marilyn,' she said. 'Your journey began that night fifty-four years ago, my child. You found your true place. You followed your heart and you cared. Now, the last part of your journey is here.'

Marilyn tried to speak but found herself mute.

'You are tired but there is a floral lady who will take your burden. You are ready to make a final journey, across the sea to a city called the end of the line. There, you will both speak freely. Tell the world of your pain so others open up too.'

Then she placed the flower on a chair and left.

Marilyn woke with a gasp.

They say your life flashes before you at the end. It had felt like that recently, with memories hitting hard, but she was sure the end wasn't here yet. It had, however, been harder these days to rise in a morning; the cold cruelly penetrated her bones in winter, and her hands wouldn't do what she wanted them to until she had wriggled them a few times, the way she did all those years ago when preparing for a movie scene.

She would be ninety in two months. But she didn't feel that old in her heart.

The mirror had a different opinion.

She stood with a groan and looked into the glass on her ornate bureau. Mary was right; Marilyn looked tired. Skin that had been pale was now translucent, which ironically gave her the very glow movie lights strived to create. She glanced at her favourite Monroe print, the black and white image of a dewy-eyed girl, carnation in hand, that had travelled with her through time and was now framed on the wall. In the top corner Marilyn had stuck the delicate trinket Mother Superior gave her many moons ago.

It made her smile, every time.

Distance had given another gift; an appreciation of that young, hungry, and hopeful woman, of the extraordinary life that a girl from nowhere created for herself as a Hollywood goddess. She had enjoyed all that she'd done in the last few decades, but Mary could be right – it might be time to slow down.

Across the sea to a city called the end of the line.

She knew the place.

There is a floral lady who will take your burden.

Was there?

Marilyn turned to go to the bathroom, knocking something from the bureau – *Icon* magazine, from a large pile. The final issue, Spring 2003, with a sultry Demi Moore on the cover.

From Ireland, via the movies and magazines and documentaries, Marilyn had watched Hollywood evolve and change. She had seen female stars garner control over their careers, even if the pay gap still existed. More needed to be done though. She read a report recently which concluded that only thirty percent of named characters in movies were female. She had imagined Stella sitting in the red velvet chair in her living room, sipping wine, saying they were still being *too quiet.*

Marilyn often heard her friend's words, carried on the breeze from the apple trees in the garden, melodic in the flow of the stream that divided her garden from the neighbouring farm: *Whatever we do with our lives, let's not be quiet.*

Darling Stella had passed away in 2003, aged seventy, from breast cancer. Marilyn had been at her side, abandoning her life in Dublin for two months. Smiles and secrets were exchanged: smiles over the times they had shared since Marilyn departed LA in 1964, the thing they had built; secrets that needed out near the end.

Stella told Marilyn the name of the daughter she had given away.

And where she lived.

'Keep an eye on her for me,' said Stella, thin and weary. 'She hasn't made much of her life, but her children, there is hope there. This is where she lives, where they live. Please... watch over them.'

Since then, Marilyn had paid someone to keep her up to date on that grown child, and on her children too. Particularly one of them; one she felt akin to. Pictures from her private investigator showed a willowy woman, a girl with slender means as her favourite book title called it.

There is a floral lady who will take your burden.

Of course – there was.

There you will both speak freely.

Would they?

Maybe it was time to emerge again; to not be quiet.

To leave the beautiful two-bedroom cottage just outside Dublin that had been home for fifty years. Number four on a quiet lane, which of course she had seen as a sign. When she first viewed it, she knew she had found the missing digit from her Brentwood house, from the 12305. There hadn't been a Mary-blue tile but there was a ghost apparently, a woman who was said to have died pining for her lost wartime love, who Marilyn was sure she heard on the stairs sobbing when it was stormy.

She lived alone here, but had never been lonely. Visitors stayed frequently for great lengths of time – sister Berniece until her death two years ago, Stella until hers, and new friends from this welcoming land (*home*, she had come to call it) that embraced this woman with a mysterious past she never mentioned.

Now, she put *Icon* magazine back on the pile and made plans. She called her travel agent on the landline – she had never been able to get on with these new smartphones – and got her to book a flight to Manchester early the next morning, and a hotel in the city called the end of the line.

For the rest of the day, she tidied up; she still had a tendency towards chaos, leaving books and clothes and cups in her wake, but she wanted the house neat for her departure. Then she packed, not much, just a weekend case.

*

In the morning, it was dark when she opened the door to get into a waiting taxi. Just as it had been that last night in Brentwood.

She often went there in her dreams, hearing the cicadas, the crickets and katydids, the hummingbirds, the distant throb of traffic, and the antique bronze windchime stirring in the tall trees. Here the sounds were more damp, dense, wet leaves moving in the night, a gentle patter of rain on the nearby moss-green lake.

Though this was only a trip, Marilyn felt she should say goodbye like she had to her first house. She had never liked goodbyes. At Stella's Los Angeles funeral she had simply said, 'For now, honey, until I see you again.'

Looking at the black silhouette of her cottage she said, 'For now, until I see you again.'

On the flight she watched tired mothers settling fidgety babies, wives reassuring husbands who were nervous flyers, young couples holding hands. Did she suddenly feel lonely in this fast-changing world that had little time for the elderly, having never had children or married again? Maybe. Most of the people from her old life were gone: Arthur, Joe, Berniece, and her mother.

But she'd had a grand life; done something she never thought she could.

A man in a tracksuit devouring his free peanuts studied her. She knew it wasn't that he saw *her*. At eighty-nine, she no longer dreaded recognition. It had continued happening occasionally for the first five or ten years after she left the movie world, but once she got past fifty-five, it stopped, as did fear of being found out.

It didn't matter now.

The world had not forgotten her, but it wouldn't know her if she walked by.

It continued to show Monroe's movies, speculate her whereabouts in documentaries, release books about her sudden disappearance, each more outlandish than the previous, all of which Marilyn rather enjoyed seeing. But she knew there would be no place now for an ex-goddess, an aging icon, a woman absent for more than fifty years.

Yet when she got out a small compact mirror, leaned in, and looked directly into her eyes, the blue and gold flecks in her irises were brilliant. They were still *her*. She snapped the compact shut. She had lived a happy life without the intrusive flash of camera, a peaceful existence without the scrutiny of the press, without the heavy weight of others' expectation.

Now, she answered only to herself.

*

At Manchester airport, Marilyn's heart warmed at the sight of seasonal daffodils in buckets. She bought a bunch; something told her the floral woman might like them. Back home, they were sprouting once again through the frozen ground around her cottage, and near Dublin's CARE, hopeful, strong.

She gave a taxi driver the address of a flat in Hull. Arrived late afternoon, under a confused sky that was grey, white, pink, and Mary-blue. The floral lady didn't answer the door. Instead it was the one Marilyn knew to be Bella. She wanted to reach out and touch that familiar face; Stella stared out of those steely eyes.

'I'm here to see Flora, honey,' she said kindly.

'Oh.' Bella looked confused. 'Do I know you?'

'No.' Marilyn smiled. 'But I know you. It's a long story, but I need to talk to Flora. Might you tell me where she is?'

Perhaps her age compelled Bella to be helpful.

'Do you know the CARE charity?' she said. 'She's staying there.'

It could not have come as more of a surprise.

Or with heavier meaning – it cemented Marilyn's intention.

It wasn't far. She had visited a couple of them over the years, though never this one. She liked the style of brick – it looked like an old building with its large windows and stone steps. Many CARE buildings had been disused before they were renovated. She loved that these forlorn and neglected structures enjoyed a new purpose.

Like the first one…

Inside, she told the lady on reception that she needed time away from the world, knowing she would be taken in. She would cancel her hotel. Once in a room, she asked the lady if she might speak with Flora Baker.

Michelle went off, and after a while returned with her.

Marilyn recognised the young woman sporting a faded pink sweatshirt that seemed like it had been worn for a while, wearing creased jeans, with hair that needed a good wash. Recognition didn't just come from the photos she had seen; she was Stella. The way she held herself, that subtle defiance in the angular elbows and straight shoulders, made Marilyn ache for her friend. The eyes too; the warmth juxtaposing the bold stance. Sometimes you met someone and got a sense of them, an immediate alliance, an impression that their future was aligned with yours. Marilyn had felt it with Stella and it led to a forty-year friendship.

Now, she did again.

'You must be Flora,' she said. 'These are for you.'

'Thank you. They're lovely.' Flora's accent was thick, unusual, magnetic. 'I don't understand. How do you know me?'

'It's a long story,' she said.

'Tell me.'

'Soon.'

'But who are you?' asked Flora.

Cursum perficio, Marilyn.

She heard this clearly.

Remembered Mary's repetition of it.

'Cursum perficio, Flora.' The words came out of her mouth. 'I'm Marilyn, honey.'

Flora sat on the bed, studying Marilyn like she was trying to remember something. 'I know those words.'

'You *do*?' Now Marilyn was surprised.

'She said them to me.' Flora was wide-eyed. 'She said, here ends your journey.'

'Who did?' Marilyn was spooked.

Flora shook her head.

'You can tell me.' She should be the one to speak so Flora felt able. Was it possible though? No. It would be too much, surely, that they also had this in common? She had always loved signs, coincidences, but this was surreal. 'Did the…' she tried. 'Did the Virgin Mary say it to you?'

Flora's face became that of a little girl who has just been validated by one attentive teacher after years of difficulties. 'How do you know about that?' she asked, incredulous.

'I don't. But she said similar to me. I saw her too.' It was only the second time Marilyn had shared this. She couldn't believe there was another witness, someone flesh and real, not written in a story.

'That's why you're here.' Flora looked suspicious now. 'Did you read about me in the paper? Did you come from Nina to get me to do the documentary?'

'No,' said Marilyn, 'I know those words because they were on a tile at a house I had.' She was surprised her private investigator hadn't picked up on Flora seeing Mary if it had been in the press. But then, it was a few weeks since the last report saying Flora was moving into a new flat again.

'*That*'s where I know those words from!' Flora leapt up; one daffodil fell from the bunch. 'I watched a documentary about Marilyn Monroe – there was a tile in her last house with those words on. That's *it!* It was driving me crazy.'

Marilyn watched Flora's delight at figuring it out.

Then she waited for her to realise what this meant.

Watched.

Saw it begin. Saw her stop moving. Turn and study what must be, to her, a frail old lady. She sat back on the bed. 'They were on *your* tile?'

'It was Mary-blue with pretty swirls.'

'Your name... *Marilyn*. You can't be... *that* one?'

'I was.' There: she had said it.

For the first time, to anyone.

Flora didn't speak. 'You can't be,' she managed eventually. 'We love you, my sister and me, we watched all your movies, growing up. I can't believe it.' She put the daffodils down and both hands over her cheeks. 'I see it, I see her, your eyes. You're alive. You're *real.*'

Marilyn smiled.

This was like the old days, meeting everyday people, which was *always* better than meeting other film stars or execs. She had been quoted as saying that she had known she belonged to the world, not because she was talented or beautiful, but because she had never belonged to anyone else. It was true. In fame she had craved the love a stable family gave, a constant mother, found neither. Except during those intimate moments meeting fans, one on one, young boys eager for an autograph, housewives who touched her hair.

'I'm more surprised that *you'd* be in Hull than about Mary coming here!' cried Flora.

Marilyn laughed.

'Can I hug you?' Flora's voice was small.

'Oh, honey, of course. I *love* hugs.'

She did. Marilyn kissed her forehead.

'Where have you *been*?' gushed Flora.

'I'll tell you another time. It's another long story.' Along with the tale of Flora's real ancestry, but that wasn't for now either. She was tired. It had been a big day.

'How do you know me? I'm nobody. I don't even have a kettle.'

Marilyn giggled. 'Why not?'

Flora was amused too. 'It broke.'

'I'm tired,' admitted Marilyn then.

'You're still so beautiful,' said Flora.

'Thank you. So are you.' Marilyn paused. 'Who is this Nina

you mentioned? This documentary?'

'Nina Ford. She made *Marilyn Only*. Did you see it?'

'Yes. I liked that one.'

It had been emotional to see old footage of her orphanage trips, recordings of moments she had forgotten captured by a fan on a Kodak Brownie 8mm movie camera; and to hear her younger voice, shy and sweet.

'Is it weird seeing people talk about you?'

'I've gotten used to it.' Marilyn winked.

'Nina's making a documentary about women who've seen Mary.' Flora looked sad. 'But I haven't talked about it, except to my sister and my friend Neil.' She smiled so brightly Marilyn saw what feelings Flora had for him.

'What's stopping you speaking to Nina?' Marilyn asked.

'It's complicated. A long tale, like yours.'

'We're made of them, honey.'

Flora nodded. 'So what now?'

'I think we're supposed to speak out together.'

'You do?'

'But maybe we get to know one another first?'

'I'd love that,' cried Flora. 'Are you hungry? Do you want some coffee?'

'Sure, coffee would be good. They have a working kettle?'

Flora smiled.

Marilyn tried to stand and faltered; Flora quickly came to her aid, gently holding her arm. 'What brought you to stay at CARE?' Marilyn asked.

'I'm a volunteer,' she said. 'But yesterday I had a... a breakdown.'

'That was me that night, all those years ago.' They headed for the door, Flora still holding Marilyn's arm. 'For now, can we keep quiet about who I am?'

'I won't say a word. I quite like having you to myself.'

And Flora took Marilyn to the kitchen, and they got to know one another.

53

Flora's turn and turning point

April 2016, Hull, England

Flora woke, momentarily confused again. Then she realised she was still in the room at CARE. This time Neil's wilting single daffodil was outshone by a brighter bunch in a borrowed vase. Had she dreamt that Marilyn Monroe had turned up *here*?

No. The splashes of yellow on the bedside table said otherwise.

She unplugged her phone from the charger Amelia had loaned her, saw two messages.

Bella: *Miss you. Can't stop thinking about your baby. When are you coming home? X*

Neil: *Will you be at work tonight? Someone cancelled, I'm filling in. X*

Flora responded to each, telling Bella she would be home today because she had to go to work, and telling Neil she'd see him there.

Work. The flat. Broken kettles.

Everyday life beckoned with its gritty realism.

Yet here in this building was a woman who once symbolised the opposite. Flora was desperate to see Marilyn again; she felt as excited as she had when she was small and knew Grandma Lil was coming over. But it was early, she should let her sleep.

She went to the dining room for breakfast.

Amelia was there. 'You OK?' she asked.

Flora helped herself to toast, nodded. Was it because she had unburdened herself to Bella about the baby, because she and Neil were good, or because of the surprise visitor yesterday? Maybe all three. 'I'm going home,' she said.

'But you'll return as a volunteer?' Amelia looked anxious.

'Of course.'

Marilyn arrived then. She had been lively yesterday, her eyes full of mischief and emotion, but this morning she looked frail. Flora was reminded that this was an elderly lady in a strange city. She jumped up, pulled out a chair.

'Thanks, honey.' Marilyn sat down with a groan. Flora couldn't believe that no one else could see it was *her*. It felt obvious, but then she viewed her with secret knowledge.

After small talk, tea and toast, Marilyn and Flora were alone.

'I've been thinking,' said Marilyn.

'What about?'

'Nina's documentary.'

'Oh.' Flora put the chipped teacup back in its saucer.

'I think we should take part together. She might not want me, when my story is from so long ago, but who knows?'

Flora wanted to please Marilyn but still resisted. 'I'm not sure.'

'What holds you back, Flora?'

'I'm…'

'You think people will mock if we talk about Mary? I understand. I only ever told one friend before you, fearing that. But finding out you saw her too... I've experienced things but this is unprecedented. There has to be a *reason*, don't you think?'

Flora had to agree. Two of the most iconic women in history had visited in the last ten days. Northern women who couldn't afford a kettle didn't have things like that happen to them. But Mary had been a poor girl with very little, and Marilyn had clawed her way out of poverty too. Perhaps it was the most natural occurrence in the world; maybe they were linked by the female experience.

Flora inhaled, let it out slowly. 'Long ago, I had a baby. Gave it away. No one knows except my sister, my friend Neil, my mum... and now you. My mum spoke to Nina for the documentary and told her. If it's used, well, it'll be public.'

'Is that so bad?' asked Marilyn. 'You did what you thought best.'

'Maybe. But there's a lot more to it.'

'Will it hurt anyone who matters?'

'Not hurt, but affect.'

'We're all affected by everything. That's good. It means we're alive.'

'I suppose,' said Flora.

'Just tell Nina as much as you want to. See where the words take you – or don't.' Marilyn paused. 'My good friend Stella always said, *let's not be quiet*, and I promised her I never would. I also promised her…'

'Yes?'

'I don't want to shock you, in case you don't know…'

'Go on.'

'Your mum Allison was adopted.'

'Oh I know that,' said Flora. 'Grandma Lil was always open about it. I do think it's why Mum had so many problems in truth.' She paused. 'Wait – how do *you* know that though?'

'My friend Stella was her mum.'

'*What*?'

'She had to give her up, just as you did your baby, and it broke her heart. But she got letters from Lillian Baker – your Grandma Lil – updating her on Allison, so she followed her life from a distance. And then yours and Bella's.'

'*Your* friend is *my* grandmother?' Flora couldn't take it in.

'*Was* your grandmother. Since dear Stella passed thirteen years ago, I've been keeping an eye on you all.' Marilyn paused. 'Mainly you. You're so like Stella. More than your mum or sister from what

I can see. She was the editor of *Icon* magazine for years, spent her life giving women a voice.'

'I love that magazine,' cried Flora. 'I still have a stack of them. Stella wrote so many great pieces about you, I felt sure she must know you – and she did! And I'm related to her!' She shook her head. This was a life-changing moment, and yet somehow it felt right.

Not a surprise.

'You are.' Marilyn's hands joined in her lap. 'Did your mum never want to find her birth mom?'

'No.' Flora paused, not wanting to be unkind.

'Go on,' urged Marilyn.

'Mum was angry at her for giving her up.'

'That's understandable.'

'I think it's why... well, she's had, as I said... *difficulties*.'

Marilyn nodded kindly. 'I know.'

'What made you find me now?' asked Flora.

'I dreamt about Mary. The first time since I saw her. She said I should come here. That we should speak freely. I think she meant about us seeing her.' Marilyn took Flora's hand, her fingers papery and slight. 'I don't think it's a coincidence that Mary came to both of us. It was because of our links. You're thirty-six. I was too when she came. That was my big turning point. It often is for women. Maybe it's your time to speak – to Nina.'

Perhaps it was both Flora's turn and her turning point.

'Can you give me time to think?' she offered, still unsure.

Marilyn nodded.

'I need to go home,' said Flora. 'I'm working tonight. I'd offer you a bed at mine but it's not fit for someone like you.'

'I'm sure your home is lovely,' said Marilyn. 'But I'm happy here.'

'If you do the documentary, will you tell Nina you're... *her*?'

'I don't know. But I will come to your club tonight.'

'You *will*?'

'Sure. I'll have a nap this afternoon.'

They had more toast and hugged again. *I'm in the arms of Marilyn Monroe*, Flora thought with a smile. *And her dearest friend is my grandmother…*

*

Later, at the flat, Bella put the pan on the hob while Flora placed the daffodils in a tall glass.

'Did the elderly lady find you?' asked Bella, and when Flora nodded, she asked, 'Who is she?'

Flora picked up an *Icon* magazine and looked at the picture of Stella in the back – how could she not have seen her mother's jaw, Bella's eyes, her smile? She moved to the red and pink painting of Marilyn, wanted to say, 'Bella, you got her right.' She longed to tell her sister that even in older age and having discarded that persona, Marilyn still exuded beauty, and that she had been watching over them because her best friend was their grandmother.

But she had promised not to reveal Marilyn's identity.

For now.

'Well?" It was Bella 'Who *is* she?'

'I'll tell you another time, I've got to get ready for work.'

54

Flora has two conditions

April 2016, Hull, England

Arriving at the club didn't cause Flora the usual dread because Neil was performing, and Marilyn had said she would call in too. It would be surreal; a Hollywood icon amidst bad tribute acts, great magicians, and occasionally lucky psychics.

Greg was swearing at someone on his phone, Georgie was wiping tables while scrolling through Instagram, and Denise was checking wires onstage. Flora paused while drying glasses, realising that there had hardly been time to absorb the last few days. She wondered if she might look back one day, from that safe distance, like we do the big things, and dissect it, marvel at the improbability, relive the intensity.

Flora spotted Pat entering the backstage room, wearing a crimson velour dress with no bobbling or bare patches at the elbows.

'She's on tonight,' said Greg. 'Packed the club out yesterday. Oh, and Sheena Turner bloody cancelled again so the Great Neillusionist is covering.'

Flora smiled.

'What?' asked Greg.

'Nothing.' She shoved her boss affectionately. 'Nothing changes, does it?'

Flora found Pat in the dusty backstage room, shuffling a pack of Tarot cards. It was strange to see her. It had been just over a week since the prediction that began it all, and Pat looked different too. It wasn't only the new frock, or her hair now cut in a snazzy bob, but her whole demeanour was charged with purpose. Mary seemed to have indirectly changed her life too.

She looked up. 'Y'alright, darlin'? Pick a card.'

Wordlessly, Flora did.

She held one up; it depicted a young man wearing a red robe, holding aloft a sceptre, with an infinity symbol hovering above his head.

'The Magician,' said Pat. 'It means you are powerful. There is an opportunity to bring your higher self into alignment and create the future you want most.'

Flora tried to keep her face mock-free.

Pat added, 'Also, it can quite literally mean a magic man.' She looked knowingly at Flora and slid the card back into the pack. 'I must thank you, darlin'. I'm booked until 2018 and I've been on *Look North* twice.' She paused, looking contrite. 'I'm sorry I sent Nina Ford to you; I were just dead excited with it all.'

Flora shrugged. It didn't matter now. 'Has it happened since?'

'Has what happened?'

'A genuine message from beyond.'

Pat looked like she was thinking about lying, then shook her head. 'That were special,' she admitted. 'But I need to earn a livin'. It might happen again, but until then, I make people happy.'

Flora wasn't sure that false messages were fair.

'Are you gonna do Nina's documentary?' asked Pat. 'I don't know if she's gonna use my interview. She paid me though, so it's all good.'

Flora still didn't know.

Marilyn was prepared to talk after keeping quiet for fifty years. Did Flora need that much time? She had been named as the Mary girl. Bella knew about the baby. But there was more. Neil said that we always know what we want to do. That's how she began to feel. One thing had been leading to another, and then another, and then another.

Five minutes until opening, so she returned to the bar.

Bumped into Neil.

'Hey Arsehole,' he said.

'Hey yourself.'

They both smiled. There didn't seem to be the right words.

It didn't matter.

Flora asked, 'Will you do your big new trick tonight or are you still hoping to go to Vegas with it?'

'I've accepted that Vegas won't happen.' His light tone felt forced. 'I'm not quite there with it yet. I need to find the right person to reveal.'

Greg yelled for Flora to get the doors open.

The stampede was sudden.

Flora felt sad that the crowd was here for Psychic Pat not Neil; he deserved a packed house. They both created illusions. But Pat's trickery was deceptive while there was a real honesty to Neil's magic.

Once Pat took to the stage in a cuddle of cheers, the lamps were relentless, calling for drink after drink.

'The spirits are strong.' Pat's hand was dramatically aloft. 'I'm getting the word ... it could be... oh, it's a strange one... magnesium... *supplement*?'

'Oh, my God.' A lamp went on and a woman in a too-tight playsuit leapt up. 'I just started on them! I was telling my friend Claire in the lavvies. It's for me bowels.'

Pat nodded; Flora side-eyed Georgie.

'Your dad's pleased and sends you love and light, darlin'.' Pat bowed her head as though in prayer and then slowly looked up, like a film camera and spotlights waited to see her face in full. 'Kettle!' she cried suddenly.

Kettle?

Flora shivered.

Then she followed her gaze to where Marilyn stood, hair neatly curled. In her hands was a box displaying a picture of a kettle. Flora hurried over, keen to get her a seat. There were no free chairs, so she found a padded one in the back, brought it out.

'Sorry,' said Pat to her confused audience. 'The kettle caught my eye. The spirits are back... I'm getting the word...'

'You look pale,' Flora whispered to Marilyn, concerned.

'I'm tired.' She shrugged. 'I'm getting old, honey. This is for you. I couldn't sleep for thinking of you having to boil a pan for coffee.'

Flora took the box; the thought of Marilyn Monroe going into Argos to get a kettle was surreal. 'You're so sweet. Can I get you a drink?'

'Oh, no. Alcohol unsettles my stomach now. Gee, this is quite a place.' She took off her coat, glancing around. 'Reminds me of the club where Ella Fitzgerald was discovered. It was always places like these where they found one-offs.'

'Neil's a one-off,' said Flora softly.

Greg was glaring at Flora from the bar. Seven lamps were on. She sighed. 'I have to work. If you need anything, just get me.'

'I'll be fine. Psychic Pat is a real character, isn't she?'

Flora put her kettle behind the bar and spent the next hour quenching patrons' thirst. Bella sauntered in, looking glorious in red lipstick and a silky black top. She ordered a beer and sat on a bar stool.

At the interval, the rush was mad.

Then it was time for the Great Neillusionist who Denise announced with gusto, despite half the audience having departed when Pat left. Flora knew Neil would have seen this and ached for the unfairness of it.

He was a talent; Pat had just got lucky.

If he felt dejected when he took to the stage in a simple charcoal suit, it didn't show. As always, he didn't utter a word. It was his strength: silence. He let his hands do the talking and they spoke fluently. He approached a table and touched it lightly with one finger – flames danced away from it. The women there leapt back with a shriek. Neil blew; the fire died. Flora smiled; earlier, these women had been bitching loudly about how 'crap' the magician was.

He pointed to a man's iPhone, and he handed it over, nervous. Neil returned to the stage and scrolled through pictures of the ocean until water – actual water – flowed from the device, spattering on the wooden stage floor. Flora had no idea how he did it.

A gasp then, echoed by others.

Good; this trick deserved such a reaction.

But Flora realised the audience were responding to something else. Marilyn had collapsed. Bella knelt by her on the floor; onlookers followed, hungry to be part of a drama. Flora plonked the ice bucket she was carrying on a table and pushed through the throng.

'What happened?' she asked Bella.

'It's the woman who came to the flat. She looked queasy.'

'*Marilyn*?' Flora touched her forehead. Her eyes fluttered open. 'Give us some space,' she yelled at the crowd. Marilyn tried to sit up. 'Take it slowly,' said Flora.

Greg told everyone to back off. 'Shall I call an ambulance?'

'She's coming around,' said Flora. 'Get her a brandy.'

She helped Marilyn back onto the chair. Colour returned to her cheeks as though an artist had painted them in slow upward strokes. 'How long was I out?' she asked.

'Not long,' said Bella. 'Are you hurt?'

'No. It happens sometimes.'

'Should we go to the hospital?'

'I'll be OK now. I'll get a cab back to CARE.' Marilyn sounded fragile.

Greg handed her a brandy and said he'd ring a taxi; she thanked him but didn't drink it.

Neil hovered close by, looking lost, like he had abandoned his stage persona and wasn't sure who to be now. 'What happened?' he asked Flora.

'Sorry I disturbed your show, honey,' said Marilyn, voice shaky. 'Your wonderful magic knocked me out.'

'Thank you.' He blushed. Then, with a frown: 'Do I know you?'

Flora was sure he must know – it seemed so obvious to her. But who expected Marilyn Monroe in the audience at your show?

'I'll make it up to you,' she said. 'I'll make sure we get the biggest crowd in for the next one.' She looked melancholy then, said quietly to herself, 'At least that was something I *used* to be able to do… But things are different now.'

Flora remembered tales she had read about Marilyn's kindness when she was a star, going out of her way to make sure new acts got a chance. Women were encouraged to always leave the ladder down for those behind them. In that way, Marilyn had been ahead of her time, and because of her, many girls had got a firm footing on a rung.

'It's fine,' said Neil. 'I just hope *you're* OK.'

'Taxi's here,' called Greg.

'I'll walk you out,' said Flora.

Outside, it was raining heavily, flushing away the old world. Flora told Marilyn to wait in the doorway and asked the driver to pull up on the path. She helped her into the car. Before Flora could shut the door, Marilyn grabbed her hand. 'You should call Nina,' she said, words stronger now, urgent.

Rain dripped off Flora's nose. 'Why?'

'I understand if you don't want to speak.' Despite the fatigue in her eyes, Marilyn spoke with determination. 'But *I'm* ready to and I think this is the way. Call her, tell her I saw Mary. Don't tell her who I am though. I might do that myself.'

'You might tell the world who you were?' Flora's heart slowed.

'I've hidden for long enough. I'm tired now. I feel like…'

'Yes?'

Marilyn shook her head. 'I should go.'

'Do you want me to come?'

'No, I'm fine. *Call Nina.*'

Flora nodded. 'If that's what you want.' She kissed Marilyn's cheek and closed the door. Watched the taxi pull away, water scattering brown sludge in its wake.

Inside, everyone was packing up. There was no point in Neil resuming his show when patrons were leaving after the disruption. Bella said she was going to meet a friend in a club. Flora found Neil in the backstage room. His head was lowered; she wanted to go and hold him but didn't feel confident enough.

'Are you alright?' she asked.

He jumped. 'Yeah, fine. I…'

'Tell me.'

'I don't know if I can do it anymore.'

'What do you mean?'

'The magic,' he said.

'But it's who you *are*.'

'Is it though?' He shrugged. 'I've been doing it for years, in places like this. How long do I give it before I get a proper job?'

'You're not supposed to have a proper job.' Flora moved closer to him. 'Imagine if Marilyn Monroe had thought that and stayed in her factory job?'

'There's nothing wrong with that kind of work,' said Neil. 'My grandad worked his whole life in a factory.'

'Don't you think *I* know that?' Flora motioned to the place. 'But some people are meant for more – and I think you are.'

'You're just saying that because…'

'Because what?'

'Nothing.'

'*What?*'

He blushed. 'Because you like me.'

She smiled. 'That doesn't mean I'd bullshit you.' She kissed him, softly. 'You'll feel differently tomorrow. You'll perfect your trick and... it'll be big.'

He shrugged. 'Maybe.'

Neil couldn't walk her home because he had an early hospital appointment with his mum, but promised he'd see her soon. That they would go on a 'proper date'. Flora smiled all the way home, despite the downpour.

At the flat she plugged the new kettle in and switched it on. It was opaque; the water visibly bubbling inside hypnotised her. It changed colour as it got hotter, from blue to purple to red, like an artist at work. Tea made, Flora got Nina Ford's card from the kitchen drawer. Despite the late hour, she dialled the number and reached a voice service.

'Nina, it's Flora Baker,' she said. 'I've changed my mind; I'll do the interview. But there are two conditions. There's another lady – a friend of mine – who saw Mary fifty-four years ago. She's never spoken publicly about it before and she wants to talk to you as well. I'll only do it if you include her. And, also... only if I can have my sister Bella at my side.'

55

'Mother of God' documentary interview (unedited), England, 2016

Marilyn Miracle, 89, Hull

'I was restless that day, you could say.'

Marilyn sits on a red leather sofa, elegant against the gaudy shade, back straight, hair curled tightly, wearing an ash grey blouse and delicate pearls at her neck. The location is made clear by the fan of CARE leaflets on a nearby coffee table. Sunlight flickers through a window.

'I'd been restless for a while. I was thirty-six – it's a funny age for a woman.' She looks to the right as though to catch the eye of someone off camera.

A soft voice – Nina's – asks if she can just look at her.

'Sorry, yes. It's been a while since I did anything like this. Anyway, that day, I'd been thinking about my career, my life, my *unhappiness*. I might never have made changes if she hadn't come into my kitchen that night. I feel sure I was supposed to come to an end that night. That's what she suggested, and it's how I've felt since. I've sensed that I wasn't meant to witness some of the big things that have happened in our world the last few years.'

'When you say she, do you mean Mary?' Nina, off-camera.

'Yes. She was in my kitchen. It's hard to see her as vividly now – it was more than fifty years ago, honey, and my memory can be fragmentary. But I know she was beautiful. That I was stunned. I felt great joy.'

'Did you believe that you saw the Virgin Mary that night?'

asks Nina quietly.

'Oh, yes. She was *there*.'

'And now?'

'I still believe it.'

'Did she have a message?'

'She told me to leave. Leave my house, my life. One thing that's curious – I've just remembered this, so forgive my rambling – is that it felt at times like she spoke in another language, yet I understood her.' Marilyn smiles, obviously pleased at recalling this. 'It's nice to talk about her. I never have, except to…' She looks to the right again and quickly corrects herself. 'She's only been here in my head (Marilyn touches her cheek) so it's freeing to share her.'

'Why did you wait so long to speak like this?' asks Nina.

'Because I was hiding.' Marilyn touches her pearls with tremulous hands. 'I used to be... someone else. Mary encouraged me to free myself of her chains. But that meant staying silent. Which I have enjoyed, because I've done things that gave me the greatest joy of my life. It's been a long time. But now I'm here because... well, none of us live forever, do we?'

She looks directly into the camera, blue eyes teary.

Nina waits a while before asking if Marilyn might return her attention to her. 'You say you used to be someone else. Who were you?'

Marilyn fidgets in the seat and another voice, male, asks if she wants anything. 'No, thank you, honey,' she says. 'I had a dear friend called Stella.' Marilyn looks nostalgic. 'She took me in when I had nowhere to go. She used to write about female celebrities.'

'You were such a female,' says Nina; it doesn't sound like a question.

Marilyn smiles but doesn't respond. 'I have another story, Nina,' she says after a few beats. 'It's as big as Mary. It happened because of her. Would you like to hear it?'

'Yes. I'm interested in how women's lives were affected by her visit. There have been common occurrences among them. One is CARE. Many women volunteered there, following Mary's suggestion. Fifteen of the twenty-two women I've interviewed.'

'CARE,' repeats Marilyn softly, a testing of the word.

'It's interesting that you're staying here.'

'Please, could I get some water?'

After a moment, a glass is handed to Marilyn by a man with headphones on; she drinks half and gives it back to him with a thank you.

'I moved from Los Angeles to Dublin over fifty years ago. It feels like yesterday. It was two years after Mary had visited, and the final of her predictions, at least at that time – that I should go to the land of my ancestors. I'm part Irish, you see, via my grandmother. And it felt good straight away. Like coming home.'

Marilyn's final words are barely audible.

Nina asks if she can adjust her microphone. Once done, she apologises and says Marilyn should go on.

'Four weeks into my Dublin stay, I went to a book group,' she says, 'The building was beautiful, but derelict. No one wanted it. I went to the auction, bought it for a steal. Then I got quotes from builders for how much it would cost to make it habitable. It was expensive but I was lucky, I could afford it. I knew that if I wanted to stay in Ireland for longer than three months I'd need a work visa, and realised this could be my way. I got some advice and I learned that if I registered a charity there, I could stay.'

'What did you do with the building?' asks Nina.

Marilyn ignores the question. 'Because of who I'd been in my other life, I wanted to keep a low profile. So my friend Stella came over a few times, she was my representation, for want of a better word, heading meetings with the press when the venture needed publicity so I could remain in the shadows.'

'What did you do with the building?' repeats Nina.

'While it was renovated, I put posters around the city asking for donations of beds, blankets, other housewares. I wanted to create a place where women could go if they were in need; to escape, to think, to recharge. Like I had.'

Marilyn takes a deep breath.

'Anyway, the one in Dublin was the first one. Stella handled things until I got older, was more forgotten, and then I could do it. She really was a star. The first sanctuary (I liked that word for it) was a real success; people were happy to volunteer, and women came for a night, for a week, for months. I wanted to open others but I knew what a vast undertaking it would be.'

Nina: 'Sounds a lot like CARE…'

Marilyn smiles. 'One evening, when I first bought the Dublin building, I was writing in my notepad – I love to scribble poems – and I saw something I'd written back in LA. I'd said to Stella that children who are abandoned require everything – that was me, you see. I hardly saw my mother and never knew my father. I'd written it down and realised that if you removed the words *who* and *are* the first letter of each word made one very simple word that was what I was trying to do: *CARE*.'

'It's *yours,*' Nina says quietly. 'And it happened... because of Mary?'

'It might be mine, but really it's everyone's.'

'Wow.'

'I'm very proud.' Marilyn beams.

'But... it's worldwide... how do you…?'

'Oh, honey, a team of people manage it all. I just receive paperwork now and again, attend the odd meeting. Once we got sponsorship in the early days and then funding, it grew, with Stella's help. Then, with the money we raised, I was able to employ a team to do the complicated things; I still made decisions, and visited some new sanctuaries, which was my favourite part – meeting the women, seeing the work done by volunteers.'

'Was it what you hoped for?' Nina sounds impressed.

'Oh, yes.' Marilyn looks around. 'When I arrived here, I was greeted with compassion and no judgement. That was what I wanted for women. So often – at least during my early career – women were blamed for every scandal even if it was the *man* who was married, even if they were barely fifteen years old and couldn't consent, even if they were promised a job and never got it, even if they tried to tell their story.' Marilyn looks emotional again. 'Now CARE is a safe place for them to go and find themselves again – like I needed to do all those years ago.'

'You said during your early career,' says Nina. 'Tell us, what career was that?'

Marilyn sits up straighter, unfurls, graceful, like a swan lengthening its neck and extending its wings, the years falling away. 'I was a model... and then an actress. I had a different surname then.'

'Would viewers know it if you told us?' Nina's voice is excited; it sounds like she knows.

'They might.' Marilyn smiles. 'They still talk about her on TV and in magazines, which is nice. Because she's still here, inside me. It's like... well, like being a mom, and she's my child. I hear her talking sometimes, so young and so hopeful. I have great affection for her.'

'Who is she?'

'My girl,' says Marilyn softly.

'But what do you call her?'

Quietly: 'She's Marilyn Monroe.'

In the bright of her blue eyes there's a flash of Monroe; a flicker of that long-gone magnetism as though a nearby switch has fired up the past; a glow, even without a movie spotlight. There's a hiss of discussion off camera, low voices overlap, movement, obviously shock at this revelation.

Then there's silence while Marilyn simply nods.

'Marilyn Monroe.' Nina's voice isn't as composed now. 'I *knew*. As soon as you started talking. I saw. Felt it. Not just the name, Marilyn. It's a popular name for your age group, but I *saw*.' Pause. 'Don't worry I'll edit this out, but I'm... I've loved you for years.'

'Your documentary about me was lovely,' says Marilyn.

'Thank you. That means the world.' Nina sounds emotional. Takes a moment. 'Can we get back to the interview?'

'Of course.'

'Why have you spoken here? Why *now*?'

'Because I dreamt of her again.'

'Who?' asks Nina.

'Mary. She said I should come here. And now I know why.'

'You do?'

'Yes.' Marilyn nods. 'I've only realised while talking to you. Isn't that something? The power of when we speak. It frees us to see more clearly. When we're listened to, we're strong, and everything falls into place.'

'I agree.' Nina's voice is still awed.

Marilyn looks off camera to the right and then returns her gaze to Nina. 'Young Flora, my new friend... I want her to take over my role with CARE. I'm tired, you see. I think my time is limited. Now I'm here with her, I see that's what's meant to happen.' Marilyn glances to the right again and laughs. 'She looks surprised, which is natural. But we can talk after this, Flora.'

'I still can't…' Nina pauses. 'Marilyn Monroe. And you're happy this will air? You're ready for the world to know where you've been?'

'If you don't mind, I'd like it to stay between us for now. But when this eventually airs, well, that's fine.'

'We can keep it quiet.' Nina sounds all business now. 'Would you like this to be your exclusive coming out, so to speak?'

'I'm not sure.' Marilyn looks thoughtful. 'But this will be the first on camera, yes. I suppose it'll be there forever, the way these things are.'

'It will. What do you-'

'I'm tired now, honey.' Marilyn smiles warmly but is pale. 'Can we take a break?'

'Of course, of course. Whatever you need. Can I get you anything?'

56

'Mother of God' documentary interview (unedited), England, 2016

Flora Baker, 36, Hull

'The Virgin Mary looked down on me from my Grandma Lil's living room and kitchen walls for most of my childhood; she was serene, pure, and perfect, everything my grandma said a woman should be.'

Flora sits next to Bella at the plastic garden table in her well-lit but dated kitchen area. Flora wears muted make-up and a pale blue shirt that has been carefully ironed; Bella is glamorous, lipstick cerise, hair piled on top of her head, smiling broadly, clearly making the most of this appearance.

Flora continues: 'On my bedroom wall though, Marilyn Monroe watched me sleep; perhaps not as pure, but definitely serene, with a tiny bird held aloft on one finger, perfect to me.' Flora shakes her head, now shy. 'Sorry. That was quite rambly wasn't it? I suppose I'm saying that I grew up alongside both women in many ways. But I never expected to see Mary... or Mar-' Flora stops, looks unsure about if she should continue.

'I don't yet know what order these interviews will run in,' says Nina, off camera. 'The Marilyn one may be the final, so we can edit your last few words out.'

'OK.'

'And maybe, for now, don't mention Marilyn.'

'OK.' Flora coughs, nervous.

Bella squeezes her leg, smile still in place.

'You're doing great.' Nina is encouraging. 'That was a lovely opening. But I have to say that of all our interviewees, you were the most reluctant to speak. Would you mind telling me why, and what changed your mind?'

'I was afraid of what people might say – and they *have* said those things, on Twitter and in other places. That I'm blasphemous, a liar, an attention-seeker. When it got out, I was scared. Then, eventually, I began to think it might be better to tell my side and people could decide from that if they believed me or not. I kind of think... well, it doesn't matter, does it? I know what I saw.'

'And what did you see?'

'Light. That was the first thing. Different to the crappy light in here.' She glances up and the camera tilts to a fluorescent strip. 'And she was *here*. In this kitchen. I thought, why me? Why this place?'

'Did this make you wonder if you were imagining her?'

'Of course. I thought I was dreaming, or that I'd lost my mind. I'm sure anyone would feel that way. But then I felt honoured. Very quickly, I just got used to it. Her presence. She talked about things she simply couldn't have known.'

'Like what?'

Flora clearly ignores this question. 'She left me a gift. I still have it.' She opens her hand and holds out some now dry, faded daffodil petals. 'I tried to preserve them as best I could. The weird thing is, that day someone else was supposed to give me a daffodil.' Flora shakes her head. 'Anyway, I look at this and I *know* she was here.'

'What did she look like?"

'Just an average girl.'

'Did she have a particular message for you?'

'She asked me to volunteer at CARE and said that in return the beautiful one would be saved.' Flora's smile then is radiant as she turns to her sister. 'I knew she meant you. Your name means beautiful. I chose it when you were born.'

Bella grins. 'That's cute. I thought it must have been Mum.'

'You were a gorgeous baby. I loved you straight away.'

'It's a common theme with the other women who saw Mary,' says Nina. 'Babies. Ones never had, ones lost, ones missed.' She pauses as though knowing this is a big question. 'What else did Mary say to you?'

Flora fidgets and smooths the material of her trousers. 'You surrendered a blessing and carry the scar deep inside.'

'Did you know what she meant by that?'

'Yes.' The word is as soft as a falling feather.

'What did it mean?'

'Mary was talking about my baby.' Flora glances at Bella again; Bella nods, once. 'I had a baby. When I was twelve. Almost thirteen. Until recently, I'd never told anyone. I'd made a promise. I'd agreed... *not* to.'

'Why was that?' asks Nina kindly.

'My mum. It wasn't meant in a cruel way. She was trying to make sure I had some sort of life. She knew I'd be judged by everyone on our council estate. We hid my pregnancy, and I gave birth at home.'

'That must have been traumatic.'

'It was. But then... I saw…'

Flora tries to hide that she is upset. Bella hugs her.

'I saw my baby. And…'

Silence. Waiting.

The sound of a cough somewhere, perhaps in another room.

'I didn't tell you all of it,' Flora says to Bella.

'Can you just tell it to me?' asks Nina. 'I'm sorry if I seem insensitive.'

Flora nods but keeps holding Bella's hand.

'My mum tried to do the right thing but there are always repercussions, aren't there? I've always had a difficult relationship with her, and it wasn't only my pregnancy – she was more interested in her boyfriends than Bella and me. What she suggested we do meant that I got to see my baby, so I can't grumble about that.'

'But I thought he got tak-' Bella starts, and then glances towards Nina. 'Sorry. I won't…'

'It was her plan from the start,' continues Flora. 'The only way for no one to know. She told everyone she was pregnant too, you see. She had these two cushions that she used, getting slowly bigger by beginning with a slim one, than a bigger one and finally both of them together, worn under stretched leggings.'

'But why would she do tha-' Again, Bella stops.

'She liked having the attention. I was stuck at home and she'd come back from the shops, beaming at how much she'd been fussed by the locals because of her cute bump.' Flora's voice subtly changes, as though someone has switched channel and it's a more serious presenter now. 'She was going to take my baby on as her own.'

'I don't understand. Where *is* he then?' This time Bella finishes her question.

Flora doesn't hide the tears streaming down her cheeks.

'What happened?' asks Nina quietly.

'I gave birth to the most incredible miracle. I fell completely in love. And in that moment I was glad that she would be living with us, in our house, just as my mum's not mine.'

'*She*?' Bella looks like someone slapped her.

'I called her...'

Flora tears the daffodil petals and then looks distraught and puts them on the plastic table.

'I called her Bella because she was the most beautiful thing I'd ever seen. And I've loved you ever since.' She looks at Bella. 'Mum isn't your mother. She's your gran. *I'm* your mum.'

Bella's mouth hangs open like it's weighted with all the things that have ever happened. 'You? But... *you*?'

'Me.'

'I can't... I don't...'

'Mum took over at first but then got bored, like she does; then I fed you in the night when she was out, I pushed you around the park when she couldn't be bothered, I read you a bedtime story because she'd never done that. No one questioned it; you were just my little sister who I liked to fuss.'

'It *was* always you,' says Bella softly. 'How could I not have known? It makes so much sense, how I feel about you, how you've always been with me... so protective.'

'Are you...?' Flora looks shy. 'Are you happy about it?'

'I am. Shocked but happy.' Bella studies Flora like she's never seen her before. 'But why did you say you'd had a boy?'

'I thought if I said a girl, you'd know.'

'Can I ask – how did your mum manage to get away with saying Bella was hers?' Nina's words seem to surprise the two women; they have forgotten that this is an interview. 'Didn't the health visitors and midwives want to check her?'

'I don't think she contacted anyone. She simply registered the birth in her name. I was a kid, I never questioned it. I was back at school a week after giving birth, changed forever, sore and yet happy that at home my baby daughter awaited me.'

Bella wipes her eyes.

'You're lucky there were no complications,' says Nina.

'I guess.'

'I think you two will want some time to talk, so shall we end for now with a question and then resume in an hour?' Nina pauses. 'I see a parallel with you and Mary. You both had babies very young. Did that give you even greater compassion for Mary?'

'Oh, yes. And imagine her life, back then. The patriarchy and the pressures. Women had no voice.' Flora touches Bella's cheek tenderly. 'I only hope she got as much joy out of her new baby as I did seeing mine… even if she couldn't call me Mum.'

57

Flora; flawed, different, a mother

April 2016, Hull, England

When Flora went into the kitchen the day after a film crew had filled it with false light, fancy equipment and a variety of people, it was the kettle that was the star of the show; Bella was hunched over, watching the changing colours as it heated, grinning like a child at a Christmas lights switch-on.

Bubbling like the water, affection simmered in Flora's heart.

The kettle clicked off and Bella finally noticed her sister – no, her *mum,* she must have thought – watching.

She smiled.

They had talked late into last night, about their 'new' relationship and what it might mean. Bella said that if Flora had looked different recently, now it was the loveliest different of all; a mum.

She then shared a new painting; it was of Marilyn and Flora sitting side by side at CARE, drawn from memory of a moment in the last week. Each woman had been brought to life with the usual reds and pinks Bella favoured, Marilyn finely sketched, soft and delicate, Flora more pop art bold, opposites that worked on paper.

'I can't believe *Marilyn Monroe* bought this kettle,' said Bella now. It was the fifth time she had said it since finding out at Marilyn's interview who she was. 'Why didn't you *tell* me?'

Flora felt guilty that she hadn't – or about their link to her yet, about Stella, her blood grandmother. She needed to. 'I was going to, but then Marilyn shared it herself. Bella, listen, there's also-'

'It's bloody surreal,' her sister interrupted. 'A Hollywood idol, not just alive, not only in Hull of all places, but she went into Argos and bought this.'

'We don't actually *know* that it was Argos,' smiled Flora.

'Aldi then.' Bella made two mugs of tea. 'No more waiting for that bloody pan.' She sank into the sofa, on the right where she always sat. Flora joined, on the left. Some things stayed the same, no matter what. The new artwork, propped up against the TV, made Flora smile; she must frame it alongside the other one.

'I can't believe Marilyn was behind CARE,' Bella continued. 'That place that was my saviour. And now it'll be yours.'

Flora sipped her tea. 'I haven't agreed to anything. Anyway, I need to tell y-'

'But that's what Marilyn wants,' cried Bella. 'The poor girl is almost ninety, no wonder she wants to retire. I wonder what it'll mean if she leaves it to you. What will you have to do? Do you reckon it's worth loads?'

'I don't care about that.'

'I know but you could leave the club, make a proper living. We could move to a better place. It makes me quite emotional. I'm dead proud of you.'

Flora touched her daughter's cheek. It was as though the revelation that she was Bella's birth mother freed her to be more affectionate; this was her baby, her girl. 'I just don't know if it's right that I... well, *inherit* it I suppose. Marilyn created it, nurtured it.' *Just like I did you*, thought Flora. 'It doesn't seem fair that I take it after knowing her for a week.'

But there was their link; Stella. She had been part of its creation and she was their grandmother. Wasn't it right therefore that it remain with family? Maybe it was the perfect idea after all.

'Who else can?' asked Bella. 'Marilyn doesn't have children. She must want you to or she wouldn't say it. You're linked by your Mary experience and that could be why she chose you.'

'We're linked by more than that,' said Flora gently.

'What do you mean?'

And she told her daughter the full truth; there had been so much recently. It was exhausting but freeing. Bella bounced in her seat, excited like only she could be; delighted that Marilyn was 'almost family' as she called it.

'Get us,' she cried. 'The two granddaughters of her best mate!' She must have realised what she had said and corrected herself. 'I mean, the granddaughter and *great* granddaughter.'

She ran to her painting, held it in joy. 'Are you visiting her today?' she asked, over her shoulder.

'Yes.'

'Now I know it's her, I see it. Can't believe no one else does.'

'I was like that too. But she wants to keep it quiet still, for now. I might take your painting to show her.'

'It's like…' Bella turned.

'What?' asked Flora.

'It's like she's a mother figure to you, and I'm glad.' Bella paused. 'Should we go and tell Mum you've told me? Maybe warn her you shared it in the documentary. She can't kick off, after all she started it.'

'I guess we should. I'd never want to hurt her. I've often wondered in recent years – especially when she wasn't bothered with us – why she didn't decide we should tell you the truth. It would have taken any responsibility off her. When you were a teen, she could have buggered off to the pub when she wanted, child-free.'

'Didn't you want to bring it up?' asked Bella.

'I never mentioned it. I was afraid. You have to understand how shame works. It silences you. I adored *you*, but the experience that led to you .... that was all wrapped up in the secret our mother... um, *my* mother had me keep.'

Flora saw herself at thirteen, running, running, running,

around the bedroom, her mum yelling up the stairs for her to give it a rest. But she couldn't. She had to shake free the hurt, exhaust the restlessness when she thought about the assault.

Flora stood now, not needing to run but to move. She went to the window and looked at the flowers in the window boxes, at the April blooms, at the tangy orange tulips and the pretty pink peonies. As always, she drew strength from their presence.

'I'm so sad that happened to you.' Bella was at her side.

Flora shrugged even though it was a flippant action after kind words about a horrible trauma.

'I feel guilty though that I'm the result of your assault.'

'No,' cried Flora, turning to her daughter. '*Never* feel like that. Your existence made it endurable. You were a light after darkness.' She paused. 'But I've often wondered, I admit, if that was the source of *your* pain. You were always so troubled, since you were a teen, we both know that. It hurt so much. I remember reading that a mother is only ever as happy as her least happy child, and that was true for me.'

'I never knew where that pain came from,' admitted Bella, voice cracking. 'It just descended on me. I know our mother's absence affected me but maybe I carried something inside, from your experience. Remember when we watched that documentary about how trauma passes from one generation to the next through genetic changes to DNA? Maybe that happened with us.' Bella composed herself, clearly struggling. 'Sometimes I felt like I wasn't in the right life. Something was off. And now, you're my mum, it makes sense. Maybe I was trying to fill the absence that was not having you in the way I was supposed to. Does that make sense?'

'It does.'

'And then it lifted. I swear, it was gone.' Bella traced a finger down the long tulip stem. 'Do you really think it was a miracle?'

'We'll never know. It doesn't matter. You're much better, however it happened. And if ever you're not... I'm here.'

'You always were. That's why you'd be perfect to take over at CARE. You *do* care. It's all you've ever done, and no, don't start dissing yourself. You've always put me first.' Bella paused. 'It's going to be hard to call you Mum though.'

Flora smiled. 'I don't expect that after all this time.'

'Mommy? *Mama*?'

'For God's sake.'

'It won't be appropriate for us to go on night's out now, will it?' said Bella.

'Stop it.'

'Can I get pocket money?'

'No, you bloody can't, Madam.' Flora took her mug to the sink and poured the cold tea away. 'You can wash these pots if you like though. I'm gonna get ready.'

'And what about Neil?'

'What do you mean?' Flora stopped on her way to the door.

'Is he about to become my step-daddy?'

'Oh, stop it.' Flora laughed heartily.

'You've got your big date tonight. Maybe he's gonna pop the question.'

'As if. We hardly know each other.'

'Will you tell him about me?' Bella was serious again.

'Not tonight. I've got six months until Nina's documentary. I'll tell him before that.'

'Do you think he'll mind hooking up with a scandalous single parent?'

Bella was obviously teasing but Flora wondered how he would take it. He knew about the baby but that had been a baby gone, not one here to be taken care of, one who would have to be part of his life as much as hers if he wanted a relationship.

'I guess he gets a ready-made family, like it or not,' said Flora.

'I'm not gonna call him Daddy, just so you know.'

'Oh, for God's sake.'

'Love you,' Bella called after Flora as she left the room.

Flora would give a relationship with Neil everything she had now. She had always been argumentative and difficult and resistant to anything serious because she was hiding something. She had feared being revealed for the shameful, ruined, unworthy girl she was.

Now, there was only truth.

There was only Flora.

Flawed, different, a mother.

But as deserving of happiness as anyone else.

58

Flora has goosebumps

April 2016, Hull, England

Neil took Flora to a waterfront restaurant, the kind she had never been to because they didn't show the prices on the menu by the door. She had heard that the portions were so small you had to have cheese on toast when you got home afterwards.

Neil was pretending to be absorbed by the menu when Flora arrived.

She realised he was nervous. This was different for them. Before now, their time together had been arbitrary, at the club or walking to her flat. Arranging a time, booking a table, that placed a stamp of expectation on the encounter. Also, how was the poor guy paying for it?

Flora decided she would order light and not drink alcohol. She wanted to put Neil at ease so she sat down, reached across the table, and patted his hand.

'What?' he asked with a smile.

'Nothing. I'm glad we did this.'

'Me too.' He looked relieved, as though he'd been told a mole wasn't cancerous after all.

'This is lovely, but the Minerva would've been enough for me.'

'I wanted to show you that you deserve everything.'

Flora didn't know how to respond.

No one had ever said anything like that to her.

They ordered food, Flora a shrimp salad and Neil a goat's cheese and cauliflower tart. Then they looked at one another, features flickering in the candlelight.

'Are you good with Vegas not happening?' asked Flora.

The money from Nina's interview would arrive next month, too late to help him. It was a missed opportunity. The money would mean many other things though. She would have a deposit for a better flat. She could help Bella at university. She could even afford to come to a place like this if she felt like it.

'I am.' He looked like he was.

'And how do you feel about your magic now?'

'What do you mean?'

'You were down about it the other night,' she reminded him.

'I was dreading an appointment the next day with my mum, which actually turned out to be quite encouraging. Anyway, I'm not sure if that moroseness pushed me on but I think I've perfec-'

The waiter brought the food then; Flora knew cheese on toast would be required when she got back. He straightened the cutlery and Flora saw that he was wearing silver cufflinks with Marilyn's smiling face on them. She thought about telling Neil that she was alive, here, and had featured in Nina's documentary too.

But she had promised to keep quiet until the programme aired.

Neil knew Flora had done the interview; she had shared that decision with him as soon as she messaged Nina, and also called him after the interview concluded. There were many things he didn't know about, including her true relationship with Bella, but wasn't that what relationships were for? To discover one another. Neil probably had secrets of his own, flaws, things he dreaded sharing.

'As I was saying,' he continued when the waiter had gone, 'I think I've perfected my new trick. This could be the one.'

'Really?' Flora stopped prodding her tiny salad. 'I've got goosebumps; your face lit up then. When are you doing it?'

'Next Saturday, at the club. You have to be there. I need my favourite arsehole in the audience.'

Flora laughed. 'I'm not working but of course I'll come. Is it a big enough venue to get the recognition you deserve? We should make sure there's a huge audience, invite the press or something.'

'I invited some local BBC presenters and emailed a few journalists. I told them–' He shook his head.

'*What*?'

'Nothing. Will you video it for me?'

Flora nodded. 'You're being very mysterious.'

'I'm nervous.'

'I've never seen you look like this.'

'I don't want to say too much,' said Neil. 'I'd like you to experience it blind.' He paused, fork aloft. 'Thank you for your faith in me.'

'The first show you did at the club, when the image on your T-shirt changed ten times, I loved how you never acknowledged those changes, like you were such a sorcerer you could do it without knowing. I've known you were special ever since.'

'Magic is letting people think one thing is happening while something else does,' said Neil. 'I blindsided the audience with my T-shirt so I could set up for the butterflies filling the room. It's a bit like lyrical dissonance.'

Flora frowned. 'What's that?' With Neil, she never felt stupid when she didn't know something.

'It's when the music and the lyrics go in opposite directions. You know, the song is bouncy, fast, up tempo, but the lyrics are at odds with this, they're sad, melancholy. Abba do it well. You fool the listener into thinking this is going to cheer them up, and then *bam*, you rip their heart out. It's a great form of trickery.'

'I like that. Not ripping people's hearts out but the cleverness of it.'

'Shall we try and keep our hearts in place?' said Neil softly.
Flora nodded.
They could try.
That was all that mattered.

59

Marilyn asks why

April 2016, Hull, England

Why?

It was a question Marilyn had often considered for many things. Why had she – a girl from an orphanage, with a mentally ill mother and an absent father – found the fame others sought but failed to achieve? Why had Mary chosen to visit her, changing the path of her life? Why had she agreed to do what she was going to do tonight?

Because. That was the only answer she ever found.

Because.

The word of her life. It stopped her having to find an absolute answer, because, really, there weren't any. Over the years, she had found comfort in signs, in special numbers, in the coincidences that gave her life rhythm and depth, in the random scribbles that she free-wrote, and in the words dear friends had said to her – *let's not be quiet* – that stuck in her head like stars on a child's reward chart.

The only *why* Marilyn knew with certainty was the reason for Flora continuing what she had built with CARE. The charity would never have happened without dearest Stella, and who better than her granddaughter to continue its journey? It was a big ask, but Marilyn was sure that Flora was more than capable.

Tonight was also going to be big.

Marilyn dressed carefully as she might have done, once upon a time, and found herself looking for one of her consolatory omens.

While she painted her eyes, the number four flashed on a TV gameshow at the same time as the bedside clock clicked onto 4.44pm.

That would do.

She had gone out yesterday and bought cosmetics for the first time in years. They were so different now, such quality in the velvety foundations, so many shades in the eyeshadow palettes. She got advice from an overly made-up young woman about the best products for an older face, mainly which reds suited thinning lips.

She then purchased the recommended items.

Afterwards, she found a small boutique in an ornate, tiled arcade in the old town, and bought an elegant, cream trouser suit and blouse; she'd always loved the simplicity of white. Finally, she had gone to a hairdressing salon and had golden streaks applied to her greying curls, just enough to add shine.

Now, when she applied a finishing coat of powder to her cheeks and peered into a tiny hand mirror, Marilyn was sure for a fleeting second that she saw *her*. Heard her voice, her tinkling laughter. She had never really gone. She had made appearances over the years, like a guardian angel on one shoulder – flashes of her smile in a car window reflection, flickers of her white dress rising in a billowing curtain, and streaks of her yellow hair in the waves of a summer sea.

'You look lovely,' said Carla when Marilyn came into the corridor.

The staff still didn't know who she was, believing the tale she had given about escaping an overbearing husband in Dublin.

'Thank you,' said Marilyn. 'I haven't dressed like this in years.'

'You said you're going to the Cave Comedy Club?' Carla seemed surprised.

'Yes.'

'Well, have a lovely night!'

The taxi was waiting outside. Though the driver had a gritty Hull accent – and the car smelled of takeaway food – because she was dressed up, it swept Marilyn back to the many limousine trips to premiers. She remembered trying to keep dresses smooth, butterflies in her tummy from nerves, cameras popping frenziedly when the door opened and she stepped out to a roar of cheers.

At the end of this journey, no cameras, just a supermarket carrier bag floating by and a not-yet-open club. She looked up; the letter M in the word comedy was obscured by a shadow. She blinked. It was back.

A sign?

Always.

She had been told to arrive early, that someone would let her in. Greg, the gruff but friendly bar manager, opened the door and offered her a drink. He gave her a table near the front. Large black and white posters everywhere showed the Great Neillusionist conjuring butterflies from the air, elaborate gold letters announcing that tonight he would be performing his greatest trick yet.

Marilyn smiled.

What he created wasn't unlike what the movies did: an illusion. She had invoked the glamour girl whose persona seduced the world. Neil conjured colourful fluttery creatures that had an audience gasp.

When the lights dimmed and the doors opened, patrons filed in, chattering excitedly; the throng didn't stop, more arrived. Marilyn wondered how the place would accommodate them all.

Flora was among the crowd, with her sister – no, her *child* – Bella. Flora had shown Marilyn the recording where she announced who her long ago baby was. Marilyn had cried, not just with joy for these young women, but because the news meant Stella now had a great granddaughter too.

While Bella was queuing at the bar, Marilyn put a hand on

Flora's arm.

'God, you look beautiful,' said Flora before Marilyn could speak. 'I feel like people might know you were her. And your *hair*. She's there…' Flora touched Marilyn's cheek. 'I can see her.'

'She's a little more lined now.'

'But that adds a delicacy.' Flora was still staring, agog.

'You look lovely too.' Marilyn thought Flora appeared like a tall flower in the emerald-green blouse that caught the light, and slim, black trousers. It was as though Stella was in the room.

None of them ever died, not really. They went on, she thought, *in those they birthed or loved.*

'Thank you.' Flora smiled.

'I've had official papers drawn up to say that CARE is yours if anything happens to me.'

'Oh, you mean I'm to take over when you're no longer *here*.' Flora looked sad at the idea, but also relieved. 'I thought…'

'Yes?'

'Well, that you wanted me to take over *now*.'

Marilyn smiled. 'I thought I meant that too. But no, I'm not quite ready... I just need to know it's in your hands, should the time come.'

'But how will I do it?' Flora looked nervous. 'I've never managed anything like that before.'

'There'll be advisors to assist you. Do you honestly think I've managed the whole thing from a cottage in Dublin, honey?' Marilyn laughed melodically. 'No, you can do as little or as much as you want, it's simply that it'll be in your name. It'll be *yours*. It's my gift to you.' She paused. '*Stella*'s gift to you.'

'Thank you.' Flora spoke quietly, despite the hubbub of the hordes.

'I had a lot of whys in my head earlier,' said Marilyn. 'Was the Mary visit and her message fate? Coincidence? Accident? Why me?

Why you?'

'And did you find the answers?'

'Because.'

'*Because*?' Flora smiled. 'That's what I'd say when my mum asked why I did certain things she didn't like.'

'That's me too,' said Marilyn. 'I might be an old girl, but I feel the same inside as I did sixty years ago.'

'You do?'

'Sure. We don't age inside, you know. Some people can't deal with the changes in the mirror but I'm at peace with that.' Marilyn grabbed Flora's hand. 'Anyway, you won't be alone running CARE one day, will you? What about that beautiful daughter of yours... and the magic man?'

Neil joined them then, as though summoned by her words. He wore an expensive black suit with slim arms and a silky lapel, narrow tie the same shade. Marilyn smiled at how Flora's eyes lit up at the sight of him. It was no wonder: he was a dashing vision with his hair slicked to one side and an aroma of musky aftershave emanating from his face.

He kissed Flora's cheek, gave Marilyn a little bow.

She remembered long ago dates, that excitement, choosing what to wear, wondering if this man might be the one. Did she miss it? Regret her more solitary recent life?

No.

Because it had been her choice.

'How do you feel?' asked Flora.

'Nervous,' he admitted.

'It'll be wonderful,' said Marilyn. 'I know it.' She was the one now beginning to feel anxious.

'The pressure's on,' said Neil. 'I'm the *highlight* and I see that the presenters and journalists I invited are here, which is great, but Jesus, if I get it wrong... I should go and chat to them in a minute.'

'I can't wait to see the big trick,' said Flora. 'He's been very mysterious,' she said to Marilyn. 'He won't tell me anything. I know he's supposed to turn into someone else before our very eyes, and I-'

Bella joined them, complaining about the waiting time for drinks. 'I could have drunk a bottle in that time,' she cried. 'Hey Neil, Marilyn.' Bella did a double take when she looked at her. 'Wow, you look nice.'

'Thank you,' said Marilyn.

'I'm going to speak to the press guys,' said Neil, 'and then I should go backstage, prepare. You OK?' He was looking at Flora.

She nodded. 'If you are, yes. Good luck.'

They hugged. Marilyn and Bella looked at one another with a smile. When he had gone, the three women found a space against the wall, beneath one of Neil's posters. Flora insisted she find Marilyn a chair from backstage but she shook her head. 'I have to go and…'

'Yes?' prompted Flora.

'I just need go and... do something.'

'Do something? *Now*?'

'Yes, I won't be long.'

'You're *going*?' Flora looked sad. 'But what about-'

'I'll be here for the trick, I promise.'

'You promise?'

'Cross my heart.' Marilyn made the sign.

Flora laughed.

Marilyn headed back outside so Flora would think she had gone. Then she re-entered via the backstage door, let in by Neil, who arrived to open it after five minutes. Grinning like two toddlers up to mischief in the night, they sneaked backstage to the dusty room where he closed the door, leaned on it, and smiled at her.

She had been here a few times this week.

After she fainted at Neil's last show, she rang the club and asked if Greg might give her Neil's number. She felt so bad for disturbing his act that she wanted to do whatever she could to ensure his next one was a sell-out; she would get the same kick out of helping him as she had all those years ago with starlets who asked her advice on make-up, or with emerging singers she could support simply by attending a gig.

She met Neil for coffee and offered her assistance.

She insisted that she had plenty of money if he needed to advertise himself, but he wouldn't hear of it. He told her about his next trick, hopefully his best he said. He just needed someone 'of stature' to feature, admitted that that would be hard to achieve 'when he lived in Hull where there aren't many big stars running around'.

Marilyn had known then that she must tell him.

Must disclose her greatest secret so that he could perform his greatest trick.

When she first said that once upon a time, long ago, she had been Marilyn Monroe, he laughed – not unkind but in disbelief – drawing glances from customers.

Over more coffee and some cake, she convinced him, resorting finally to speaking how she had as Lorelei in *Gentleman Prefer Blondes*.

Then his face had been a picture. 'It really *is* you. But how? Why here? Where did you…?'

More stories shared; more coffee.

More Neil attracting attention with his over-the-top reactions.

More Marilyn calming him down.

'Does Flora know?' he asked.

'Yes, but I swore her to secrecy. Shall we surprise her? I have an idea. Let me tell you…'

After that, they met every other day to rehearse.

Neil had built a wooden platform that was painted black and would be positioned centre stage. On it, a mirror was mounted at a slant, reflecting the floor. This would also be black for the spectacle, making it appear like it was simply the area behind the small podium. Marilyn would be hidden behind this while Neil stood on top of it. He would pull an inky silk sheet up over his frame and then drop it to reveal that he was now Marilyn.

It was up to her to bring the magic of Monroe.

To create a jaw-dropping climax.

It looked basic until he applied his skills to the performance, his willowy movements, his quiet artistry, the quick drop as she got into position at his side. And when the lights and smoke were added, she grew excited. But now she was afraid she wouldn't give the effect he needed. That it would not be the showstopper he wanted.

That they would not even recognise her.

Neil approached her, shaking his head. 'I seriously can't believe that I'm going to change into *you*.'

'Did you talk to the journalists?'

'Yes.'

'Did you tell them it's me?'

'No, I want that to be the big surprise. But I assured them that one of the biggest stars in the world is going to be here tonight. Trust me, it was *very* hard convincing them to believe me. I still don't think they do. I think they're here to watch me fail and then write about the deluded magician who thinks he's Dynamo. I said that I'd give them my fee for the night if I'm lying.' Neil ran a hand through his immaculate hair and Marilyn told him not to. 'Do you think you can you *be* her again, after all this time, at your…'

'My age?' Marilyn winked.

That was the only part of the trick they hadn't rehearsed –

what she would do once revealed. She said she needed that to be spontaneous. Instinctual. That it was how she had always worked.

'I didn't mean *your age* as an insult. You still have that ... special something.' He blushed. 'You look beautiful tonight, and wearing white is perfect, especially with me in contrasting black. And your hair!'

'It's been so long. Will the younger generation know who I am?'

'Marilyn, you're still one of the most loved women in the world. I think when you disappeared, you became a myth. The mystery elevated you into the stratosphere even more. There's always some new documentary with *shocking* new evidence about where you are. I loved your movies as a kid, I told you.' He took a breath. 'I think they'll know who you are.'

'Maybe,' she said softly.

'If you can be her.'

'*If*.'

'Smile at me,' he said.

She did. She tried to find the right one as she often had, lowering her top lip to stop the shadow from her nose ruining the look. It was what had always created the tremulous effect.

He shivered. 'Wow. I don't know how anyone won't recognise you. Now remember, I'm going to distract them with the doves while you get into position right before the finale. OK?'

She nodded.

He looked at the clock. 'Two minutes. God. I feel sick.'

She held his shoulders and made him look at her. 'I got like you before every single scene,' she said kindly. 'I'd often throw up into a bin in my trailer. That's why I took hours and hours to get ready and was always late – I was petrified. Now, I look back, and I think that those nerves made me alert, made me strive to be better, to be great. If we're not nervous, we're not present, eh, honey?

You'll be magic.'

'Thank you.' He looked around. 'Will you be alright in here until it's time?'

'Sure. I'll keep the door open a crack so I know when.'

The muffled sound of an announcement then.

Marilyn closed her eyes, feeling briefly dizzy.

When she opened them she was alone.

For a moment, she was on a movie set and the director was waiting impatiently for her to emerge. She had often wondered if she kept people waiting as punishment for those who had kept *her* waiting – the mother who didn't turn up for a visit, the father who hid in the shadows.

Let them wait, she had often thought.

She had let them wait many years now.

But it had not been punishment. It had been necessary. For her wellbeing, her sanity, her control of her own destiny. She would not be late for this. She would ensure this lovely young man had his moment, if it was the last thing she did.

Then it was time.

60

Marilyn is wonderful

April 2016, Hull, England

The audience were *oohing* in delight at the dozens of flapping doves that Neil evoked from his hands.

Marilyn emerged from the backstage room, sure she would be seen, even in the shadows. She looked for Flora but couldn't see her. No matter. Flora was there, she knew that. So Marilyn crawled with aching bones to her spot, as she and Neil had practised over and over. She had hidden her exhaustion well. Now it didn't matter; it was the final time.

Neil was on the box.

The room fell quiet.

Dove feathers fell like snow by Marilyn's feet. She felt dizzy again and feared not being able to stand gracefully. But as Neil pulled the inky sheet up over his body, she rose behind him, in position, knowing that as soon as his face was hidden, that would be it, fast, sheet gone.

Marilyn instead.

She remembered being so nervous before stepping out in front of the cameras that she broke out in a vicious rash. She often missed her mark – the exact spot she was supposed to stand on for her lines – causing the director to violently curse.

But there was no such guide tonight.

She was the character of her own making.

Could she be *her*, one last time?

The room was deathly silent.

Neil dropped the sheet, falling deftly with it, hidden now.

Just her: *her*.

Becoming Marilyn Monroe had never been about the make-up, though that helped shape her. It had never been about the wiggly walk and the breathy voice, though they had defined her. It had never been about the trembling smile, though that had brought her most to life.

She was the mystery woman in the mirror at the orphanage, promising another life. She was a friend when she opened doors and a foe when she ended up trapped behind them. She was an alter ego that Norma Jeane created but struggled to control. And she had been quiet for a long time.

But now she spoke; she sang.

'I wanna be loved by you, just you, nobody else but...'

Marilyn's voice faltered; she feared it was too quiet.

But the room was holding its collective breath, like an orchestra waiting for the conductor to give the signal. She relaxed into the performance.

The moment.

She recalled her time at the Actor's Studio with Strasberg, who taught her *The Method*. In this, students were required to recall a parallel real-life event that conveyed similar emotions to the ones the scene demanded, an approach more conducive to a theatre production than a busy film set. But the intimacy of the method, the focus on self, appealed to Marilyn. She had thrown herself into it, drawing on past trauma to breathe life into a current role.

Now she drew on a past woman.

Flicked on the rusty switch and gave her light.

'Nobody else but you,' she sang. 'I wanna be loved by you, alone...'

The audience began to respond.

Phone cameras winked.

She heard mumbled words, phrases, gasps; *is it, it can't be, it's her, it's Marilyn Monroe, no, you've been drinking, we're imagining it, it can't be, it is, I swear, it can't be, no, I tell you, but is she real, did he magic her up, yes, she is, it's her, even if it's an illusion and he made us think it, it's her…*

'Boop-boop-a-doop!' she sang.

Now applause began, whooping, cries of her name, a surge near the front, constant light from phones that were recording. She remembered the warmth of that adulation, how it kept her hooked on fame. Now it was a reminder but not an addiction; now she could enjoy the brief adoration and then let it go.

She felt dizzy again, staggered a little, one side of her body numb.

A blinding and sudden headache overwhelmed her.

The words forming in her throat died.

Falling, falling, *falling*.

Hands caught her as she did: Flora.

'Get her into the backstage room.' A male voice – Neil.

Together, they lifted her.

Marilyn surrendered to the safety of their support. It felt like when the nuns at the Angels of the Immaculate Mary had carried her. A door shut, the air changed, the audience noise became a distant clamour. Bella was speaking fast, asking Flora what was wrong, what they should do, was Marilyn breathing. Marilyn could see three silhouettes, but they were blurred.

So there were four of them.

Four of them at the end.

'Don't leave me,' she cried, suddenly afraid, feeling five years old, like when she had called desperately for her mother.

'I'm not going anywhere.' Flora grabbed her hand. 'Neil's ringing for an ambulance, but I'm here. So is Bella.'

'Why can't I see? What is this pain in my head?'

'I don't know,' admitted Flora, 'but lie still, and hold onto me, I won't let you go, I promise.'

'Did they…?' Marilyn tried.

'Yes?'

'Did they love his trick?' She fought to keep her eyes open.

'Oh, yes, they went crazy. They were all recording it, and journalists were fighting to get the closest, calling people on their mobiles, yelling that Marilyn Monroe was here, in a bloody club in Hull.' Flora laughed. 'You're gonna put him on the map, Marilyn, you really are.'

'I'm so…'

'Don't speak now. Just rest.'

'Glad,' she managed. 'Was I…?'

'Shhhhh, Marilyn.'

'But was I… any good?'

'Oh, yes,' said Flora, right by her ear, breath like a safe promise she could sink into. 'You were…' Flora paused as though finding the right answer. 'Wonderful.'

It was the perfect word.

'You gave such joy with your films, you know,' said Flora. 'And you brought that magic again tonight. But it's your kindness we see, what you've created with your charity; you lifted women with the movies, but she you saved them with CARE.'

'You'll do it now,' Marilyn managed.

'Not quite how you have.'

'Why not?'

Flora smiled and winked at Marilyn. '*Because.*'

Because.

And Marilyn closed her eyes with all the answers she needed.

61

Flora sits with her flowers

April 2016, Hull, England

The morning after the show, Flora sat in her window with the flowers.

A single tulip wilted among the vibrant others. She caressed its weakened stem, willing it to life, watering the soil around. When it remained lost, she cried with abandon, inconsolable even when Bella found and held her.

'She was ready to go,' said Bella, stroking Flora's hair as she calmed a little.

'The tulip?'

Bella giggled, gently, despite the pain. 'No, Marilyn. It was her time. I think that's why she did it, don't you?'

'Came here you mean?' Flora sniffed, wiped her nose.

'That too. But I meant the trick. Her one last time in the light, you could say. What a way to go, eh?'

They had gone in an ambulance to the hospital with Marilyn; by the time they got there, she had passed, peacefully, a small smile on her painted lips. In that relaxed state, she looked glorious.

'We only just got her,' said Flora, 'and we've lost her already.'

'But weren't we privileged to have had her even for a moment?' asked Bella.

'I guess.' Flora sat up straight, shaded her eyes from sudden sun that peeked out of the clouds. 'I kept seeing her, you know, in recent weeks, before she arrived here.'

'What do you mean?

'I kept seeing this woman, blurry, as though through an old net curtain, often kneeling at flowers. I think now it was her. And then she arrived with secrets. Great secrets. Look what we know now, and we never would have done otherwise.'

'Exactly. And look at what she did for Neil. He's all over social media today. I reckon this will send his career into orbit.' Bella looked pointedly at her mother. 'So don't be sad. Be excited. She brought us the truth about our ancestry, and she helped Neil, and now you have CARE to think about too.'

'Oh God, that's scary. I can't think about it yet.'

'You don't have to. I reckon it'll take weeks for them to do whatever they do when someone dies.'

'But the... *responsibility*.'

'You were made for it,' said Bella.

'Was I?'

'Hell, yeah. You've always taken care of people. It's you. Now it'll just be on an epic, mad, crazy, worldwide scale...' Bella smiled.

'Not helping,' said Flora.

Seeking comfort, she glanced at the two images on her wall: Grandma Lil's idol, and her own.

Mary on a small cloud, palms open and welcoming, tiny gold stars circling her head and a ring of roses at her feet; serene, pure, and perfect, everything Lil said a woman should be. Marilyn, a golden-haired woman, large daisy above one ear, small smile playful, with a tiny bird held aloft on one finger.

Both perfectly imperfect humans.

Both, hopefully, at peace now.

'No, don't think about CARE yet,' said Bella. 'Let's just sit here. With the flowers.' She paused. '*Mum*.'

Flora smiled.

Then they did.

And the sun blessed them both.

62

Newspapers and magazines, 2016

Like Dynamo, who the Great Neillusionist quotes as being his idol, Neil (in his everyday guise) is a shy, working class, northern magician who stuns with his silent yet swift turn of hand.

He came to prominence following the now viral trick where he disappeared and in his place, Marilyn Monroe emerged. The trick in itself was average, one often done in much flashier ways, but the genius was in revealing the long-missing Hollywood Goddess, aged almost ninety and still able to evoke the ghostly remnants of that young actress.

The act's notoriety was helped by Monroe's demise shortly afterwards – footage of the dazzling magic trick was shown on every news channel across the world when her death was announced.

The Great Neillusionist is currently enjoying the start of what hopes to be a long run at the MGM Grand in Vegas, where stars big and small beg to be his latest reveal in the finale of each show.

MagicWeek

Local woman, Flora Baker, 37, who featured in Nina Ford's new documentary, *Mother of God*, has announced her engagement to the Great Neillusionist. She plans to join him in Las Vegas where they will wed in an intimate ceremony.

The couple have been dating since he revealed the long-missing legend Marilyn Monroe to the world at the Cave Comedy Club in April of this year.

The actress sadly died just after, but not before leaving CARE – the worldwide women's charity that it turns out she built – to Flora. The two women formed a friendship after discovering they had both been visited by the Virgin Mary, coincidentally when each of them was thirty-six and 'feeling lost'.

Though she spoke about her divine experience in *Mother of God*, Flora has been reluctant to talk publicly about it again.

Since taking on CARE, she lives in South Cave with her daughter Bella. She now regularly travels with her to visit CARE sanctuaries across the world.

Our exclusive source, Psychic Pat, told us that Flora 'doesn't like the limelight, but enjoys a simple life, encouraging women to find their voices'.

Hull Daily Mail

Review of *Mother of God* documentary – Nina Ford (October 2016) ★★★★

In this artfully shot and at times emotional documentary, which weaves grainy footage of women sharing their visitations by the Mother of God with Pop Art colourful animation of the Virgin Mary through time, we get a sense that Ford has her own divine message. That of women's trauma, and being silenced.

But despite this – and the heavily religious theme – there is no heavy preaching here; no discussion of theological issues; no polemics about the supernatural (Mary's virginity) or extensive details of doctrine (was Mary herself immaculately conceived?) or overtly Catholic language. It also gracefully avoids that other tedious vocabulary: the suggestion that these women are insane, were hallucinating, or are lying.

Ford is respectful while not pandering to her interviewees; she obviously respects the stories from these mostly working class women but her questions probe harshly enough that we're left satisfied they have been interrogated. We're left believing these women did indeed witness a miracle. Unlike other atheistic documentaries that condescend religious audiences, this film relaxedly participates in an awe of the faithful.

The concluding interview is one that has had much press. After Marilyn Monroe emerged from a black sheet in a Hull club six months ago during a magic trick and passed away from a stroke just a short time afterwards, she has not been out of the headlines. One senses that Ford sees Monroe as an icon of the same stature as Mary, especially since in her previous film – *Marilyn Only* – she explored the Hollywood star's life in a similar way, via the direct female voice.

Though it's not her final appearance – magician the Great Neillusionist was host to that – this documentary exclusively shares the actress's last interview, and in it (speaking about her life-changing visit from Mary) she is ethereal, elegant, and utterly enrapturing.

In short, she is wonderful.

The Guardian

Author's Note

I've always wanted to write this book. I've loved Marilyn since I first saw her on a poster in HMV when I was twelve. I bought it and hung it on the wall above my bed. She looked down while I slept, a sort of glamorous, heavy-lidded guardian angel.

I'm still haunted by her.

I've read every book released (some good, some bad), watched every documentary, and seen every film. I wrote to her sister Berniece Miracle twenty-five years ago. She sent me a signed picture and a letter in which she thanked me for 'keeping Marilyn's memory bright'. I visited Hollywood with my sister Claire and we saw her last house, her grave, and I placed my hands inside her handprints at Grauman's Theatre.

But what *is* it about her?

Why is the world still obsessed?

For me, beyond a fascination with how she gave herself to the camera, stepping literally through the lens and into the real world, it's the things we have in common; the things myself and *many* other women have in common with her.

She is us, and she *isn't* us.

Like Marilyn, I have a difficult relationship with a mother who has a lot of mental health problems and often left us to go into a mental hospital. I had an absent father in my later childhood. Like Marilyn, I spent time in the care system. We were both abused as children. We are both working class and had a limited education, which meant we had to work twice as hard to achieve half of what anyone else might.

The question I've been left with, after a lifetime of loving her, is what *might* have happened? What might she have gone on to do and to be if she hadn't died in 1962, aged just thirty-six, with a whole life head of her? What was her other destiny?

She has been portrayed as a victim, as a survivor, as a goddess, as a problem, as dumb, and as bright, but I wanted to write the sensitive and intelligent woman in charge of her own destiny.

I hope you like it, Marilyn.

Acknowledgments

Thank you to my early beta readers Madeleine Black, Lynda Harrison, Carol Lovekin, Gill Paul, Claire Lugar, and Chris Bridges. Your comments and thoughts, as always, helped shape what the story became. I'm grateful also to John Marrs and his Other John for their advice and support with this book. Thank you too for the encouragement from Amanda Prowse and Laurie Ellingham, both in pushing me to go ahead with this, and with pointing me in the right direction to make it happen. Thank you Wayne Kelly for, essentially, *making* it happen, for the beautiful cover, and the care and time with my novel. And to my agent, Emily, for giving me the freedom to explore this project.

Thank you to all the book bloggers, readers, reviewers, book groups, festival organisers, librarians and bookstore owners who have made the first ten years of my career as an author such a joy. This would be twenty-five pages if I named you all, but you know who you are, and you know what you mean to me, and this one is for all of you.

Thank you to my sister Claire for all your love and support – this book is about two sisters who are *so* much more, and you are.

If you want to also read them, some of my favourite Marilyn Monroe biographies include:

My Sister Marilyn by Berniece Miracle
Goddess by Anthony Summers
When Marilyn Met the Queen by Michelle Morgan

Marilyn and Me by Susan Strasbourg
Norma Jeane by Fred Lawrence Guiles
Marilyn by Gloria Steinem
The Last Take by Peter Brown and Patte Barham
My Week With Marilyn by Colin Clarke
Marilyn Mon Amour by Andre De Dienes

About the author

Louise Beech is the author of eleven novels and a memoir, *Eighteen Seconds* (2023). Her debut, *How to be Brave,* was a Guardian Readers' Pick; *The Lion Tamer Who Lost* shortlisted for the Romantic Novel Awards 2019 and longlisted for the Polari Prize the same year; *Call Me Star Girl* was *Best* magazine's Book of the Year; *This Is How We Are Human* was a Clare Mackintosh Book Club pick; and the audiobook of her memoir, *Daffodils,* shortlisted for the Audies23. Her thrillers, *End of Story* and *Lights Out,* are written as Louise Swanson; the former was chosen by Sophie Hannah as a Book of the Year in the *Daily Mail*, and the latter was reviewed by *The Times.* Her debut play, *How to be Brave*, toured Yorkshire venues in 2024.